SCOOTER

SCOOTER

A NOVEL

Mick Foley

ALFRED A. KNOPF NEW YORK 2005

THIS IS A BORZOI BOOK
PUBLISHED BY ALFRED A. KNOPF

Knopf, Borzoi Books, and the colophon are registered trademarks
of Random House, Inc.

Library of Congress Cataloging-in-Publication Data
Foley, Mick.
Scooter / Mick Foley.— 1st ed.
p.   cm.
ISBN 1-4000-4414-6 (alk. paper)
1. Bronx (New York, N.Y.)—Fiction.   2. Fathers and sons—Fiction.
3. Baseball fans—Fiction.   4. Boys—Fiction.   I. Title.
PS3556.O39173S37 2005
813'.54—dc22   2004061592

Manufactured in the United States of America
First Edition

For my father

Acknowledgments

Thank you first and foremost to my editor, Vicky Wilson, for believing in me, challenging me and knowing what was best for me long before I did.

To Luke Janklow and Barry Bloom for their encouragement and feedback from the book's conception to its completion.

To my publicist Gabrielle Brooks for her enthusiasm and energy.

To Dr. Russell Hamilton for his knowledge of leg and foot injuries, and to Lisa Pappalardo for her insight into trauma units and emergency rooms.

To Mark Dehem for sharing his Joe D. story with me.

To Steve Feldman for giving me a policeman's tour and history of the Bronx.

To all of the people willing to share their knowledge and remembrances of the Bronx. From the staff at Sacred Heart, to Jack and Peg McCarthy, to the gang at the Smithtown Library to the staff at *Back to the Bronx* magazine, the help of many people was invaluable. As was Jill Jonnes's book *We're Still Here: The Rise, Fall, and Resurrection of the South Bronx.*

I was very fortunate to have a cavalcade of people more than happy to talk baseball with me.

Thank you to my old buddies, John Imbriani, Scott Darragh and Steve Zangre for pointing me in the right direction.

Thanks to Robbie Dromenhauser for filling me in on open tryouts and the New York–Penn League.

Thanks to former Mets Bud Harrelson, Ed Kranepool and Ron Swoboda.

ACKNOWLEDGMENTS

Thanks to former Yankees Reggie Jackson and Dave LaPoint and to front-office man Stanley Kay.

A special thanks to George Steinbrenner for his friendship and generosity.

And thank you in advance to Joe Torre and Yogi Berra for having a sense of humor about their roles in my book.

Author's Note

I have tried to make this book as authentic as possible, to both the borough of the Bronx and the game of baseball. In a few instances where the facts could not fit the story, I used creative license to simply make things up.

SCOOTER

1964

[1]

"Dad, what's a dick?" I was four years old when I let that question loose on my unsuspecting dad, but oddly, I don't think I've given that somewhat strange inquiry a second thought until recently. I'm not sure what seems odder—the ridiculous nature of the question or the fact that my dad never batted an eye upon its delivery. Didn't bat an eye, didn't crack a smile, didn't even turn his head. Instead, he paused, measuring his words, and softly said, "That's a person who does bad things, son, kind of like a jerk."

That was the Bronx in 1964, aboard the Third Avenue El train that was only part of a long journey from the northeast corner of the borough to Highbridge, which was just a little northwest of Yankee Stadium, where I lived in a small three-bedroom house on Shakespeare Avenue.

Thirty days earlier, I'd come home from school to find my mother in a state of near shock, my father sitting by her side on our faded red love seat, his shoulder her only visible means of support. My little sister's slapping soles and happy babbling stood as a stark contrast to the dark aura that hung heavy in our tiny living room.

My father broke the news. My grandfather, a fireman for over thirty years and my roommate for my entire life, had been in an accident. His head, face, chest and arms had been severely burned, and his chances for living were questionable.

I had never been alone before that night. Surrounded by my grandfather, I'd always felt safe. Maybe I should say surrounded by my grandfather and Joe D., for his visage was everywhere. Grinning down at me from every conceivable angle. Following through on his textbook swing as he watched another shot sail out of the seemingly endless confines of Death Valley in left center. His arm around Marilyn, who had played a part in prompting my surprise dick question.

Joe DiMaggio scared me that night. To a young child all alone, he appeared to be glaring, his awkward grin seemed to be taunting me, the gaps in his smile looming large, impossibly large, as if they could inhale a young boy and leave not a trace.

I longed for my grandfather, his soft touch, his smell, his sound. The touch of his thick, calloused fingers tousling my hair. I missed his soft, gentle brogue, an ode to his ancestral homeland, even though his ancestors had left Ireland a century before. An accent like his was not uncommon in Highbridge, a strong Irish enclave, but the brogues, like the Irish, were starting to fade and within a short time, like the Irish themselves, would disappear from its streets.

Grandpa used to say that my father had a map of Ireland on his face. Which, after some confusion, I came to learn meant he had traditional Irish features. Fair hair, rusty blond but not quite red, freckles and green eyes. My map wasn't quite so detailed. I think I had my mother's face, dark, almost exotic. The result, I'm told, of Spanish blood passed through my veins some centuries before, on some forgotten branch of my mother's Irish family tree.

I was never sure of Grandpa's map. To me he never looked Irish, or of any other ethnic group, for that matter. He was Grandpa, after all, which meant to my young, unknowing eyes he'd always looked just . . . old. He was old, but I missed him.

I missed the Scooter as well. Phil Rizzuto, my namesake, was, from April until fall, like a third roommate. A third roommate who showed up each night around seven and wished happy birthdays to strangers and once in a while mentioned the ball game. An old Philco radio, from which the Scooter's voice would emerge, sat on a small table by Grandpa's bed. That night it was silent . . . and I missed the Scooter.

I lay awake thinking about Grandpa. Long after the hour when the crack of the bat and happy birthdays to strangers would usually lull me to sleep, I thought of that man. I used the prayers that I'd learned at Sacred Heart Church. I used them over and over, until I knew they would work. I prayed for all his late-night screams to stop. Those infrequent, mournful cries that had been frightening me for as long as I could remember. Those screams that left him cold, but sweating. I prayed for those burns to all go away. So that Grandpa would be back. Back in our house and back in my room. Where he belonged.

I got out of my bed well before dawn. I turned my head from side to side, studying Joe D.'s various likenesses, hoping he wouldn't decide to swoop down for the kill. I looked out of my window. First across the street at the three-story brick walk-ups, where during daylight hours mothers rested their elbows on pillows to watch over their kids. I looked to my left down the steep hill that led to P.S. 114. The hill where I'd sat on my grandfather's lap as he steered the Flexible Flyer. Where my little-boy laughs had come out in great clouds of steam. Where my mother had waited, with her hands on her hips, saying her child was too young to sled down such a steep hill. This winter, she said, she might reconsider. But when this winter came, would Grandpa still be alive?

I grew up thinking that my mom babied me, because she wouldn't let me have the run of the streets like other kids did. But on that first night without Grandpa, I needed my mother. I needed her warmth, her love, and the scent of Wrigley's Doublemint Chewing Gum and cigarettes with each breath she let go.

I walked out my door and into the hall that separated my sister Patty's room from mine. I looked for my sister inside her room, though I knew better. She was nearly three now, but she still slept in a crib in my parents' room, a subject that for over a year had been a bone of contention between my mom and my dad. A bone, it turned out, that my mom always got. For despite the fact that my father had spent two full weekends of the previous summer wallpapering Patty's room with a pattern of fairies and field mice, the little girl remained a fixture in my parents' bedroom.

Weekends were not something that my dad parted with lightly.

Weekends meant ball games and ball games meant beer, and my father loved both. Nothing extreme, just a six-pack of Ballantine, the Yankees' proud sponsor, over the course of nine innings. Then would come dinner, and my father would glow, from both his game and his beer. Back in those days the Yankees didn't lose often, but I think more than the outcome, the game's timeless rhythm put him at peace. I always hated for Sundays to end, for I knew that when they did, my dad had to go to work across the river in Harlem, walking a beat from four until midnight.

Sure enough, no sister there. I proceeded with care down the short hall. Still on the lookout for Joe D. I had heard of the way he patrolled center field, how surefire doubles met their end in his glove. How he was so fleet of foot that he never needed to dive.

I opened the door. As quietly as possible with two shaking hands. I heard a head stir.

"Scooter, is that you?"

"Yeah, Mom, it's me."

"Are you okay?"

"I'm a little bit scared."

I could almost hear her smile in the darkness. She said, "I guess you'd better come here."

I practically dove into her arms, then faded off into sleep as she tickled my back.

"Dad?"

"Yes, son?"

"What does 'fuck' mean?"

We were walking down 167th, only a few blocks from home, and we hadn't talked much since we got off our train. In fact, I think my father had been silent since shedding some light on "dick's" definition. His reaction, again, was slightly low key, considering the subject.

"That's when someone does something bad to somebody else. It usually concerns money. Kind of like cheating."

[2]

My grandfather couldn't have visitors for those first thirty days. I guess due to the threat of infection. He'd nearly died that first night. My dad had grown silent and sullen during the course of that month. On a couple of nights I heard beer tabs in the darkness, a prescription for sorrow after a long night of work.

My dad had rejoiced when he'd gotten the phone call. My grandfather's life was no longer in danger. He'd been transferred to Bronx Psychiatric to undergo testing, but at least he was alive and, better yet, could have guests.

My father woke me up early on the day of our visit. He didn't smile often, at least not in matters that didn't concern a ball game. But on this day in question his smile was a wide one.

"Scooter, wake up."

I blinked once or twice and then turned off Grandpa's Philco, which I had placed next to my bed a week after he'd left.

"Hi, Dad," I said.

"Guess who we're seeing today?"

"Grandpa," I said, my voice high with excitement.

"You betcha," he said, then he glanced around my room, allowing his eyes to take in every single shot of Joe D. "Yes, we're gonna see Grandpa, but we're gonna see someone else too."

My dad was so excited that I thought he might cry. Just seeing Grandpa would be the absolute best, but my dad was holding a secret, as if things could somehow get better.

He said, "Go ahead, guess."

My mind drew a big blank. Once again, my dad's eyes darted around the room.

I shook my head, clearly puzzled, then said, "I don't know."

My dad's face formed a frown, but it was quickly erased by a grin even bigger than the one I'd awoken to. "I'll give you a hint—he's on your wall."

"Batman!" I yelled. "I'm gonna meet Batman!" I looked over my bed at a picture of TV's newest sensation that my mom had cut out of the paper and taped to the wall.

"No, Scooter, not Batman." My dad played it off as if he was amused, but even at the age of four I could hear the disappointment in his voice. This was his moment, and I was in the process of ruining it, all due to Bruce Wayne's alter ego.

I looked at the walls. Aside from Batman, a faded, yellowed snapshot of a pretty teenage girl and a 1959 photo of my father in the *Daily News,* the choices were slim. There was a photo of me, in front of the Babe's monument in the outfield at the stadium, looking just a tad more than terrified, I think due to the fact that I thought the Sultan of Swat was buried right there and that I was posing for photos on top of his grave. After that, there was no one except—

"Joe D.?" I asked, with a level of enthusiasm usually reserved for the discovery of lima beans on one's dinner plate.

"That's right. Joe D.," he said, making up for my lack of excitement by doubling his own. "But it gets even better. Guess where we're meeting him?"

I had no idea, and told him as much. My answer didn't faze him. My father was on a roll now, savoring a high that usually came only with a frank and a cold one during our yearly pilgrimage to the stadium, and neither my ignorance nor my apathy was going to slow him down. "Today!—You—and I—are going . . . to . . . Freedomland!"

"Freedomland!?" I yelled.

"Freedomland Indeedomland!" he yelled back.

I temporarily forgot about my poor grandfather, so blinded with excitement was I. Freedomland was like a dream. Farther away from home than I'd ever been. All the way on the other side of the Bronx. I had begged my dad to take me there for as long as I could remember, ever since hearing "Mommy and Daddy, take my hand, take me out to Freedomland" on the radio. Ever since hearing Johnny Horton sing the Freedomland theme song, "Johnny Freedom," on the jukebox at Rossi's Sandwich Shop. Today the dream was real. My father seemed to feed off my euphoria, detailing with relish just how our day would proceed.

"We'll head down to Cozy Corners for a new ball and a coffee. How 'bout an egg cream while we're at it? Then we're off for the train to Gun Hill, take the bus to Baychester, and *BAM!* Before you know it, you're merry-go-roundin' in Kandy Kane Lane. Then after you've had more fun than one little guy can stand, *BAM!* We go see Joe D.!"

[3]

The day went just as my dad had planned. *BAM!* I rode the merry-go-round in Kandy Kane Lane. I didn't know then that Freedomland was in its dying days. That I'd never see it again. It didn't occur to me that 1909 Cadillacs didn't belong on the Civil War battlefield, or that Elsie the Cow was at the World's Fair. I only knew that souvenirs were a quarter, and my dad was in the mood to spend. A mood I'd never seen him in before, and would never see again. Sure enough, I had more fun than one little guy could stand, and then, *BAM!*, we went to see Joe D. with Grandpa's old Philco tucked underneath my father's arm.

My dad had told me how he and Grandpa used to wait for hours after games for Joe D. to emerge. Just to see him walk by on his way to the car. Just to say hello, maybe get him to sign a yearbook or a ball. But Joe D. never emerged. My grandfather wondered if the stadium had some secret underground passageway so that Joe D. could escape undetected. Kind of like the secret exit from the Batcave, I guess.

They had never met Joe D., but they sure had met a lot of other guys. Yogi. Larsen. Lopat. Bauer. Mantle too. My father showed me his collection a few times. Two decades of Yankee royalty, their signatures scribbled on a cavalcade of memorabilia—yearbooks, scorecards, ticket stubs, balls, gloves, Spaldeens, even a Krum's menu. But the crown jewel of my dad's collection was his photo of the Scooter, 1950, the year he won the MVP, posed with my dad, both of them smiling.

The Scooter had driven in the winning run that day, bunted it in, a suicide squeeze, and when he posed for the picture, he let my dad hold the bat. Then he walked away. He just walked away and let my dad have the bat.

My dad got his bat. I got his name. Why couldn't Rizzuto have taken DiMaggio's tunnel on that fateful day?

But on this day, for the first time, my father would see the great Yankee Clipper. Just as soon as he waited in a line several hundred feet long, where die-hard Yankee fans all waited for the greatest living ballplayer to write down his name. All except the guy right in front of us, who had nothing to be signed. Which struck my dad as rather strange.

"Whattaya want Joe to sign?" he asked the guy.

"Nothin'," the guy said.

"Nothin'?"

"Nah, nothin'."

My dad hadn't inherited his father's brogue, but he didn't have a typical "Noo Yawk" accent either. Very few people in Highbridge did. I escaped somewhat unscathed as well. Some Bronxites, however, including my mother, didn't get off quite so lucky. This guy, the "nothin' " guy, may have been the unluckiest of all.

My dad didn't quite know what to make of the guy, who didn't have a kid with him and didn't appear to be a connoisseur of amusement park rides. The guy was definitely there to see Joe D., yet had "nothin' " to sign. It didn't make sense.

A few more minutes went by. Joe was in sight now, or at least the green curtain that he was sitting behind was in sight. Apparently, you had to pay to see Joe. There were no free peeks at the Clipper. Even the "nothin' " guy had paid his two bucks—it was a shame that he'd leave with "nothin' " to show for it.

Curiosity finally got the better of my dad. He didn't want to ask, but I guess he felt like he had to.

"Whattaya here for if you don't want Joe to sign?" my father asked.

The guy smiled. Not a friendly smile, just a little corner-of-the-mouth smile. He was a big guy, much bigger than my dad. I thought there might be trouble. After a tense moment, the guy seemed to relax. His smile even became friendly.

"Hey, buddy," the guy said, "I just wanna shake Joe's hand."

The guy and my dad then proceeded to reminisce about great

Joe D. moments. Great Joe D. hits, great Joe D. catches. Great Joe D. wives.

Gradually, the curtain got closer. I could see Joe's silhouette as he wrote down his name, could see the pen performing its elegant arcs, could see the cigarette as he brought it to his lips for a long, refreshing drag. We were next. Yes! We were next! I'd never even seen Joe play, but we were next. His pictures scared the crap out of me, but we were next. I could hear Joe's voice, rich and resonant, as he spoke to the guy in front of us—the "nothin' " guy.

"What would you like me to sign?" the Clipper asked.

"Nothin'."

"Nothing?"

"Nothin'."

"Excuse me?"

"Nothin', I got nothin' to sign."

"I've got a piece of paper here. I'll just sign that."

"No, I don't want nothin' signed."

I could see Joe's silhouette stiffen. I could see the silhouettes of Joe's two beefy security guards stiffen too. When Joe spoke, it was with agitation.

"If you don't want me to sign anything, why are you here?"

I could see the nothin' guy shrink. Even from a seated position, Joe D. suddenly loomed much larger than life. Much larger than the recipient of Joe's very well-mannered bile, who now fumbled for words.

The "nothin' " guy finally said, "I just wanna shake your hand."

"You want to shake my hand?" Joe asked, his disbelief mingling with sarcasm.

"Yeah, how 'bout it?" I could see the guy stick his arm out.

A deep voice rang out, very official. "Mr. DiMaggio, would you like me to remove this man?"

"No, that's okay," Joe said. He now sounded intrigued, slightly amused. "This gentleman just wants to shake my hand. Isn't that correct?"

"Yeah, so how 'bout it?" The guy stuck his hand out again.

"Hold on a moment," Joe said. He was having fun now, toying with the big guy, sitting back and watching him squirm. He was like a fish on Joe's hook and Joe was going to reel him in, just as he had done in his youth on the docks of San Francisco. It was just too bad that Freedomland's San Francisco area had closed down. The irony would have been incredible—Joe D. baiting and hooking this poor slob right on Fisherman's Wharf.

I could see Joe put his arms behind his head. He leaned back and said, "Let me get this straight. You paid two dollars to get into the park. Then you paid two dollars to stand in line. Then, after standing in line for quite a while, you tell me that you just want to shake my hand. Is that correct?"

"Yeah, Joe, that's right."

"Why?"

"I got my reasons."

"I would like to know what those reasons are."

"No, Joe, I don't think you do."

"Yes, as a matter of fact I do." Joe sat up now. He wasn't quite as composed. The fish was fighting back. Joe reached for a verbal harpoon. And hurled it. "Sir, either you tell me now or I'll have you escorted from the park."

"You really wanna know?"

"Yes."

"Ya sure?"

"Yes, I'm sure."

The guy let out a breath of air. Then let Joe have just a little bigger dose of truth than he was prepared to handle.

"I just wanted to shake the hand that shook the dick that fucked Marilyn Monroe."

The Clipper jumped up and stormed off through a steel door and slammed it shut behind him. I wasn't sure where it led, an office perhaps, maybe a closet, but I was reasonably sure that things started breaking behind that steel door.

"Dad, why is Joe mad?" I asked.

My dad didn't say a word.

The big guy who wanted "nothin' " signed didn't look so big as he was being whisked away. He was kind of doubled over, maybe from the punches that Joe's two security guards directed at his midsection. I hadn't seen punches thrown in quite a while. My mom didn't let me watch bad shows on TV, and my dad was under strict orders to get up and switch the channel when one of baseball's bench-clearing brawls broke out.

Following the "nothin'" guy's departure, Joe D.'s security informed the line that the autograph session was over. Refunds were offered. But my dad didn't want a refund—he wanted Joe. I watched my father's face as he contemplated his course of action. Wrinkles on his brow, adding a decade to his twenty-seven years. Biting down on his lower lip, a mannerism that would become increasingly more prevalent in his demeanor as the years went by. His way of fighting off natural instincts of aggression in favor of a cooler head.

"Scooter, stay here for just a second," he said as he stepped out of a line that was fast dissolving and approached the protective layer of Joe's men.

My dad put a hand on one man's broad shoulder. The hand was slapped away. My father tried again. Again his gesture was rebuffed. My dad reached for his pocket. His holster, I thought. My dad's drawing his gun. I could almost read the headlines. A DEATH AT FREEDOM-LAND. But when his hand came out, it didn't hold a gun. It held a badge instead. A badge that got the guy's attention and a sympathetic ear for my father's real-life woe. When my dad returned minutes later, the line was all but gone. Gone except for me, and a somewhat angry fan who was yelling at Joe's door that Ted Williams should have been MVP back in '41.

"Joe will see us in a little while," my father said.

A little while, it turned out, was quite a while. Forty-seven minutes, to be exact. Long enough for me to replay the day's events in my mind several times. I thought of the egg cream, the train, the bus, the rides. I thought of the big guy who didn't want nothin' signed and the sound of things breaking behind the door Joe had slammed. But I kept coming back to the way I had felt when my dad reached for his badge. I had really believed that he was going to spray Freedomland full of lead. And I thought it would have been justified. But pulling a gun was against my dad's nature. I had heard him explain on many occasions how he intended to put in twenty years on the force without ever firing. It was an intention that had put him at odds right away with his father-in-law, a retired First Grade detective in New York's Four-O district in Motthaven, a close Bronx neighbor of Highbridge. Apparently, my mother's father had amassed an impressive arrest and body count during his days on the force, and he had showed very little understanding or respect for my father's somewhat more humanitarian approach to law enforcement. My dad walked a beat on the mean streets of Harlem, and he did so without fear and with a heartfelt belief that every life was worth helping. I guess a Joe D. tantrum at the fun park was not such a big deal after all.

The security guy put his hand on my dad's shoulder. "The Dago will see you" was all that he said.

I followed my dad, who had the Philco under his arm, as he made his way to Joe D.'s steel door. I looked at Joe's curtain as I passed it by and wondered if Grandpa might like a few of Joe's smoked butts to keep in his room. I thought that he would, but I was too scared to ask.

The heavy door opened, and Joe D. himself looked straight into my eyes. He didn't look goofy or awkward like he had in '41, when he'd hit in fifty-six straight. And I was reasonably sure that he wouldn't inhale me. He just looked sad and lonely, sitting behind an ugly gray desk whose contents lay scattered and broken and battered on the dirty tile floor. There was a hole in the wall that looked newly formed.

Joe D. spoke with a whisper, his voice barely audible as he expressed his regret at what had transpired. Then he expressed his remorse for my grandfather's health. "I hope this will help," said the Clipper, as he took the ball from my father and rolled it in the palm of his left hand until he found the sweet spot. When he picked up his pen, I could see his right knuckles were bleeding.

Joe signed his name with the ease of a man who had done such a task thousands of times. As he did, I studied his hands and saw one drop of blood make a long, lonely trip from the wound's point of origin to the tip of his finger to the point of his pen. Black ink and Joe's blood became one and the same as he looped his last "o," and it wasn't until later, on our short cab ride to Bronx Psychiatric, that the "o" became smudged and the red scarred the white sphere.

[4]

I wasn't prepared for what I saw in room 317. The sight of my grandfather lying in bed, his face swathed in gauze, not a trace of skin showing. I wasn't prepared for the sounds of that place either, distant screams that seemed to pull at my feet, as if trying to drag me through concrete, to unknown horrors below. I wanted to leave, to get out of that place, and I started to tug on my father's coat sleeve. I loved my grandfather, but this wasn't him. This man was a monster, a mummy, a ghoul. I tugged the sleeve harder.

My father glanced down, more hurt than annoyed. "Say hello to your grandpa" was all he said. But I couldn't speak. I just turned away. The thing in the bed couldn't speak either. Was it even alive?

My dad did the talking. He talked to a ghoul. He talked to an unseeing, unfeeling, unmoving ghoul. The Bronx Bombers in five, the Cardinals couldn't stack up. Gibson's heat was no match for Whitey's best stuff. Flood couldn't lace the Mick's shoes in center. He placed the old Philco on a shelf by the bed. Game number one of the '64 Series began the next day. He thought Grandpa might like to listen. But Grandpa was gone. And the thing in his place wasn't responding.

My dad's hands were shaking as he reached for Joe's ball. His red, swollen eyes were rimmed with welled tears. He looked like he'd aged since we entered the room. His voice shook when he spoke.

"I got somethin' for you."

He took out the ball and rewrote the day's history as he fought back his tears.

"I saw Joe D. today, Dad. Yeah, can you believe it? Me and Scooter saw him. I took Scooter to Freedomland, he had the time of his life. You gotta see the place, Dad. You'd love it, I swear. Scooter helped put out the great fire in Chicago. He wanted to help so he could be just like you. Then, as we're eatin' Chinese in San Fran, Scooter tugs on my sleeve. I say, 'Scooter, hold on, I'm tryin' to eat.' But he tugs on my arm, so I look up at your roommate and he's pointin' out in the street, over by the Seal Pool. So I look where he's pointin' and who do I see? Joe D. 'Yeah, Joe D.' I know Joe likes his privacy, but I couldn't resist, so I walk on over and I say hello and I tell him my father is his number one fan. And I'll tell you what, Dad, Joe couldn't have been nicer. He even pulled out a ball and signed it for you. And I got it right here. Isn't that just how it went, son?"

I'd never once heard my dad tell a lie, let alone ten in a row, but in spite of that fact, I nodded my head. I don't know why. It's not like the monster could see me. Or hear one word that my father said. My father held out the ball . . . and the thing moved its hand. At first it moved slowly, hardly at all, but it moved just the same. The hand started to rise. I felt a lump in my throat. My father lowered the ball. The thing's hand met it halfway. The thing was my grandpa, and he was touching the ball. My dad wrapped Grandpa's fingers around Joe D.'s smudged ball and, just for a moment, the hand held it there. Then the hand slowly lowered and put the ball to its heart. My knees went weak and I thought I would fall. I leaned on my father's leg to help me stay up, and he reached down for me and stroked my short hair. I looked up at my dad and there were tears on his face.

[5]

My father was silent the entire way home, my two poignant questions being the trip's only exceptions. A few kids were playing stoopball as we approached our little blue house. Darkness was falling and Shakespeare was quiet, almost eerily so. My dad waved to a neighbor, whose day probably hadn't been quite as hectic as ours. The lights were all out, meaning no one was home, but my father wasn't alarmed. Friday was my mom's day to go shopping, with my little sister in tow. They usually killed a whole day on the Concourse, going to stores, painting their nails and, depending on what time and what feature was playing, catching a movie at the Paradise and an ice cream at Krum's. They were usually back around nine o'clock.

My dad tucked me in at eight thirty-five. I awaited my story, but no story came. I had to settle for a kiss on the cheek. He started to leave, but something was bothering me and it just couldn't wait.

"Dad," I said, as the door started to close. At first there was nothing, and I feared that my call had come just a little too late.

The door slowly opened. Thank goodness for that. I had information too important to wait. It had to be heard.

"Yes, son?" my dad said.

I fumbled for words. I needed just the right way to express what had been bothering me all the way home. "Um, um."

"Yes, son, what is it?"

"Well, I just wanted to say that uh, um—"

"Go ahead, Scooter, just let it out."

So I did as my dad told me—I just let it out. "Dad, I don't blame Joe."

"Oh," said my dad, thinking over my words. "What don't you blame Joe for?"

"For shaking that dick."

My sudden confession must have caught him off guard, for he put his hand to his mouth and swallowed real hard. Then he covered his eyes with the hand and rubbed his eyebrows with force, obviously mulling over the depth of my thoughts. Finally he said, "Uh, Scooter, which dick did Joe shake?"

"The one that fucked Marilyn!"

How could he ask? It was so simple. There was only one dick it could possibly be. I looked at my father for some sign of agreement, but he was looking up at the ceiling and shaking his head. Shaking his head like he didn't agree. I pleaded my case.

"Dad, if that dick fucked my wife, I'd shake him too! Can't you see? Don't you—"

My dad cut me off. "Scooter, you're right. I don't blame Joe either. Now go to sleep, buddy, okay?"

"Okay, Dad. Good night."

My dad shut the door and walked down the hall. I heard his footsteps on the stairs as he made his way down to the living room, where he would no doubt ponder my words in the comfort of his rocking chair, with the companionship of a Ballantine beer. I heard the distinctive pop of a tab being pulled. Then a small laugh, then another, and then great gales of laughter that were still at their peak when my mother got home at ten minutes to nine.

1969

[1]

I turned nine in June of '69, and my day of birth was heralded the way it always was—with a yearly trip to see the Bombers in the House That Ruth Built. We saw just one game a year, for although my dad's status as a cop could have yielded him a ticket at any time, his own Spartan code of ethics did not allow him to take freebies. I often used to wonder about the mighty Babe and why he'd built the house so strange. It seemed as if I sat behind a rusty girder in section 315 every time I saw a game. I think my dad preferred that section in the upper mezzanine because of Pop the peanut vendor, who, unlike other vendors that loudly shopped their wares, just said "Peanuts" softly, so you almost had to read his lips.

So every June I'd see one game by peering out from behind Dad's pet girder, and I'd eat Pop's special peanuts while my dad pounded Ballantines. My dad looked like he was in heaven with his beloved beer and Bombers, while I took in the slow, dull games and cursed Babe Ruth's building skills. He may have been a great hitter, but he'd built a lousy house. No wonder he hit so many out—that right porch was so damn close—five sewers, maybe six.

Our '69 excursion took place on Mickey Mantle Day, when sixty thousand jammed Ruth's house to show their love for the Mick. My dad loved Mickey too, although he said the Mick had cut his career short by swinging for the fences on every single pitch. With his speed, he could have been an all-time great—if he'd just learned to slap it up the middle.

That seemed to be my father's sole solution to curing baseball's woes, which by '69 were plentiful. Microscopic batting averages and even smaller ERAs had sent the game's brain trust searching for answers.

New ballparks sprung up around the country, funded by the public and, to the naked eye, almost identical. But new ballparks couldn't hide the truth: Fans found baseball dull. So, to celebrate the game's hundredth year, some changes had been made.

Lower mounds, a larger zone for strikes—that would do the trick. Home plates moved out, fences moved in and fans could no longer sit in the center-field bleachers. If the players could just get a better look at a better choice of easier pitches and didn't have to hit the ball quite so far, things would be just fine. Especially if those closer fences were at parks built in places where Negroes didn't live.

My father didn't like the changes—he said the old rules were fine. What needed changing wasn't rules, it was batters' minds instead. They had to learn to slap it up the middle. Or punch it through the hole. Or spray it all around.

The terms were interchangeable when my father barked them out. Which he'd done all through the summer, whenever he could find the time. I was set to start playing in a league as soon as September rolled around, and my dad tried to get me ready. I don't know how he found the time. With all the hours that he worked, his days off were now quite rare. I'd overheard him many times when he'd gotten home from work. Things had been extra tense in Harlem since '68, when Dr. King and Bobby Kennedy were killed, and as a result, there was overtime to fill.

He no longer walked a beat, but drove a car and was breaking in a rookie partner. He still sometimes walked to work from Shakespeare, over the 145th Street bridge, but he told my mom the trip now brought him fear, and he had once almost drawn his gun.

For my mom, the solution was quite simple: Move the hell away. Take an easy job somewhere in the suburbs, where Negroes posed no threat. He could still be a policeman, just one without the stress. But my father wouldn't hear of it. He had made a vow to serve—and little things like homicide and drugs weren't going to keep him from his calling.

So my mom proposed a compromise, one that she was quite persistent with. Keep the job in Harlem, but move the family somewhere safe. Most of Highbridge was still Irish, but it was less so every day. Our house was in the shadow of the projects, and the public schools were taking on a darker shade. Sure, the Catholic schools, where every self-respecting Highbridge Mick sent his kids, were mainly white, but the Bronx as a whole was no longer safe for kids and my mother wanted out.

She wanted Dad to change—to make arrests instead of friends. Make detective, bring home more pay, and leave the Bronx behind. It was the least that he could do, after all she'd given up for him.

My mother's detective father, with his multitude of arrests and the overtime hours that came with them, had earned a handsome living. Handsome enough to live on the Grand Concourse, the Park Avenue of the Bronx. Handsome enough to lavish money on their only child, until she got pregnant by a common street cop. Then the cash flow abruptly stopped.

There had been, I've been told, a few early attempts at reconciliation, but the combination of my father's on-the-job pacifism and their daughter's premarital activities had been too grave an offense for the devout Catholic sensibilities of my maternal grandparents.

For the first few years there were birthday cards and Christmas gifts, but then those disappeared, and when the couple chose to move, a forwarding address never made its way to our house.

My mother lived with her decision, but said she couldn't live without some things.

New things, nice things, things a plain old cop could not afford. Alexander's wasn't petty cash, and the subways weren't safe. So overtime bought Mom a car, a beautiful '67 candy-apple-red Dodge Charger. Monday became her new Concourse day, and as soon as Patty got out of school, they'd hit the road and get back at nine, with new hair, new nails and brand-new things.

So with my mother gone and my dad at work, I had Mondays to

myself. Mom insisted that I stay inside, because things weren't safe on the street—there were now Puerto Ricans up the block. Compared to other streets, Shakespeare was quite dull—I think it was the hill. I was older now, I could sled in snow, but the hill killed the thrill of sports.

Stickball, boxball, stoopball—all the major games—weren't much fun when the Spaldeens were gone, and the hill's sewers were unforgiving. Those balls cost a quarter each, which wasn't cheap in '69, and Shakespeare could swallow four an hour, which made the games quite rare.

Sometimes I would walk a few blocks to Nelson, where my friend Jim Gray lived. Jim's dad would play stickball for hours, throwing Spaldeens to any kid who cared to play. He had the coolest knack for throwing pitches within one inch of a kid's swing. A kid couldn't help but be a hitter when Will Gray did the pitching.

My father caught me playing stickball one day when I was eight. He said the game was poisonous to any kid who played real ball. He said he saw Willie Mays play with kids in Harlem back in '62, on his way to the Polo Grounds. The "Say Hey Kid" fanned three times that day, and my dad said the stick had killed his swing. He said Willie's stickball habit had struck down a promising career.

Stickball is a game where a hit is judged by distance. If a guy had quite a swing, he might be a four-sewer man. I think that's why my dad disdained the game. You didn't slap Spaldeens up the middle. Or punch them through the hole. You didn't spray them all around. You simply hit for power. I saw my dad play only once, when I was six years old. Kids were playing a rare game on the hill, and the Yanks had just dropped two on a Sunday. My dad may have had a few too many Ballantines when he took a turn at bat. A two-sewer man at best.

"Spaldeen" was the accepted name for pink Spalding rubber balls. It was the same in every section of the Bronx—in all the other boroughs too. In my entire life's existence, I have heard only one person call it differently. My mother. She called them "little soft pink balls"—which seems kind of gross now that I'm older.

[2]

Nine times out of ten, Mondays were for Grandpa. He had lived through his tough ordeal—not just lived, but thrived. His intellect was keen and sharp, his wit was warm and loving. He seemed to find hope where hope could not be found, and made sense where none existed.

But though he'd emerged from death's door with his spirit energized, his face and head bore the scars of his ordeal. A few tufts of gray were all he had now where a full head of hair had been. Thick white bands of scars poured down the right side of his face, like a flow of angry lava that had devoured all life in its path. His right eye simply did not exist, nor was there any sign it ever had. There was no eyebrow, or eye socket, just opaque tissue stretched tautly, like the covering of a drum. The tissue then ran down his neck and disappeared into his shirt. I never saw the rest, as his shirts were always buttoned to the top.

When I was four, I thought he was a monster. As he lay in bed like Boris Karloff's mummy, I had really wished him dead. But with each visit he grew less horrible, until my eyes no longer saw a wounded freak, but a gentle soul whose smile had gone untouched.

And that's what I always saw when I saw Grandpa—a smile, and then the scars. The accident had changed him, that fact was evident—not just in how he looked, but in how he was—as if he existed on a higher plane somehow. He never moved back home, but he got an apartment on Townsend, just a few blocks from the house. My dad took down all the Joe D. stuff and put it back up over there. The sacred ball from Freedomland was placed in a glass case on the TV set that my dad had bought for Grandpa's birthday.

Twice a week for several years, my dad and I went there. Then came the winter day in '68 when I heard Grandpa and my father yelling. After that, our visits stopped.

I asked my father why one day, but he kept it to himself. He just said the old man could not be forgiven, that what he'd done was far too wrong.

My dad said, "You don't go against the family, son," as if that shed any light at all. "And that old man's not my father. It's about time you found out."

"No, I guess I'm not," the old man said in response to my sudden accusation. His apartment was forbidden, of that I was sure. My parents had both been very clear in making that fact known. But I felt I had to see him—I had nobody else. My mom had shopping, my dad had work, and my sister had my mom. So where did that leave me? With a street I couldn't play on, with a few friends I couldn't see.

My mother pulled away in the Charger and I headed for Townsend. The old man tried to hug me, but I pulled away from him.

"You're not my grandpa," I said, in a voice much tougher than I really felt. My anger turned to tears, but I would not accept the old man's open arms. If this old man wasn't my grandpa, then who the hell was he?

He looked old and pathetic, shaking, close to tears himself. Standing with his arms still open wide, as if I was going to reconsider and give him a hug.

"Who are you?" I yelled.

His voice quivered when he spoke. "I'm afraid I can't say."

"Why not?" I screamed even louder.

"Because—because—I made a promise to your dad."

"Oh, yeah?" I said, my little boy heart beating fast, new courage rushing through my veins. "I've got a promise too. I swear that you won't see me again, ever, you . . . freak!"

I raced for the door, opened it up, then turned to face him. I was leaving him forever, but I needed one more shot. A way to hurt him deep and for a long time, just as his lies had done to me. I saw the TV—I could smash the thing to bits. Tip the damn thing over, so he couldn't watch his stupid games. Or better yet, the Joe D. ball, the one from Freedomland, I could throw it in the river, let Joe sleep with the fishes. Why had my father wasted his time and money for a pathetic fraud like this?

Instead I reached for what was closest, a framed photo on the wall. Me and the old man at Cozy Corners candy store. Sharing an egg cream and a smile. I had been just a little kid. Just a little fool. I threw it to the floor. I slammed the cheap wood door behind me. But just before it shut, I heard an old man's desperate yell.

"I'm your father's uncle!"

I tried to open the door. The stupid thing was locked. I pondered knocking hard, but my aggressive streak was gone. I tapped meekly.

"My sister's husband was a war hero. He flew some pretty major missions—he helped lead the raid on Tokyo." He paused as if imagining the raid, smiled sadly, then continued. "He came back in '45, right before the war was over, just to pay a visit to your grandmother. And—he was stabbed to death for seven lousy dollars. He had roses in his hand. Clutched tightly—as if he'd rather die than give up those roses for his wife."

He looked directly at me, as if trying to reach right to my soul. Trying to judge if I was ready for the words he had to say.

He said, "I'm going back on a promise, Scooter—one I made to your father long ago—when you were just a baby. I'm telling you now because I love you, and I think your father's gone from me for good. Understand?"

I nodded.

"I don't want to lose you, Scooter, you're the only blood I've got." A tear fell from his eye. "I had the house in Highbridge—I tried to move my sister in. But she was independent, a proud Irish girl, wanted to make it on her own. She moved out of Hell's Kitchen, a place on Fifty-ninth, and took her baby uptown just below the Polo Grounds. I used to wonder why. Then Christmas Eve I take the train, stop by for a visit. Your dad was just a little boy, maybe two or three. I knock outside, no one comes, but I hear your father crying. The door is locked, but I make it give, and—"

"Had Santa come?" I asked.

The old man smiled at my innocence, then said, "No, old Santa hadn't come. I bet I just beat him there. Otherwise I do believe Santa would have put some heat on. That apartment needed Santa. No tree, no gifts, no heat at all, and your poor father had no clothes."

"But how?" I said in disbelief. "Wasn't your sister there to help him?"

"Oh, she was there," the old man said. "She was there alright. But she wasn't there to help him."

"Why not?" I said.

"Well, Scooter, my sister couldn't help, because she was sleeping on the floor. I didn't know just what was wrong, until I saw blood trickling down her arm."

"Did someone stab her too?" I asked. "Just like they'd done to him?"

The old man bit down on his lip, just as my father did so much. He stirred a cup of tea and went on with utmost care. "I think she'd kind of stabbed herself."

"To kill herself because she missed him?"

"In a way, yeah, in a way. She made lots of little tiny stabs, died a little every time."

"What did you do, Grandpa, what did you do?" I had called him Grandpa by mistake, and it had not gone undetected. He was smiling when he answered, on the verge of tears again.

"I brought him back to Highbridge, where he's been ever since."

"What happened to your sister?"

"Oh, I tried to help, but she wouldn't help herself. She gave your dad up without a fight. Then one day she was gone, she just seemed to . . . disappear."

It was getting late, and I was a little scared that my parents would be mad. Even though my dad was in his uptown squad car and my mom was shopping up a storm. I had deliberately broken the rules, and I needed to go home. But I really liked my father's uncle and I didn't want to go.

"Do you think I could visit you again?" I asked.

"Well, I don't think that you should try . . . but . . . if you happened to walk by and by mistake walked up the stairs, and accidentally knocked on my door . . . I'd be glad to let you in."

"And . . . could I . . . still call you Grandpa?"

"I wouldn't have it any other way."

He opened up his arms, and this time I ran inside them.

I'd been born Scooter O'Brien, but following the fallout of '68, my father forbade any mention of the old man, prompting the rather unusual process of surname relocation. My dad reclaimed his true father's roots, and from that point forward, I was known, legally and otherwise, as Scooter Reilly.

[3]

The Bombers never really had a chance in '69. The two they took on the Mick's big day put them up to 29–29, but the Orioles were on a roll en route to 109 wins and were a sure thing for the Series.

When the Yanks were sold to CBS in '64, the league feared the network's cash supply would render all of baseball helpless. The league was in for a surprise. For according to my grandpa, the game had passed the Yankees by. Sure they'd won it all in '61, Roger Maris's year of 61. But they were soundly spanked in four games straight in '63 by Koufax and his crew, and in '64, as it turned out, the Cards did indeed stack up. By '66, the Yanks were shot, and my grandpa knew just why.

"We all end up paying for our sins," he said. "The only question's when."

My grandfather saw the game of baseball as if it were the game of life itself, as if all of life's great lessons could be explained in baseball lore. Most of Grandpa's knowledge sailed just a little north of me, but I kept my ears open just the same. Because once in a great while, I found something I could keep.

"Our boys are paying for it now. Paying now for moves they made, or didn't make, since the color line was broken."

I never had the nerve to tell the poor old guy that I didn't like the game. He seemed to sometimes speak a foreign language, one he'd passed down to my dad. As for me, I knew *"BAM," "BOOM," "POW,"* and cursed the day *Batman* left the air. I really didn't know about the line that Robinson broke, or what color it had been. But my grandfather didn't stop his words. He had more knowledge to hand out.

"After other teams saw Jackie Robinson play, they knew that things had changed for good. But the Yankees didn't see it, and the game just passed them by. Mantle bought them time, because his game was speed and power, just like the Negro Leagues, and they finally brought up Elston Howard in 1955. They could still pick Kansas City's pocket, but after Maris, that connection died out too, and then they sabotaged the minors to make the books look good for CBS."

"Grandpa," I said.

"Yes, Scooter."

"You know all that stuff you just said?"

"Yes."

"Well, I don't understand any of it."

"Any of it?"

"Not really."

The old man shook his head and smiled. "Well, let me see how I can explain it all a little clearer."

"Okay."

"All you need to know is that the guy who used to run the Yankees thought a white family from White Plains wouldn't want to sit next to a Negro from the Bronx. And the team is paying for that now."

"Well . . . did they want to sit together?" I wasn't being smart. I just really didn't know.

"Scooter, three years ago Red Barber was fired by the ball club after over thirty years of service. He was fired for announcing that only four hundred fans had showed up for the game. All those empty seats were blue that day—they weren't black or white. That family in White Plains wants to see good baseball, just like that Negro in the Bronx."

Oh my goodness, I thought I understood. Once the old man knew

I didn't talk the talk, he made a lot more sense. But this new sense left me confused.

"Grandpa?"

"Yes, Scooter, how can I be of help?"

"Well, if all of that is true, why does my father still get so upset when they lose?"

Grandpa's words came gushing out. "Just because he loves them. And that's what love's about. He probably loves them more than ever, even though they've let him down. He loves them unconditionally. World Series or the cellar. And sometimes I think that love like that can make a person blind."

"It makes them blind?" I yelled. I thought I'd better tell my dad. It would be hard to drive the squad car if the New York Yankees made him blind. Thankfully, my grandfather cut me off before I could say anything even dumber.

"No, not in that way. I mean love like that can make someone blind to others' faults. Even when those faults seem obvious. Do you think you understand?"

I thought I did—and I thought I'd show him what I'd learned.

"You mean like how I love you even though your face looks really weird?"

Grandpa smiled. He didn't look weird when he smiled. "Well, that wasn't what I was thinking of, but yeah, I guess that's not a bad example."

If the '69 Yanks were indeed paying for their earlier sins, then the '69 Mets seemed to be reaping the harvest of seeds they had planted since their birth in '62, as the team had emerged from league laughingstock to bona fide contenders when August rolled around.

Even in their woeful days the team had pulled in decent crowds, and with a brand-new stadium unveiled in '64, the upstart Mets, not the mighty Yanks, had become the New York team to see—for everyone but my father.

It wasn't so much hate he showed as it was a genuine refusal to acknowledge their existence. My mother once suggested that he take me out to Shea. He simply didn't answer her. She said that it was nicer, that the streets of Queens were safe. But my father wouldn't hear of it.

So it came as a surprise to me when he woke me up one night.

"Scooter, Scooter—Scooter, hey, wake up."

The clock read three a.m.

He said, "Guess what the two of us are gonna do tomorrow?" The words seemed kind of slurred.

His tone was one I recognized, though just vaguely, as it had last surfaced years ago. Then it came to me—Freedomland back in '64, when we'd gone to see Joe D. Maybe that was it.

I said, "Are we going to see Joe D. again?"

I couldn't see him in the darkness, but I could smell beer on his breath. A lot of it. He grabbed both my arms and shook me to emphasize his words. "Well, only if the Clipper is sitting right behind the Giants bench with you, me and my partner."

Even in my sleepy state, I knew this couldn't be. Giants football hadn't started yet, and besides, my mom thought the game was violent. He kissed my cheek and said, "You'll see," and let me fade back off to sleep.

It never did occur to me, even after waking up the next morning, that these Giants were the baseball type and the seats he spoke of were in Queens.

[4]

My dad had done the guy a favor, that's the only reason he gave. And in return the guy was giving us two seats meant for his mom and dad, who were visiting from California. I asked my father if the favor was a big one, and he really didn't say. I thought it must have been kind of big for the guy to replace his West Coast parents with a kid he'd never met.

The guy turned out to be my father's partner, the rookie I'd heard mentioned. For a guy my father hadn't known too long, they seemed like the best of friends. I liked the guy immediately, and I think he liked me too. My father said his name was Vinnie, but he called himself the Dago. As in "it's the Dago's treat tonight." I knew I'd heard the name one time before, but I could not recall just when. Oh, well, I thought, it must be a common name, there must be a million Dagos in New York.

We lived ten miles from Shea Stadium, maybe twelve at most, but the Dago picked us up at four for a seven-thirty game. It didn't seem to make much sense. Until the Dago cleared things up.

"Hey, kid, your dad said he'd come watch a real ball team, but only under one condition."

When the Dago smiled he showed off huge white teeth that lived in the shadow of his nose, which was pretty big as well. Everything about the guy was big: his voice, his arms, his thick dark hair, his car, even the gestures with his hands. He made steering seem like an afterthought, the way he used those hands.

I was too shy to ask what the one condition was, so the Dago filled me in.

"He said he would come to Shea, but only if I didn't drive on any Robert Moses roads or bridges."

"Oh, come on, Vinnie," my father said, half amused, half mad. "Spare the kid the politics."

I didn't know it then, but trying to get from the Bronx to Queens without a Moses road or bridge was like trying to sail without a boat. So as a consequence of my dad's demand, we carved out a lengthy trail, from Jerome Avenue to the Macombs Dam Bridge, through Harlem, then downtown. All the way to Chinatown, where he caught the Brooklyn Bridge. Then side streets through North Brooklyn until we crawled on into Queens.

I knew my father hated Moses, but I thought he meant the Bible guy. I never realized the devil could be the guy who shaped New York. But to hear my father tell it, as the Dago's old beat-up Caddy inched its way along, all the city's ills fell in one guy's lap, especially when dealing with the Bronx.

He said the borough's white flight to the suburbs could be traced to the Cross Bronx Expressway, which drove an eight-mile stake right through the city's heart. It ripped out the guts of Tremont and cut out Soundview's soul. It trampled right through West Farms' bowels and cut the throat of Morris Heights. So, after thirteen years of devastation, which uprooted a quarter million lives, Robert Moses got a new notch on his gun and the Bronx got a bullet in its head.

The Dago disagreed. "Come on, Paddy, it wasn't Moses who chased all the Jews and guineas out. It was the spics and the spooks together. It was like they planned the whole thing out."

"Oh come on," my dad moaned. "They moved in when the whites moved out, that's why housing prices dropped. Runnin' to the suburbs on roads that Moses built."

The Dago laughed at my father's pain and gestured wildly with his hands. "So now we learn the truth. That's why you won't move out to the Island, like your wife wants you to. You don't wanna take the LIE or the Northern State. Come on now, that's the truth."

"That's part of it," my father said, as we paused at a red light. Passersby stopped to look at the sweaty white guy yell. "Vinnie, maybe roots don't mean much to you, but they sure as hell do to me. You wanna leave Clason Point for White Plains, fine for you. Your parents want to move out west, fine for them too. But roots still mean a damn to me and that's why I'm stayin' put. I grew up in my father's house and I'm gonna die there too!"

Man, my dad was really passionate about his house—too bad my mother disagreed. The Dago lived in White Plains. Did he like Negroes from the Bronx?

The Dago played off my father's pride. It was like a game to him.

"I don't know, Paddy, I don't know. You think you're safe over there in Mickland, but I could see the projects from your house. Someday soon, I swear to you, all those spooks and Puerto Ricans are just gonna come spillin' over Highbridge like some science fiction blob. And you're gonna be up there on your roof, as that tide of Harlem rejects rises, sayin', "I should have listened to the Dago.""

The Dago's words made my father laugh—I think part of him liked to play this game. "Jeez, Vinnie, I can't believe I let you talk like this in front of my kid." Then he turned and said to me, "Scooter, don't listen to this guy."

I said, "Some Puerto Ricans moved in up the block. The girl is really nice." I'd never heard of spooks or spics, but I knew what Puerto Ricans were. I was glad I could contribute to the conversation.

"See what I mean?" the Dago asked. "The groundwork's laid. They'll call their people in San Juan. They'll say, 'Come on in—no, there's no work, we just cash our welfare checks.' And in they come on cheap one-way flights. I just hope that girl you know can outrun her fastest uncle."

"Alright already," my father said. "You're gonna scar the kid for life. We're goin' to a ball game, right, so let's start talking ball."

"Good idea," the Dago said, with both hands in a rare position—on the wheel. "But if you ever do move to the Island, I've got a foolproof way to find your town."

"Go ahead, let's hear it."

"Well, you get the Island paper—*Newsday*'s probably the best."

"Okay."

"You look through the sports pages' high school section—you follow me so far, Paddy?"

"Yeah," my father said.

"You look for the records of each school in basketball—this method only works in winter. You with me back there, Scooter?"

"Uh-huh."

"You find the school with the worst record . . . and that's where you move."

"Jesus Christ!" my father yelled. "Let's start some baseball talk."

The Dago's unique race perspective had brought us into Queens. It was like a different world out there, like a wilderness or prairie. The talk did indeed turn to baseball—kind of.

"So," the Dago said, his white teeth gleaming in the rearview. "You're named after Rizzuto?"

I nodded my head in agreement.

"I don't know what's stranger. That your old man did that in the first place or that you still speak to him."

"MVP in '50," my father said, sticking right up for his man. "The fact that he's not in the Hall of Fame is a lowdown dirty shame."

The Dago threw both hands up in the air, even though we were moving somewhat faster now. It looked like we would make the trip in about two hours. "I'm not sayin' he couldn't play—though I personally never seen him. I'll have to take an old guy like you's word for it. But Jesus, Mary and Joseph, I'd rather hear nails across a chalkboard than hear that sawed-off guinea announce a game!"

"What's the matter with him?" my father asked, his tone a shade defensive. As if it had never crossed his mind that my namesake had a fault.

"You want a list?" The Dago laughed. "Well, here we go. He never talks about the game. He wishes about a hundred happy birthdays every day, then drives home midway through the sixth. Though for that I should be thankful. Then he goes off on wild tangents. Like the other day I'm listening, drivin' in to work. During yet another Yankee loss—what are they, twenty under five? He starts talkin' about squirrels in Yogi's attic when there's two men on, no one out."

"So, what's wrong with that?" my father asked.

The Dago turned to his right, so that he wasn't looking at the road. His hands were still in full gesture mode, but my father didn't seem concerned. He was focused on the Dago. The Dago seemed to bring the kid out of my dad.

"I'll tell you what's wrong, my Irish friend. I don't give a damn about a squirrel problem in Yogi's attic, when I got a coon problem in Harlem."

My father sunk low in his seat, he was trying not to laugh. The Dago put his hands back on the wheel, looking very happy with himself. I didn't see what was so funny—I felt kind of bad for Yogi.

The Dago wasn't through yet, nor was Yogi for that matter. "I'm glad the Yanks had no more use for Berra—he's been good for the Mets—not to mention me."

"Oh, come on, you don't know Yogi," my father said, his face perplexed, not seeing he was being set up by the Dago.

"Yeah, I know," the Dago said, real casually, before reaching for a punch line I wouldn't get for another seven years. "But when the Dago's with a lady, and things are, you know, ending a little quickly, I think of that poor bastard Yogi, until my big guy settles down."

The Dago laughed. My dad did too. Really hard. I didn't have a clue. Years later, I laughed hard too. Shea was coming into view. My dad was still doubled over when he pretended to be mad.

"Jeez there, Dago, that's gotta be the sickest thing I ever heard." He paused until he could sit up straight again, then turned slowly to his left. "Besides—St. Louis just got this kid named Torre who could stop a boner in its tracks."

The Dago pounded on the dashboard. My father held his gut. The two looked like epileptics, the way they jerked and seized. The Dago gave the parking guy a dollar and we pulled on into Shea.

"I'm gonna call the paper, got a headline for the *Post*. IRISH COP MAKES JOKE—WORLD COMES TO END—whattaya think of that?"

My father held my hand as we walked on toward the game. A game that would change my life. I had no idea that fate was shining through as the sun went down. I tugged my father's sleeve.

"What is it, son?" my father asked, his face content, filled with an ease I rarely saw.

"Does Yogi have a coon problem too?" I asked.

"No, probably not in his neighborhood," my father said, and then we went to meet my fate.

[5]

"What the hell you think you're doing?" the Dago asked my dad.

My dad was gluing on a moustache.

"I don't want anyone to know I'm here," my father said. I thought he might break out and laugh as if this were another joke from the car, but his voice betrayed no humor.

The Dago shook his head and took a giant swig of beer, then gave a giant burp. He had said "the Dago's treat tonight" and had set about proving it. We kept our cache of Dago stuff on top of San Francisco's dugout, closer seats than I'd ever dreamed, far from Babe Ruth's rusty girders. I took a bite of hot dog number two and washed it down with soda. My dad followed suit with a soda of his own, which seemed slightly odd. I'd never seen him at a game without a cold beer. Not that the Dago didn't offer, he did, but my dad had said no. He said Rheingold tasted like Tom Seaver's piss, and besides, he'd told his wife he wouldn't drink. The Dago asked my father how he knew what Seaver's piss tasted like, which I'd been wondering also. My dad had also shunned the peanut guy, because his name wasn't Pop.

All in all, the scene was kind of weird on that August night at Shea, sitting next to a stranger with a fake moustache who wanted neither beer nor nuts. Watching my father with a soft drink was like watching Gandhi sink his teeth into a Big Mac.

The Dago broke the silence while my father studied Mays swinging in the batting cage.

"Your father says you're playing Little League this year," he said, as Mays popped one up into shallow right.

"Uh-huh," I said, with a dog-stuffed mouth—it was the best I could offer.

"You gonna be a pitcher like your old man?"

"No," I said, my mouth now free. "The coaches pitch." Then, "I didn't know my dad could pitch."

The Dago said, "You're probably right, but that's not the way he tells it."

My father grabbed me by the shoulder and pointed to the field, where a Mays grounder was dribbling slowly to the mound. "You see there, Scooter, that's what stickball did, it took away his timing. That lack of discipline killed his career." A month later, Willie Mays hit career home run six hundred. No telling what he could have done if not for that damn stickball.

"By the way," the Dago said, "I've got a question for you, partner."

"Go ahead," my dad replied while he sipped his Coke with joyless care, as if it contained trace amounts of Seaver's urine.

"Well, if you won't ride on Robert Moses roads, or go through Moses tunnels, or over Moses bridges, or swim at Moses beaches, why did you agree to come to Shea?"

My father had his eyes on a tall well-built black man who had just replaced Mays in the cage. My father took a casual bite of hot dog and said, "Whattaya mean?"

"He built this place," the Dago said, not exactly quiet but downright subdued for him.

The dog dropped from my father's mouth. The soft drink left his hand and splatted on his lap. He said, "Tell me you're joking."

"I could, but I'd be lying. I thought everybody knew." He opened up both big arms as if trying to give the world a hug and said, "You're sitting in the House That Moses Built." Hey, the guy might have been the devil, but he'd built a nicer house than Ruth.

"I think I'll have a beer," my father said.

"Hey, buddy—give this man a Rheingold."

The gloom disappeared instantly with one great wood and sphere collision. A crack loud enough for all eyes to take notice. It exploded like a shotgun blast that echoed through Shea's canyon. The white ball propelled majestically against a purple twilight sky.

I'd heard tales of Mantle blasts that seemed the stuff of legend. The '60 shot that left Forbes Field, or the one in '63 that clipped the facade in the Yankees' upper right while still on an upward path. Experts say it might have gone 620 if its flight hadn't been impeded. Well, I'll swear this one was longer. It left Shea Stadium completely; it simply disappeared. I wished I'd brought a tape measure, I'd have measured it right then. Except I didn't bring one, or know what one was, to tell the truth.

"Fuckin' McCovey," the Dago said, filled with awe at what he had just observed.

I riffled through my scorecard (my dad always insisted I keep score) to see who this Fuckin' player was. McCovey, Willie, there he was. Fuckin' must have been his nickname.

My father shared his two cents with us on what we had just seen— after all, he was a learned baseball man. He was still looking at the sky, retracing the missile's path, when he said, "That is one strong nigger."

I had heard that word a time or two by that point in my life, but never from his mouth. I would hear him say it again, four years later on an ugly night that shook my world, one I wish I could take back. I had thought the word was evil, but now I wasn't sure, for if McCovey was a nigger, I knew being one was good.

My father poured a Rheingold down his throat, too quick to taste the Seaveresque stuff. The Dago took out a wrinkled five and bought three more beers for my father. I saw McCovey approaching. His smile was wide, his manner seemed warm, as he accepted teammates' hands. I'll never know why he looked at me, because I hadn't called his name. Others did, but he looked at me instead and raised his bat in the air. He rolled it across the dugout roof with a quick motion of his wrist. By the time the bat had rolled halfway, he had vanished out of sight. I reached out in anticipation, but just as I could almost touch the wood a pimply teenager made a dive across the roof and snatched it from my hands. My father put down his beer and flashed a badge, but Pimples turned and ran. He almost made it too. But my dad fired up from his seat and made a diving save before Pimples could get free.

At that moment, Patrick Reilly wasn't just a dad with a fake moustache and a soda stain on his slacks. He was the Packers awesome Nitschke, and Shea was Lambeau's frozen tundra.

My dad was halfway through making a citizen's arrest when the Dago talked him out of it, saying the kid's face was punishment enough. I will never forget the way that bat felt when my small hands tried to grab it. The handle was thick, I couldn't quite grip it, but the feeling was magic to me nonetheless. I thought my dad was like Arthur, who pulled Merlin's sword from the stone, instead of a cop who took a big bat from a pimply-faced kid.

To say it was big was a gross understatement. It barely had a taper to it, like a giant rolling pin without the handles. My dad said he'd never seen another bat bigger. He said the Babe once used a 54-ouncer, but this one seemed larger, like a Bunyanesque club. The Dago said something about the bat in his pants being bigger, but I wasn't really listening. I was too filled with the magic of my Arthurian sword.

My hands felt electric through the first half inning, and I wouldn't have guessed that anything could ruin that buzz. But when the Mets jogged off the field, I knew I was wrong.

"Oh my God, it's John Marshall," I said softly, as if to myself.

I knew it was him as soon as I saw that leg kicking high into the air. I reached for my father. "Dad, it's John Marshall."

"Who?" my dad asked.

"Him, look, John Marshall, the pitcher tonight, you know, the guy with the bat."

The Dago said something not meant for my ears, and the two cops started laughing. But there was nothing funny about the guy on the mound. Nothing at all. I didn't know much about the Giants' star pitcher, except he kicked high when he pitched and he clubbed catchers into unconsciousness.

For millions, the sixties could be summed up in great photographic images. Like the grimace of Oswald as he took a bullet in Dallas. Or maybe for some it was the naked girl screaming in terror in a land far away. Or Hendrix at Woodstock or the first step on the moon. Me, I had two of those images. Two baseball photos that explained the whole decade for me. That filled me with dread and kept me awake, especially after Grandpa moved out. One was a *Sports Illustrated* cover of a player from Boston. His eye had been shattered and the whole thing was purple. The other photo was of the guy on the mound. But he didn't have a glove or ball in this picture, he instead held a bat. Which he had just brought down on the head of the Los Angeles catcher. Over and over and over again.

God, how I feared him when he walked into the dugout, only a few short feet from me. I longed for the safety of my dad's special girder, the upper-deck safety I'd known till this game. And when Marshall was batting, I thought the Mets' Jerry Grote must have been the world's toughest man, to squat down behind a man with such a violent past.

The Dago added fuel to my fire, saying, "John Marshall will get you" and sharing laughs with my dad. My dad, I have to point out, had dropped his grudge against Rheingold and was tossing them back at a rate of one every inning.

The game lasted fourteen. Which meant fourteen beers for my father. Who no longer seemed fearful of anyone seeing him there. His moustache was gone, he'd put his glasses away and his old battered hat had been replaced for the night. Replaced in the seventh inning by a cheap plastic Mets helmet. Hey, if the Dago was buying, who was my dad to say no? And when the Mets took the field in the bottom of the fourteenth, nursing a 1–0 lead, the team had just found their new number one fan.

My father was chanting and cheering his heart out. "Let's go, Mets!" he kept yelling while the Mets' new pitcher warmed up.

Tom Seaver was out, a new guy was in. The guy seemed kind of thin to be throwing so hard.

The Dago put a big hand on my father's cheap helmet and said, "This kid throws some heat."

My dad put his beer on the dugout and briefly stopped chanting. "Heat's overrated, trust me, this kid from Texas, what's his name, Ryan, he'll be out of the game in a year or two tops. Got no control."

"I don't know," said the Dago as Ryan finished his warm-ups. "I hear at his best he throws ninety-nine."

All of a sudden, I longed to talk baseball. Fourteen innings this close to the action had made me a fan—at least for one night. "My friend's brother throws ninety," I said.

"Ninety?" my dad said, surprised at my claim. He didn't even look at the field as Mays took ball one. High and away.

"That's what she said."

"Who said?" asked my dad. Ball two rolled to the wall; it had missed Grote's glove by a foot.

"Nina Vasquez," I said. "The new girl that moved in. Her big brother Manny pitches for Taft." William H. Taft was the area's public high school. If you were Irish in Highbridge and your family had money—any money—you didn't go there.

The Texas kid missed just low with ball three. The Dago spoke up, saying, "Damn, ninety's fast."

"I told you," my dad said, "heat's overrated. Now let's watch the game."

The ump called ball four on a pitch that looked good, Mays trotted to first, and Willie McCovey walked to the plate.

Willie hadn't done much with his turns at bat, one for four and a walk. But for me, every swing held the promise of another Shea missile, and I fell in love with his swing, from his heels every time. My dad had seen how he grimaced with each step that he took. He said he admired that—how he played through the pain. "Just like Mickey," he'd said. But just like that damn Mickey, Willie swung for the fences; they'd both have done a lot better if they just slapped singles instead.

Now the whole game came down to McCovey. Who was facing this kid, who made Grote's glove pop. Ryan came with his heat. McCovey swung from his heels. Grote's glove popped—the Mets were two strikes away.

The Mets needed this game, they were gaining ground on Chicago. Ryan wound up, the pitch was just high.

My dad was perturbed. He said, "This isn't baseball. This is silly kid stuff. This kid Ryan throws hard, McCovey swings hard, where's the mystery? They might as well just take off their pants and see whose dick is bigger!"

"I think the colored guy would win," said the Dago, then laughed at his own joke.

Ryan threw hard. McCovey swung hard. Fouled off, one and two. The crowd noise was huge. Above the roar of the crowd my dad could barely be heard. But by God, he was trying. And when he was heard, he was near incomprehensible. The consequences of fourteen Rheingolds were becoming apparent.

"Drop the curve, drop the curve!" my drunk father yelled. Thinking, I guess, that the thin kid from Texas was going to let my dad call his game. Ryan came with the heat. Just a shade low.

I was enthralled. I'd been coming to games once a year for six years. I'd seen hundreds of games on our old black-and-white. I'd heard hundreds more on my grandfather's Philco. I loved a lot of things about baseball. The taste of a dog and the roar of the crowd. The smell of cut grass and the sight of old fat guys in uniforms chewing tobacco. Singing along with "Take Me Out to the Ball Game." Most of all, the look of pure bliss that came over my father when his third or fourth beer took effect and he was munching Pop's peanuts. But I'd never loved baseball. Not the game itself—not for a second. Not until now. For with the count two and two and Nolan Ryan throwing fire and Willie "Fuckin' " McCovey swinging from way down at his heels, I suddenly got it. Man vs. man. Power on power. It wasn't a game. It was a life or death contest.

Ryan brought heat. Low, in the dirt. Grote walked to the mound. I poked my dad's shoulder. I had seen something strange.

"Dad, why did Willie Mays take such a strange lead?"

"Whattaya mean?"

"Well, Dad, Mays looked like he was hiding behind the first baseman. I think he was holding on to his belt."

Grote was walking back to the plate. My father adjusted his cheap plastic blue helmet. "That's because the big bastard hits so hard. He could ruin a face with one swing of his bat."

"Thanks, Dad," I said. My dad's mouth hung wide open, unlike his eyes, which were partially closed.

My nine-year-old heart was pounding as Ryan rubbed up the ball. I held Willie's bat and briefly considered offering it back, as if my big magic bat held some solution for fire.

Ryan brought smoke. Willie swung from the heels. I heard the crack of the bat and looked for the ball. Looked for the streaking white sphere against a black starry sky. Hoped someone had brought the tape measure that night. They'd surely need it.

Willie threw down his bat. But he never headed for first. Instead, he walked slowly toward us as the Mets faithful went wild. How could this be? Then I saw the white sphere. It was in Grote's glove. The crack I had heard had been ball meeting glove.

McCovey approached. I shouted his name and waved my huge bat. But he didn't see. He just flipped his brown Giants helmet into the dirt and disappeared from my view.

I never saw him again. But the lesson I learned has never been lost. Fight strength with strength. Never fear losing, only fear losing faith. And most of all—always swing from the heels.

[6]

Falling into the backseat of the Dago's beat-up Caddy was my dad's last conscious act of the evening.

We drove slowly through the parking lot. Cars were beeping loudly, yelling out their oaths of loyalty to their team. I looked back at their biggest fan, passed out cold, and laying long strings of stale Rheingold farts, but still with one hand on the cheap blue helmet. Wouldn't want to lose an obvious keepsake like that.

The Dago didn't talk until we left the lot, content to let the radio play. Lindsey Nelson on the postgame show made me hunger for the Scooter and the squirrels in Yogi's attic.

Finally, he turned to me. "Hey, Scooter, you know it's getting late, so I'm gonna ask you just two important questions."

"Okay," I said.

"First question. Do you think that I should drive all night, or you wanna be in bed in fifteen minutes?"

"Be in bed," I said.

He turned onto the Grand Central. I soon saw a sign for the Triborough Bridge. "You'll be home in no time," the Dago said. A few minutes later, we caught the Major Deegan to the Bronx. He still hadn't asked his second question.

"Uh, Dago?"

"Yeah, pal?"

"Um, did you have another question?"

"Yeah, I guess I did—you sure you want me to ask it?"

"Okay—sure," I said, but I wasn't sure. The Dago's voice had gotten soft. I wasn't used to it. I was afraid he'd try to sell me drugs; my dad said drugs were everywhere.

"Scooter, look . . . um, did your father ever say why, uh . . . I was taking him with me to the game?"

"He said he did some kind of favor for you."

"Yeah, that's true," the Dago said. "He sure did me a favor." With that, the Dago changed the FM dial and started patting the dashboard, adding percussion to the Stones' "Honky Tonk Woman."

I turned the dial down myself. "What was the favor?"

The Dago turned the radio off completely and let the car slow down to a crawl. He locked his eyes on mine. "Last night . . . your father saved my life."

I thought for a moment that he might laugh, or burp, or fart, or make a reference to his penis. He did none of the above.

"I got those tickets special for my parents' visit. But I gave 'em to your dad 'cause without him, my folks would be goin' to my funeral."

He pulled in front of the small blue house. The family home for fifty years. My prone father posed a problem, or so I thought, until the Dago took control. He draped my father over his shoulder as if he were a child. The cheap blue helmet fell off his head and made a cheap blue helmet sound on the street. I picked it up and followed the Dago to the door.

My mother was up waiting for us, not appearing to be overjoyed. "He said he wouldn't drink."

The Dago laid him on the couch and draped a blanket over him.

My mother's face was softer now, after watching the Dago tuck him in. "Thank you for taking care of him," she said.

"Mrs. R., I'd do anything for him. I owe that man my life. Good night now, ma'am, good night there, Scooter. The Dago's gotta go."

I shut the door, then turned around to see my mom with hands on hips. "What did that mean—'I owe that man my life'?"

I wasn't a good liar, so I fumbled through the truth. My mom seemed lost for words. She turned to where my father lay, knelt down, and placed kisses on his cheek. I slipped away in silence, when I heard her softly cry.

[7]

Grandpa rolled McCovey's bat around his worn and calloused hands, like a jeweler sizing up a stone. He even put a ruler to the barrel, just to make sure the monstrous piece of lumber didn't exceed major league specifications.

"Well, I've seen some blasts in my day," he said, going through the motions of a swing, "but that one takes the cake. A shot like that's a thing of beauty."

"My father doesn't think so."

"No," my grandpa said. "I don't suppose he does." I loved listening to the old man talk. His accent and his way with words made even simple statements seem profound. "No, I think that in your father's mind enough balls punched up the middle could stop the war in Asia."

I had heard about that war—just enough to not ask questions. My parents didn't fight much, but every now and then the war's mention set them off. If not for Vietnam and money, they seemed like a perfect pair.

"Grandpa?"

"Yes, my boy?"

"So . . . is punching singles bad?"

"Of course not," Grandpa laughed. "I've seen a lot of singles that were things of beauty too. That's the way I taught your dad to hit— compact swing, hands choked up on the bat, slap it all around."

"Yeah, I know," I said without emotion. "That's how he taught me too."

"Listen, Scooter," the old man said, now leaning on the bat, his one eye staring into mine. I took this as a cue to listen up—a baseball lesson was on its way. "I think everyone should learn to use the swing that's right for them. In your father's case, that swing was short; he liked to keep the ball in play. Who's to say if yours won't come from the heels. You never know until you try."

"You mean disobey my father?"

"No, not deliberately, but a lot of things of beauty never live to see their day."

The old man was pacing now, looking at old photos of Joe D., channeling his wisdom.

"From '43 to '45, the game was down, our boys were in the war. Joe D., Williams . . . Greenberg too, attendance really suffered. In '46, the boys were back along with all the fans. But something about the game was wrong. I just couldn't put my finger on it . . . until I sat in center field . . . for the colored all-star game. Colored stars took on the major league's best, and fifty thousand showed. Feller versus Satchel Paige—I don't remember which team won. What I remember was the different styles, how each Negro seemed unique."

This stuff was way over my head. So I let it fly on by, nodded every couple seconds, and watched a new show on TV. Grandpa's words kept coming. I just didn't pay them too much heed.

"Sometimes it's too much coaching that kills the fun of the game. The Negro boys developed on their own, without a coach to change their way. Of course, when the Dodgers took a chance on Robinson, the colored kids got to show their stuff."

I loved my grandfather, but this baseball stuff was getting old, especially when compared to Mike and Carol Brady. And Mr. Brady's wisdom didn't need to be dissected.

"Even pitching's suffered. When Marichal is retired, the high kick might be extinct."

Grandpa's latest words grabbed my attention, cutting off Mike Brady cold, right in the middle of a grandiose gesture. I had heard a name that gave me chills.

"Who did you say?" I asked. "Who's the guy who kicks his leg?"

"Why, Juan Marichal, of course."

"I think you mean John Marshall."

Grandpa smiled. "Yeah, I think you might be right. My mistake, I must have—"

I cut the old man off. "But isn't Marshall bad?"

"No, in fact he's very good. Why, besides Koufax and Bob Gibson, I'd say he's the—"

"But he kills catchers with his bat!"

"Listen, Scooter, I think—"

"I've got the picture, Grandpa. He's got the weapon in his hands. He's swinging it over and over and over, making sure the catcher's gone for good." I went on this way about the heinous scene, until no further words would come. That picture had been haunting me since I was just a little child. Keeping me from finding sleep, so I just lay awake sometimes—now that my mother said I was too old to climb in bed with her.

My sister was almost eight in '69, and she got scared at night sometimes. She'd seen a picture in the paper of a blond actress killed in California. The actress had been beautiful, but she had met a grisly end, and my sister feared that she was next. She would bang on my parents' door, crying, terrified. My mother always let her in.

Grandpa put his hand on mine and put the bat down on the kitchen table. Then he turned the Bradys off, just as the family's faces played a game of tic-tac-toe. He sat down next to me. I had rarely seen him look this serious. Not since that day I learned about my dad. His scars seemed somehow thicker now; I swear that I could hear them stretch when he turned to speak to me.

"Back in 1965, John . . . Marshall's country was at war. He still had family over there. Now what he did was inexcusable—though he said the catcher's throw had nicked his ear. But that catcher's still alive."

"He is?" I asked in disbelief.

"Oh, yes, alive and well. What he suffered was a two-inch gash— he was better in a week. But the very face of baseball . . . well, that wound wasn't quite so quick to heal. And John Marshall's very name—it was ruined on that night. Now listen to me, Scooter." My eyes and ears were glued on him. "Because this is difficult to say."

"Okay."

"A man can work all his life for what he thinks is right."

"Uh-huh."

"But history doesn't recognize events that it finds dull. One's own epitaph is written by moments that circumstance defines. Moments of achievement—and ones we wish we could have back. Do you understand?"

I nodded that I did.

"A two-inch gash on the head requires a stitch or two, but a soul sometimes just won't heal—my goodness, this bat's heavy."

I wanted to hear more about unhealing souls and epitaphs and history, but I didn't dare press further. So I talked about the bat.

"Do you think Dad would mind if I started swinging like McCovey?"

"When is your first game?"

"The season starts next week."

"Maybe for this season you should do as your father taught you."

"After that?" I asked.

"Well, after that we'll see."

I picked up McCovey's bat. Its mighty barrel dropped to the floor, as if it was made of steel and the old carpet was magnetic. "Do you think I'll ever grow up enough to use this bat?"

"It's a big one," Grandpa said, his voice less strained, his scars not quite as thick. "But I have an exercise that you can do that might help you do just that."

A magic trick for a magic bat? This sounded too good to be true. "Okay. What's the exercise?"

"When you get back home, check the basement by the furnace. Next to my old uniform there should be an old weight set. Might be kind of rusty now, but it really doesn't matter. Bring a five-pound weight next time you come and I'll show you what to do."

"Will it work?" I asked Grandpa.

"It made Hank Greenberg who he was."

I could hear the sound of evening Cross Bronx traffic as I walked from Grandpa's apartment to my house. Were things really so much better then, before Moses came along? A group of Negroes laughed at me as I crossed Jerome at 170th. By doing so, I'd left the Melrose section and was once again on Highbridge ground. Were Negroes ruining the Bronx? Or was it the Puerto Ricans' fault? Or maybe it was the spics and spooks instead, like the Dago had proclaimed.

Nina Vasquez came from Puerto Rico—I didn't think it was her fault. She always spoke to me when I walked by, even though she was almost two years older than I was. I thought the way she spoke was beautiful, especially when she said my name. Her voice, her skin, her hair, her eyes—all of it was beautiful. Why wouldn't she be wanted on our block? Especially when her brother could bring the heat at ninety?

I liked the Irish girls of Highbridge too, in their own way things of beauty. But they seemed to be so plentiful, like singles up the middle. Nina was no simple single; she was a rocket flying out of Shea.

I thought of the fifty thousand fans at Yankee Stadium who had seen Feller take on Paige. Did any White Plains families sit in the crowd that day? Or did that guy who'd sealed the Yankees' fate not hear about that game?

I'd been relieved to find out John Marshall hadn't killed that catcher after all. It's too bad he'd had a problem with his foot; I guess those souls would be hard to stitch. I laughed out loud as I made a left on Shakespeare, two blocks from my house—and saw another Puerto Rican flipping cards out by his stoop. It wasn't him that made me laugh, though. I saw kids flip cards almost every day. I was laughing about how I was going to change my swing, once I learned Hank Greenberg's magic trick.

[8]

I had never really thought about my mother's boobs until I saw them at the park. When I was little, maybe three or four, I had asked her if she'd nursed me. She said she'd tried it once and it made her nipples sore. It was the only time a talk of ours had drifted to her nipples. Indeed, until I saw her boobs pushed up almost to her neck at my team's fifth baseball game, I don't think I gave those boobs a second thought. But at Macombs Dam Park, the way she'd dressed made not thinking about them difficult.

It was a Monday, Concourse Day, and although my sister went to Sacred Heart with me, she'd awoken with the sniffles. So she'd stayed home from school and joined my mom on her weekly credit card bonanza. They had stopped off at the Ascot Theatre on the Concourse and 186th. The Ascot wasn't quite as grand as the Paradise—it had no goldfish in the lobby—but it showed old classic films and my mother seemed to like it.

She had seen *Gone with the Wind* and apparently it pleased her enough that she bought some vintage clothes and wore them to cheer me on while dressed up as Scarlett O'Hara.

I had never known that breasts could heave until Big Will gave infield practice. My mom pulled up along with Patty in the Charger and every eye turned toward her. My little sister was dressed up too, but at her young age nothing heaved, except perhaps my stomach.

Lots of questions crossed my mind as I took in my mother's little fashion show. The one that seemed most obvious was simply "What's she doing here?" Macombs Dam Park was literally a next-door neighbor of the Yankees. In fact, it was not at all unusual for some overzealous Yankee fan, with a few beers too many in him, to relieve himself on Macombs Dam grass after checking out the Bombers. As best I knew, my mother's car had never ventured south of Highbridge. That car had eyes only for the Concourse, and only north of 170th. This was like another world to her, though we were only six blocks from our home, and she wasn't exactly incognito when she finally chose to travel south.

I think she'd only acquiesced to Little League when Big Will stopped by one day. Saying he was going to coach the boys and that he'd keep an eye on me. Big Will even said he'd drive me, which made my mom give in. But not before my father put his arm around Big Will and said, "I can't be there much because of work, but make sure he slaps it through the holes."

I had made my father awfully proud with the reports about my games. I had six hits, each one a single, in twenty-one at bats. I didn't tell him about my six errors out in right field, where Big Will had no other choice but to play me. If Rizzuto's glove had indeed served as a vacuum, then mine was like an iron skillet with a hole; it was a place where sure outs got a stay of execution. I also didn't tell him that my average, good as it might seem, was the second lowest on the ball club. All due to Big Will's arm.

Will, as I mentioned, had a unique talent with a ball. Which he had showcased on the street with Spaldeens, but which carried over to the field. Will would let each kid take practice cuts and then throw the ball right to the bat. You couldn't miss his pitch by accident; you almost had to try to whiff.

So I choked up on the bat from the right side of the plate, took the short, compact swing like I'd been taught and tried to spray it all around. Thanks to Will, I did—I just didn't do it very well. Most of my choked-up, compact swings yielded little dribblers, and even though I had some speed to first, I grounded out most of the time.

But all that stuff was in the past as far as I was concerned. The choking up, the compact swing, the wimpy hits—all ancient history. For that stuff had come before my meeting with McCovey and the old man's revelation about Greenberg's exercise.

I had brought the five-pound weight to Grandpa's house, just as he had asked. He had cut a length of broomstick and knotted twine around it. He looped the twine's other end around the weight and knotted that as well.

From wooden stick to metal plate, the twine measured only twenty inches. "Just like Greenberg's," Grandpa said. He had me grab the stick and instructed me to hold my arms out straight. It seemed a bit too easy and I couldn't, for the life of me, see how it could help my swing. But Grandpa made me roll the weight up the twine, and when I did, my forearms burned.

Lowering it inch by inch was just as bad, and I begged to put it down. Grandpa said that Hank had begged his first time too, but he'd learned to stick it out and hit fifty-eight round-trippers in 1938, just two shy of Babe Ruth's season record. Grandpa said he would have broken it if he could have gotten more pitches he could reach. But back in '38, the major leagues, if not the world, just weren't quite prepared for a Jewish home run king.

I thought my forearms were on fire when I woke up that next morning. I couldn't even tie my shoes or write my name correctly. The pain was just intense. But it was sending me a signal. My muscles had grown stronger. Like the ghosts in Charles Dickens's classic Christmas tale, the magic of Hank Greenberg's exercise had done its thing in just one night.

The game was just about to start when a drunk stumbled out of East 161st onto the far end of the field. Nothing special there. After all, when you gotta go, you gotta go. But when the guy peeing in deep center field is the guy that you call Dad, the mundane gains new meaning.

The fans on hand had been treated to views of, first, my mother's breasts and now my father's penis. My new swing was going to be boring by comparison.

"Play ball!" the umpire yelled.

All the guys used metal bats but me. Aluminum was light and sounded cool and made a high-pitched *ping* on contact. Bill Billingsworth led off for us and lined a Big Will pitch to center for a single. Another perfect pitch from Will resulted in a deep fly ball to left. A well-hit ball, a well-made catch—one on and one away.

Will's son, Jim, or J.W. as he called him, stepped up to bat. Jim was like the Babe to us; he hit for both power and average, and patrolled center like Joe D. Big Will's first pitch was perfect, as was the swing his son completed. That high-pitched *ping* filled the air and the ball flew off the metal. The next sounds to come were leather meeting bone and an anguished groan from Will. The ball had clipped our coach's shoulder and ricocheted to shallow right. His frightened son threw down the bat and ran to check on Will.

But halfway there the wounded Will barked an order to his son. "Run it out, run it out! Don't worry, I'll be fine." Once safe at first, time was called and Will embraced the boy. "Good work, son. Quite a hit. Sorry Dad got in the way."

The game resumed, one out, one on, but Big Will was not the same. He tried his best to gut it out, but he could barely raise his arm. A couple throws missed their mark, and it was clear that Big Will's day was over—just as my father reached the stands, oblivious to both my mother's presence and Big Will's situation. There was no standard protocol for the crisis that befell us. There were no long or short relievers warming up in the bullpen. No bullpen either. Just as my father strode up to the bench, Big Will asked the fateful question: "Can anyone here pitch?"

I saw my father look around with both hands in his pockets. I could feel a few fathers start to stir, but no definitive moves were made. I looked back once more at my dad and saw that a pocket was now empty. Haltingly, he raised his hand, like a schoolboy not quite sure of his answer. Big Will gave a word of thanks and handed him the ball.

My father looked uneasy as he shuffled to the mound. Bronx ball fields had no infield grass, so he raised small dust clouds as he went. For a guy who loved the game so much, the field seemed like a foreign land. He didn't even have a fielder's glove out there and he looked frightened, almost naked.

The first batter was Tim Johnson, who looked at my father's first feeble toss—way outside and in the dirt.

My dad just yelled out, "Sorry!" and bit down on his lip. His next pitch was even slower and bounced a yard from home. I saw Mr. Johnson shake his head and laugh into his hand. My mom was sinking low in shame; a few more inches, she'd be prone. I felt my stomach tie itself into a knot. It hurt like hell to breathe.

My father took a deep breath and threw, slow but down the middle. I think his accuracy surprised the Johnson kid, who looked at a called first strike.

"That's okay," my father said to Tim. "You'll hit the next one out."

The next one found its mark as well, but this time Tim was ready. The metal bat announced its presence as it smacked my father's pitch. A hard ground ball right up the box; a sure base hit for Johnson. A sure base hit if not for my father's hands, which dropped quickly to the dirt. His hands were bare, but nonetheless, he came up with the ball. Which he fired to second, where the shortstop made the grab, stepped on the bag and blooped the ball to first. They got Johnson by a step.

My father patted J.W.'s back as he headed to the bench. "Thataway to hustle, kid," he said, then shouted encouragement to Tim. "Way to make a little Bingo, son, you'll get 'em next time up." My dad exuded confidence as he jogged back to the bench.

My mom sat up a little. Mr. Johnson wasn't laughing anymore. My stomach lightened up a bit, but it still felt kind of strange. As a general rule, coaches don't steal children's hits, or turn double plays on their own team.

I took my place in right field, and God was with me as he spared me any chances. As I approached our bench, my father asked me for my glove so he could better hide his pitches. When I handed him the glove, I assumed that he was kidding.

Rico Torrez led off the second. He had an accent just like Nina's, but it didn't make me feel quite the same way when he spoke. His English may have been a little tough to understand, but his baseball comprehension was quite good. He was a big kid, kind of chubby and a little slow of foot. But he could send the ball for quite a ride, usually far enough so he could waddle down to first.

My dad's first pitch was a little low, at least according to the umpire. My father thought it was right at the knees and raised an eyebrow at the call. The second one was Rico's pitch to hit. Even Big Will couldn't have aimed it any better. Torrez sent it for a ride, but got under the pitch just slightly so that the ride was strictly vertical. Up, way up, the baseball went, almost out of sight. Every eye from both teams strained to see its flight until a man's voice filled the air.

"Got it! Got it! I got this one!" Oh, no, it was my dad, who had drifted into shallow left and was now calling for the ball. Apparently the shortstop hadn't studied baseball etiquette and was trying for the putout, despite my father's clear-cut yells. My dad was taller than the kid, however, and plucked the baseball from the air.

My mother's breasts were now unnoticed. Every eye was on my dad, who started pitching from full windup, his left leg cutting through the air. And that baseball started doing tricks that I'd never known it could.

I swear he threw a knuckleball to Schwartz that danced three times in the air. The poor kid hit the deck on an 0–2 curve that must have broken at least a foot. Mrs. Schwartz consoled her shell-shocked son with a meaty hug and then filled the air with Yiddish curses that I was pretty sure were meant for my father.

But my father didn't notice. He barely even acknowledged Big Will when he walked out to the mound to appeal to my father's better judgment. My dad dismissed our coach with a couple nods and a wave of his hand. As it turned out, Big Will's collarbone was broken and his arm would never be the same. His gift was gone, taken away inadvertently by his own flesh and blood.

My father had no time for petty annoyances like broken collarbones. Not when he was caught up in the zone. He had told me stories about how the great ones had an ability to tune out everything around them, except the job at hand . . .

. . . And the job at hand was me—it was my turn to bat. My poor mom looked terrified, but she clapped and yelled my name. And for the first time my father noticed her, but he didn't seem to care. My sister shouted in her little voice. She waved and called my name. "Scooter, Scooter, Scooter." She did look kind of cute. My dad was rubbing up the ball, blind to my dilemma. I had to make a big choice right away, one that could cause repercussions. Should I choke up on a small aluminum bat to please my dad? Or should I find a swing that was my own and try to please myself? I bent down and picked up McCovey's giant bat and walked slowly to home plate.

The thing looked like a caveman's club inside my tiny hands. I felt like Barney Rubble's little kid, the one who was stronger than his dad. I wished right then that I *was* Rubble's kid—stronger than my dad. I had said a prayer and done one day of exercise—I thought that made me ready.

My dad looked truly puzzled when I walked past the right side of the plate. I could almost see him leave that zone of his and reenter the real world. For a moment I felt bad for him; he was watching his own hopes go floating by. He'd dreamed about a son who would live to claim unfinished fame, not one who spit in the face of tradition. The same guy who had just caused Schwartz to cry now seemed on the verge of tears himself.

A weak voice called my name. "Scooter. Scooter, what're you doing?" Silence was my answer. "Scooter, come on, put away that bat." I slowly shook my head. Once more he tried to change my mind. Once more I shook my head. I thought my forearms would explode, trying to keep the bat off of my shoulder.

He went into his windup. I wondered what pitch would be on tap. One that sunk? One that curved? I hoped that I'd be ready. My father gave me neither. He came instead with heat, a fastball I did not so much see as hear.

The catcher did his best to suppress a scream. Which could not be said for my mother, who gave my dad an earful. Nothing profane like

Mrs. Schwartz's tirade, but not exactly sweet nothings either. My dad didn't even look her way. Instead he looked at me sadly and called out my name. "Scooter . . . please, don't ruin this for me." Again I didn't speak. Again I strained to keep McCovey's bat aloft.

He went into his windup and came with heat again, even faster than the first. Again I didn't see it. Again my mother yelled. "Dammit, Patrick, stop it!" My sister got her two cents in. "Daddy, no. Daddy, no." He disregarded her.

I heard the catcher whimpering, trying to suppress his pain but failing. My dad no longer tried to talk to me; instead he glared in pure contempt. I knew the next one would be even harder, and I knew I didn't have a chance. But I also knew that I wouldn't go down without a fight. I was facing Nolan Ryan, and although Macombs Dam wasn't Shea, and I was surely not McCovey, I also knew that I could not go down unless I did so swinging.

I never saw the pitch. From the time it left his fingers, I shut my eyes completely. Shut my eyes . . . and swung. And heard a telltale crack echo through the park. I still have no idea how my feeble swing found my father's pitch. But find the pitch it did, and I was instantly rewarded with a feeling of such utter joy, a high that words cannot do justice to. Euphoric. Beautiful. Too damn beautiful to interrupt with a stupid thing like running. From my hands up through my forearms, which no longer burned but buzzed, to my shoulders, to my heart. Each fiber was rejoicing. My legs didn't want to spoil the moment. For years to come, I would regard that feeling as the greatest of my life. An elusive high I could but taste, if only in my memories.

"Run!" I heard my mother yell, which broke me from my high. But before I did, I took one last look as the ball sailed through the sky.

Like I said, my speed was good, a trait I'd gotten from my father. Grandpa said that Dad could fly, and as I dug for first I saw my father prove it. He was following the baseball's path, a foxhound on the chase.

The other team's right fielder may have been even worse than me. He stumbled in pursuit two times and then got off a lousy throw. Far short of the cutoff man, but the cutoff man was moot. For my dad had run at least fifty yards to get the ball on one small hop. Now he turned to face the infield and saw the second baseman wave his arms.

I had just rounded second base when I caught on to my dad's plan. He didn't even entertain the thought of throwing to that kid. Instead, he set his sights on home. If this guy could run down criminals, he could surely beat his son. He hit infield dirt as I rounded third. I looked home and saw the catcher blocking it and thought I could put my shoulder into him, just as he caught my father's throw.

Then I saw my father's face, and in that instant I knew there would be no throw to home.

Ten more feet. Three more steps. One less than my dad. The catcher stepped away from home as I went into my slide. I could almost taste the sweet bouquet of victory—that ethereal communion of sneaker touching base. Until my dad took flight.

He looked like Charlie Hustle—arms extended, body parallel, flying through the air. I saw his glove touch my cleat, mere inches from home plate. I didn't hear the umpire make his call—I only heard my dad.

"Yer outta there!"

My mother came running to my aid, holding my hand as I struggled to my feet. She wiped away my muddy tears and gave her little boy a hug. It was the closest I had come to being nursed since that time I'd made her nipples sore.

As I made my way off Macombs Dam field, I had no way of knowing what had just been lost. That in addition to my would-be homer, part of my childhood had been robbed from me as well.

[9]

We'd been home since half past seven. My mom had stopped at Daitch's Dairy store and let me pick out my own half gallon of vanilla. I ate until my stomach was the only thing that hurt. She'd even let me skip my bath, so I fell asleep in my uniform, my face a blend of ice cream, dirt and tears.

My father usually didn't argue much. He tended to let my mother have her way. Except about that whole Long Island thing, which was where he drew the line. So my mother got to win a lot; she just won in a house she didn't like, in a city she despised.

Yelling, fighting, the heavy stuff—they didn't go that far. I'd have known it if I'd heard it, because on summer nights in Highbridge, with heat and tempers running high, I heard fights through open windows. Thank God my parents didn't fight like that. At midnight, when my father stumbled in, that situation changed.

My mother wouldn't let him in the bedroom—so he kicked the door in instead. My mom was not impressed.

"You showin' off your cop skills? You gonna break your handcuffs out?"

"You wanna dress up like a slut?" my father yelled. "I'm gonna treat you like you're one. Come on, get on the bed."

"Why, so you can try to get your little weenie to work?" My mom was way off base on this one. I knew my father's little weenie worked fine—I'd just seen him peeing with it at our game.

Apparently that weenie comment changed my father's mind, because his aggression backed off slightly. He now seemed more hurt than mad.

"How do you think I feel? Huh? How do you think I feel? I take a walk to see my son and then I see my wife. At a park she said was too dangerous to play in, and she's dressed up like a slut." Then he got sarcastic. A slurred sarcastic "Excuse me, sir, how are you? Would you care to meet my wife and her tits?" Sarcasm yielded to new anger. "Goddammit, Molly, what were you thinking?"

"I was thinking that it might be fun to play dress-up with your daughter. I was thinking that she might enjoy some culture outside of Phil Rizzuto's jock."

I knew quite a bit about the Scooter, but his jock remained a mystery. Despite the fact that her claim had no merit, her delivery was good and it kept my dad off balance. So far she had taken my dad's best blow (the hypothetical tit introduction) and was counterpunching well.

"Besides, who cares if someone meets them? You haven't introduced yourself to them in weeks."

Oh, a deliberate low blow. My father, for all his earlier bravado, was now clearly on the defensive.

"Well, maybe I'd have some energy left for you if I wasn't putting in so much goddamn overtime so you can do your little Concourse thing."

"I gave up everything for you, Patrick. And God knows, I don't ask for much."

"You don't ask for much?" my dad repeated, his tone once again sarcastic. "Paintings, clothes, furniture. That's not much? Maybe not for your father, Mr. Body Count, but it's too much for just one honest cop."

"Not for a detective."

"I'm trying, Molly, I'm trying. But these things don't happen overnight."

"No, I guess you're right," my mother said. "They don't happen overnight. But they don't happen *ever* if you don't start making some arrests."

"Arrests are not the answer."

"They are if you're a cop."

"You don't understand the problem."

"You don't make arrests. I think *that* is the problem."

"Five million Negroes moved up north due to Jim Crow and the loss of jobs. They settled into Harlem because—"

"Spare me the history lesson, Patrick. Your job is not to understand criminals. Your job's to lock them up. Yes, the Negroes need some help—I hope they get it too. But that is not . . . your . . . job. You are not a social worker. You are not a politician. You are a cop. You arrest the bad guys, who just happen to be Negroes. And if a Negro puts your life in danger—you shoot him. Understand?"

"Yeah, I understand," my father said. "You want me to kill some people so you can move out to Long Island."

"That's not what I said, Patrick."

"Sure thing, let me kill a couple people so my wife can have her half an acre."

Verbal fights, like a boxing match, are all about momentum. My dad had seized the moment and had staged a minor rally. He then made a tactical mistake.

"Beautiful Long Island, home of Robert Moses. Building ways to get to parks—that's why they call them parkways. Oh, Moses loves his parks. Jones Beach, Flushing Meadows, even named one for himself—Robert Moses Park. He built two hundred fifty parks but only one in Harlem. And you wonder why the crime rate is so high. People have no place to—"

My mother cut him off. Cut him off and started yelling. "Look around you, Patrick. Look around the Bronx. It's full of parks. Some that Moses built. So why is this place such a shithole? The parks aren't even safe for kids. Glass is everywhere. People shooting up. This place is full of criminals but we're the ones in jail. I'm afraid to let Scooter out to play. Puerto Ricans three doors down. What's next? A colored family? Oh, it's coming soon, Patrick. Mark my words, they're coming soon. But you refuse to let us go. Every day that you don't sell the house is a day that you lose money. They're burning buildings for insurance now because no one wants to buy. South Bronx now, but our turn's coming soon. It's just a question of when. And if your family is still here when it happens—"

"You wonder why I dressed up today? Because I wanted to feel special, because you don't make me feel that way anymore. Yes, I wanted men to look at me, because you don't anymore. I wanted to be beautiful, because you never tell me I am anymore. And maybe if I dressed up as a Southern belle, I could pretend just for a little while that I didn't have to go to bed in a shithole like the Bronx."

"Are you through?" my father asked. I sensed the fight was over. My dad had been knocked out. But in answer to his question, she wasn't through with him just yet.

"I'm twenty-eight years old and I—am drying up. Sometimes I hate my life. But no matter how bad things looked, at least I knew my husband loved his kids. Until today."

"That's not fair," my father said.

"Oh, it is," my mother answered. "You might be embarrassed by my breasts, but I am embarrassed by your heart. What you did today was shameful. You destroyed your little boy. You ruined his big moment. You trampled on his joy."

"But he didn't do things like I taught him, he—"

My mother snapped at him, "The very fact that you're defending what you did today hurts me most of all. I don't want you in this room."

There wasn't any door to slam, not in the literal sense. But something came between them then, and even though our day of reckoning was still a couple weeks away, things were never quite the same.

[10]

When I awoke the next morning, my dad was asleep beside me in bed. His breath was hideous. Not beer, like the weekends, but something far different—bitter and vile. I lay there awhile, wanting to move but not quite sure I should, worried that my dad would start up where he'd left off.

In a way, I longed for Joe D.'s old photos. His young, goofy smile was somehow more elegant than nail holes, hooks and faded, stained walls. If given the chance, I'd have traded Dad for Joe D. I doubted Joe D. would have climbed into my bed.

My father awoke with a single long yawn and a chain of short farts. I feared the worst. Not from the farts, but my dad. My father rolled over and faced me, his awful, strong breath inches away.

"I'm sorry," he said.

Somehow that word didn't seem like enough.

"Scooter, please, can you forgive your old man?"

I was just nine years old, not very practiced in the ways of forgiveness. But somehow I knew that telling him "yes" would let him off way too easy. He'd robbed my home run. Didn't let me complete the last step of my journey. He'd made me cry like a girl in front of my sister. What I wanted to do was kick him out of my room, like my mother had done. She had shown guts, stood up to a cop and told him to leave. I wished I had guts like my mom's. But I was still just a kid. So I stayed silent instead.

He climbed out of bed on unsteady legs. He was clad only in boxers, his body wiry and strong. His arm was still scarred from where the bullet had entered before I'd been born. It had happened at work, the same day he'd met Mom. She was his nurse, and the attraction was instant.

My mother used to tell stories about my father, the hero. A hero who stole dreams from his son. He didn't look too heroic as he fumbled about with his trousers, nearly falling two times before getting them on.

The scar wasn't much to look at. Just a small, faded pink circle of flesh on his right shoulder. Why all the fuss? My grandfather's scars put his to shame. I was still staring at this little girl scar when he tried once again to get rid of his guilt.

"Hey, listen, Scooter, I know you're mad—and I don't blame you either. I wish I could say that I know how you feel—but hey, I never hit a ball like you did. You know what I mean?"

I was still on the scar. It seemed even smaller and wimpier. His attempt at kissing butt had fallen flat on its ass.

"Maybe I was a little bit hard on a few of those kids. Maybe at your age the game should be fun."

My head was still hung. My dad's scar looked like a bee sting—or a little pinprick. It was no badge of honor—not like Grandpa's scars were.

"But hey, Scooter," my dad said with phony excitement. "Did you see the break on that curve that I threw to Schwartz?"

I let out a laugh. I didn't mean to, but it somehow snuck out. Right until that moment that his heat had whizzed by me, I'd been proud of my dad. Not for trying to be Cy Young in a game of fourth graders, but because of the things he could do with a ball. I had heard about curves that dropped off the table, but I'd never witnessed it live, until Schwartz hit the deck. Even the sight of poor Schwartz's mother, cursing in Yiddish, had been kind of funny.

My dad seized the moment and sat down on the bed. He said, "Listen, Buddy, I know I was wrong. For a while I guess I forgot the game wasn't about me. But you know, when I saw you hitting lefty, holding that bat, I just kind of lost it. I don't know why."

I waited in silence for him to go on. Wanting to hear what his excuse could possibly be. Wanting so badly to believe in his words.

"I think it was that game, you know, with Vinnie at Shea—I don't think we should have gone."

"Why not?" I said.

"Because it wasn't right, that's why."

"Why not?"

"Because the Mets aren't our team. Hey, I know what you're thinkin'. We had fun that night. Isn't that right?" I nodded my head. "But just 'cause it's fun does not make it right. Listen, as you grow up, you'll see lots of things that look fun. You'll see other people do them—you'll want to too."

"Dad, isn't this the same talk we had about drugs?"

"That's right," said my dad, clapping his hands, as if he'd just made his point. Though his point seemed kind of pointless. "Because the Mets are like drugs. They're both bad addictions. Hey, I can see why a young kid could get hooked on the Mets. They're handsome, they're young, they're kind of successful."

I was really confused. "But Yogi's a Met. He's not handsome *or* young."

My poor father winced like he'd taken a Smokin' Joe Frazier hook to the stomach. "I'm talking about loyalty. The fact that you stick with the one that you love. Even when things aren't perfect. You love your team, for better or worse—and I don't care what his hat says, Yogi's a Yankee—always has been, always will be."

"Mom thinks Fritz Peterson is handsome and he's a Yankee."

"Look, Scooter, we're gettin' off track. I don't know how to say this, so I'll just blurt it out." He was edgy now, sweating. The sweat that ran down his neck smelled like his breath. "That game made me feel sick!"

"I know. Mom said you threw up."

He looked up at the ceiling and shook his head. Like he had five years earlier, when I'd offered my opinion on the Joe D. dick-shaking dilemma.

"Scooter, that's not what I mean. What I mean is that game made me think less of myself. Like I'd let myself down. I went because Vinnie really wanted me to. And I thought, what the heck, the game sounds like fun. And it was. But that doesn't change the fact that it was wrong. I tried to put that night out of my mind. I threw out that helmet. I threw out the tickets. I threw out the scorecard. I'd blocked it out of my mind. Then, I don't know, when I saw you up there, holding that bat, it all came rushing back."

"I don't want to throw out the bat," I said in dismay.

"Of course not," my dad said. "No, that bat was a gift from a very nice man. A man who might be league MVP. Hey, who knows—that might be the same bat that he used in this year's All-Star Game. He hit two out that night."

I smiled at the thought.

"Can I watch the Mets?"

"Sure, you can—when I'm at work. And I'll tell you what. If the Mets keep it up, we'll watch the Series together."

"At Shea?" I yelled out.

"No, not at Shea. At home on TV." He got very quiet. He sat down on the bed once again and put his arm around me.

"Listen, son, I'm trying real hard . . . to let you go your own way. But there's three things I need . . . three things I won't . . . allow you to do."

I got ready.

"One. Never do drugs. Do you understand?"

"Uh-huh."

"Two. Don't go to Shea—at least until you're eighteen."

"Alright."

"And three—please don't let me see that bat in this house. You can use it when you're alone in your room. Keep it hidden in your closet. 'Cause I don't want to see it. It just hurts me too much."

"So, you say your dad took the mound?" my grandfather asked.

I had just finished filling him in on the whole crazy story—and all the old man could say was "Your dad took the mound?"

I thought he might ask how it felt to send the ball flying, or what went through my mind when I saw my dad on the run. Instead, he just marveled at the idea of his son on the mound. I was kind of insulted.

I said, "Yeah, but so what? What's the big deal?"

"Well, he swore he would never pitch a baseball again for the rest of his life. That was June 17th . . . 1959."

"Again, after what?" I was no longer insulted. I was intrigued instead.

"Oh, it's quite an old story. I'm not sure he'd want me to tell it."

"Grandpa, my father doesn't want you telling me *any* stories, remember? If I ever got caught, I'd be in big trouble."

"Scooter, you've made a good point," my grandfather said. "Let me see, let me see. Where to start? Where to start?"

I looked at him intently as he gathered his thoughts, pulling the past out of mothballs, his one eye twinkling grandly.

"Your father was quite a pitcher. He could make that ball dance at will. Like he had a string on it, like it was his own little puppet. He had everything, except for the speed. He didn't have a good fastball—high seventies tops."

"That's not true," I said. "That thing came at me fast. It was like a shotgun had sent it."

My grandfather smiled. "I'm sure that is true. But remember there, Scooter, back then he was pitching to boys who were almost grown men. From big league distance. Sixty feet, six inches. But to a nine-year-old boy from forty-five feet, I'm sure that it did look like it was shot from a gun."

"Is ninety fast?" I asked.

"Yes, it sure is. Why do you ask?"

"We have a new neighbor who I heard is that fast."

"All Hallows or Hayes?"

"I think it's Taft."

My grandfather nodded. He knew without knowing that this kid wasn't Irish.

"No doubt about it," he said, "ninety is fast. Very fast. But speed is seductive. Many a scout has fallen under its spell. It's also misleading. It only tells partial stories."

"What does that mean?"

"Take your dad, for example. He had master control over three or four pitches. Every one coming from the same point of release. Knew how to change speeds. Knew the minds of the hitters. But as good as he was, not a single scout saw him pitch."

"You mean that my father could have pitched in the bigs?" This was even cooler than finding out he'd saved Vinnie's life. You know, Vinnie the Dago.

"Hold on, Scooter, hold on, I didn't say that. But I do know that your father never got a fair chance."

"Because of his speed?"

"Among other things. He played at All Hallows, a smaller school, back when all the attention was on Cardinal Hayes and Monroe. Monroe put out Greenberg—and that Kranepool kid too, the one on the Mets. Where was I now?"

"My dad at All Hallows."

"Yeah, okay, thank you. All Hallows, yeah. Small school, didn't have their own field, so they played their games at Macombs."

"You mean where I played?"

"That's the one. But on the bigger field—across the street."

I nodded my head.

"Anyway, when your dad is a senior, he's got a great won-loss record, low ERA, very few walks. But nobody cares. The scouts are all looking at another kid on the team. Lost some big games, given up far more runs. But the kid can throw hard—maybe high eighties. He's a pitcher and a shortstop, just like your dad. So your father, he—"

"Did my dad punch balls up the middle? Was his glove like a vacuum?"

"Indeed, he had quite a glove," my grandfather said with a smile. "But I'm afraid as a hitter, he mostly hit weak grounders to second."

I laughed hard out loud. Grandpa did too.

"Where was I again?" he said, scratching his scarred head.

"The pitcher who threw hard, the high-eighties guy."

"That's right, thank you, Scooter. Well, your father and this guy— his name was McHenry—they got to be friends. So your father helps the guy out, takes him under his wing. Teaches him all the little things that he's learned. And McHenry becomes the talk of the Bronx."

"And my father got mad?"

"No, not at all. You know your dad. He loves to help people."

Yeah, that was true. He'd helped out the Dago by saving his life.

Grandpa got up from his seat in the kitchen and walked the few steps into his bedroom. He was back moments later with a newspaper clipping. The headline read, O'BRIEN NEAR PERFECT. I looked at the date. May 18, 1959.

"I'm going to say something here, Scooter, and I don't want you to think that I'm out of my mind."

"Sure, Grandpa, okay."

"But I firmly believe that there are moments in life when people transcend that which is thought to be possible."

"What does that mean?"

Grandpa squinted his eye and leaned in real close. I leaned in a bit too, so I was mere inches away when he whispered the news.

"It means that one day at Macombs Dam Park, on May 17th ten years ago, your father was as good of a pitcher as any man's ever been."

"Really?" I asked. "In what way? How?"

"He was like a man among boys."

"Like he was at my game?" I asked. After all, he had been impressive. At least until I had taken him deep.

My grandfather laughed and sat back in his chair. "No, not quite like that," he said. "I mean his control, always great, was nothing short of amazing. His breaking ball, always sharp, was now simply lethal. And his fastball, his weakness, must have gained ten miles per hour. For six and a third, he could do nothing wrong."

This was amazing. I hadn't heard of pitching this great since . . .

well . . . a week ago, when he was striking out Schwartz. "Did something go wrong?" I asked.

"Well, a high school game is seven innings, did you know that?"

"No."

"Well, through six and a third, your father is perfect. No runs, no hits, no walks, no errors. He's struck out thirteen, only one guy's made decent contact. All Hallows has scored two. So the score is two to zero. There's one out in the seventh. Count's oh and two. Sinker, right at the knees and a lollypop curve that the guy missed by a foot. I thought maybe your dad might waste a pitch in the dirt. But he came with the heat. He kicked that leg high, almost like our friend Marichal, and he brought in the fastball. I swear it must have been ninety. The guy takes a swing, catches the bottom of it with the top of his bat. Pops the thing up, way up, almost straight into the air. Your dad says he's got it, but McHenry at short is calling him off. Calling real loudly—'I got it! I got it!' Except he didn't get it, it bounced off his glove."

"And the guy got to first?"

"Not just to first. That ball went so high, the runner rounded the bases."

"He hit a home run?"

"No, not even a single. They ruled it an error. He walked the next man, then got the next batter out."

"So he decided to quit so he could go out on top, because he'd pitched a no-hitter?"

"No, that wasn't his logic," my grandfather said. "What some viewed as a triumph, he saw as failure."

"Why? I thought throwing a no-hitter was good."

"They are good," said Grandpa. "No, they're not good, they're great. But unfortunately, Scooter, for your father, a simple no-hitter was not great enough."

"Why not?"

"Oh, he thought that the news of his perfect game would have drawn lots of attention. That word would have traveled around and he'd get a look from the scouts. Unfortunately, a two-to-one no-hitter doesn't have the same aura as that rare perfect game."

I had to agree.

"To make matters worse, he felt that McHenry had made the error on purpose. So as to not share the glory."

"Did he, you think?"

"I'm sad to say, Scooter, I think that he did. He broke poor Patrick's heart, then took the skills your dad taught him and got to the bigs—for a year, maybe two, then he threw out his elbow. Now he sweeps the floors at the Terminal Market."

"Why couldn't my dad have just gone back and had more of those moments when he was in a trance?"

"I don't know," my grandfather said, smiling a little at how I'd butchered his word. "We never found out. He swore never to pitch. Even stopped watching baseball for over two years, until Mantle and Maris made a run for Ruth's record. Of course, that's not what he'd say. According to your father, it was Richardson punching balls through the holes that got him back into the game."

[12]

I don't know why the Series had me hooked. I didn't really like the Mets, and upon a closer reevaluation I didn't think the team was all that handsome. I thought my dad was way off base. The girls at Sacred Heart had crushes on Tom Seaver, but the other Mets were not amazing as far as good looks went. My mom thought Fritz was Seaver's equal, and I think Yogi's presence on the Queens team may have tipped the whole thing in favor of the Yankees.

But the Yanks were on vacation or working second jobs, while the Mets' business was unfinished. The Yanks had finished 80–81–1, good for fifth place out of six. The Mets had shocked the baseball world with their drive in the late season. From nine games back in mid-September to league champs by season's end. They'd gone on to top Atlanta's Braves in baseball's first year of divisional playoffs, due in part to a game three gem by the skinny kid from Texas. My father had dismissed Ryan's game as just freak luck; he still gave him two years tops.

Maybe I was interested because my own baseball team had folded. Big Will's shoulder hadn't been the only casualty that game. Rico Torrez had to quit when his family moved to Boston. And the Schwartzes' lawyer sent my dad a letter wanting money, claiming emotional duress.

I think the team's collapse was a relief to me somehow. I didn't have to live up to my father's dreams or see men stare at my mom anymore.

I found myself enduring sleepless nights as I ran endless replays of McCovey's mighty blast in my head. I thought about my mini-reenactment, and how great the contact made me feel. He'd won the MVP award, finished just ahead of Seaver. And sometimes, when I knew the house was quiet, I'd take his bat out of the closet. I kept doing Greenberg's exercise so that one day I'd be ready.

My father said he'd fix the broken door when he got a little free time on his hands. I hoped the free time wouldn't come too soon, as I'd come to enjoy the open access to their world. Access enough to conclude that both my mom and my dad were crazy. Crazy in a good way, but crazy nonetheless. That dress is an example. The way they'd fought after my game I thought my father hated it. But thanks to my lack of sleep and their lack of a door, I found out I was wrong.

For when he came home late at night, he started asking her to wear it. My mom got even weirder. She asked my father several times to cheat her out of money.

The sporting world's top showcase took place on weekday afternoons in 1969. No one stopped to wonder why—that was just the way things were. The younger generation questioned Vietnam but left the Series' dubious start times alone. It was not until two years later that the Fall Classic played in prime time, under the lights.

The result was no one saw it—at least not working dads or kids. I heard that Queens schoolteachers brought TVs into class so that kids could watch the games at school. One kid at Sacred Heart asked Mrs. Carson, our teacher, if she might do the same. I think it was the only time I ever saw Mrs. Carson laugh.

The Bronx was Bomber country—at least that was the theory. But in practice, you could almost hear the thud of lifelong fans jumping off the Yankee bandwagon. The Yanks had been a dynasty, but the dynasty was over. The team had stunk since '65 and the horizon held no hope. Bronxites loved their ball club, as long as they were winning. Loyalty moved crosstown, on roads that Robert Moses built.

The Orioles had won game one, which was no surprise to most. Even worse, the Mets' wives had been made to sit in right field's upper deck. Imagine the indignity of Nancy Seaver in the nosebleeds. I knew right then the Mets could pull it out; they'd win this one for Nancy.

I missed game two because I saw a Sunday matinee of *True Grit* at the Crest. I was sad to see the theater suffering from neglect. The screen was torn, the popcorn stale, and my shoes stuck to the floor. My mother heard it would be closing soon. I really liked that place. The Mets won game two 2–1 to pull even—one apiece.

If the Series as a whole did indeed declare my independence, game three marked another rite of passage.

I was running down 168th in the Sacred Heart three o'clock stampede. She was walking up the hill, coming home from public school. Our paths and fate both crossed. She was with her friends and two years older and I thought she'd pass me by without a word. But that wasn't Nina's way. She said hello, called me Scooter, which caused the little Irish kids to laugh. The next day in school they teased me and tried to imitate her voice. They couldn't imitate her kindness, though, or the way she made me feel.

Her English was fluent, although her accent sometimes made it difficult to follow. But I had no problem with three questions that made my body weak.

"You wanna walk with me, Scooter?"

"Okay."

"You gonna watch the game?"

"Uh-huh."

"You wanna watch with me?"

She lived on the second floor of a three-story walk-up that, like most of the apartments in Highbridge, had been built in the early 1900s, when the completion of New York's subway system had made the Bronx explode almost overnight. She had flown to this country with her family when she was still a baby on one of those cheap one-way fares that the Dago had made fun of. In many ways the Puerto Rican exodus that started with the failure of the island's sugar crop of the 1930s was reminiscent of the Irish, who had escaped the famine in their country back in the 1800s. Both groups arrived tired and poor and at the bottom of the U.S. social barrel.

The Irish journey over had been tougher. They'd come in former slave ships, not on planes, and their passages were traced by schools of sharks that swam behind, dining on their dead.

But the Irish spoke the language and rose up New York City's ladder after building its sewers, roads and subways with the sweat of their brows. Puerto Ricans showed up in New York City without the benefit of the language, and just as labor jobs left town on forty thousand miles of interstate that had been paved in '58. Roads that led to places where no unions had emerged.

Nina's father left town as well and didn't leave a lot behind him. Just a wife with two young mouths to feed in an apartment shared with rats and roaches on Harlem's east side. Until Spanish Harlem swelled and nearly burst and Mrs. Vasquez crossed the river to the Bronx, where they replaced a fleeing Irishman who was moving to a year-old place called Co-op City, which stood on the grave of Freedomland.

Her mom worked sixty-hour weeks, trying to create a better life. If the scouts were right, she'd get that life, not from sixty-hour weeks but on the strength of her son's ninety-mile-per-hour fastball.

Nina's brother, Manny, was seventeen, handsome, and in possession of a bright future. He seemed to be perpetually smiling, at least until he cast his eyes on me. He didn't seem to like the sight of an Irish boy inside his house. He was in the darkened living room, eating a pizza with his friends. The dull glow of the game's seventh inning served as the room's only light. Manny offered us no greeting—or slices, for that matter. Just a stare and Spanish whispers followed by laughter that was loud.

I sat down on a tattered love seat. Nina sat down beside a three-legged cat with no tail that was lying on the floor. One of Manny's friends lit up a cigarette that smelled a little strange.

I used to look up at the scoreboard when my dad took me to the games. A sign said, COME TO WHERE THE FLAVOR IS, and a rugged cowboy smoked a butt. It looked like a great place to live—the place where that flavor was. The kind of place where "the Duke" might hang his hat.

Nolan Ryan wound up for the Mets. His throw popped Grote's glove. Manny nodded to his friend. All three looked impressed. Then Ryan threw a curve that was lined foul into the stands. Manny shook his head and smirked. Nina stroked the cat.

I don't know why I spoke at all, probably nerves, I guess. Even as it was slipping out, I knew that it was stupid, really stupid.

"My dad can teach you how to throw a curve."

His two friends laughed and cursed in Spanish. Tommy Agee made a great catch in the outfield. The ball looked like a scoop of Krum's vanilla protruding from his glove.

"Oh, you probably know how already," I said. Kind of a question, kind of a statement. Equal parts stupid and ill timed.

I thought Manny might be angry. Or might laugh and make me wince. Instead, I saw him smile. "You gotta fastball like mine, you don't need no fuckin' curve."

The three friends slapped palms the way athletes did before the high five was invented. I vowed to never speak again. Nina looked up from her cat.

"You wanna sandwich, Scooter?"

I nodded yes. I'd kept my vow.

Nina got up from the floor. Shag carpet, old and grossly green.

I heard a knife clang against a jar. My eyes were locked on a commercial I can't remember. I only know I looked at it as if it was the most important message ever sent. I didn't dare look up at Manny.

Nina returned with a sandwich on a paper plate. Peanut butter and banana. My mom said it was Elvis Presley's favorite, but he liked it fried in lots of butter. He must have had to give them up to fit into black leather for his comeback special on TV.

Nina didn't sit down on the floor. She left the cat alone. Instead, she sat down next to me on the love seat with her leg barely touching mine. Her body felt electric. I took a bite of PB&B, the one she'd gone to great lengths to make for me. It was wonderful, just like her. Some guys on TV played baseball.

She gathered up her long dark hair and let it fall over her left shoulder. Then she turned to her right to look at me, her hair no longer an obstruction. When she spoke, I saw her jawline move. It struck me as majestic.

"Scooter?"

"Yeah?" I had broken my solemn vow. But vows meant very little when her leg was touching mine.

"Can I have a bite?"

I handed her the sandwich. I could have sworn her thumb touched mine when the handoff was made. I looked at her mouth as she took her bite. Oh, my God, it was more than I'd dared dream. I had just assumed that she'd bite down on virgin bread, but that was not the case at all. Nina Vasquez chose instead to journey down the road that I'd just traveled. Her mouth clearly touched the bite I'd made—she was almost kissing me by proxy. She knew it too, I could tell—the way those big, dark, soulful eyes looked at me as she chewed.

I don't think she knew my life had changed as she swallowed the bite. I wondered if this was one of those moments Grandpa spoke of, where one transcends or whatever. Because I thought I'd just transcended.

I took the sandwich from her hands—the one with two bites missing. I put our special sandwich on the paper plate and placed the plate onto my lap. Where it covered my first erection.

I think the Mets won 5–0.

[13]

Game four was Nancy Seaver's day. I couldn't have picked five Mets out of a police lineup, but I could spot Tom's wife a mile away. The cameraman seemed drawn to her like a mouse to cheddar cheese. Or my mother to an Alexander's sale.

I watched the last three innings with my sister and my mom, who seemed quite impressed with Mrs. Seaver.

"Do you like Nancy's hair?" my mother asked, referring to her stylish golden bob.

"Yeah, I guess," I answered. Although I preferred hair that was much darker and cascaded down the back.

"I like it too," my sister said.

"She really is quite a looker. Don't you think so, Scooter?"

"Um, yeah," I told her. And I guess she was, if you liked that blond-haired light-skinned thing.

"I think I'll color my hair like hers and wear it in a bob." My mom a blonde? With her dark features?

"A handsome young couple," Curt Gowdy called the Seavers.

"They are indeed," said Lindsey Nelson, who my father used to say was no Rizzuto.

Ron Swoboda made a diving catch in right field that Nelson called "a lulu." My grandfather later called it Swoboda's "one moment"—the one he'd be remembered for forever. Father Time would forget about his so-so stick in favor of that catch.

Jerry Grote scored in extra innings to give the Mets the win. I don't remember Grote's face because the camera cut to Nancy.

"Nancy is a happy, happy girl," Nelson said. "Tom Seaver has his first World Series victory ever as the Mets go up three games to one."

My mom looked slightly puzzled as she watched the postgame scene unfold. I thought something might be wrong.

"Mom?"

My voice shook her from her daze. "Yes?"

"Are you alright?"

"Yes, Scooter, I'm fine, I was just thinking . . . I think Fritz's wife is prettier. I really like her hair."

I really didn't know what Fritz's wife looked like and didn't really care. I can't recall a single Yankee's wife in 1969, nor had I paid it any heed. But the subject made me wonder, "What did Yogi's wife look like?"

As important as the New York baseball wives' hair duel seemed, my father's situation was far more vital. For, as Nancy Seaver showed her happiness, my dad was being rushed to a hospital in Midtown.

He was putting in some overtime at Bryant Park on Fortieth, next to the New York Public Library. Helping out at the city's other major scene that day—an anti–Vietnam War rally. The actions of the marchers brought out supporters of the war. Both sides clashed. My dad stepped in and was nearly knocked out for his efforts.

The culprit was a swinging book, newly checked out from the library, which caught him on his small Irish nose and broke it in three places.

To say my dad was in some pain that night would be an understatement. The bedroom's broken door let me hear his tortured moans. My mother's soothing words seemed to offer little comfort, until she made him take the doctor's pill so that he might rest a little.

[14]

The Dago had a gift for me when I bounded in the door. I had sprinted home from Sacred Heart, my eyes alert for Nina. I'd been thinking about what happened at her apartment that day and couldn't get her off my mind. At first I thought I'd tell my grandpa, but then decided I should keep that moment just for me.

I was a little sad I hadn't seen her, but was in high spirits nonetheless. For game five was a big party and the Dago was on hand. The Amazin' Mets could win it all and my dad was going to watch. He'd have to watch with swollen purple eyes, but I was just thankful he was there.

My little sister seemed thankful too, the way she nestled next to him on our new leather love seat. The Dago sat on the couch, looking very comfortable with a busty blonde by his side. I took a seat on the floor, within hair-tousling distance of my injured father.

"Go ahead," the Dago said, taking his arm out from around his girl so as to better gesture with his hands. "Go ahead and open it."

The umpire saw shoe polish in inning six and granted the Mets' Cleon Jones a pass to first. My dad was up in arms.

"Jeez!" my dad yelled out. "That thing didn't touch him!"

Despite my father's protest, the tying run was on first base. And despite a face worthy of Lon Chaney's best efforts, his attitude seemed great.

I opened up the Dago's gift. It was a baseball card—Joe Torre. At first I didn't get it. The Dago tried in his own way to make me understand.

"When you get a little older, you need two things in your wallet. One of them's this Torre card."

My father and the Dago howled, though I think the joke escaped my mother, who stepped into the kitchen to get the boys another beer. Judging by the piles of empties—Ballantine, not Rheingold—she'd made many trips that day.

A surprising crack from the bat of the Mets' Al Weis put an end to the Torre-inspired laughter.

"Holy shit!" the Dago yelled. "The little Jew just hit it out!"

Indeed he had. A two-run shot to tie the game had sailed over Paul Blair's head in left.

"Way to go, you Jewish bastard!" It was the Dago's line, of course. The blonde looked at him with starstruck eyes; her guy was quite a catch.

"Hey, Molly," my father said. "How 'bout gettin' us a beer?" He opened up a little bottle and shook two pills into his hand. "This is to help kill the pain if the Mets go on to win." He popped both in his mouth and swallowed them with spit.

The camera showed a happy Nancy Seaver, for no apparent reason.

My father turned to me. "City's gotta crack down on these hookers, son." In retrospect, it might have been the most wit he'd ever shown. But even as the Dago's laugh filled the room with its sheer size, I couldn't help but think that inside those swollen eyes, my dad looked kind of funny. His eyes seemed kind of glassy.

Next, the camera showed Joe D. sitting in the stands, looking either bored or stoic. I looked at my dad and saw him smile. I thought of Co-op City and what it once had been.

I wish the big leagues played only seven innings like my dad's team in '59. They could have ruled game five a tie—after all, it's just a game.

For in the interim that existed between the schoolyard game and Shea lay the undoing of my future—an inning and a half.

I wish the flow of beer had stopped. Instead, it picked up steam. But beer was merely an accessory to the crime of stealing boyhood dreams. I think it was the glassy eyes that made me shift the blame to the bottle he'd been given to take away his pain. A man who had seen many young lives broken from the crippling hold of drugs fell into its trap unknowingly, with a doctor's willing pen. He always preached about the needle, making sure I'd stand up to its lure. But he didn't realize narcotic highs could come in other forms.

So as the eighth unfolded, my father basked in the warm glow of his buzz. And after nine years as the NYPD's man of peace, he spoke of the virtues of his gun.

Cleon Jones doubled off the wall to begin the inning's drive. A few years later, he'd be found sleeping naked in a van with someone other than his wife. And that's how he'd be remembered—not for his '69 heroics.

"I swear to God," my father said, his words tough to decipher. "If the goddamn Mets win this thing, I'm gonna put a bullet through this screen."

"That I'd like to see," the Dago said, with a wild gesture of his hands. "I bet the devil skates in hell before you draw a gun."

My mother shook her head in mock contempt and lit up a cigarette. Took a drag and let out smoke. She said, "Vinnie, don't encourage him. He's drunk enough to shoot himself."

The Dago coughed a couple times and waved the air to clear the smoke. "Hey, Mrs. R., ya mind smokin' that thing in the kitchen? That stuff's bad for the Dago's lungs." Then he turned to his blonde, nudged her with his elbow and said, "You know the Dago likes a healthy set of lungs."

My mother took her butt into the kitchen, rolling her eyes as she went.

The Dago lifted one butt cheek off the couch and let out a mighty fart. "Yeah, that's what I'm talkin' 'bout!" he yelled.

"Oh, gross," my sister said and scurried to the kitchen, where the thick plumes of cigarette smoke seemed a safe haven from the Dago.

"Scooter," my mother said, "sit next to your father so he doesn't do anything stupid."

The Mets scored two runs in the inning on a Swoboda blooper into shallow left and a Jerry Grote infield single. Our TV set's future didn't look too promising, at least not according to the Dago.

"Looks like pistol-packin' time," he said, which drew a reprimand from my mother.

The Dago threw up the hand that wasn't on his girlfriend's butt and said, "Hey, Mrs. R., your husband saved my life—ya think I'm gonna let any harm come to him or his TV?"

My father stumbled up the stairs, presumably to take a leak, but he bounded down a minute later packing heat, waving his pistol and threatening Mets.

"This bullet's got Seaver's name on it," he bragged.

My mother stepped into the living room and tore into him. "God-damn it, Patrick, put the gun away and sit down!"

My father looked like a scolded puppy as he sat down on the love seat. "Molly, I was just kidding," he said. "It's not even loaded. I just took all the bullets out." He set the empty gun in his lap.

The Dago coughed. "Hey, Mrs. R.—the cigarette?"

My mother walked back to the kitchen, just in time to evade another Dago fart. "Oh, that will leave a mark," the Dago said.

I heard my sister laugh. My mother told her farts weren't funny, which seemed at odds with the Dago's self-congratulatory chuckles.

Frank Robinson was forced out at second for the first out in the ninth in a play that nearly flattened Mets shortstop Buddy Harrelson. The Dago said Robinson would have been safe by a mile if he'd been running with a television on his shoulder with a cop chasing him. My father wondered why anyone would name his child Buddy.

The other Robinson, Brooks, flied out to Swoboda. Two down, one to go.

Curt Gowdy gave his take on things. "If they get one more out here, you're going to see one of the doggonedest sights you've ever seen."

Davey Johnson swung on a 1–1 count.

"There's a fly ball hit out to left," Gowdy said. Cleon Jones, the future naked van sleeper, caught it for out three. "The Mets are world champions!"

"Look at this scene," Gowdy shouted, as fans surged onto the field. They were climbing over fences and dropping from the outfield stands like paratroopers hitting foreign shores.

My sister ran into the living room yelling, "The Mets won! The Mets won!"

The Dago jumped for joy. The blonde joined in and they all jumped: my sister, the Dago, the Dago's girl, the Dago's girl's boobs. My dad just sat and stared, disbelief etched on his swollen features. The euphoric glow was gone.

Then my father saw a group of fans hovering around home plate, digging at Shea's dirt, attempting to uproot a souvenir. Like a pack of hungry jackals gnawing on a carcass.

I saw his eyes turn from sad to angry in that moment. The blatant theft of home plate, in full view of the television cameras and his NYPD brothers, was just too much for him to take. The callous disregard for authority was like a slap to my father's face. A slap that staggered him enough that he nearly fell off of the love seat. The gun he thought was empty had one bullet left and with a mighty blast that bullet fled the barrel and life was never quite the same.

I never heard my sister scream. The shot was just too loud. But I saw the terror in her tiny eyes and I saw her mouth go wide. I cried out, "Oh my God!" and tried to run to her but was paralyzed with fear. The Dago's mouth hung open as if petrified in mid-Met cheer.

My mother was the only one who moved—springing into action to save the child she loved. The world seemed to move too slowly when juxtaposed with her. Perhaps it's within these moments that heroes thrive and cowards fall. I knew my mother was the former when she pressed her hand against the wound. But the gunshot was a gaping hole, and her hand was overcome by a steady stream of blood that quickly pooled up on the floor. It was one of the doggonedest sights you've ever seen.

"I need towels!" my mother yelled. I got up to lend a hand. Until I realized the wound was mine and I couldn't feel my leg.

The Dago's blonde was the first to gain her bearings and volunteered her denim coat, which quickly turned to rust. The Dago hovered uselessly and my dad began to cry.

My mother yelled, "He's losing too much blood! I need towels, lots of towels!" The blonde headed for the bathroom.

I tried to feel my leg but there was no answer coming. I looked down with fading vision and saw my mother's arm was red.

My father finally stirred and, still crying, found his feet. He stumbled to the telephone and my mother disappeared. He was lifting the receiver when a shiny, blood-soaked hand pressed it down. Maybe he was too stoned to speak, maybe just too drunk. Or maybe he was petrified by the eyes that greeted his. Or the voice that sealed my fate. My mother's voice. Firm but calm. Direct but gentle.

"If this gets out, Patrick, you'll never make detective."

My father's mouth was moving but words would not come out. Tears ran down his swollen cheeks as he struggled to be heard. His attempt was not successful.

About this time my vision failed, but not before I saw the Dago come to life, poised to ruin everything. The blood was pumping out in squirts with each beat of my heart. It felt oddly peaceful to feel my world fade into black. But not before the Dago seized the moment and my mom. He shook her in his big strong arms and said he was going to make that call.

I was so proud of my mother, the way she stood up for her rights. Her voice was even firmer now, but her words were downright soothing.

"You said he saved your life, Vinnie. Remember? Now how about saving his? If word gets out, this family's done. Is that how you repay him?"

He never made the call. My mom was in her moment. She was transcending what others felt was possible. She kept her cool. She took control. She gave guidance to the others. Her thoughtful words continued to soothe me as she laid out her plan.

"Vinnie, take off your belt, I'm gonna make a tourniquet. Be ready with excuses in case a neighbor heard the shot. What's your name—?"

The blonde said, "Jane."

"Jane, thank you for the towels. Try to keep my daughter calm, play dolls with her upstairs. And Patrick, go up to bed. You're useless to me here."

1973

[1]

Ten months' time would pass before I would step outside our front door, and when I did, the steps were slow and filled with fear. Ten months without the outside world. Ten months without a single word from Grandpa. Ten months without a talk with friends, a Cozy Corners egg cream, a movie at the Crest, a Rossi's meatball hero or a sled ride down the hill. Ten months without the Dago's wit, Nina's smile, Pop's peanuts or a harsh word between my parents.

Indeed, those ten months were a time to heal. A time for my father to accept responsibility for what he'd done to me. A time for him to accept the role that alcohol had played in the shooting of his son. For him to accept that he and Ballantine would have to end their partnership. A time for him to dedicate himself to nailing perps and slapping cuffs, instead of making friends with Harlem's worst. A time to find solace in his family and comfort in his pills.

I listened to his tearstained pleas and tried to absolve him of his guilt. But the truth remained—the guy had shot me. I was nine and maimed for life.

The shot had hit me on my leg's right side, an inch below the knee. Before resting in the carpet, the bullet found the time to ruin me. The artery was severed, as the blood spurting might have indicated. If not for the Dago's belt and my mother's knowledge, I would have never made it. A nerve was severed in that leg as well, a nerve that runs from knee to ankle. The peroneal nerve, which supplies sensation to the foot. I could vaguely feel my right big toe, but the other ones were numb.

I often thought about that gunshot and the panic that ensued. Screaming, crying, fear and pain—but none of it from Mom. She seemed more myth than mom that day, as if she'd been lifted from a fable. Like Pecos Bill or Bunyan's axe or McCovey's magic bat. Maybe game five of the Series had been my mom's day, not the Mets'. They were nine guys working toward a common goal, not one person who transcended. For truly, in that moment, she was at her very best, turning disaster into triumph, giving life back to her son.

To compare my parents was inevitable, their actions on that day. My father almost took my life—my mother rescued me. My father took away my health—my mother did her best to heal. My father faced his fate with tears of pity—my mom with selflessness.

I guess I should not have been surprised, for selflessness seemed to cling to her, like a skin she'd never shed. From her Concourse heritage to her hours spent at my bedside, her life was one of sacrifice, placing family needs above her own.

I was healed at home and schooled at home, both a tribute to my mother's will. She taught my little sister there as well, and our house became our world.

Our Highbridge home was under siege and the house was my sole refuge, like a foxhole on a battlefield. I clung to it for safety, knowing if I ventured out, I might not make it back. Sure, foxholes were unsightly, but there were no other options. Not until the siege was through.

The Reillys would stay safe and warm while the battle raged outside. We knew that our Shakespeare house would have to do until the smoke cleared. And then I'd climb out of Highbridge hell and find heaven on Long Island.

For only there could we find true peace and calm, a housing-tract oasis. Soft green grass, cool blue pool, and middle-class white faces. Everyone was doing it—why be the last ones to join in? Leave the Bronx, hurry up, don't be the last white guy on the block.

Thanks to Mom, I knew all this. Her lessons didn't end with math and English. She taught lots of helpful things about spics and spooks and coons. Enough to not feel too bad when I saw Nina walk sadly away from our stoop. My mom had spared me from her threat. She'd be okay. After all, lots of other spics had moved in by '73. She could hang out with her kind and leave the nice white kid alone.

Still, I thought about her smile sometimes and how I had felt when I was with her. I sometimes asked my mother to skip the jelly and slice a banana up instead. Then I'd take two bites and close my eyes and imagine she was there.

Other times, I faced the facts—she was only a temptation. I'd learned about that stuff at Sacred Heart. Eve and her damn apple had screwed it up for all of us. I wasn't about to let Nina and her sandwich make things even worse.

I wish I had known back then that what I felt was not temptation but the longing for a friend.

My mother was my nurse and teacher, and she performed those duties well. But she also filled my head with fears and let them ferment while she shopped. No longer on the Concourse, for its shade had turned too dark. The Paradise was falling victim to neglect, and stores were closing down.

So my mother quickly aimed her car away from the Concourse and toward Manhattan. She filled our house with useless but expensive junk and then cursed the mortgage people. Why couldn't they approve our loan? Can't we buy a house with no down payment? To her it seemed that paradise was just a cruel mirage. We were sinking in our Shakespeare sand while we watched Long Island drift away.

So when I finally did limp out our door, it was as a wiser, weaker child. I knew that Highbridge was hell on earth and that I was powerless against it. I watched in vain as my sister walked with the other Irish kids up 168th to Sacred Heart. Then my mother said good-bye and sent me down the hill to public school, to face monsters she had created.

Manny Vasquez, as it turned out, could have used a fuckin' curve. He'd been a ringer at All Hallows and had made scouts clamor for his fastball. But by his second year in Class A ball, people had caught on that the kid had no other pitch. It wasn't that he couldn't, he just flat out wouldn't give another pitch a try.

Now, personally, I respected that. To me, that's what the game is all about. Eliminate the guessing. Eliminate the off-speed stuff. Take away the batter's right to choose. Just give the guy a stick and let him take his cuts, swinging from the heels on every pitch. Yeah, I respected Manny as a pitcher, even if as a person he was nothing but a dick. Not the kind Joe D. shook either.

Unfortunately for Manny, guys don't make the bigs based on what I think. Maybe Koufax had got away with nothing but fastballs at the tail end of his career. His arm was slathered with hot pepper sauce and he got by on fastballs and guts. But Manny wasn't Koufax.

Maybe, if not for prejudice, he would have been allowed a few more years. If not for discrimination he could have been taught to throw the curve. After all, this was the early seventies; before Messersmith pled his case for free agency and zeros started adding up on major leaguers' checks. Back then prospects had to supplement their income by working other jobs. Even future Hall of Famers went to work after hitting Series homers. I heard Yogi sold men's suits. I wonder just how many souls were haunted by the memory of Yogi measuring their inseam.

Manny worked a side job too. Selling heroin in Syracuse. He was busted once and did thirty days. Word got out quickly in the minors. On the second strike, he was gone, washed up at twenty-one.

I sometimes wonder where life would have taken him if he'd only listened to my words. If he'd just taken a short walk down the block and let my father help him out. He might have thrown his heat and a curve my father taught him, inside Yankee Stadium.

Or maybe he just weighed the economic factors and figured he could make more money selling smack in Highbridge than throwing fuckin' curves in Syracuse. Whatever the case, Manny Vasquez became a major player in the fast-growing world of Bronx gangs and drugs.

As '73 came rolling around, Highbridge was Hispanic, at least to a large extent. The Irish had been leaving at a fairly steady pace, until the Spellman-Latham murders at a bar in '71 sent them sprinting for the suburbs at a speed belying white genetics.

Meanwhile, on Manhattan's Upper West Side, my dad's friend Robert Moses was cleaning out the slums. Guess where the refugees took off to? Mott Haven, Melrose, Highbridge—each with extra room. For every sprinting Irishman selling out at record lows there was a Puerto Rican family waiting for a cheap roof over their heads.

Property values tanked. Rental business sank. Rates were rent-controlled, but the costs of maintenance spiraled ever higher. A Mideast oil crisis tripled fuel costs, but the price of rent stayed flat. Landlords tried to refinance, but bankers' ears were deaf. And tenants came to feel that paying rent was just an option, as was moving without payment.

Buildings started burning. If tenants wouldn't pay, perhaps insurance companies would. Arson was big business and fire engines screamed. Four blocks a week went up in smoke—proud blocks reduced to blackened shells. Robert Moses had the antidote. He thought the place was beyond repair and said, "People living here must be removed."

Still, our family remained. My father still held on to roots. Too proud to flee, too poor to move, or maybe just too stoned to notice.

It was in this war-torn atmosphere that the heroin trade was nurtured. What had started as a tiny spark among new arrivals in the fifties was fanned and fed by disregard and cops who turned their heads, and it burst into a red-hot trade in the early 1970s.

My father used to rail against its ravages and issue threats about its use—all with pupils that were pinpricks. He let me see *The French Connection* so I could learn a little more. I thanked him for his kindness but didn't have the heart to tell him that I didn't need a silver screen with which to see the stuff when I had P.S. 73. In '73, I was in middle school, and in addition to pens and books, students came to school with needles and spoons.

I'd see Manny Vasquez there quite often, hovering by the fence that divided the outside world from our institute of knowledge. But a chain-link fence was no match for Manny, and I saw the hand that had once gripped baseballs gripping dollar bills instead.

Manny wore Diablo colors and the word was you didn't mess with him. Word was a guy named Nicholls had, and as a result no longer lived.

To his credit, Manny's trips to middle school were not simply ones of commerce. In fact, he himself rarely made the trades. Instead, he came as a recruiter, seeking numbers for his game. And his numbers were successful—for as a mere matter of survival kids had to play the game.

At first the gangs were seen as heroes, like fabled outlaws of the West. The press seemed taken with them and the good their deeds had done. For in their infancy these new Bronx gangs harassed junkies and their pushers—until they saw the potential of the business and started dealing it themselves.

After all, these guys were businessmen and they were entitled to a living in a place with no livings to be made. The Italians, Jews and Irish all had left the place (with the exception of my dad), but they'd taken their jobs with them. And where was a minority to get a break when there were no breaks at hand? The Italians had sanitation. The Irish had both fire and the police. The Jews had schools and civil service. What was an entrepreneur with darker skin to do?

Heroin—the wonder drug. Developed at the century's turn in Germany by Bayer—the folks who brought you aspirin. It was seen as a cure-all for colds and asthma, bronchitis too—who knew it was addictive?

I saw Nina only rarely. I'd been at P.S. 114 when she was in middle school. Then when I moved up, she entered Taft. She still had a smile to offer me, but it seemed to have lost some of its warmth. I still thought that she was beautiful, but her face and manner seemed plagued by sadness.

Word was out on Nina too—you didn't mess with her. Not with Manny as her brother, lest you meet the fate of Nicholls.

I sometimes thought about that time I'd seen her walking away from my stoop. What she would have said, how she would have smelled and how she would have made me feel.

Word had gotten out on me as well. I was a guy you didn't mess with, unless you wanted blood spilled on your hands.

I used to get beaten up quite regularly because I was a white kid with a limp. By some standards I lost badly, but by my own score I did well. For it mattered not who won or lost to me. All that counted were the blows. Had I taken the best they had to offer? Had I thrown my best as well? I might go down, but I'd go down swinging—always from my heels. And as I got a little older, those swings of mine grew harder. I might not have landed many punches, but I tried to make them count.

I didn't care if they wore colors or if there were two or even three. I didn't fear the pain so much as going down without my swings. Eventually the fights all but stopped. No one wanted to sport a shiner from a white kid with a limp. And I learned a neat new trick that brought with it respect.

[3]

He had bit his lip for hours, or so it seemed to me, as he stared blankly at the sports page on a cold March afternoon.

"Patrick, are you okay?" my mother asked.

He bit down a little harder.

"Patrick?"

Nothing but a stare.

I was busy watching television, a *Brady Bunch* rerun. Although their network time was up, the three blondes with hair of gold like their mother (the youngest one in curls) and Mike Brady's three boys of his own were now setting an example, five syndicated days a week, of how groovy life could really be, even in the hectic seventies.

It should have been wonderful escapist television. No mention of Vietnam. No Watergate. No OPEC oil embargo. Just simple, wonderful words of wisdom and a hot sitcom mom. Except the words didn't seem so wonderful or wise anymore. And the latter-day Brady Afros seemed just a bit misguided, even by the standards of the day.

My father just kept staring at his paper as if the sheer will of his gaze could make the letters rearrange themselves in ways that he approved. My mother scoured her paper too. She'd started getting Sunday's *Newsday* and was perusing high school sports. My mom was like a little child at Christmastime with a wish list just for Santa. She didn't want a choo-choo or a dolly that could pee. What she was looking for was towns. Glen Cove, Westbury, Oyster Bay. Prioritized in order according to their basketball record. Baseball season was coming now, but according to the Dago, baseball win-loss records were misleading. White kids could still hit the ball and they were better coached in fundamentals.

I didn't see the Dago much after that day in '69, and his name was rarely mentioned. When I did see him, he seemed to have changed a bit—he wasn't loud or funny. He would just say hi and wait in silence, save for a mention of the weather. Maybe it was because I'd grown, but he seemed much smaller than my recollections. He didn't call himself the Dago any longer and he'd even gotten married. I once asked him if he still saw the big-boobed girl (I think I phrased it differently) and he didn't even answer. If I'd had a thing for blondes, I think I might have liked her.

"Mom always said not to play ball in the house."

Man, is that the best *The Brady Bunch* could offer? Playing ball in the house? Maybe it seemed cutting-edge stuff back in '69, but I needed something stronger.

Maybe, "Mom always said not to get drunk and put a bullet in your son's leg." I got up and turned the Bradys off. I was sick of television. Besides, I had a new book from the library that had been taking up my time. No, not *The Joy of Sex*—although I did usually snag it from my parents' room on Fridays, after Mom and Patty took off for Manhattan. The pictures looked a little weird but I thought I'd like to someday give some of it a shot.

The book was *Marilyn,* its author Norman Mailer. I didn't see what all the fuss about her was, but I guess millions did. I was ready for a little Joe D. insight so I could better understand his rage at Freedomland.

I didn't see my grandpa much, and when I did, he seemed really frail. The past few years had been tough on him, especially when he learned the origin of my limp. The revelation made him want to go and seek out justice, but I convinced him silence would be best. My parents may have had their faults, but they were the only parents I had. Who would have taken me and Patty in if the justice ruled was harsh? Grandpa? He offered willingly, but I told him I'd pass. Patty was hanging in at Sacred Heart and I was being left alone at P.S. 73. A move would mean more beatings, which I wouldn't really mind, as long as I could take my swings. But to uproot my little sister would only add to her mounting fears.

She was now eleven but still cried out in the darkness. It wasn't schoolday pressure or even Shakespeare's changing face. Instead it was *The Exorcist* that kept her up at night.

I was halfway up the stairs, a slow and labored chore, when my father finally spoke.

"The sons of bitches traded wives!"

"What?" I said.

"The sons of bitches traded wives!"

A fact that had already been established.

"Who?" I asked.

"Peterson and Kekich!"

Oh, *those* sons of bitches. "Why?" I asked.

"Who knows why!" my father ranted. "Who knows why anyone does anything these days! Maybe it was drugs! Kekich seems the type to me. California hippie, jumping out of planes."

My mother sat in silence, *Newsday* in her lap, her mouth hanging open wide, as if in shock. Then she shook her head.

"What do you mean they traded wives?" she asked.

"Oh, not just wives," my father said, his face growing red, his neck veins trying to break free. "Houses too, kids and dogs, let's not forget the animals."

"I can't believe it," my mother said.

"Oh, believe it. Believe it, it's all right here. They're calling it a life swap. They did it in the summer after dinner at some writer's house!"

"I just can't believe it," my mother said, treating the new life swap as a funeral. She seemed to be taking the news of this development awfully hard. "I just don't understand . . . why Fritz . . . would ever give up Marilyn."

"Goddamn Kekich, that's why—screwing up his head. Two years after Fritz won twenty."

"I wouldn't blame him too much, you know, that's quite a trade for Mike."

[4]

The Yankees didn't suck—I think that point should be made. Maybe public opinion disagrees, but I disagree with public opinion. Hell, they won ninety-three games in '70, good for second place. The year Dad discovered Thurman Munson, the Yanks' new pride and joy. They'd been okay that next year too, and just missed out in '72. They looked to be the favorites leading into '73, before those sons of bitches' life swap ruined everything.

Sadly, those Yankee teams that didn't really suck played to empty seats. Despite the August pennant run, attendance dropped below a million for the first time since '45—back when all the top boys were fighting for the country—Joe D., Ted, Greenberg, even Phil Rizzuto.

The crosstown Mets, the Moses Mets, doubled those weak numbers. Despite the inability to duplicate their feats of that one magic summer. Word had gotten out on the Bombers—you didn't want to risk your life to see that team. Maybe watch it on the TV, listen to the Scooter wishing strangers happy birthdays. Be a loyal Yankee fan—but do it from a distance.

The fans were not the only ones who didn't want to see games played in the Bronx. The Yanks themselves made a threat to jump over to New Jersey. Hey, why not? The Giants did it and they found heaven in the swamplands. The thought of losing both Bronx teams was too much for Mayor Lindsay, who said that cash-strapped New York City would love to help the team. Although the Big Apple was bobbing up and down in a monstrous sea of debt, the mayor promised a new stadium to make the Yanks stay put.

Even with that sweetheart deal, CBS had seen enough. Apparently the TV guys had tired of sniffing jocks and, much like Highbridge Irishmen, sold out at a loss. A Cleveland shipping magnate came in and made the save, buying the most storied franchise in sports for a bargain basement price.

My father was still up in arms over that whole life swap thing even when the season started, imploring the new Yanks owner to show some moral fortitude.

"I know the new guy wants to stick to building ships," my father said, "but I think he needs to get involved sometimes."

I rarely watched the ball games with my father anymore. They brought back thoughts of simpler times, and the memories made me sad. Instead, I learned to hide between the covers of my books. Stories could transport me to places far away. Places where loving dads didn't shoot their kids. Places where the hero sometimes got the girl.

Sometimes I'd turn on Channel 9 if the Giants played the Mets. The past few years had been tough ones on McCovey—he was merely mortal after all. His painful feet had sidelined him; some days he couldn't walk. I sometimes wondered if I was the cause, in some weird King Arthur way. Too bad he had to play the field instead of just showing up for swings.

The Yankees had a guy like that—who was paid only to hit. A new rule had been instated where a guy batted for the pitcher. A designated hitter—baseball's greatest job. Not so for McCovey, though, for his league had opted out. So by process of elimination, Ron Bloomberg became my hero.

I had not been to a baseball game since that night in '69. I think my father's gun had destroyed more than just my leg. It had claimed a few more casualties, including traditions of my birthday. Perhaps he sensed after all this time that I had never really loved the game. Or maybe he just couldn't bear to see how slowly I climbed the steps.

In spite of that, I reminisced a lot about that day in Little League. How magical my hands had felt when the heavy wood made contact. Sometimes at night when Patty didn't cry and I was sure I was alone, I would pull that bat out of my closet. I would roll it around in my hands, feel its strength and try to summon Willie's power. I would pull out Grandpa's Greenberg thing and do it till my forearms throbbed and hot tears streamed down my face. The weights were now much heavier and I learned to block out all the pain. Maybe one day I would hit again, send a ball into the sky. In a game where there were no fielders, where I wouldn't have to run.

I didn't miss the double plays, the nice line drives or the singles up the middle. But I somehow felt the game call to me as I approached my thirteenth birthday. I might have longed to see Big Ron, the new DH, aim for the Babe's short porch. But I think, in truth, the thing I longed for most was to see the game work its wonders on my dad. So it came to pass that I asked my dad to celebrate my entry into teenagehood with a return trip to the stadium.

Upper mezzanine, right behind the girder. As if we'd never gone away. Sixty thousand screaming fans on hand to see the Yanks take on the Angels. Sixty thousand fans? Yeah, that is correct. I guess I should qualify my remarks about attendance. It's true no one wanted to risk their lives to see a ball game by traveling to the stadium. Unless of course it was bat day, in which case lives were gladly risked.

White Plains whites and Bronx blacks alike jammed the stadium for a chance to take home wooden souvenirs with a Yankee name engraved. Somewhere in those last few years the word "Negro" was replaced. "Black" was in and it was beautiful and Afros were the rage. Some black 'fros reached mountainous heights, though none seemed to climb as high as the latter-day Mike Brady's.

I got my bat—a Horace Clarke—until my father flashed a badge. He hovered over personnel until they finally found a Munson. I really didn't care so much but my father was insistent. Because Munson guarded home plate with his life while Horace bailed out into center field when turning double plays.

My dad's eyes lit up during batting practice when he saw his favorite guy, Pop the peanut vendor, slowly mumbling his wares. My dad was in his glory, sort of—with his peanuts, frank and soda. I hadn't seen him look so out of place since he shuffled to the mound at Big Will's game. Some things aren't meant to be. Gandhi with a Big Mac. Mike Brady with an Afro. My father with a soda.

A scoreboard sign said SCHAEFER BEER—Ballantine was gone. Schaefer claimed it was the one beer to have when you're having more than one. I wished right then that my dad could pop a couple tabs instead of popping pills. For no amount of pain pills could replicate that look he got every year in June, when he and I sat behind Ruth's girder and he had a cold one in his hand.

A brilliant *crack* filled the air and stirred me from my daze. A horsehide sphere had been launched into space and it was heading for the nosebleeds. Not quite in McCovey's league but brilliant nonetheless. A lucky fan made the catch in right field's upper deck. Although by the way he grabbed his thumb and yelled in pain he might not have felt too lucky. I turned to see the batter. It was Ronnie, my DH. Tall, handsome and well built, he could have been a hero to all the borough's Jews. Like Koufax had been in Brooklyn. But all the Jews had fled the Bronx, not counting Co-op City.

"Too bad he can't field or hit the southpaws," my father said, his words ruining the moment like an alarm clock cutting off a wet dream. I was a veteran of those things, having had exactly one. The dream's vision had been hazy but I thought the girl was Nina and we were doing things I'd only read about.

"Scooter?" my father asked hesitantly.

"Yeah?" Bloomberg hit another blast, not quite as impressive as the last. It bounced into the right field seats, kind of like most of Roger's had that year he broke Ruth's record.

"We're gonna move out to the Island."

"Oh?"

"Yeah, I think we gotta go. Your mother's right—Highbridge isn't a place for kids."

"But what about the money? I thought you said we were broke."

"I'm workin' on that now. I've been savin' up these last few months and your mom's been cuttin' back."

"Is that why you've been gone so much? Working overtime?"

My father usually volunteered for extra duty when extra cops were needed. Thanksgiving, St. Patrick's Day and rallies like the one at Bryant Park.

But most cops put in extra time for extra money when they'd made arrests. And you couldn't make detective without some bookings on your record. So I guessed that all his extra hours had been spent in that pursuit. My father and the Dago, both slapping cuffs on perps.

"Doin' what I've gotta do to get us outta here." His voice was strained, his answer vague, but I bought it at the time.

"What about the Moses roads?" I asked, which caused my dad to smile.

"That must seem kinda crazy, huh?"

"A little bit," I said.

"Look at that," my father said, pointing to the field. Munson had just lined a nice one up the box; he'd punched it through the hole. "Scooter," he continued, "I think I've got a plan."

"Yeah?"

"Yeah. We're thinkin' about Manhasset, just a little ways from Queens. A little place with a nice backyard, maybe room there for a pool."

"Yeah?" I was starting to sound like McCartney and Lennon on the chorus of "She Loves You" with all the "yeah, yeah, yeah."

"Yeah! It's just a couple blocks from the train station. I'd take the railroad to Penn Station, then catch the number one train straight uptown."

"That sounds great, Dad," I said, and in fact it really did. "Mom must be really happy."

"Oh, she is, she is," my father said, sounding like he needed his own words to convince himself. "They've got great public schools. Great shopping too."

"Shopping? Wow, Mom must really be ecstatic," I said sarcastically.

"Scooter, don't you be too hard on your mother. She's given up a lot for us."

"Like the Concourse?"

"Don't hear about the Concourse too much these days, but yes, that is one example. You need to think about her more, son."

"Oh, I think of her each step I take, Dad."

Only the singing of the anthem killed our awkward pause. I wished he would have bought a beer. Instead he popped two pills.

Somewhere in the first the pills must have done their work, for my father broke his silence and started providing running commentary on all of the nation's pastime's finer points.

"Look at that guy on the mound throwing all that heat. Kid'll never make it. Watch Thurman punch it through the hole." The kid was Nolan Ryan, a California Angel now, and he sat Munson down on strikes. Bloomberg fared no better, but at least he took his cuts and didn't have to field.

My father pointed to the Yankee dugout and said, "Scooter, look at that."

I saw what appeared to be about twenty guys scratching their nuts and spewing brown streams of tobacco.

"You see it?"

"I think so."

"Whattaya think?"

"I think that tobacco's kind of gross."

"No, not that. I'm talking about the pitchers. Peterson and Kekich. Ya see 'em?"

"Yeah," then, "so?"

"Look at how they're sitting."

Kekich sat with one leg crossed. Peterson's legs were spread. "Uh-huh," I told my father, not sure of what he meant.

"Can't you feel the tension?"

"I guess." Even though I couldn't.

"Can't blame 'em, can you? What're they gonna say? 'How's your wife been since I screwed her? Don't you love how she sucks . . . ' " His voice trailed off mercifully, never finishing its final words, which I thought I could guess, though I'll never know for sure. All I knew from looking at my dad was I had a junkie on my hands. He fumbled with his nuts—no, not the way the dugout Yankees had. I'm talking about Pop's peanuts, but my father couldn't manipulate the shells. They slipped from his fingers and fell unceremoniously to the concrete floor.

I had never seen him quite this bad or heard him talk that way. I had once imagined Nina using those same words and I thought I would have liked it. Somehow, hearing my father talking dirty didn't touch those same emotions.

"The whole thing's a disgrace. It's a stain on the Yankee legacy. That's what I think! How 'bout you?"

What I thought was that Yankee Stadium was the last place I cared to be. Except for Ryan's heat and Bloomberg's blast, this was the worst birthday on record. Limping up to the mezzanine to sit behind a girder while my junkie dad talked dirty wasn't my idea of fun. I had kind of lost my sense of humor the instant the bullet hit my leg, but now I had a single thought that seemed quite humorous to me.

"Well, Dad, I saw a picture of Mrs. Kekich in the paper."

"And?" my father asked, his head a clumsy prop on a neck that couldn't figure which way it should droop.

"And . . . I think that was quite a trade for Fritz."

Nothing. Not a thing. I thought it was pretty funny.

My father tried to take a pill midway through the sixth, but I politely asked him not to. By inning eight he seemed okay, at which time we had to leave. He had to be at work by four; he could take the C train there. I'd be forced to limp alone through treacherous turf, but I really didn't care.

My father's buzz was gone and without it he was sad. He came clean with a confession as soon as we had spun the turnstile.

"I've been coming to some games."

"Which games?" I said, though by his tone I thought I knew.

"These games, Yankee games. I just thought you should know."

"Okay, fine," I said, although I didn't really mean it. My father grew defensive.

"Hey, everyone else does it, why not me? Why not take free tickets? What's it gonna hurt?"

"What about your overtime? What about saving all that money?"

"I have been saving money. I'm just goin' about it . . . differently. And we'll be in that house out on Long Island, just you wait and see."

"Sure, I'll wait, Dad, and hopefully I'll see."

Some of the sixty thousand were streaming out now too. I smelled hot roasted pretzels and heard vendors making late-game sales. Then I saw my father crying for the first time in a while. There used to be a time, following game five, when he'd done so every day.

"Scooter, I been coming to these games this year tryin' to get back something that I lost."

I let him get it out.

"Since you got shot . . . since I shot you . . . I've had this hole inside my heart. And I just thought . . . if I could see this place . . . sit in these seats . . . I might feel whole again, just for a couple hours. This place was always magical . . . when my father took me here. But that magic . . . I can't get it back . . . I think it's gone for good."

He turned and walked away. I didn't call him back. I was stunned by what I'd heard. Not just about hanging out at games when he was thought to be at work. But mentioning my gunshot wound—it was a thing that wasn't done. It was always called "my accident," as if I'd slipped on a banana peel. As if the thing was my fault. As if I was to blame.

He had also mentioned Grandpa, whose name had been forbidden. And how did he save enough money for a mortgage if he had no overtime?

As I walked up Shakespeare's steep incline, Munson bat in hand, I saw Willie Gomez on his stoop. He had kicked me in the ribs two years before and as a result I'd spat up blood. But I'd caught him with a wild right hand when next we met and now the two of us were cool. He invited me to hang out with a couple guys he knew—maybe show them my cool trick. Usually I read books at night, but this time I agreed.

[5]

My dad's favorite book was *Slaughterhouse-Five*, by Kurt Vonnegut. He'd read it the way some people read Bibles—perusing its pages, looking for meaning in each of its words. In terms of significance in the Second World War, he found the bombing of Dresden unequaled. Some looked to Pearl Harbor or D-day or Iwo Jima. My father saw Dresden. Simply because it showcased mankind at its worst. The bombing accomplished little. Dresden's strategic location wasn't all that vital. It was a matter of killing just to prove that we could. My dad said he knew cops like that. Which is why he had vowed never to draw his weapon. A vow he'd broken just once during his thirteen-year career.

He used to show me photos of Dresden in ruins. It looked like the Bronx—at least the blocks that Gomez and I walked to get to our party. Remains of charred buildings. Bodies strewn on the street. Sleeping in doorways and puking in alleys. Smoke filled the air. Another landlord paid off; another piece of the Bronx relegated to history.

We were joined by Gomez's brother and his two friends. Willie carried a small canvas bag. He had two years on me, even though we shared the same grade. His academic career had been briefly derailed by a short stay at Goshen for a beating he'd given to a candy store owner who wouldn't sell him a beer. He'd been eleven years old and was using a Gene Michael bat that a friend gave him from bat day. Gomez had said the beating he gave was the most solid contact that a Gene Michael bat had ever been part of.

Willie's brother and friends were all seventeen. They bought beer with no ID and no problem. The candy stores that hadn't yet barred up their windows and moved the hell out were willing to sell to any person with money and a prospective hair on their sack. They didn't ask questions.

Willie's brother was Rico, who was a member in proud standing of the vaunted Diablos. Rico gave me a can. I'd never had beer, except for a bitter Ballantine swig that my dad offered me once. One swig was enough to point out to me that beer was no good. Yet here I was on the street with one in my hand. Walking tall toward the projects among the junkies, the pimps, the hookers and the winos.

I took a long sip of my beer in its paper bag wrap. Damn, it was bad. But hey, it was almost my birthday and I needed some fun. It had been a tough day. My dad had lost that old magic. Munson went down on strikes to that flamethrower from Texas. And Fritz and Mike were feeling the tension. I needed this beer. I pounded it down. My very first beer. I lifted the can out of its paper bag home. My goodness, a Schaefer—the one beer to have when you're having more than one.

"Hey, Willie," I said.

"Yo," Willie responded.

"Can I get one more?"

"You gonna show us that trick at the party?"

"If you get me a beer."

"Hey, Rico," he said to his brother, who was the man with the cans. "Another beer for the Scooter."

I had killed a second beer by the time we arrived at the projects. All of a sudden my small house on Shakespeare looked like the governor's mansion. The place was horrendous. Jack Lord could have had Danno book five guys in the front lobby alone. Kojak could have had a field day in there. Barnaby Jones could have—no, I think these guys would have handed Buddy Ebsen his ass.

The place stank of urine. I guess these Bronx high-rise dwellers would rather piss in the hall than walk up the stairs. I saw a needle injected, its lucky victim's eyes rolling when the dope found its mark.

Our middle school junkies got high under toilet stall cover, but these guys had no shame. They just sat out in the hallway, their backs to the wall, chasing their dragons, savoring their vomit like a wine taster's bouquet.

We climbed the stairs to floor seven, hearing the alternate worlds of small babies crying, old couples fighting and young lovers screwing with each passing floor.

I arrived at floor seven a couple minutes after the rest of my crew. I guess the guys just couldn't wait for the little white limper. As a result I was lost, following the pulse of the music like Hansel and Gretel and their trail of bread crumbs.

I heard the sounds of Tito Puente, a far cry from my mom's trendy music and my dad's Nat King Cole. I walked into the doorway and stepped into the light. A red flashing strobe that made seeing things tough. My eyes tried to adjust, but damn, it was difficult with the glare of the light and the beer in my brain. At last I saw something. A chest with some hair. Right in line with my eyes. He wore a cut-off denim vest. Same colors as Manny Vasquez and Willie Gomez— Diablos. Man, he was big. His voice when he spoke seemed awful big too.

It said, "Get outta here, white boy."

I said, "Okay."

It said, "Get your ass movin'."

I said, "Okay."

It said, "Now."

I said, "Okay."

I think the next step would have been physical and it would have caused pain had Gomez's brother not come to save the day.

"Wait. Wait, Ese, don't you know who that is?"

The big voice said, "Fuck should I know?"

"This here is Scooter," Gomez's brother told him.

"Your name's fuckin' Scooter?" the big voice inquired.

I nodded my head.

The big voice said, "Well, that changes everything. Turn down the music." When the music was down he addressed the crowd, which numbered right around twenty and whose ethnic background didn't look to be Irish.

"Ladies and gentlemen, damas and caballeros." The big voice paused, waiting for just the right moment. "Fuckin' Scooter is here!"

A few people laughed. Most could not have cared less. The music returned. Roberta Flack was on now, singing about the first time ever she saw my face. Willie gave me a beer. It wasn't a Schaefer, but I liked how it tasted. I saw an attractive young lady dancing slowly to the music. I kind of liked it here now. The beer, the music, the people—who needed Long Island? I was feeling good in the projects.

A new Diablo approached, said, "Scooter, my man," gave me a beer, then walked away. Just a well-meaning gang member doing good deeds anonymously before moving on.

I waved to the stranger as he strode away and that's when I saw her. Nina. Alone in a doorway, a beer in her hand. Her makeup was heavy, too heavy, it seemed. But that was the look of the times or at least of the place. Still, she was beautiful and I felt my heart pound when I saw her smile—shy, almost apologetic. I wondered if she was always alone—if the threat of brotherly vengeance kept boys at bay all the time.

It wouldn't keep me away, I decided. I was too drunk to care about things like staying alive. "Hi, Scooter," she said as I approached in full stumble. A few couples were dancing slowly to the music and I wanted to join them, to hold Nina in my arms and recite every heartfelt lyric of the song about the face.

Nina leaned forward, touching me softly on the shoulder as she prepared to whisper in my ear. Maybe she was going to ask me to dance. "Scooter, get the hell outta here." Not quite what I was hoping for, even if her breath did feel nice as she was making clear the fact that she didn't want me anywhere near her.

"What?" I said, hoping that I'd simply misheard her.

"I said get the hell outta here."

No, no mistake about it, she wanted me gone.

Nina smiled sadly. "Scooter, you trust me?"

"I guess so," I said.

"Then leave."

"But I'm having fun," I said. "Besides, it's my birthday."

"Then here's a gift for you, Scooter. Get the hell out! Go home." She was no longer whispering, but her tone wasn't angry. There was an urgency to it, like she really truly wanted me gone.

"Why?" I was getting defensive.

"Because I know why you're here, Scooter. You're tonight's entertainment. They're gonna make a fool out of you—and I don't want it to happen. So just . . . go home."

I pondered her request, odd as it seemed, but was cut off by the big voice in the Diablos' vest.

"Ladies and gentlemen," it called. "Damas and caballeros. How many you know my man Scooter?"

The crowd cheered a little. I guessed they were ready for my unique brand of entertainment.

"Scooter, don't," Nina said.

"I gotta go," I told her and walked to the room's center so the big guy could place a tattooed arm around me.

"It's come to my 'tention that it's fuckin' Scooter's birthday."

"Happy Birthday, fuckin' Scooter!" someone yelled. Hey, it was Manny Vasquez with his floppy brown suede hat and a big smile, wishing me well. Not such a bad guy after all. I waved to the former minor league star.

"It's also come to my 'tention that fuckin' Scooter here never been drunk."

More clapping. Hey, I just realized, I shared McCovey's '69 nickname.

The big Diablo guy had a way with these people. They were starting to care about me. One such caring soul replaced my old beer with a new frosty one. Some kind of longneck.

"Let's give Scooter some 'couragement as he drinks down that beer."

Manny started to chant. "Scoo-ter, Scoo-ter, Scoo-ter—" The whole room joined in. All except Nina. Just jealous, I guessed. Jealous that little Scooter up the block was somebody special. I didn't need her support. I had a whole room of it. Another beer found my hand.

The big voice started up once again. He was like one of those old Negro preachers spreading the word. But the big voice wasn't selling salvation, he was selling my virtues and I basked in the glory of his words.

"An' it has also come to my 'tention that my man fuckin' Scooter has got a great talent that he would like us to see."

Oh, man, this was great. I was going to be a star. I took off my right sneaker, my red faded Chuck Taylor. Then took off my sock. Willie handed Big Voice a foot-long two-by-four, and I seized my cue and the moment and lifted my foot so it could rest on the block. Willie handed Big Voice a six-inch nail—nice, strong, thick and silver. Let the street junkies have little needles; I'd take a real spike.

I said, "Make sure it's clean." Big Voice dipped the big nail into a tall glass of vodka. At least I thought it was vodka, it could have been Tom Seaver's piss for all I knew. Man, I was beaming. Nothing like being accepted as one of the guys. Big Voice took the hammer from Willie.

My finger was shaking, but I think I got it to stop just long enough to point to the spot. There was a little scar there to show him the way. Hell, this wasn't my first barbecue. I was a veteran at this. I knew how to make friends.

The cheer started low. But, oh, did it grow. Man, it got loud.

"Scoo-ter, Scoo-ter, Scoo-ter!"

I wished my father was here. He would have had a tear in his eye just like on Mickey's big day.

"Scoo-ter, Scoo-ter, Scoo-ter!"

It felt great to fit in. I scanned the roomful of faces. Happy, ecstatic, busting with joy. Manny was beaming. Then I saw Nina. Shaking her head. As if to say no. What the hell for? Hey, she had lots of attention. She was Manny Vasquez's sister. Word was out. You didn't mess around with Nina. She already had status. Why be such a bitch just because I was gaining my own? I didn't need Nina. I had this whole room.

I saw the hammer go up. Way up. Maybe Big Voice thought he could win his girlfriend a stuffed bear at Playland up the highway in Rye. I thought just for a moment of Joe D. at Freedomland signing the ball.

The hammer came down. I didn't feel a damn thing. But I knew by the cheer that the trick was successful.

"Scoo-ter, Scoo-ter, Scoo-ter!"

Man, life was good. Then I saw Nina shaking her head, a stupid tear on her face, trying her best to rain on my parade. She tried to smile but failed. God, she was useless. She backed into the darkness and was once more out of my life.

I woke up around seven in a spare lot on Nelson Avenue next to an old rusted-out Buick, four blocks from my house. I walked home, my head pounding, the two-by-four slapping the asphalt with each step I took.

[6]

I could see traffic crawl on the Cross Bronx Expressway. My grandfather's window offered a perfect view of this Robert Moses masterpiece. The road that enabled motorists to pass through the Bronx without spending a dime in it, leaving nothing behind but the exhaust from their cars.

The old man seemed so old now. A term of endearment had become all too real. His scars had aged too. They'd taken on color, contrasting now with the pale hue of his face. They made me uneasy for the first time in years. I should have been empathetic; after all, I had scars of my own. Most of them were just mental, but they were painful when stretched, just like my grandfather's were.

He seemed like a relic from the past I had known. A symbol of life before game five was played, when life was still fun. Maybe my visits, more sporadic with time, were like my father's trips to the game. Looking for magic and finding it gone. Words used to seem natural when I'd come to this place, and silence did too. But now, as I watched him attempting to scramble eggs without burners, I didn't feel much like talking or staying at all.

"Grandpa, I need to go home," I said, lying to him for the very first time.

Averting his gaze from his futile egg effort, he looked over at me, using his one eye to study me closely.

"Is that so?" he said.

"Uh-huh."

"Or is it something else?"

"No, uh, no, Grandpa, I just have to get going."

"Have to . . . or want to?" he said, that eye glaring intently, as if boring a hole right through my conscience and into my soul. I swallowed hard, opting not to talk, letting him continue this odd inquisition.

"Or are you thinking you might be just a bit old to visit an old fool like me." His brogue was soft and gentle, but nonetheless, the effect of his words weakened my knees and put a lump in my throat.

"No, I uh, just, uh . . ."

"Perhaps you were thinking that these eggs might cook quicker if I turned on the stove?" With a flick of his wrist, he turned on the burner. I struggled to speak.

"Grandpa, what are you, some kind of mind reader?"

He smiled warmly, his intensity gone, his gaze once again focused on scrambling his eggs.

"Just a second there, Scooter, I'll have these eggs done in a jif."

Hadn't he heard me? "Grandpa, I asked if—"

He chuckled softly, using the laugh to let me know I'd been heard. "Don't worry, Scooter, your grandpa doesn't read minds."

"Oh, good, for a second you scared me. I thought—"

"I read faces, Scooter."

That second was back. I was scared once again. Slowly I asked, "What does that mean . . . reading faces?"

"Oh, don't let it bother you. Everyone does it. Looking at faces, studying expressions for signs of deceit. I just do it better than others."

"What, like you have some kind of special gift?" I asked.

"I'm not sure if it's a gift. Sometimes seems more a curse than a blessing. I only know that after my little . . . accident, I could see things more clearly with one eye than I ever had with two."

He dished up the eggs, which were a bit undercooked, but I tore into them anyway. Home-cooked meals had become a rare commodity, so I didn't complain. I looked at the old man stirring his tea contentedly. He sure loved his tea—as well as his Scooter. So why was there a coffee machine, brand spanking new, on a new shelf on the wall, as if the thing was some hunter's prize seven-point buck? I had to know why.

"Grandpa?"

"It's a new Mr. Coffee."

"What?"

"You're wondering why I have a coffee machine even though I never drink coffee. Right?"

"Uh-huh." Man, this was weird.

That's when it hit me. Mr. Coffee. Joe D. He was their pitchman. It made perfect sense. Grandpa told me one time that Joe D. had a half cup of joe and a Camel unfiltered after every inning. Maybe Joe D. liked coffee so much that the stuff was named for him.

"Can I tell you a secret?" my grandfather said with a slightly mischievous tone.

"Sure," I said, wondering what the old man had up his sleeve. Maybe he was planning to drag out a toilet that Joe D. had pooped on.

"That Mr. Coffee?"

"Yeah?"

"Was a gift from your dad."

I didn't know what to say. The two hadn't had any connection since that day long ago.

His grin seemed a mile wide. "Isn't it grand?"

"Yes, it is, Grandpa, it really is nice."

The old man sat down and speared a bite from his plate. What a strange thing—a coffee machine bringing such joy.

"It came on my birthday, along with a note. It said maybe he'd call me or try to stop by. Scooter, I tell you, I wait every day."

I thought back to bat day and my father mentioning Grandpa for the first time in years. Maybe the stadium had magic left in it after all.

"That's really cool, Grandpa, that you love Joe D. so much that you put it up there."

My grandfather smiled. His one eye was now twinkling. If not for the scars, he'd have looked downright handsome. Hell, I thought he was handsome regardless. He then shook his head and looked into my eyes so I knew a great lesson was coming.

He said, "You've got it all wrong."

"I do?"

"Yes, Scooter, you do. You see, I didn't put that sorry contraption up on that shelf because of my love for Joe D."

"You didn't?" I was a small child once again. No bullet in my leg, no nail in my foot.

"No, I put that sorry contraption up on that shelf because of my love for your dad."

I thought I might cry. If I wasn't thirteen and trying awfully hard not to, I think I would have.

The old man leaned forward and whispered, "Can you keep one more secret?"

I nodded I could.

"Oh, but this is a big one."

"Uh-huh, I can keep it."

"Okay, here goes."

I waited and wondered, what could it be? Was the old man gay? Is that why there'd been no Mrs. O'Brien?

"Scooter, this is a little bit tough—"

I knew it wasn't a sickness, but still—it was gross.

"I never . . . liked Joe D. too much."

"What!" If I'd had a drink in my mouth I'd have surely spat it all over. "But how could that be? Joe D.'s everywhere. He's all over the house! I thought you loved him!"

Who was gay now? I was mourning the loss of Joe D. in my life.

"I just loved the game, Scooter, I just loved the game. I didn't have any one favorite, I just loved the game."

"But what about all those pictures?" I asked, waving both my arms wildly. "Or the ball on the television, the one that we got you when you were hurt?"

"Oh, I love all those things—the ball most of all, because it came from you both. But what I loved was the thought, not the guy in the pictures. Well, it could have been worse. They could all be of Yogi."

I laughed at the name and started to tell a little story about Torre, but wisely reconsidered.

"Listen, Scooter," he said, "your father and I were both huge baseball fans. I just loved the game and I'd go anywhere to see it played well. Yankee Stadium, Polo Grounds, even Ebbets Field. Why, if I'd have had the means I'd have gone to Shea as well. But my brother-in-law, your father's real dad, loved Joe. The Yankees and Joe. That was it. He thought anything else was a complete lack of loyalty.

"Your dad was just a wee little guy when his father was killed. He didn't know much, but he sure knew Joe D. I thought he'd had things too tough already, losing his dad and then his mom too. He barely would talk those first couple years, barely would eat, hardly slept a wink either. Then opening day, 1947, I'm watching the game and Joe comes to bat and your dad starts going crazy—you know, in a good type of way. So I just . . . played along. And from that moment on, in the little guy's mind, Joe D. was my hero. I just let it be."

"Were you ever in love?"

The question caught him off guard. I think he'd drained all his emotion and energy during our talk about Joe D. He struggled to speak. He tried once, then twice, like Nina had weeks earlier, attempting to smile. He finally cleared his throat, then spoke with great effort.

"Why, yes. Yes, Scooter, I guess I was."

"Can you tell me about it?" I made extra careful not to assume that the love was a her. I tried to keep my mind open.

"There's not much to tell. It was quite a long time ago. Sixty-two years. I don't remember that much."

"Well, then, could you maybe tell me why you and my father don't speak?"

"I'm afraid that I can't."

"Why not?" I asked, a little bit upset that the secrets that mattered were not mine to know. I truly was thankful for the truth about Joe. The Mr. Coffee thing touched me. But I shouldn't have been made to sneak across town through horrible neighborhoods just to be touched now and then. It should have been a simple walk across my little bedroom. I should have fallen asleep to the ramblings of Rizzuto. I should have known all about the pretty girl in the picture.

"Scooter," he said, his voice breaking up, his one eye rimmed with tears. "I'm a very old man. I'm not feeling well. The story behind my falling-out with your dad is his story to tell. Not mine. I don't have that right. And my story of love is not one I feel up to sharing just yet."

A tear fell from the eye. He wiped it away before it could gain any momentum, as if destroying the tear could deny its existence. Struggling, he said, "I'll tell you just this. When you find that one love, you hold on to it tight. Don't let it go. Help it, protect it, keep it from harm—but Scooter, I warn you, you might get only one chance. Don't let it go."

[7]

I jumped on the four train to 167th, then limped up to Shakespeare as fast as I could. Faster, in fact, than I'd thought I could move. My mother once claimed that my injury was just mental. That I could walk fine if I could just clear my mind. For a few hundred yards I thought she might have been right. I swear I was sprinting as I approached Nina's apartment. Like my grandfather said, I might get only one chance. I could not let it go.

I practically ran up the stairs. My heart thumped in my chest, my lungs screamed for air and my good leg was on fire, but I just about ran. The hallway was dark, but I could see paint peeling badly. A small plastic wrapper with white residue hid in the shadows. Tools of the trade for a scumbag like Manny. I knocked on the door, waited a moment, then pounded much harder.

The door slowly opened. I saw the face of a stranger and brown cardboard boxes throughout the small room. I smelled frying chicken and heard the telltale sounds of slow-motion bionics, which could mean only one thing—Steve Austin in action. Six million taxpayer dollars hard at work. I wished that someone could rebuild me, make me stronger, faster.

The stranger said, "What you want?"

I said, "Can I talk to Nina?"

The stranger turned, said something in Spanish, heard Spanish words back and said, "Okay, come in."

I'd picked up some Spanish during my last few years as a High-bridge minority and I thought I detected a few words I knew. Like "white boy," "nail," and "foot."

I got a better look at the room and I saw it was bare. Like my room had looked after Grandpa was gone. A few hooks and nail holes, that was just about it. That Grinch guy left more when he raided Who houses. Three girls were loading odds and ends into crates. Not quite the scene I'd imagined when I played it out in my head as I journeyed from Grandpa's. I thought I'd catch Nina alone and she'd fall into my arms, though I had not much more than a sandwich and a boner from four years earlier on which to base my whole image.

Nina emerged from the hall. God, I loved when she smiled. A beautiful smile that could brighten the darkest of days. Too bad for me she wasn't wearing one now. I tried to stay strong nonetheless. This was my chance; I would not let it go.

"Nina."

"Scooter, go home!"

Not quite what I'd planned. The words seemed pretty direct, not much room for maneuvering. Still, I thought that I'd try.

"Nina, I was hoping that—"

"I said 'Scooter, go home!' " This was not going well.

"But I thought that—"

I guess I must have looked awfully pathetic, for her demeanor softened a bit. Not a lot, just a little, just enough so my leaving was no longer demanded.

"Scooter, come here." She motioned me to the hallway, then into her room. I got no sense whatsoever that this request was romantic, so thankfully I didn't treat it as such. I think if I'd dared make a move she'd have slugged me and besides, up to that point in my life, the only sexual moves I had made were performed on myself.

Her room was in boxes, except for a poster of Roberto Clemente, which still hung in a frame. So aside from Clemente I couldn't get much of a feel for her likes and dislikes. Though I thought at the moment I was one of the latter.

"Scooter, look out that window."

I did.

She said, "What do you see?"

I saw lots of things. Too many to list. I said, "Um, I'm not sure."

"Wanna know what I see?"

I nodded my head.

"I see your house, Scooter, that's what I see."

I didn't know what she meant.

"I see your father take off. I see your mother and your sister leave every Monday. I see them come back with a car fulla crap. Then sometimes at night I look for your father as he walks up the street. Slowly, head hanging. I see all those things and I know exactly what happened."

"What do you know?" I asked, aiming for defiance but falling way short, sounding frightened instead.

She yelled, "Don't lie to me, Scooter, I know what went on!"

I put my head down.

"I'm watching the game—I hear a gunshot. I knew, I just knew it had come from your house. I yell out your name. Manny turns up the volume. I go to my room and I look out my window and I can't see very much, but I see lots of people movin' around. Looks like panic to me. So I call up the cops."

My head was still down. My eyes were both closed. But as she was speaking, I could see it so clearly. I had run this thing through my mind so many damn times, but never this clearly. Never before had the blast seemed quite so loud. Never before had I felt the shot enter or seen the perfect round hole before it began squirting blood.

"A few minutes later, I see the cop car pull up. Cops jump out, real fast, hands on their guns. Ready for trouble. Your mother walks out and I swear to you, Scooter, soon's they see it's a white lady they slow their asses down. I open the window, try to hear what they're sayin' but can't make it out. All I know is they talked for less than a minute, then they were gone. No way they take the word of some Puerto Rican over your mother."

I turned my back to her then, not wanting to hear the same truth I'd faced a long time ago. She put her hands on my shoulders and I wanted so badly to lean my head back, to somehow convey that the slightest touch of her hands could make my whole body warm. Instead, I hung my head forward, not wanting to risk any further rejection. Had I really come over to proclaim my affection just to have my world shaken and turned upside down?

She leaned close to me so I could just barely feel her breath in my ear as she continued to speak. It was a paradox of sensations. So close yet so far. The proximity begged for dirty thoughts, but instead she came clean.

"Every day, Scooter, I walked to your house. Every day for three weeks. Every day I was told you didn't want me around. One time you looked through your window—you remember that day?"

I nodded my head. Tears formed in my eyes. My body shook softly. I wished that those hands on my shoulders would wrap tightly around me, but instead they dug into my shoulders, years of trapped anger, finally set free.

"I thought you might look for me, might wave one more time. But you know what I got?"

I knew.

"Nothing. And you know who else came to see you, to check on you, to see how you were?"

I knew that answer too.

"Nobody! Now, after four years, you invite yourself over on the day that I move?" Now she was yelling, clamping down on my shoulders, displaying a strength I hadn't known she had. "Why? To say 'good luck'? To say 'see you later'? 'See you around'? 'Hasta la vista'? Or you wanna show me your little trick with a nail? The one where you lookin' at me like I'm some piece of garbage?"

"I didn't know you were moving!" I just yelled it out, bringing the words up like a shield to deflect further pain.

Nina's hands, so harsh moments earlier, turned gentle again and turned me around ever so slowly. In all of that anger, I'd failed to take notice of her body pressed tightly to mine. I wish I could have frozen that moment, saved time in a bottle, as the Jim Croce song said.

"You didn't know I was movin'?"

I shook my head slowly. My chin was still down, my throat was in knots and the tears in my eyes hadn't yet started to dry.

"Then why are you here?" She put her hand to my chin and lifted it slowly, making me look where I hadn't dared.

"Why are you here?" she asked again softly, looking straight into my eyes and, I thought for a moment, straight down to my soul.

I bit my lip like my father and shook my head slowly. When my head finally stopped shaking I said, "I really don't know."

Which was a great big lie. I knew why I'd come. I'd come to tell her I loved her. To hold on to her. To never let go. Maybe it's better that I didn't let those words fly. I didn't really know love. I'd never been given the chance to let love really grow. Never allowed myself that one special freedom. But I knew that for a few shining moments Nina had made me feel special. In that brief slice of time when Nolan Ryan threw heat and her body threw warmth, when sharing a sandwich became an intimate act, Nina Vasquez set a standard for enduring emotion that no one else had come close to.

I was only nine at that time. Too young to feel the hot need of desire, the longing of lust or the primal urges of sex. But I swear, in that moment I felt Nina's warmth, her kindness, her strength and her heart, and it gave and still gives me a feeling of greater consummation than all of the backseat high school high jinks and *Joy of Sex* suggestions rolled into one.

She was moving to Rockland County to a house that her mom had saved up for without help from big brother Manny, who was opting to stay in Highbridge to look after his business. Because business was booming.

I thought I might never see her again, until she let a tiny ray of hope shine on me. She had a new job, one that would bring her back to the Bronx a few nights a week. She worked as an usher down at the stadium. Maybe she'd see me.

The last thing she said before I walked down those stairs, almost walking on air, was "Don't put no nails in your foot, Scooter. Don't be anyone's fool. You're better than that."

Then she gave me a hug. A hug that almost replaced my thoughts of game three as my all-time favorite memory. The way her thick hair, as black as the night, brushed at my face. The way her body, warm and soft, pressed into my chest. And the scent of her skin, combined with a perfume that I never could guess, stayed on my sweatshirt for the next several months. Perhaps because I no longer wore it outside, or inside for that matter. Or washed the thing, ever. I just took it out and breathed in its scent when I wanted to feel close.

I saw Manny the dealer and a couple of friends as I came down the stairs, all wearing their colors. "Hey, Scooter," he said, "how 'bout I show your pig father how I curve my fist into his mouth?" The friends both laughed, far too loud for such a stupid comment.

"Okay, I'll pass that one by him," I said. Then I left.

I was almost to my house when I heard Manny's voice. Yelling. "Leave my fuckin' sister alone."

[8]

I helped soothe my sister when she started to scream. Sure, she had seen her doll's head turn around and puke up pea soup. I was just lying back down when I heard my father come in. I couldn't recall the last time he'd bothered to check up on me. But that's just what he did, pushing the door open and saying my name.

"Scooter? Scooter?"

"Yeah?"

"Can we talk?"

"I guess so," I said. My father was beaming. A narcotic buzz, or could it be something else? I think the odds were it was a combination of both.

"Listen, I've been doing some thinkin'."

"Yeah?"

"Yeah. And I know that back in June your day at the stadium didn't turn out so great."

"It wasn't so bad." Sure, it was a lie, but only one of the little white kind. Besides, my dad didn't read faces.

"Did you know that after this season they're tearin' the stadium down? Gonna try to rebuild it."

"Uh-huh." I'd heard Rizzuto mention that fact, in between tangents and wishing happy birthdays to strangers.

"Well, it got me to thinkin' that maybe you and I could be part of history by goin' to the last game of the season."

"You want to go to the stadium?" I asked, my voice one long high-pitched rush of air.

"If you want to come."

"Yeah, I'd love to." Boy, would I.

"Alright, then, let's do it. Tomorrow morning I'll go down to the stadium and pick up three box seats—the best they have, no more mezzanine."

"Can I come with you?"

"Sure," my dad said. "Wow, you're excited about this."

"I just love being a small part of history." I paused for a moment. Something didn't add up. "Dad?"

"Yeah, son?"

"Why the third ticket? Is Vinnie planning on coming?"

"No. Actually, Scooter, I was thinking my father might want to go."

[9]

The stadium had a date set with the wrecking ball as soon as the Bombers were finished with their season. For a while that looked to be the last week of October, as the team turned it on in June, to sit atop the AL East, heading into summer.

But alas, it wouldn't last. An early August melee with the Red Sox seemed to be the turning point of sorts. It turned winners into losers and by September the Yankees were done.

Meanwhile, out in Queens, the Miracle Mets, version '73, were making a bid to become the worst team to ever get into the Series. Coming from eleven back in August to move into first in late September with a mere .500 record, the Mets had once again energized the city. "You Gotta Believe" became their slogan, which I found kind of tiring, but I got a little laugh each day when I saw their manager, Yogi Berra, in the paper.

The renovation of the stadium would take a full two years to finish. During that interim period, the Bombers would be playing their home games out at Shea. My father had forewarned me that this would be our last ball game for a while. There would be no Shea trips for him.

The Yanks were set to play Detroit on the last day of September—the last day of their season, by virtue of their falling apart down the stretch. My father had indeed picked up three box seats for the contest, but Grandpa would not be coming. My father was too proud to take a walk and my grandfather was too poor to buy a phone, so as a result I became the intermediary, making the arrangements for this overdue reunion. Somewhere in this process my mother found us out and the resulting fight was nasty.

She unloaded all the classics. Questioning his manhood, heralding her sacrifice, laughing at the old man's scars. When it came to verbal battles, my mom was like McCovey—swinging from the heels. Not caring if her charges missed the mark sometimes, just as long as the ones that didn't miss landed hard. My father didn't even bother swinging. He never took the bat off his shoulder.

So we had an extra ticket. The Dago turned us down—something happening at his church. That seemed to be his hangout now. We thought about my sister, but my mother said, "No way." It was bad enough to have the men both risk their lives, let alone her little girl. Besides, she'd need to save her strength for Monday; shopping could be tiring. Mom had been planning out our new home in Manhasset and she needed window treatments. Also, *Serpico* was playing and my mother loved Pacino. She said my father would look good with longer hair once he made detective.

My dad and I made small talk as we walked down Shakespeare Avenue and turned onto Jerome. My mind was kind of wandering—the way minds do when they're in love—wondering if I'd see her, wondering how she was.

My dad was talking about Hank Aaron—how he would break

the record of the Babe. He swore that Willie Mays would have beaten it if that damn stickball hadn't screwed him up. The Say Hey Kid called it quits one week earlier at Shea with a measly 660 to his name.

I thought about the metaphorical teenage game of baseball that awards bases for making moves on girls. A kiss was like a single. A breast fondled was two bases. A triple meant you'd gone a little farther and a home run was—self-explanatory. I didn't like the game. It made kisses seem so wimpy, like a ball slapped up the middle. Kisses weren't wimpy, at least not the ones I dreamed of. They were far from wimpy singles. They were McCovey blasts at Shea. Shooting stars across a moonlit sky, that's what kisses were.

The blow struck me in the temple as we were crossing through an underpass that led to Macombs Dam Park. By the time I gained my bearings, there was a blade pressed to my father's throat.

A black man held the knife. Wild Afro, jaundiced eyes, a large scar across his cheek. His filthy clothes contrasted with brand-new white PRO-Keds. From his stance behind my dad, he could have slit his throat at any time. It was up to me to save the day. Up to me to do something, anything, to help my father out. But no help would be forthcoming.

To this very day I can't explain why, just when I was needed most, my courage took a hike. I sometimes use a groggy mind to justify my failure to react. But after all this time I still find all excuses to be useless. I had limped to Yankee Stadium and failed to bring along some guts.

I was thinking about charging in and swinging from my heels when the black man with the knife made a move for my father's wallet. I saw my dad resist, a move of sheer stupidity that could have meant his life.

" 'Less you wanna die, give me the goddamn money," the black man hissed, half tough, half scared to death.

My father wasn't scared. Not the slightest bit. "You can have the money, not the wallet."

"Gimme the goddamn wallet." I saw the blade make the slightest indentation in my father's naked neck. I closed my fist and thought to pounce, but my body wouldn't move. Three men stood inside that overpass—two were scared to death. The one who wasn't had a blade pressed to his throat.

"You're not getting my tickets," the fearless one said.

"Tickets? What tickets?"

"The Yankees game," my dad said calmly, with just a bit of disbelief, as if every self-respecting knife-wielding junkie should know the Yanks' last game was going down.

"Yankees? Motherfuckin' Yankees?" His voice was high and incredulous. His knife hand dropped slightly toward his side. I prepared to make my move—but didn't. Why, I'll never know. "Keep the fuckin' tickets, just gimme the goddamn cash."

Which is exactly what my father did. He reached into his wallet, his badge clearly on display, and handed our somewhat cooperative attacker all his cash. Seven lousy dollars. He'd risked his life for Yankees tickets and seven lousy dollars.

I don't imagine I'll forget the man's parting words as his PRO-Keds slapped the gravel, looking to get as far away from the crazy white man and his cowardly son as quickly as was possible. "Motherfuckin' Yankees!"

"Scooter, you okay?" my father asked, checking his throat for signs of blood and finding none.

"Yeah, sure, Dad, I'm okay." Besides being a gutless coward, that is. "How 'bout you?"

"Sure, sure. It's just a shame a kid like that's gotta steal to buy some groceries."

I may have been just thirteen, and though I'd grown up way too fast those past few years, I couldn't claim to know it all. But I knew that bastard was no kid and what he wanted wasn't food.

My father's face lit up as we began our trek across the park. "Damn," my father said.

"What is it, Dad?"

"Well, I've got an extra ticket. I should have offered it to him."

"You're kidding, right?" But I knew he wasn't. And odd as it might seem, I could picture my dad sitting right next to our filthy junkie mugger inside Ruth's house, pointing out the error of his criminal ways, as well as the fine points of the game.

We walked through center field, mere feet from where my dad had once relieved himself before throwing knuckleballs to Schwartz.

I watched two teams of Little Leaguers do their thing. Nine years old, I guessed. I thought about Big Will and where his family might be. Then I heard the distinctive sound of ball meeting aluminum, and turned to see its source. The ball rolled far past the outfielder, whose cutoff throw was futile. For before the ball could reach the infield, the batter was at home. Jumping into waiting arms, living out a childhood dream. No father diving for home plate to chop those dreams in half. One team was all Hispanic, the other, all but one. Each one the next Clemente, who'd been a hero to the end.

So my dad had tagged me out. He'd been a little drunk that day. Those days were gone; he hadn't had a drop since '69, not even at the games. So he took his little pills, who could begrudge him that? Sometimes when things were going bad I'd felt the gnawing of temptation. An urge to disappear into a safe cocoon, to leave the real world for a while. Sometimes I thought the junkies had it made, aside from puking up their guts and harassing motorists with squeegees. Sometimes I thought their one-track lives looked pretty good.

My father popped a pill. I think he deserved it. As we were heading for the turnstile, I saw him look away. Looking at a businessman who seemed on the verge of tears. The guy was riffling through his pockets, though his search seemed in vain.

"Watch this," my father said to me. "Watch me make this guy's day."

My dad approached the business guy, who seemed a bit disheveled. The guy was still looking through his pockets, as if the hundredth time might be the charm.

"Excuse me, sir," my father said.

"Huh?" was the disheveled guy's reply.

"I can't help but notice that you seem upset. Is there something I can help you with?"

"No, not unless you've got an extra ticket."

My father's face lit up. "As a matter of fact, I do." He loved this kind of thing. If it wasn't for my mother spending all his money, I could see my father as a philanthropist giving hard-earned money to the needy.

"How much?" asked the disheveled guy. "I've only got a couple bucks."

"I'd say just a buck will do."

The disheveled guy got out the buck and forked it over quickly. "Thank you, sir," was all he said. But for my dad no thanks were needed. The joy of helping sloppy businessmen was thanks enough for him.

My dad put his arm around me. I could see the pills had done their stuff. He smiled conspiratorially, as if he had the scoop on Watergate. He waved that dollar bill as if he'd just won the lottery.

"Half is for the program. You'll want to keep score for sure today."

"And—" He had left me hanging for a reason. He had big plans for those last two quarters.

"And—the other half's for peanuts. Wait till Pop sees us!"

"But we're sitting in the boxes. Pop's way upstairs in right."

"You don't think Pop is worth the walk?"

To tell the truth I didn't, but I didn't want to poop on Pop's parade.

We should have never walked up there. Security was extra tight due to the historical value of the game. At first they wouldn't let us up. I guess they must have had a flood of four-dollar box seat holders sneaking up to the dollar-fifty seats. Finally they relented when my father flashed his badge. I was looking everywhere for Nina, my dad was looking everywhere for Pop. I was searching for my one true love, the thought of her full lips, brown eyes and raven hair filling my stomach with warm fuzzies. My dad was searching for the peanut guy, whose incoherent mumbles, gray hair and ruddy nose filled his mind with weird nostalgia.

Pop was MIA. Whereabouts unknown. We were missing batting practice. The place was now half full. Not bad for the last game of a lackluster year, but not good for fifty years of memories. My father asked security if they could let him speak to Stuart Irving, the director of concessions. I have no clue how he knew that.

We missed half of the first inning waiting for Stuart to show up. When he did, he seemed a little frightened, having never been interrogated by a cop. He said he didn't know a "Pop."

"Come on," my father said, his patience growing thin. "Of course you must know Pop. He's been here since I was just a kid, twenty years at least. Sells peanuts, upper mezzanine, speaks so softly you can't hear him."

"Oh, you must mean Spencer," Stuart said, relieved that this questioning was over. "Spencer's gone. He moved to Queens. I believe he sells peanuts at the Met games."

The director of concessions must have sensed my dad's sorrow at the crosstown defection of the peanut guy.

"I'm sorry about Spencer. I didn't know just how beloved he was. But if you'll only try another vendor, I'm sure you'll find the peanuts taste the same."

What the hell did Stuart know? We bought some peanuts anyway and made our way down to our seats. First-base side, about ten rows back—my father had done well. The businessman had a beer in his hand and was cheering the team on. It was the second inning now. We opened up our peanuts. Dad said they tasted bad. I couldn't tell the difference, but I pretended that I could.

The businessman took out a dog and ingested half with just one bite. If my dad had driven a little harder bargain, I could have had a hot dog too. The guy hadn't finished chewing when he opened up his mouth.

"Come on, Fritz! Come on, Fritzie!"

Fritz was on the mound. Mike Kekich had been traded. Apparently that life-swap thing had been causing tension after all. Despite the tension, Fritz and Mrs. Kekich had persevered, which meant—she might be here. I'd be on secret Mrs. Kekich lookout every time I looked for Nina.

When the seventh inning rolled around, I was batting zero for 2. No Nina Vasquez sightings. No Mrs. Kekich either. But hell, that was better than Ron Bloomberg, who was zero for 3 so far, or even Thurman Munson, who wasn't even in the lineup on this historic day. Instead, Duke Sims, who wore the Yankee pinstripes for a grand total of nine days, took Munson's place behind the plate and entered baseball's annals as the last man to homer in the storied stadium.

The Bombers had been clinging to a slender 4–2 lead when Detroit's engine started rolling, producing six runs in the eighth. Fritz was not the loser, having given up the ball to a preacher named McDaniel who mailed out flyers to ballplayers called "Pitching for the Master" and probably didn't have too much in common with Fritz Peterson when it came to swapping lives.

My father couldn't concentrate on the runs that crossed the plate. He was watching our disheveled friend, who produced a wrench, a hammer and a screwdriver from within his jacket's inner pocket. He may have forgotten about his ticket, but he certainly remembered to bring his tool kit with him.

"What on earth you doin'?" my father asked as the disheveled guy commenced working, his back turned to the game.

"Bringing me a souvenir," the guy replied. "I told my kids I'd get a seat."

"Like hell you will," my father said.

"Like hell I won't."

My father flashed his badge. "I'll have to place you under arrest."

The disheveled guy laughed out loud. "What ya gonna do about all the other souvenir collectors?"

My father looked up at the stands. The box seats had been calm, but there was lots of action in the nosebleeds. Thousands upon thousands—all digging up the past.

It was like some strange hybrid of vandalism and a scene from an Esther Williams film. The ones where swimmers' moves were synchronized, in an underwater dance. These Yankee fans were dancing too, in a vast ocean of blue seats. Looking for special gifts to load into station wagons bound for White Plains.

My father turned around to watch the game, replacing one debacle with another. He took out his little brown pill bottle, shook it around a time or two, then put it back inside his pocket. He didn't want to kill this pain; he wanted to embrace it. He let the hot-dog-eating business-man have his way with the seat he'd rented for a dollar. I looked down at the peanut bag, still full but empty nonetheless.

A routine fly to center sealed the Yankees' fate. The ninth was gone and so was all respect and decency, as twenty thousand stormed the field at 4:41 p.m.

My father's eyes were free of tears, but I could tell that he was cry-ing. I didn't need evidence to know how he felt inside. He looked out at the sea of bodies like he was looking at the rubble of Dresden. Mankind at its worst, killing fifty years of memories just to prove it could.

White and black, Hispanic too—it really didn't matter. They were all in on the destruction. I hadn't seen such a huge display of racial harmony since that sappy commercial where they all sang in a circle about wanting to buy the world a Coke.

My father leapt to a standing position as if fired from a cannon.

"Oh, my God!" he yelled. "They've got ahold of Ellie!" I looked quickly at the riotous scene and saw just what my father meant. Elston Howard, the Bombers' first-base coach, who back in '55 had been the first Negro to wear the Yankee pinstripes, had first base in his hands and was fending off three souvenir-seeking fans.

Luckily for Ellie, the cavalry was on its way, in the person of my father, who climbed over ten rows of four-buck boxes and gladly joined the fray. He approached the would-be bag thieves and showed off his fighting skills, not by swinging from the heels but by slapping singles up the middle. Quick jabs and combinations that snapped the heads and the will of Elston Howard's tormentors and sent them on their way.

It was like the glory days of *Batman*—all that was missing was my mother yelling, *"BAM! BIFF! POW!"* as Wild West punches found their mark. My dad had beaten back the bad guys and Ellie's base was safe.

My father wasn't finished, though, not when he spotted third. The bag had been pilfered by a Mick with a beer belly who was lumbering through the outfield, heading for his family's outstretched arms so he could take the base home to the suburbs. Come on, Dad, you can do it!

My father bounded for that outfield like it was the plains of the Serengeti. A cheetah on the move looking for white-collared prey. Come on, Dad, you can do it! I was caught up in the struggle of doughy banker with third base and stoned father on a mission when I smelled that perfume I couldn't guess and forgot all about my dad.

"Nina!" Oh, God, she looked so beautiful in her dark blue usher outfit sitting next to me.

"Scooter. This is a surprise. A good one, though. I'm glad that you could make it."

"I've been looking around all day. I thought I'd never find you."

"I'm glad you did," she said, smiling kind of shyly. She wore just a little makeup, not like the project party, just enough. She was perfect.

"I'm glad too," I said, hoping for more prophetic words, but those were not forthcoming.

"Your father with you, Scooter? I see him here sometimes. He don't know me, though."

I pointed to the outfield. "That's him, holding third base in his arm." With his other hand he held his badge aloft, wielding it like a protective shield, trying to part the sea of fans like Moses had. The other Moses. The Bible guy.

"He takes that cop stuff pretty serious, huh?"

"Yeah, but he's only used his weapon once."

Nina placed her hand upon my knee, sending hot flashes through my body and letting me know in her own way that she knew just what I meant.

"You know, Scooter, we used to think one day we'd see Manny on this field."

I nodded in agreement and was glad her hand was on my good leg, so I could feel her thumb caress it and could feel the tingling in its toes.

She said, "Guess sometimes things don't work out like we think."

I tried to speak but couldn't. For the second time in one day my courage took a hike.

"Kinda like you, Scooter."

Nothing, not a peep.

"I used to think we'd get together."

My throat was dry, my hands were sweating. Still, words escaped me.

"Well, since you ain't sayin' nothin', I guess I'd better make a move."

Her full lips were upon me. But mine were stiff, like sticks glued to my mouth. But, man, she was persistent and I finally willed myself to use those *Joy of Sex* suggestions, and to my surprise, it worked. My goodness, I was kissing. It was strange but wonderful. It only lasted seconds, but in that time I thought I knew what heaven was and I found the guts to speak.

"I love you, Nina. I always have." Wow, that came out of nowhere. Actually, it came straight from my heart, but its blinding speed and suddenness took us by surprise.

"That what you wanted to say last month in my room?"

I nodded very slowly and hoped my mouth wouldn't get me in more trouble.

She kissed me one more time. Cradling my lower lip between her teeth and looking straight into my eyes.

My dad was climbing up the steps toward us, holding a Yankee cap aloft like a marine holding up the U.S. flag on the peak of Iwo Jima. I looked at Nina's hand, which was writing numbers on my scorecard. My father was now close, a mere three steps away.

"You call me sometime, Scooter."

My father's face was beaming. Behind him, thousands still roamed the field, leaving havoc in their wake. But his had been a job well done and he deserved the pride he showed. He waved the cap at me. "A gift from Elston Howard. I helped him out a little."

I said, "I know, Dad. You were great."

He was oblivious to Nina, though she was sitting in his seat. There was no other seat beside me; it had left with our disheveled business friend, who'd left behind hot dog wrappers as the only proof he'd ever been our friend at all.

Nina stood up slowly and said " 'Scuse me" to my dad. Then

said her words like poetry, floating like a butterfly into the South Bronx air.

"Hello, my name is Nina. I used to be your neighbor and I just gave Scooter his first kiss."

She smiled and was gone. Heading back to work while the thousands wrecked the house.

I said good-bye to my father as he took the C train west to work, having secured a two-hour reprieve so he could watch history with his son. I watched that graffiti-covered eyesore whisk him off to do his thing. My father and the newly pious Dago, an odd dynamic duo.

I took the number four train north for thirteen blocks so I could spill my guts to Grandpa. To let him know I didn't let him down—I would hold on to my one love. I clutched my rolled-up program like it was a sacred scroll.

[10]

"I want to know about your love."

I had just finished telling the old man about the Yankee game, carefully avoiding the part about his son being robbed while I played the gutless coward in the background. Grandpa was ecstatic, slapping my back, slapping his knee and looking about a decade younger than he had when last we'd met.

That didn't make him ready to confide in me the one memory he most treasured.

"It might be best if you don't know," he said.

"But why? I just told you about mine. Besides, what could it hurt to tell me?"

He pondered my words for several moments, as if entertaining the idea that telling me his story might actually hurt a lot.

"Scooter. You are a thirteen-year-old boy who's been beaten up at school for the color of his skin. Your father put a bullet in your leg that means you'll limp for life."

"So?"

"So, do you forgive him for that bullet?"

"I don't know. I guess so."

"If you have to take a guess, you don't."

"Okay, so sometimes I'm still mad," I said, not sure where this was leading.

"Scooter, look at me and listen, because this is perhaps the greatest question I can ask you."

"Okay."

"Your father—do you think that he forgives himself? Do you think he'd give up everything in life to have back that one moment in time?"

My throat closed off immediately, making swallowing tough and talking even tougher. I gave a quick shrug of my shoulders.

"Do you think he ever will?" Grandpa asked. "Or, do you think that after a lifetime of helping people he'll remember only that he put a bullet in his son and that thought will haunt him till he dies?"

"Like Marichal and that catcher?" I said, thinking back to a past lesson.

"Yes, like Marichal and Roseboro. Scooter?"

"Yes, Grandpa?"

"I'll tell you just this once and then I'll never speak of it again."

I nodded. Grandpa bowed his head and rocked silently for a minute. He then lifted up that tortured head and let his tale spill out.

"I guess I was fifteen when I started working at a garment factory, Triangle Shirt and Waist. Cleaning up some garbage, running errands, things like that. Does that name ring any bells?"

I told him it didn't. He nodded silently. Paused a beat, continued.

"Back then, New York was like a sponge soaking up the different cultures. It had more Irish than did Dublin, more Italians than did Rome. It was the largest Jewish city in the world. All these groups had it tough, but I think the Jews, they had it worst.

"And oh, these groups, they hated each other with such passion.

The Irish fought the Italians until they married them. Then both fought the Jews until they fell in love as well.

"Parents clung to their traditions and their children did what children do."

"Which is?" I asked.

"Which is—they didn't listen."

"Like the way I swung like McCovey, instead of slapping singles?"

The old man smiled. "Ah, the game always gives examples." This was going well. Not so difficult for Grandpa after all.

"Now, Scooter, eventually traditions changed, but back in 1910, romance between those races was thought to be taboo."

"Races?"

"Oh, you forget that things have changed. We have baseball on TV. We have astronauts in space. We take craps in indoor toilets."

"You had to take a crap outside?" I asked. "In the cold?"

"I think we're getting off track a little bit, don't you?"

"I guess, but didn't you guys freeze?"

"Enough about the crapping, Scooter. This story's hard enough for me without you examining my feces."

I laughed at Grandpa's statement. The last laugh of the day.

"I used to see this little girl walking in and out of work. Just a year my junior, but a tiny thing she was. The girls were teenagers mostly; some weren't even that. They worked long hours, awful hours, six days every week.

"They were paid by piece of garment, so they never slowed their pace. No air-conditioning back in those days. Eleven-hour days, not a single break.

"But still, this little one had a smile for me when I saw her now and then. I found myself thinking about that smile and made it a point to see it more often. Sometimes we'd sneak a word or two, she didn't know a whole lot more. Her name was Katerina—it gave me pleasure just to say it, even by myself.

"Well, in 1910 the girls went on strike to protest these awful hours they worked. The strike, it didn't work, but it made my boss very nervous.

"So after this strike was finished, I had added jobs to do. Lock the doors and fire escapes to keep out union people. Girls couldn't even talk. If the boss heard them, they'd be fired.

"Scooter, as you might imagine, that didn't make me well liked among the girls. But Katerina kept on smiling and made my heart do little tricks. Flips and flops, little things to make me think it might be love.

"A Jewish-Irish thing would have been bad enough, but when you throw in how I earned my pay, any love would be condemned. But my little one kept smiling. So one day, Scooter, I followed her, and when she was almost home, I found the strength somehow to talk to her—and that's how it all began.

"After that, every day we'd find a way to get away. A minute here, a minute there, every moment was a treasure. And knowing no one knew our love made that treasure even better. For it was only ours to share.

"I didn't make a lot of money, and most of what I did make went to help buy my parents food. But anytime I had a little extra, I'd put those pennies in my bank."

That last one startled me. "Pennies?" I said. "You put pennies in your bank?"

"Now, Scooter, maybe pennies don't mean too much in 1973, when a seat out in the bleachers is going for a buck. But back in my day pennies weren't laughed at. They were the building blocks of wealth."

"So what did you do with all your pennies?" I asked.

"Well, Scooter, the nicest thing about pennies is that they grow up to be dollars. And dollars multiply when enough pennies have been saved. And when I had the necessary dollars, I bought my little girl a ring."

"What'd she do then, dump you?" I asked, trying to be humorous.

Grandpa shook his head. His head that bore his scars that prevented him from traveling anywhere. I wondered if he really would have gone to the Yankee game that day.

"No, she didn't dump me, Scooter. Who knows, perhaps she would have—but she never got the chance.

"March 25th it was, just shy of five. Another hour left at work. I had the ring in my pocket to give her when we walked. I don't know how we could have worked it out—perhaps we couldn't have. Her parents were strict, from what she'd told me. I had only seen them once. But I knew this was it, my one true chance at love. When it's the right one, you just know. I was going to hold on to it. I would have never let it go.

"How it started, I don't know. Some think a small pile of discarded cloth went up and that it quickly spread. I was down in the factory's basement when I heard about the fire. But we'd had four small fires the year before and no one had been hurt.

"So I walked outside with all the rest, never thinking it was bad. Till I saw those flames bursting high. Till I saw the smoke clouds in the air.

"Fire department tried to help, but ladders only reached up to the sixth floor. Tenth-floor girls all got out; came down the fire escape. But God help me, Scooter, the eleventh floor was locked. Locked tight. I knew, because I'd checked it twice.

"Remember when I told you about your father's perfect game? How sometimes people rise up beyond what we think is possible?"

"Uh-huh."

"Well, I think that maybe other times, for reasons I don't know, people seem incapable of just the simplest things. And maybe their inaction is the biggest act of all. I know I could have saved her, but I stood there, motionless."

I thought about the junkie who had robbed my father and how my inaction was to blame. He could have easily killed my father, but I stood motionless. Incapable of simple things, like protecting those I loved.

"A large crowd had gathered on the pavement by the time the girls began to jump. Bodies hitting concrete, the thuds too loud to be for real. Girls were holding hands, jumping, three or four at the same time. The smell of human flesh—burning—too horrible for words.

"I kept looking for my Katerina, praying that she'd lived. That somehow, by a miracle, she'd been on the other floor. But—there were no miracles that day.

"I couldn't even find the strength to check the girls dead on the street. To glimpse the charred and broken bodies, to see if my little one had flown.

"One hundred forty-six girls died that day. Teenage hopes, teenage dreams, all gone before their time. Including my sweet angel, who'd met death at my own hands."

He put his head down and cleared his throat, trying not to cry. He failed. For the next few painful moments, I looked at his scarred head as it gently shook and I wondered about his tears. I wondered if his missing eye still made them and where those missing tears would go with no eye to set them free. Grandpa regained his lost composure and bravely carried on.

"The next day, when the blaze was over, the little bodies lined the street. Families came to claim their little girls so they could get their grieving under way. I saw her parents from a distance. They kept walking back and forth. Some bodies were still smoking, some were bitten on by rats. And there'd been bodies found by the door, the very door I'd locked. Piled up, broken bodies trying to get out. Those girls had been burned the worst. Some were identified only by their rings. But my Katerina's parents kept on walking—they couldn't find their little girl. My goodness, Scooter, they didn't know their little girl! Her body was too damaged! They couldn't—"

"Stop it, stop it, Grandpa. Stop, I heard enough." My God, I couldn't take it. I didn't want to hear another word. I always wondered about Grandpa's screams. What on earth they were about. Now I thought I knew.

"Scooter, Scooter, I can't stop, because you need to know. And I will never speak another word of it, once this day is done. And I know that you will want to know and I can't let you ask me one more time. So I'm going to finish talking and you'll just have to hear."

I nodded that I'd try, and for the first time he moved his chair. Moved it next to me. He put his hand on my right shoulder and closed his eyes, as if to summon inner strength.

"There was a procession in Manhattan to honor those we'd lost. Almost half a million gathered to pay respects to the teenage girls. There was no absence of the races. Everybody grieved. Everyone's the same deep down, I think—we all need to mourn.

"I saw her family at this service walking by, a casket close behind. I don't know if she lay in it. And the anguish on their faces—was beyond what I could grasp."

"I took solace in our church. Father Condon was a blessing. But what I had done was too big a job for rosaries, Hail Marys or Lord's Prayers. Oh, I still did those things every day, but I needed something more."

"What did you do?" I asked.

"I looked out for her family. The subway lines my dad helped build made the Bronx grow overnight. A short trip under the river meant a whole new life for some. A better life, a place to grow, to raise a family. Katerina's family moved there, and I did my best to help them until the Cross Bronx moved them out."

"How'd you help them? By buying groceries, running errands, things like that?"

"No, Scooter, I never even met them—I didn't want to cause them any further pain."

"Then how?"

"By fighting fires in their neighborhood. Right here in Melrose, actually. Back then, in 1913, until Moses built his road, this whole area was Jewish. Eastern European. I moved into Highbridge with the other Irish, but I fought my fires up here. Trying, I guess, to do some good, so that perhaps one day I might forgive myself."

[11]

Grandpa got up slowly from his chair, crossed the room, and picked up Joe D.'s ball. He held the ball with utmost care, like a mother with a newborn. I could see where Joe had signed his name; I could see the rusty smudge.

The old man looked at me intently. "It's the greatest thing I own. Give it to your dad. I want for him to have a piece of me, until we meet again."

"Okay. Alright," I said, getting up to take the gift.

"And tell him that I love him and I think of him each day."

"I will, Grandpa."

I gave Grandpa a big hug, put the ball in my jacket pocket. Then, clutching my beloved Yankee program, I headed for the door. I had the strangest thought—about the Wise Men in the manger bearing gifts for Baby Jesus. Simple things that meant so much because of the spirit in which they were given. A rolled-up Yankee program, a Joe D. ball and a brand-new Mr. Coffee. Simple things that meant so much, just like the Wise Men's gifts. Gold and myrrh and frankincense. I wouldn't know the last two if I stepped in piles of them. But the thought of gold jogged my mind and I thought quickly about my grandfather.

"Grandpa?"

"Yes?"

"What happened to the ring?"

He heard but did not answer.

"Grandpa?"

He turned his back and walked away.

"Did you ever get a chance to give it to another girl?"

He turned around and faced me, now seeming very old, as if he was dying right before me. "There were no other girls," he said, the words a labored whisper. "She was my only love."

"What about the ring?" Dammit, that was stupid! But by the time I realized, it was much too late. The damage had been done.

I wish that he had let me go without telling me the answer. After all these years I truly think it would have been better left unsaid. "I kept it in my dresser drawer for almost fifty years. Then—I gave it to your father.

"And he—gave it to your mother on their wedding day."

[12]

I could have either walked the seven blocks or hopped a train and walked just two. I chose to take the longer walk, perhaps to clear my head. I had such a battle of emotions fighting in my brain.

It had seemed like such a wondrous day by virtue of that kiss. But the truth about Grandpa's love had hit me very hard. As had the vision of my father suffering all those setbacks in a row. It seemed the mugging was the least of them, in terms of how he suffered, compared to the peanut vendor's mutiny and the vandals at the ballpark. He looked to be a boxer who's been staggered by some blows. Wandering around on queer street until the last one puts him down. Like when Frazier took on Foreman and came out the worse for wear. Even though the first-base save had been a late-round comeback for my dad, he'd still looked dazed and weary as he took off on his train.

Guilt weighed on my mind as I turned right onto 170th from Grandpa's street of Townsend. Why didn't I feel worse? God knows I wanted to. I wished to submerge myself in Grandpa's grief, to completely feel his loss. But Nina's kiss made total grief impossible, because it kept moving to the forefront. Past my staggered dad and Grandpa's loss, to become my top news of this day.

A few blocks later, I stopped fighting it and gave in to happiness as I approached Jerome Avenue. I tried not to let emotion get the best of me as I dodged cars and junkies on the avenue. I made it and relaxed as I saw my block approaching.

I was thinking about our kiss when the pistol split my eye. The first blow didn't put me down but it made it hard to think. Who would want to hit me half a block from my home? Darkness was just falling; kids were playing in the street. Hispanic girls jumping rope and singing songs that sounded sweet.

I could kind of see my house from there, but my focus was real hazy. Then I saw the face of Manny Vasquez and a flash of moving steel. This time I went down.

I heard children's voices and, in my weakened state, couldn't really tell if it was screams I heard, or cheers.

The next voice I heard was Manny's.

"I told you, motherfucker," he snarled through pearl-white teeth. "Leave the girl alone. But you didn't listen."

For the second time in just eight hours, I was motionless. At least this time I had reason, getting the shit kicked out of me.

But in a way I wasn't motionless, for all the while I lay there, I kept my program tightly clutched. So even while he kicked at me and spat out angry words, I took solace in the knowledge that I had his sister's number.

It seems that what I'd heard had indeed been cheers. For although this pusher dealt out junk and ruined countless lives, to these kids he was a hero who only dealt out candy.

At last I heard real screams, coming from my sister. "Mommy, Mommy, Scooter's hurt!" But Manny played Jan Stenerud and kicked a fifty-yarder with my nuts.

"Motherfucker, don't let me see you no more," he said, pearl-white teeth close to my ear. " 'Less you come for business."

My mother came out running, to the dismay of all the children. Seemed like the show was over. It was, save for the encore, which saw Manny grab his crotch and tell my mom that she looked good. Then he strutted off into the darkness throwing Hershey kisses to the kids.

[13]

My sister hovered over me as my mom pressed cotton to my eye.

"Does it sting? Does it sting?" Patty asked.

I'd been left lying in a pool of blood and my nuts were grapefruit-sized, but my sister's main concern was if the alcohol was hurting.

"Back away," my mother said. "Give your brother space to breathe."

Despite my weakened state, it did feel kind of nice to have my mom's attention for a change. She usually doted on my sister and left me to the wolves.

My mother spread the wound open with her fingers. She winced, my sister screamed. "That's quite a gash," my mother said. "Split right to the bone."

"That's gross," my sister said.

I said, "Mom, tell Patty to get lost."

She took a look at the other gash and declared it even worse. "You might have to see a doctor, Scooter. These are really bad."

My mind shot back to where it often did, game five in '69. She hadn't deemed me doctor-worthy when I had a gunshot wound in my leg. But now she was the perfect image of concern, cleaning up my blood.

"It's all coagulated. Scooter, usually brow wounds don't result in this much blood. Are your testicles alright?"

"Scooter hurt his testicles," my sister squealed. "Scooter hurt his testicles."

"Mom, make her go away." Fortunately, she did. Unfortunately, the line of questioning had not yet run its course. "Are they sore? Are they swollen? Could they use a little ice?"

I answered with three yes's, then told her to never say the word again.

We didn't have an ice pack, or ice cubes for that matter. But I accepted a bag of frozen raviolis and slapped it on my aching nuts when my mother went upstairs.

I had never seen my mother sew a thing in my entire time on earth. When clothes got holes, they got thrown out or my dad took them to a shelter. But my mom returned with sewing thread and a needle for my wounds. And I thought of a few of Julie Andrews's favorite things while she went to work on me.

Some mothers are good cooks; some join the PTA. Some are good with homework, and some keep a tidy house. My mother batted zero for 4 when it came to those mundane things. But brother, could she stitch up wounds without novocaine or pause. Indeed, she was an artist. I looked upward from my kitchen chair while she sewed, her hands moving like a conductor's, leading a symphony of thread.

We had an overhead fluorescent light that seemed to bounce off of her finger. Shooting starlike sparkles in the air—or maybe I was dizzy.

"Mom?"

"Yes, Scooter?"

"Back when I was . . . hurt . . . four years ago, did a little girl come ask for me?"

My mother never missed a beat, moving quickly with the needle, patching up her son. The sparkles were so pretty.

"I don't know, four years is a long time, hon. I really can't remember."

"Could you try a little harder?"

I felt a slight tugging on my eyebrow. I recoiled a little bit. This whole stitching thing was not pleasurable, for the eyebrow wasn't numb. But that last tug had really hurt me.

"Okay, I think we've got that eyebrow done. It took eleven stitches. Now I'll start the other one. It's right above your cheekbone, so this might hurt a little bit."

"Mom, about the girl?"

"Like I said, I don't remember. Now I need you to hold still."

"OW!" My skin felt like it had torn. I saw her hands, so skilled before, grow clumsy while she worked. A distinct transformation, like scientist Bruce Banner changing into the Hulk.

"I told you to stay still, honey. Or else it's going to hurt." Her tone was sweet, perhaps too much so. It made me feel a little sick, like a kid on Halloween who overdoes the candy corn.

I should have been more cautious, with a needle waving before my eye. But I kept thinking about Nina at age eleven, trying hard to visit me.

"Mom, I really need to know. Did Nina visit me?"

I felt another tug but swallowed back my pain.

"If you're talking about that Spanish girl, yes, she came by here once."

"Once?"

"I don't know, once or twice. Really, what's the difference?"

"I'll tell you what the difference is," I said, my insides knotted up with anger. "I would have liked her company."

She let her hands rest from the task at hand and I saw what had made the sparkles. A diamond ring, a good-sized rock, though I couldn't guess the carats.

She smiled and leaned in close to me. I could smell smoke and Wrigley's Doublemint on her breath. "Honey, that was a tough time. The neighborhood was changing. I just didn't want to see you running with the wrong crowd. I was trying to protect you."

I got up from the stool, the gash half stitched and bleeding slightly. I threw the pasta ice pack on the floor and slowly backed out of the kitchen, the threaded needle swinging gently on my face. Tickling me just slightly.

She lit a cigarette and took a long drag, giving me a good look at her diamond as she did so.

"That's quite a ring, Mom," I said. "Dad catching lots of criminals?"

She blew out a cloud of smoke and opted not to answer.

"What happened to the other ring—the one you used to wear?"

She smiled and poured more of her maternal syrup on me.

"Honey, that was just a little ring. I think you would agree I deserved something better."

"What did you do with it?" I asked, hoping that she'd saved it, so after all these years it could be back in Grandpa's hands.

"I pawned it down at Miller's—a couple weeks ago."

Upstairs in my bedroom, I lay down and blinked back tears. I wished I had a way out of my problems, a way out of all the pain. A magic pill or potion that could change my life for good. I felt the needle dangling, tickling me a little. I pulled it forcefully and felt blood ooze down my cheek. It didn't tickle anymore.

I reached into my jacket pocket and found that Joe D.'s ball was gone.

I reached into my closet and came out with Thurman Munson. Yellow, cheap and light—maybe twenty-eight ounces. I felt it in my hands and took a quick swing at my dresser, scattering coins and trinkets, sending a framed photo crashing to the floor. No, it wasn't right. Kiddie stuff, too light. I threw it on my bed.

I reached back in and grabbed McCovey and withdrew it like a broadsword. Wielding it with anger, I held it aloft with a shaking hand. Heavy, like a club, awesome—it was perfect. I looked down my arm and willed the shakes to end, took notice of my corded forearms. Four years of rolling up increasing weights, for what I'd not been sure. But I knew there was a reason. And now it was apparent.

I felt the bat in both my hands. I wasn't nine years old anymore. Fueled by pain, anger and Hank Greenberg, I'd swing it from my heels. And what I hit—I'd hurt. I saw a picture of Phil Rizzuto. On a kiddie bank from the Money Store. Rizzuto was their pitchman and the stupid thing had been a freebie. I swung with all my might, blasting Rizzuto's smiling face. Holy cow! Look at all that money fly. Pennies, nickels, dimes and quarters. And some bills were drifting to the floor—two fives, a ten and eight singles. I stuffed the bills into my pockets. Most of my life savings, going to a noble cause.

My sister looked at me oddly. Scared, but only slightly.

"Scooter, why are you acting so crazy?"

I glared at her and limped away, blood now running across my cheek and down my neck. I would have never harmed the spoiled child, but I didn't like her either.

I stumbled down the stairs, feeling a pounding in my swollen balls with every clumsy step.

My mother sat at the kitchen table, savoring the last few puffs of another cancer stick. She used to just smoke socially, but within the last few years she'd become a two-pack girl.

"Honey, where are you going, out to play some ball?" A statement so damn stupid it didn't merit a response.

I emerged from my house on Shakespeare like a ghoul from a B movie. Matted hair damp with blood, stitches in my brow, plasma clinging to my face—hobbling down the chalk-marked streets, taking swings at phantom kneecaps.

Shakespeare had grown quiet now, just a few kids playing jacks. They eyed me with suspicion, but not with fear, as they'd just seen this white boy take a beating. Certainly I knew better than to go crawling back for more.

"You know where Manny went?" I asked, trying to sound like a buddy.

"Screw you, blanco," I got back. It sounded funny from a nine-year-old.

"I'll give you both two dollars."

They gave blanco the directions. All the kids knew where Manny was, how else could he do business?

167th Avenue and Nelson, second floor of a 1912 walk-up. It's where the Highbridge Jews once lived, along with well-off Irish.

Now the place had gone to hell, but at least it had some tenants. The apartment houses on either side had both gone up in flames and now served as shooting galleries for the undiscerning junkie. I wondered if Manny's pearly whites would look as nice if McCovey's barrel found them.

He wasn't hard to find. I just followed the guitar chords of Santana. Pounding and pulsing loud enough so he wouldn't hear the clanging of a ladder.

I huddled on that fire escape and thought of all the reasons why I should. Knowing that once I broke that glass there could be no turning back. I let the day's events jolt my mind—too much to deal with in one day. Macombs Dam Park, disheveled friends, riots on the field, love's first kiss, burning flesh and the save made by my mother. Then I looked through the window at Manny in the shadows. Buttocks moving up and down, doing things I'd never done. He'd split my eye, he'd split my cheek and kicked me in the nuts. But most of all, he'd tried to take Nina from me; trying to nip love in the bud.

That's the thought I tapped into while I tapped the bat into my hands. I closed my eyes and thought of Nina, then swung right through the glass. I knew my act was justified. I needed this release.

His gun lay on the same cheap table as Joe D.'s sacred ball. Perhaps if he had reached for it right away, he would have had a chance. He instead reached for the sheets. He chose silk over steel and his covered ass was mine.

I took three swings—all from deep down and each one found its mark. First came Manny's table, the one where the pistol sat. I felt the cheap wood shatter and the piece and ball both fell to the ground. I kicked the pistol to the corner, just as I'd seen McGarrett do, and put Joe D. in my pocket, right where he belonged.

The next swing took out the TV set, and that one-eyed cop Columbo finally shut his mouth. Then from way down deep I went up high, like that guy who'd nailed my foot. I came down on Santana and silence filled my ears. Eerie, deadly silence so thick I felt the fear.

Manny tried to hide beneath layers of machismo. Saying, "What the fuck you want?" but meaning, "Please don't hurt me, Scooter." Propped up by his ego and his girlfriend in the room. Had it not been for the girlfriend, I could have got Manny to squirt some tears. Then I saw her telltale veins and shaking hands and I knew I'd walked in on a deal. No love here, strictly business, exchanging fluids instead of money.

If only I had had the strength, this whole story would be different. The strength to cope with problems, the strength to deal with loss, the strength to stand up to my mother and the strength to hold on to true love tight. But I didn't have that strength. Didn't have it and didn't want it. What I wanted was release. A release that only Manny Vasquez had. So when he replaced his primal fears with macho prose, I was ready for the dealer.

"The fuck you want?" he asked, shaking underneath his sheet. His colors lay feet away, but the respect they brought was gone. The girl beside him puked on herself. Perhaps from fear, but probably not.

I held the bat aloft, wanting badly just to hit him but wanting even worse to just feel high. I hesitated for a moment, knowing that my answer would change my life for good.

"I want you and me . . . to do some business."

My father had laid down three simple rules in the aftermath of our one day at Shea in August 1969. I broke one that night. For, at a quarter to eleven on the last day of September 1973, Manny Vasquez took me up the block and, in back of the broken-down Highbridge Community Center, got me higher than I'd dreamed was possible.

I guess I was a novice, so it took a couple times. But as soon as I felt contact, I knew I was hooked. I knew that against my better judgment I'd be Manny's biggest mark. Always craving the hard stuff, not the useless junk. I would go on to other dealers, spending every penny earned and driving endless miles, all searching for that high. But Manny Vasquez on that night became the standard-bearer for me.

After, I was wasted—hands shaking, brain buzzing from his stuff. I began to laugh and he did too and the Shakespeare misunderstanding seemed like a long, long time ago.

He spat into the foot-long grass. I spat a gob of blood. I'd been so damn preoccupied that I hadn't had a thing to eat since one o'clock, when I'd scarfed down all of seven peanuts before agreeing with my father that they didn't taste as good as Pop's.

"Yo, blanco," Manny said.

"Yo, Manny," I said.

"You wanna do this thing again?"

"Whenever I can afford it."

"Then you do one thing for me."

"Okay."

"Leave the fuckin' girl alone."

I thought about this one prerequisite, but not for very long. I gave a hurried answer and I let go of my true love.

I walked on air for those two blocks, from Nelson to my home. The pain I'd felt a few short hours before had been replaced by sweet surrender. I floated in the door and leaned McCovey's axe against the wall. I looked up at Rizzuto's bat and took it from the wall. Comparing this little stick to my mighty oak was like comparing a baby's penis to the Dago's. At least from what he'd said. I'd actually never seen it. Or had the urge to either.

I sat down with my father's bat; it felt like balsa wood to me. Then with one swift move, I brought it down and broke it on my knee. I never felt a thing. That's for you, I thought, you diamond-buying son-shooting prick.

I walked out to the kitchen and put my mushy ice pack in the freezer. My mom could heat it up and eat the raviolis some other time. I chugged half a quart of milk before I saw it had gone sour. Half a quart had gone down fast, but it came up even faster. Splashing on our ancient tile, white milk with bloody swirls. I grabbed a pack of matches before floating up the steps.

I saw my rolled-up program and held it to my face. I could fairly smell Nina's skin, could almost taste her kiss. I looked at the numbers she had written. Seven simple numbers. She was just a call away. I slowly pulled the cover off before I lit the match.

I don't know which came first, tears or fire, and I guess it doesn't matter. But I swear that I heard Nina scream as flames engulfed her writing. And I know that I was crying still when I drifted off to sleep.

[15]

I awoke to Patty's screams. Maybe Linda Blair's head had spun around again or maybe it was *Serpico* and the mere thought of dirty cops. Then I heard the crashing sounds and thought we had a burglar.

I thought of McCovey's bat, but realized I'd left it leaning against the wall of our tiny living room. I then heard the anguished cries and I knew it was my father. He must have found the bats. I'm not sure which one hurt him worse—the bat that he'd been given, broken clean in two, or the forbidden bat of Willie's, which must have taunted him in his time of sorrow with its potency and strength.

The house was under siege from a man whose temper rarely flared.

The cop had come home from his Harlem shift, seen Rizzuto's broken bat and was now tearing up the place. He'd grabbed hold of my McCovey and was doing bad things to his house.

In and of itself, the bad things didn't scare me. It was the screams that accompanied them. My father, for just the second time, was letting loose the N word and was doing it with force.

"No nigger bats!" he yelled. I heard a giant crash—the TV, I guessed—and another awful yell. "No nigger bats!" A window broke and my father laughed with manic glee before continuing his battle cry. "No nigger bats! No nigger bats!"

I made it down the stairs, a slow trip that was quite painful. My high was gone and everything was achy. My head, my hands, my face, my ribs, my wrists, my nuts, my fingers.

I got a good glimpse of my father surveying all the damage and contemplating more. He held McCovey in one hand and a quart-sized bottle in the other. Brown, with a white label—most of it was gone.

He hadn't had a drop since that day in '69. He'd probably gotten hammered with the Dago, toasting the death of the old stadium, and come home a happy drunk, until he'd seen Rizzuto's broken bat.

He took a giant swig and muttered to himself. He held the bat aloft, his back still turned to me, sizing up his prospects. He chose my arts and crafts, like I really gave a crap. "No more nigger bats!" Wham! There went my cup I'd made in pottery, shaped like Marty Feldman. "No more nigger bats!" Wham! The butter churn from woodshop that never really worked.

He then eyed my sister's papier-mâché menagerie, things she really liked. "No more nigger bats!" Wham! The giraffe was history. I finally got mad. Take it out on me, but not on Patty's things. I approached him from behind, telling him to stop. Without bothering to turn, he threw me to the floor with strength belying his small frame.

"No nigger bats!" Wham! An elephant was gone.

I was lying on the floor, not hurt but taken aback, when I saw her little feet run past me. Clad in bunny slippers, those little feet were moving quick. I guess she'd seen that last swing pulverize her pachyderm and it had upset Mommy's little girl.

"Daddy, don't!" she screamed.

My father brought the bat back with the intent of bringing it down on some helpless paper pet. "No nigger—"

The swing never reached its destination. My sister's head got in the way and the bat seemed to land a glancing blow, sending her stumbling backward for a step or two before she fell, as if in slow motion, crumpling to the floor.

Thank God the blow had not been too bad. He could have really done some damage, the way he had been swinging. My father, for his part, began to overdo his sorrow. He dropped to his knees, wailing and moaning, shedding the type of tears usually reserved for the shooting of his son.

He scooped Patty up in his arms, looking, I thought, to play the hero by carrying her upstairs to her room, where she'd no doubt wake up the next morning with a pretty decent headache. Although it would probably pale when compared to the monster hangover awaiting my "nigger bat"–wielding father when the sun shone down on Highbridge.

I'll never know what made me do it—the awful thing that I did next. But when I saw my father with her in his arms, and saw McCovey lying free, I picked up the giant bat without thought or hesitation.

I've thought about it every day since that night. A million times, probably more. I still don't have an answer, only random guesses.

Maybe I did it for love. The love of Patty. The most far-fetched guess of all, though it's the one that yields the only comfort, the only one that doesn't paint me as a selfish, vengeful child.

Maybe I was too high to be blamed. I didn't know what I was doing. But that simply is not true. I knew—and I liked it. I can't blame the high, because I simply took too much pleasure in doing the deed. I'm both responsible and accountable for my actions of that night.

Maybe I just had to act. Maybe I simply didn't feel I could just stand by helplessly for the second time that day. Perhaps I really did believe that any action trumped inaction. That when my epitaph is written, history will remember me as a man of bold action and will conveniently forget that those bold actions resulted in such misery.

Or . . . maybe it was hate. Hatred—the least random of my guesses.

I hated where my life had gone since October 1969. And where it should have been. Hidden from the world while my gunshot wound was healing. Limping off to public school to pay the price for my white skin. Driving spikes into my foot just to make a couple friends. And letting go of my one true love to forget about all the rest. I hated him for that.

I would never go to college. I could never be a fireman or a cop. I would never know the thrill of stepping on home plate. And I'd never share a sandwich or a kiss or feel truly needed in the world or smell the perfume on her skin. I hated him for that. God, I hated him.

I think my heart was simply filled with hate when I picked up McCovey's bat. My father was in the wrong place at the wrong time, with the wrong son with the wrong emotion. I hated so many things about him, his weakness most of all.

How he couldn't stand up to my mother, even when she was wrong. How he'd stood blindly by when the bullet hit my leg. How he'd let her take my grandpa, how he'd let her pawn the ring, how he'd . . .

My father was approaching me, but seemed oblivious to my presence. Oblivious to everything, perhaps, except his own pathetic guilt and sadness. Tears were streaming down his face at a pace that seemed too fast to be for real. Indeed, if not for the minor blow to my sister Patty's head, it would have struck me as quite comical. I thought those too fast, almost comical tears must have clouded his vision, for he was heading away from the stairwell's promise of two waiting beds. Instead, he seemed headed for the front door, as I started from the heels.

I focused on a special spot two inches from his knee. The same place I'd been shot. It seemed appropriate. I studied as that spot arrived, tracing it as if it was a fastball fired from a grown man at a nine-year-old on that field in '69. On that day four years before, I'd closed my eyes and swung. My hit was strictly luck—coincidental contact.

The contact in our living room was not coincidental. Nor was the intent that launched it. For even if the swing itself was not pre-planned, the hatred that delivered it had been nurtured for four years.

It was a perfect swing. Long stride, level path, nice hip rotation, eyes always on the target. The follow-through was somewhat flawed, though through no fault of my own. My father's bone got in the way. I swear I heard that bone shatter when the sweet spot found his tibia.

It felt so damn good to do. I didn't have regrets—not even when I saw him pitch forward to the floor, somehow managing to hold on to Patty as he went. He never dropped the unconscious girl—I'll give him that much credit. He had a good glove up the middle.

No, I didn't have regrets. Not even when I heard him scream. No, I simply closed my eyes and imagined that bone was a baseball, sailing against a purple twilight sky. Back, back, way back. All the way back to my days of innocence, when I didn't need a Manny Vasquez to get me high. That ball is outta here.

I kept my eyes shut and circled Macombs Dam bases, imagining that my father's guttural wheezes were the cheers of my adoring fans. Chanting my name as I headed for home. "Scooter, Scooter, Scooter." God they felt so real. I heard my mother's voice so clearly, chanting my name. "Scooter?—Scooter?" It was my mother's voice. But it was not my imagination. I opened my eyes. "Scooter?" Calling from her bedroom.

"Mom?" I called.

"Scooter, what's all that noise?"

I struggled for a way to explain what I had just done. For the first time, it occurred to me that my actions were not justified, at least not to an outside party.

"What's that noise?" my mother repeated.

"Um, nothing. Dad just fell."

"Is he alright? Should I come down?"

"He's alright, Mom. Go back to bed."

I had headed for the stairwell during my brief, dishonest discussion with my mother, leaving my father behind me. The screams had stopped, leading me to think he'd passed out from the pain or the whiskey, or possibly a combination of both. I turned to face my drunk, unconscious father and looked straight into his very much conscious, very pained, very mournful eyes.

Somehow he was standing, with my sister in his arms, struggling to speak.

"K-k-keys."

"What?" I'd heard his word, but couldn't comprehend how he was standing, let alone what that word meant.

"Car keys. Mother's car."

I'd hit his leg with a tremendous blow. I'd been swinging for the fences and I'd had my pitch to hit. I had heard that damn bone break and was sure that he'd stay down.

But there he stood before me with my sister in his arms. He then began to walk. Hobbling, hopping, staggering—but he never did go down, and he never faltered with my sister as he headed for the door. He paused for just a moment to take my mother's keys off a hook and then staggered to my mother's Charger as fast as his condition would allow.

He laid Patty in the backseat, then gunned the engine, leaving Shakespeare in a squeal of burning rubber.

My mom had heard the tires squeal and had looked to see the scene outside. The sight of her beloved car taking off was one she didn't like. She pushed her window open and shouted out into the night.

"That's my car, you bastard!"

[16]

"Your father used to be religious."

That's how my mother greeted me when I emerged from sleeping three hours following the worst day of my life.

I had taken a short much-needed shower to get the blood out of my hair. I could have stayed in there an hour and let the hot water try to wash my sins away, but I had to see my sister to check on how she was.

I looked at my face in the mirror. A well-done job above my eye, which was now swollen and deep purple. Half an angry gash below it, thread embedded in the wound. I took out a pair of tweezers and, with hands that never did get steady, commenced to pull the thread out of my cheek with jerking painful tugs. The wound sprang back to life and looked a little like one of those vaginas I'd seen in *The Joy of Sex.*

I poured alcohol inside it and repressed the urge to scream. Then I slapped on half a dozen Band-Aids and hoped they'd stay stuck. The little strips were strictly ornamental, as I doubted they would heal me.

I replaced the past day's clothing with beige corduroys and a Bobby Murcer T-shirt. Then put on my same jacket and limped down to face the day. That's when I saw my mom, sitting at the table with her ashtray, informing me of my father's faith, followed by some smoke rings.

I didn't bother to acknowledge her. I had other things to think about, like my sister in the hospital and my father, who was probably there as well.

I was also thinking about my stomach and how it ached inside. Not just from repeated kicks, but also from lack of food. I had one dollar left and I hoped that I could pick up something decent at the new bodega on Cromwell on the way to see my sister.

I tried to get out of the house, but my mother's trip down memory lane wasn't over yet.

"Of course, he wasn't too concerned with God when he had my legs up in the air." She laughed, like the thought of her legs up in the air was funny.

I winced like the thought was sick. "Why are you doing this?" I said.

"So you can appreciate my sacrifices."

"I know all about the Concourse, Mom."

"Do you know all about abortion?"

I wish I hadn't turned around, but her last line was like a car crash; I simply had to look.

"Sure, everyone was doing it, even though it wasn't legal yet. My parents, of course, forbade it, being the devout Catholics they were. Threatened to leave me high and dry with nothing if I did. And then my parents left me anyway—high and dry with nothing."

"And do you regret not getting it?" I asked.

"Of course not, honey, not a single day," she said.

"Thanks, Mom, that's nice to know," I said and opened the door.

"Scooter, please don't go." I paused for just a moment, giving her time to get up from the table and hold my battered face in her soft hands. "I'm still here, Scooter," she said gently. "Please remember that. I'm still here. I could have had it all and I gave up everything. You remember that, Scooter. I'm your mother and maybe I'm not perfect, but I'm the only one you got—and I'm still here."

"I'll see you at the hospital?" I figured that was where my dad had headed in my mother's shopping car. Since my little accident, he'd been cautious, almost paranoid, about his children's health. I figured he had brought Patty there for observation, and may have had his leg looked at as well.

My mother frowned in thought. "It will be tough without a car—streets aren't safe, you know. I'll have to catch a cab."

"Okay. I'll see you in a while."

She kissed me on the nose, which she hadn't done in years, and I walked out into a chilly autumn morning. A light rain was falling and the sky looked ominous. The worst, I knew, was yet to come. I wished I had a heavy coat instead of my old Yankees parka. I felt inside the pocket. Joe D.'s ball. Damn, it could get ruined in this weather.

I was walking slightly better. My grapefruit balls had shrunk; I had checked them in the shower and they were down to tangerines. I was just a block from Cromwell when I saw a new store on Jerome. It had replaced Murray's Deli, a Bronx tradition for nearly thirty years. This new place was offering cash for valuables. I walked in and got ten bucks in return for Joe D.'s ball. Ten more bucks for Manny Vasquez.

The lady at admissions put down her *New York Post.* "Can I help you, please?" she asked. Puerto Rican, very pleasant. About my mother's age.

"Um, yeah, I'm here to see Reilly."

She put her head down for a moment, perusing paperwork. "Patrick or Patricia?"

"Both of them—if possible."

She put her head down once again and sadly shook her head. "I'm sorry," she said, looking up. "You can't see either yet."

"Why not?"

"They're both in ICU."

"ICU?" I asked, not comprehending just what those initials meant.

"Intensive care."

Intensive care? In my sister's case this made little sense. It had only been a glancing blow. But my father? That made no sense at all. I'd seen him walking. I'd seen him drive a car.

"Excuse me, ma'am," I said. "There must be some mistake. My father only hurt his leg."

"Not according to this file. It says he had an auto accident."

My knees buckled and I thought I might fall. My eyesight became hazy and I took deep breaths that hurt my ribs as I tried to gain my bearings.

The lady at admissions was looking at her *Post* when things got right again. The front page had a large photo of Yankee Stadium with twenty thousand idiots dancing on its grave. There was a much smaller photo up above it, of a man I thought I knew. Postage stamp size. Was it? Yes! Yes, it was! My father's partner in the paper. The Dago in the *Post*. The front page no less. I looked up at the small headline that accompanied the photo. COP KILLED IN HARLEM SHOOT-OUT.

Like most Bronx hospitals of the time, Morrisania had been forced through necessity to become a good trauma center. Baseball bats weren't just for baseball anymore and surgeons had employed their "Saturday Night Special" kit immediately—a series of saws, drills and scalpels that allowed rapid access to the brain. Burr holes had been drilled to allow brain pressure to release, but the blow had been a far more vicious one than I'd realized and the swelling had been bad.

She'd been out of the operating room for several hours but had yet to regain consciousness. Her prognosis was a cloudy one—only time would tell.

My father had carried his daughter in and had gone back to his car. He had called in a robbery in progress on a woman who'd been beaten, and even though the Bronx was not his precinct, he'd taken off in pursuit.

He had hit a telephone pole at eighty, with no sign of slowing down. The Charger had been totaled, along with much of my dad's body.

I called the house on Shakespeare and caught my mother as she was headed out the door.

"Mom, come quick!" I pleaded. "Patty and Dad are both hurt bad—and Dad's partner died last night. Please come quick!"

I put myself in my father's shoes, on the worst night of his life. A fighter who'd been staggered. One blow from going down. He sees his best friend die. Grieving for his partner, trying hard to numb the pain. Coming home intoxicated for the first time in many years. Expecting to find comfort in his home and finding Rizzuto's memory in pieces. Was Vinnie's death the final blow or was it seeing the Scooter's broken bat?

Then the man who had been color-blind lets out some racist words. And pays dearly with his daughter's health and payback from his son.

I thought through these things for hours inside a smoke-filled respite lounge. Sometimes looking for my mother so I could be wrapped in her arms. In spite of all the sadness and the anger and the hate, part of me was still a little child looking for warmth when things went bad.

My mom had always favored Patty, and that fact had always hurt me. Now I just hoped that Patty would get better so I could tell her that I cared. I'd been so focused on self-pity that I never even tried to get to know her. I prayed for extra time together. Got right down on my knees like Grandpa used to and prayed to God to give her time.

Grandpa! He could help me. But he didn't have a phone. The subway stopped at 167th, just a couple blocks away. I could have been in his room in fifteen minutes, but I didn't want to take the chance of missing the arrival of my mother. Besides, I couldn't bear the thought of seeing Grandpa, knowing what I'd done with Joe D.'s ball. He would have taken one quick look at me and known I'd hocked the ball.

It never crossed my mind as I sat in that waiting room to give the pawnshop guys a call. Tell them I'd screwed up and I'd be right by to buy it back. At worst, they'd charge a couple extra dollars and I'd learn from my mistake. But by the time I thought of doing so, a couple days had passed. I never even got the chance to bargain because it had been sold within a day. Gone and lost forever.

I waited twenty minutes for the chance to use the phone. A Puerto Rican lady was using it and was shouting words of anguished Spanish. Although my Spanish wasn't strong, I could make out "son" and "stab." All the while I waited, I tried to think of Nina's number. Calling on my powers of recollection to get in touch with my one love. My recall powers failed me, for all I could feel was her number up in flames and hearing screams that seemed too real.

I picked up the receiver and saw a teardrop had run down it. I was not solitary in my grief. At least not at Morrisania, for there was plenty there to go around. I closed my eyes and willed the numbers to come into my head. The numbers never came and I didn't know her mother's surname, which wasn't Vasquez, like her children's.

A nurse tapped me on the shoulder. My father wished to see me, but he wasn't doing well. Aside from all his injuries, his mental state was tenuous. The nurse said he was despondent and despite his agony he was begging her to stop the morphine.

The injuries were serious. She thought that I should know. So while we walked to the ICU, she did her best to list them.

Impact with the steering wheel had done extensive damage to his torso. Sternum crushed, a punctured lung, five ribs broken, ruptured spleen.

The tibia was fractured right below the knee. Actually, "shattered" was the word she used. She said the doctors had never seen a bone so completely devastated. She said the swelling had caused occlusion of the blood vessels.

"What does that mean?" I asked.

"It means he might lose his leg."

We walked right past my sister's room. "Couldn't we go back?" I asked.

"Not without a parent."

I felt a lump inside my throat.

"Can I just look at her?" I asked. "I won't try to go inside."

The nurse acquiesced with a soft smile.

Patty seemed so tiny lying there. A little girl all alone, despite the monitors and beeping. No parent there to comfort her. A father who had put her in this condition and a mom who couldn't walk five blocks. And a brother too caught up in envy to learn just who she was.

The nurse gently touched my arm, then led me three doors farther.

I thought of Joe D.'s ball the second I saw him. God, I wish I'd had it so it might work its magic once again. The way it had incited movement inside Grandpa when I was convinced he was a ghoul. I really thought that stupid ball could have made my father whole again.

Not in terms of body, for clearly he was maimed. I refer here to his spirit, which seemed beyond repair. Lying in that dismal room, I truly saw a broken man.

"Scooter . . . please . . . come here . . . I need to . . . talk to you."

The nurse put her hand on my shoulder and told me not to stay too long. My father had been through a tough ordeal and he was going to need his rest.

Moving to my father's side was among the toughest things I've ever done. It was difficult just to see him there, fighting off his pain. For God's sake, take the morphine, I thought. You've been through enough. If medicine's the issue here, there will be time for weaning later. Take a drink, a pill, a spike, anything to spare me this.

I could see the scar from his old gunshot wound on his right shoulder. He'd been a hero on that late September day in 1960, chasing a murderer eleven blocks, with a bullet in his arm. He'd made the arrest without drawing his gun, and somehow made it back to work the following night. A murderer's bullet couldn't stop him, but his thirteen-year-old son could. It didn't seem right. In fact, on that day, nothing did.

I tried to talk but found the going tough. Besides, what could I do or say? "Sorry" probably would have been a start, but it completely skipped my mind.

My father forced out painful words.

"I told the truth about . . ." I thought my heart might stop. "Your sister."

He took labored breaths and spoke. "Not about . . . my leg. That will be . . . our secret." I could have sworn he winked. Was it possible that even as he lay in monumental pain he was trying to ease my own?

"Thank you, Dad," I said, happy to have broken free from the restraints of silence.

"I lost . . . my way . . . son."

"Which way, Dad? Which way? What do you mean?"

"I looked . . . the other way."

"Which way?" I asked again. He was speaking to me in puzzles, the way Grandpa did. But I sensed that when I figured out the mystery, I would find that things I thought I knew had changed.

"I know what my father meant."

"Daddy, what's that mean?" I hadn't called him Daddy since I was just a little child.

"An eye for an eye," he said, and then he turned his face from me. "An eye for an eye," he said again.

"Dad? Dad?" My voice was breaking as I said it. A voice didn't answer. But I had to get it out. "Dad, Dad?" I was going to shake my father, but man, he'd been through enough. But I wasn't going to leave before I said my piece.

"I'm sorry that I did this." I could see him fighting tears. "And I'm sorry about Vinnie."

He gave in to the sorrow and then pushed a button for the nurse. I left before she got there.

I heard a voice in Patty's room. Soft and low and heartfelt. "We're not sure," I heard it say.

I took a look inside. A doctor of some kind talking to—my mother. Thank God she'd finally made it. Perhaps she couldn't get a cab. Not too many cabbies risked taking fares in the Bronx. And walking could be dangerous.

My mother's head was down. I couldn't see her face. But something about her seemed different now, probably just her grief. I heard the doctor say, "Worst case," and then I saw her body shake and I knew that she was crying.

The doctor softly said, "Brain damage," and my mother fell sobbing to the floor.

That's when I ran to her, and above the doctor's objections, I helped my mother off the ground.

"I'm her son," I said.

"Then I'll leave you two alone."

"Mom, I'm here, I'm here," I whispered and I stroked her long dark hair. The hair seemed somehow different. I helped her to her chair and wrapped my arms around her, probably more for me than her. I smelled her blend of cigarettes and Doublemint and it reminded me of childhood. "Mom, I'm here, I'm here."

She let her tears fall on my shoulder then sniffed back more tears, trying to regain her composure.

"Scooter, honey, let me up. I've got to get myself together."

"You look fine," I said, and in truth she really did. I'd been mad at her so long that I'd forgotten just how beautiful she was.

"I'll only be a minute. Stay here with your sister."

I watched her leave through the doorway, and I pulled a chair close to my sister. I watched her little chest breathe in and out and I gave thanks for all those breaths. She was just a tiny thing. Delicate but pretty. I guess I'd never taken the time to notice. I reached out and touched my sister. I held on to her hand. Held on to it and stroked it until I guessed an hour had passed. That's when the difference hit me.

Her hair! Her hair was newly styled! This was Monday, shopping day, and while her little girl and husband were stuck in the ICU, my mother had gone shopping in Manhattan and had a stylist do her hair.

I didn't know if I should cry or scream. In time I would do both. At least I would look her in the eye, just to let her know I knew.

I never got the chance. Her minute never ended. The woman who'd said "I'm still here" that morning gave up motherhood for good.

1977

[1]

I fully understood that smoking cigarettes at tryouts was not the fastest way to make the team. I think that's why I did it. I already had the "dirtbag" label, so why not take this chance to solidify my image? Truth was, I didn't smoke, but since I hung out in the smoke shed (an architectural wonder of plywood and steel tubing) with other kids who smoked, it was just assumed I did. Which was fine with me. I got the dirtbag reputation without the tar and nicotine.

Still, I was smoking on that butt as I walked across the field, making sure to exaggerate the limp a bit, just to dig myself a bigger hole. I lit another up as I stood and watched the white boys swing their metal bats and throw grounders to each other. Even then I didn't draw too much attention, except for the little snickers and witty observations that Long Island high school athletes were bound to make at guys like me. Lots of dirtbags wandered by and watched the jocks do their jock thing before heading for the woods to smoke doobies after school.

I drew a little more attention than the average by-the-numbers dirtbag, if only for the fact that I got in fights a lot. And won most of them too. I couldn't stop their comments, but I could hurt the guys I caught.

Still, it wasn't until a half hour's time had passed that I felt true repercussions. How dare I sit and watch them stretch their groins when there were so many unloved cigarettes waiting to be smoked? That's when the coach approached me and asked me how I was.

"Fine, thanks for asking, Coach," I said.

"Is there a way that I can help you?" he asked, trying not to let my presence bother him. But I could tell it did.

"Yeah, I'm trying out for baseball." At least a dozen players laughed.

I took a long drag on the butt and threw it to the ground. The same move I'd seen the Duke use to great effect in *The Quiet Man*.

The coach looked a little baffled, like maybe this was some kind of joke that his players had put me up to. The coach's name was Frederick Henrick—blond, handsome and athletic. His players called him Barney, although never to his face. I think because his wife's name was Betty. She was rumored to be gorgeous.

I exhaled a last rich cloud of smoke, which tag-teamed with the steam to provide a lasting visual. It was very early March with the temperature near freezing, and the field had a dusting of fresh snow that had fallen in the morning.

I was glad I had my work boots on instead of the cleats the others wore. And I wouldn't have traded my quilted flannel for all their satin jackets.

Henrick scratched his head and said, "Let me ask you something."

"Okay."

"Now, Slim, if you're really trying out, then why were you not stretching?"

"I don't care too much for stretching, Coach, and Slim is not my name." I believed it was a reference to my somewhat ample waistline. Which had filled out quite a bit since I moved out of the Bronx.

Someone yelled, "It's Scooter!"—which made the others laugh.

"What's your real name, Scooter?" Henrick asked.

"That is my real name, Coach." Henrick spun around, checking the faces of his team. A couple players nodded, affirming my statement. The others didn't know.

"And this is not a joke?" he said.

"No, sir."

"Then I'll tell you what there, Scooter. We're about to run a couple laps around the fields. How about coming with us?"

"I'm sorry, Coach, but I can't run."

"Oh?"

"Hurt my leg when I was nine."

"Then how about calisthenics? Can you show me a couple push-ups?"

"I can't. I hurt my hand."

I thought the guy might hit me. I'd heard he used to do some boxing and that he'd been pretty good. A jabber and a mover, kind of like a singles' man. If he hit me, I was ready. He might kick my dirtbag ass, but at least I'd go down swinging.

Instead, he asked me about my bag. "What do you have in there . . . Scooter?"

"My bat."

"Your bat? In an army duffel bag? How about your glove, where's that?"

"I didn't bring one." I still thought he might drill me.

"Kinda tough to play the field without a glove."

"I don't play the field," I said.

"You don't, huh?"

"No, I'm the DH."

The players suppressed laughs with varying degrees of success. Some laughed into brand-new Rawlings mitts. Others turned their heads. If not for my reputation as a puncher, I doubt they would have bothered with the attempts at subterfuge.

The coach bit down on his lip, not to stop the urge to laugh but because he finally got it. I really wasn't kidding. I wanted to DH. He turned to face the team.

"Guys, this young man would like to be our designated hitter. So I'm going to ask him to sit down and smoke some cigarettes while you run, exercise, sweat and work your butts off. Then when the rest of us are done, I'll let the DH take some swings. How does that sound, Scooter?"

I gave a quick nod of my head. Sounded good to me. His sarcasm was so subtle that it had flown right past me. I sat down and lit up while the others ran their laps.

There was a part of me that really wanted to play baseball for the team. I didn't really like the game, but I had financial problems to consider. But I knew my choices weren't good, which is why I'd been providing my own alibi.

Cigarettes, greasy hair, work boots and a flannel. I knew they were mistakes. I'd even worn my thermal undershirt a little high so my gut protruded just a bit. I would give him every reason to cut me from the team. So at least I'd have that much going for me—that I hadn't tried my best.

This Long Island thing had benefits, like no knives or guns in school. Instead, students had their cliques, which were sometimes just as bad. Football cliques and baseball cliques and cliques for school cheerleaders. Math club cliques and chess club cliques as well, to mention just a few.

The clique itself was not as important as the simple need to fit in somewhere. I'd seen kids who'd been cast out and it really wasn't pretty. I think former jocks had it the worst. Their whole persona lay in jock life. And then once that life was over, for whatever reason, that persona was exposed. Like salmon swimming upstream, most of them just never made it.

That's where the extended dirtbag family came in, cradling the castoffs who couldn't fit in anywhere else. Showing them the tools of the trade—the dirty denim jacket and the army surplus clothes. A cheap black concert T-shirt always helped, along with way too many hickeys. That's all there was to it. Cigarettes were optional. It didn't matter if you smoked, just as long as you pretended.

The dirtbag ranks were filled with kids who'd made the teams in junior high. Kids who'd played sports for most of their young lives. Who simply couldn't make the cut at a big school like North Milton. Eight hundred kids in every grade. Kind of tough to beat those odds. Unless you wanted to run track. You might be bored as hell and you might run till you collapsed, but at least you could fit in.

No, I didn't want to get cut, but if I did I was ready. I had the butts, the hair, the limp, the boots, the flannel. Five really good excuses.

I thought I had the talent. All I needed was the shot. This team had no power and I knew that I could help. Their best hitter, Dan McCarthy, was out for three weeks with a broken jaw. They had a couple decent pitchers, but no one overpowering. Not like Lake Grove did. I'd heard they had a guy who threw high nineties and was sure to make the bigs.

Henrick's team was a victim of the school's lacrosse tradition. The lacrosse team got the best athletes, the titles and the glory. The baseball team drew tiny crowds, little press and a few good athletes now and then.

I had never seen lacrosse. It wasn't real big in the Bronx.

I didn't smoke cigarettes as I watched, though the coach had given his approval. I'd already displayed proof of my defiance. Instead, I watched them play. Not bad but nothing great. A group of single hitters swinging late on batting-practice pitches. Taking fifty-mile-an-hour floaters to the opposite field. These guys didn't have a prayer against a guy who threw real heat.

I put the duffel bag on my knee and hoped that I'd be ready. My hand was really hurting and it had been a while since I had swung. But this was my only chance. I'd have to block the pain out.

"Okay, guys!" Henrick yelled. "That's enough. Let's call it quits. Suitor, get the bases. Blaustein and Betcher, get the balls."

What was going on? What had happened to my chance? Perhaps he'd just forgotten. I got up to let him know.

"Coach?"

"Yeah?" he said, turning toward me. "Oh, Scooter, how can I help you?"

"Well, uh, I thought I was going to take some swings."

"Not today there, Slim."

I felt my damn throat tighten up. I willed myself to be a tough guy. For the last seven years I had. But sometimes maturity betrayed me and that little boy came out.

"But you said I could DH."

Henrick shook his head. "You're kidding, right?"

I shook my head and hoped he couldn't see the embryonic tears gaining life in both my eyes.

"Look . . . Scooter . . . go back to the smoke shed. I'm sure you're wanted there. The ball field is for athletes, and . . . I don't want you here."

"You said I could hit." Damn, I know he heard my voice crack.

He turned his back and walked away.

God, where was my fortitude? Had my balls suddenly fallen off or disappeared? I was in a field out in Long Island. This was child's play to a city kid like me. I'd been shot, been pistol-whipped, been beaten up for being white. I'd been through far worse than this. Why was I so scared?

I knew why I was scared. It came to me right then. I was out of money, luck and hope. I needed this one chance.

"You're a goddamn liar, Henrick." It wasn't full-force swearing, but it got the coach's attention. He turned around and glared.

"What did you just say?"

Here goes, I thought. My last chance. I didn't know which path to take. Sincere, just ask him please. Nonchalant, come on, Coach, give a guy some swings. I settled on direct.

"You're a goddamn fuckin' liar." I threw in that extra word for emphasis and I thought it was effective.

The players who'd been walking off had a sudden change of plans. They scurried toward the two of us to see what would transpire. Henrick knew nothing of my record of not playing well with others. But the other players did. Was I going to throw a punch? Or would Henrick fire the shot? A dirtbag had tried to test him once and had to have his nose repaired. Luckily the kid's father was a plastic surgeon and the kid was good as new.

Henrick cracked a smile. Did he appreciate my candor? Were we going to share a laugh and slap each other's backs?

"Go ahead, Slim, grab a bat."

A murmur from the crowd. We had a little showdown there. The dirtbag and the athlete. Pumas versus Timberlands. Like the shoot-out scene from *Shane.* Alan Ladd and Jack Palance.

Two kids asked Henrick for the chance to pitch, as I turned to get my bag. God, my heart was pounding and my hand was having trouble closing. I picked up the duffel and struggled with it slightly, as if it were bolted to the ground. I walked slowly toward home plate.

The coach himself was on the mound. He wasn't about to let a child do a man's job. He didn't want a kid like Betcher or Blaustein to do his dirty work.

Macombs Dam field came rushing back as I took McCovey from his bag. Seven and a half painful years had passed since that fateful day, but it felt like yesterday. Like I was a tiny boy with a sword more myth than fact and I'd never get it off my shoulder.

"Holy shit," one kid said when he saw the size of it.

Even Henrick missed a beat. His eyes opened in surprise for a split second before he found his game face.

If only I was healthy. If I only had my hand. I placed it gently on the bat. Like a decoy on a pond. Meant to create the impression that the thing was usable. But decoys couldn't fly—and my right hand couldn't close.

He went into his windup. Good form, decent kick, fastball, maybe seventy. Hittable, hittable. I swung and almost cried. A line drive into left field, enough to raise some eyebrows, but the pain almost brought me to my knees.

The team whispered to each other and I tried to find the will to place my hand on the handle again.

Henrick kicked and threw. I could tell just by his face that this one would be faster. It came in at almost eighty. It wasn't pitched so much as served. Waist-high and down the middle. A banquet for the batter. A swing, but not a good one. No longer from the heels. I didn't have the strength. Or the threshold to withstand it. Solid contact, up the box, to goddamn center field.

Henrick looked impressed. The players looked unhappy. The right guy wasn't winning. At least not in their minds. I thought I was a failure. If I hadn't used the F word I could have told him I was done.

Maybe I could try again next season, without the greasy hair and cigarettes.

Instead I dug back in. Here it came—low eighties. I lined it foul just wide of third. Damn! McCovey went the other way two times a decade. I'd done it twice on just three swings. I was thoroughly embarrassed.

I dug into my reservoir of nothingness. The place I tried to travel where pain did not exist. Where I visited each time I took Greenberg's weights out of my closet. Where I went to hide the burning, the nausea and the pain. Where I dumped the lactic acid that flowed within my arms.

Henrick wound and fired. Seven times. Mid-eighties every time. I tried to grip the bat. Seven times I swung. Seven times I heard the telltale *crack*. Seven low line drives to right.

Sweat poured down my face, even with the temperature at thirty once the sun had dipped below the trees. A few players clapped for me. I heard minor oohs and aahs. The coach called it a day.

"Come over here," he said.

I placed the bat inside the bag and limped out to see the coach. Oh, no, he had his hand out! Anything but this. He was going to shake my hand.

"Scooter, put it there."

I put it there, and although his grip was not meant to test me, it brought vomit forth so quick I didn't think to fight it. Instead I let it fill my cheeks, like Dizzy Gillespie on a solo, until the burst was over and I drank the vile stuff down. I wouldn't let him see me puke.

The coach shook his head in disbelief. "That's quite a swing you've got."

"Thank you—thank you, Coach," I said, turning my head slowly so he wouldn't catch the scent of puke.

"But it looked like you were having trouble, like you were almost swinging with one hand."

"Um, well, like I said, I hurt my hand."

A lightbulb seemed to click on inside his head. "Which is why you couldn't do the push-ups."

"Yeah."

"And when you said you couldn't run—that limp's for real too?"

"Yes, Coach," I said, my eyes tearing up against my will. "The limp's for real too."

"And your name is really Scooter? That's your given name?"

"Yeah."

"Okay, then, Scooter, see you later."

I turned and limped away, biting down hard on my lip so as to circumvent the crying process.

I was almost out of earshot when I heard Blaustein break the news.

"Coach—that's the guy who hit McCarthy. I saw him last period in metal shop, cutting his cast off with a hacksaw."

[2]

Without a doubt, the old man rescued me as surely as if I'd been caught up in a blaze and he'd given me the breath of life. I was thirteen, without a parent, or a sibling, or a clue and no one else to turn to.

My father was a resident of Morrisania for almost thirty days. His prognosis wasn't good, at least as far as walking went. Eventually, we'd come to look like twins, with matching limps—each a victim of the other's hand. Bookends, in a way, with volumes full of suffering tucked between the two.

With my father on the shelf and my mother on the lam, I would have been bound for social services had Grandpa not showed up. A recluse with a tortured face and past, who cut through mountains of red tape and paperwork by simply not accepting "no."

My father's hand was shaking when he signed away his son, due perhaps to pain, the withdrawal from his pills or the sight of Grandpa in the room. I left the two of them alone, so I don't know what was said, but I know they talked for hours and neither face was dry when I went back into the room.

My father asked the whereabouts of Joe D.'s magic ball and I had to tell a whopper and say I'd lost it in the beating. I deserved his scorn, not sympathy, but there was no reason he should doubt me, not when I had the wounds to prove it. In time the wound on my cheek became an angry scar, a tribute to my former borough. But at the time it seemed a mark of lies and shame, like Hester Prynn's scarlet letter. My grandfather, of course, saw right through me.

For the second time, an accident resulted in homeschooling. The first time I learned about the three R's from my mother, as well as intolerance and hate. Grandpa taught me differently, always borrowing from the game.

Mathematics, history, even science—he found a way to work in baseball themes.

I became something of a math whiz by figuring batting averages and earned run averages, and learned of biology and physics by breaking down the components of a Sandy Koufax curveball. The sad plight of the Negro Leagues told me hard facts about our country's heritage that textbooks failed to mention.

If it was Grandpa's hand that rescued me, then it was my sister's brain that moved us from the Bronx.

My father's swing had changed her in ways beyond my comprehension. I couldn't understand how one blow to the head could manifest itself in so many complications throughout her little body.

Physically she looked the same to me when she was given her release. Except for one eye that seemed to be gazing constantly at a world that was her own. Her hair was still the same—shiny, dark and long. Hair just like my mother's before she'd checked out of our lives. Nose and mouth, teeth and smile—they all seemed to be the same.

The difference in the way she talked was the biggest shock to me. The singsong voice that used to tell on me and call me names was now slurred and very soft, like Pop without his peanuts. I wished that she could have called me names again or tattled on me for stupid things. I would have held on to every insult and taken my punishments with glee.

Her speech, her gait, the way she wrote—all of it had slowed. As did her rate of burning calories, so that she slowly put on weight. A heavy child with a simple mind in a world that could be cruel. Starving for acceptance and affection and finding very little to consume.

Ultimately, it was my father's visit to her new school that resulted in the move. The smell of shit and urine, but most of all a cigarette that a teacher calmly puffed, savoring its smoke, while a child not three feet away banged his head until he bled.

A law was passed in '75 that gave the handicapped more rights. For the first time, federal funding helped these kids escape their zoos. My father tore into his special education research like my mother reviewing high school hoops.

It was strange how quickly cash was saved without my mother's needs. My father was on full pension and the old man helped as well. They set their sights out on Long Island in the town of North Milton. We settled down on the low end of a high-end town in a giant tract of quarter-acre lots and houses not much larger than the one I'd grown up in.

It was just a short walk from the high school, one that focused hard on special needs. My sister would be happy there, in a school free of the crime and hate that plagued the Bronx. And I'd be just another white kid, albeit one with quite a scar and limp.

Grandpa never made it; he died a week before the move. Natural causes were the reason given, but I think it was a broken heart. Broken just by looking out at all the fires consuming blocks that he once risked his life to save. Broken also, I've come to think, by the grandson he had saved. A grandson who sold his Mr. Coffee to get a quick fix from Manny Vasquez in the same abandoned lot on Nelson that he'd awoken in once with a board nailed to his foot.

A few days after Grandpa's funeral, his own place went up in flames. I think he would have rather gone that way, to better know the fate of Katerina, who'd remained his one love until the end.

I guess I had never really seen the Bronx until I left it, looking out the window of our cab as we crossed the Triborough Bridge. Smoke was everywhere, as if from giant industry. But this industry was arson and the smoke we saw was just an average day, just a few of the thirty-four thousand fires that scorched the Bronx in '76.

The situation had grown worse since Nixon eliminated federal spending, putting an end to Bronx renewal funds sometime in '73. The place no longer spiraled downward; it just free fell into an open pit of poverty, gang violence and street drugs.

My father never even mentioned the bridge and roads of Robert Moses that we utilized on the way to our new home. He was stubborn but not crazy, and looking at it burn, I knew you would have to be crazy to remain there—crazy, or black, or brown, or poor.

It was only fifty miles. An hour with no traffic. But it was a whole wide world away. A world of green grass, white skin and smokeless skies—a world where we could thrive.

[3]

The first cut is the deepest. Some teams had just one round of those brutal, life-defining moments. Other sports, like baseball, had a few. For some players it was easy; they were as good as on the team. On the basis of their merit on teams in years past or because they kissed the coach's ass.

For other kids, the total scrubs, it was relatively painless. They knew their chances going in and had accepted life in nerdland. At least these kids had backup plans like college and careers. It was for those poor souls caught in between that cuts could be so damaging. For those were the ones who put their faith in sports and saw their faith squashed like roadkill squirrels, based on a few swings of the bat.

I had been the smart one, prepared with alibis. Other kids didn't have the foresight to let their hair grow long and greasy and smoke butts while on the bench. So when they didn't see their names on Henrick's paper taped to the inner pane of the coaching office glass, their social lives were all but lost. Time to trade the ball field for the smoke shed and accept a smoke and knowing look from those who'd already traveled down that path.

I refused to join the masses who made the trip to Henrick's window before the ring of opening bell. Sprinting for that sheet of paper as if it was a piggy's trough at feeding time, instead of a public gallows, which for most of them it was. I saw Betcher in homeroom; he was one who didn't have to check.

"You make it?" Betcher asked.

"I don't know, I didn't check." Teenage apathy and bravado combined, although deep inside my quilted flannel I knew that I had neither.

"So, you gonna look?"

"Yeah, maybe when I go to lunch." A North Milton indoor record. No one in the school's seventeen-year history had ever made it all the way to lunch without looking. I'd solidified my alibi. Not only was I a dirtbag, I didn't even care enough to check.

By nine o'clock I'd heard rumblings. My name was being tossed around by athletes for something other than my fighting. Which was a first for me. Now I was the kid who swung the giant bat and had hit line drives off of Henrick. Still, according to those guys who'd checked not only for their own names but for mine, the dirtbag didn't make it.

I made the trip at lunchtime. Those guys who'd checked had been correct. I didn't make the team. Henrick couldn't look me in the eye when he saw me through the glass. Instead, he bent down to tie the laces of shoes that looked tightly laced to me. Then he turned and headed for his private shower and I turned to my own private hell.

I shrugged it off in Milton's hallways when asked about the team. I shrugged it off when I helped Patty pick up books she'd dropped and walked her to her class. But I couldn't shrug off the emptiness that clung to me like a parasite. And I couldn't wait for school to end so I could go into my room and use up all my tears. At least I'd get the chance to finally wash my hair.

I was in psychology learning Freud's theory of transference when our teacher, Mrs. Fish, was summoned to the door.

"Scooter?"

"Yes?"

"You're wanted in Dr. Foley's office." The school's director of athletics. A hush fell over the classroom.

Foley's office meant trouble, at least if you weren't a top jock. Which, according to the cut list, I most certainly was not. This guy Foley hated dirtbags, and rumor was he'd once tried to tear the smoke shed down with a winch hooked to his car.

I was escorted to Foley's office by a hulking black custodian named Wally Wheet. Wheet had played defensive end at Alabama and was considered a sure thing for the NFL before a botched neck surgery ended his career. He'd gone from holding sixty thousand fans in the palm of his massive hand to cleaning urinals, but no one dared make fun of him—at least not to his face.

Foley's dark Irish eyes were scowling, as it seemed they always were, when I opened the door. He was partially obscured by stacks of magazines, but I saw that crew cut and those eyes. Magazines stacked at angles that seemed impossible, like Pisa's leaning tower. *Coach,* and *Sport,* and *Coach and Sport,* and others of their kind. Then I saw Janet Lupo's face stare at me from somewhere in the pile—*Playboy*'s Miss November 1975. Okay, maybe I'm kidding about the *Playboy.*

"Come in, Scooter," Foley said, his voice deep and commanding, like Robert Mitchum from the movies. "Okay," I said, then slowly shuffled in, hoping that my thick scar and reputation would precede me. I saw Henrick in the corner of the room.

"Scooter, would you like to take a seat?" Foley asked in such a way I knew that saying no was not an option.

Once I was seated, Foley stood so that both he and Henrick towered over me, like two battleships and one dinghy setting up to make some waves.

"Now, Scooter," Foley said. "Do you mind if I ask you how you got that name?"

"Sure, after Phil Rizzuto. My father idolized the Scooter."

"Couldn't he have named you Phil?" he asked.

"Yes," I said. "I guess he could have." As if I hadn't asked myself the same damn thing a thousand times before.

Foley smiled. "I like that. Myself, I named my son after Mickey Mantle."

"Lifetime average .297, career homers 536."

Foley looked at Henrick with a grin. Had I really made a good impression? But why the hell was I in here?

The proceedings then commenced. Henrick started off the inquisition.

"We've done a little checking on you, and I must say, your past is something of a mystery. But since you've been at this school, we've found a few odd things."

"Oh?" Just how odd, I wondered.

"Yes," said Henrick, pulling out a sheet of paper like an archer sizing up an arrow. "Let's see. In this school year you were detained eleven times and suspended seven others—all for fighting. Including breaking my best player's jaw. Would you like to tell me what all this fighting's for?"

"Not really," I said.

Henrick glanced at a pissed-off Foley and let him take over. Foley paced in a tight circle, then let his voice pick up volume in a hurry. "He said what the hell's the fighting for?"

"No, he asked me if I wanted to tell him, Dr. Foley. It's two completely different things."

I once saw smoke come out of Grandpa Al Lewis's ears on a *Munsters* episode. Foley looked like he might do the same thing in his office without benefit of camera tricks.

"Listen to me, son. I don't know what you got away with in your last school," Foley said, "but here at North Milton that smart mouth is going to cost you. Because here in—" I cut the fuming Irishman off with a little volume of my own.

"I didn't get away with much, Dr. Foley. I got beat up for being white. I got beat up for my name. I got beat up 'cause I limped. And I got this right here (pointing to my cheek) 'cause I kissed a girl. So I'm not all that worried about North Milton."

Henrick thrust his little sheet of paper for the big AD to see, nodded, and then whispered, and I think I heard "the Bronx." Foley looked at me with borderline respect as if looking at a survivor of a shipwreck. I took this as a cue to speak a little more, which I did at a slightly lower volume.

"McCarthy got beat up for calling my little sister names."

Henrick spoke up now. "A broken jaw for that? Is that what all these fights are for?"

"Yeah."

"Doesn't that seem a bit extreme?" he said.

I thought on it and said, "Not really. That's my policy. You hurt her, I hurt you back. McCarthy should have known it too—he just thought I wouldn't call him on it."

Henrick seemed confused. "But all they do is tease her. There's really not a lot of harm in that."

"That's because you don't hear her cry, Coach." Then, "Is there anything on your paper there that says my sister is retarded? Because she is and that's what McCarthy called her. And it hurt. Her and me, it hurt us both."

Henrick sat down. He clearly had not counted on just where this talk had led us. Foley took over again.

"Scooter, let me see your hand." I handed him the good one. "The other one," he said.

The hand was wrapped with an Ace bandage. I had planned to take it off if I'd made the team.

"We checked with the school nurse. She told us that last week you went to the hospital for a broken hand."

I nodded that I had.

"Broken in three places."

"Uh-huh."

"Can I ask you a question, without getting back a useless answer?"

"Yes."

Foley took his time. He was still standing high above me, but he no longer seemed so large.

"Coach Henrick told me about the practice yesterday—about your turn at bat—and what I'd like to know is how the hell you swung a bat so well with a broken hand."

I thought of how best to answer that. "I don't know," I finally said.

"Weren't you in a lot of pain?"

"Yeah, I was," I said.

At this point, Henrick returned to his sheet and stood back up, allowing Foley to sit down, somewhat bewildered at the course of the proceedings.

"Scooter?" Henrick said.

"Yeah?"

"We've also noticed that you're absent quite a bit."

"Yeah, I guess."

"Could you tell us why?"

Let's see. I didn't want to flat-out lie, but I didn't want to spill my guts out either.

"I do some traveling," I finally said.

Henrick flashed a conspiratorial smile and went into litigious over-drive, like he'd just dug up dirt on me.

"Scooter—in these travels of yours—did you ever go to Marist College in Poughkeepsie?"

Uh-oh! This wasn't good. I felt the foundation of my secret life begin to crumble. "Uh, let me see, Poughkeepsie—Poughkeepsie—yeah, I think I have been there."

"About three weeks ago?"

"Yeah, I guess so." He was on to me! He was on to me!

"Do you know who Joe McGann is?"

I squirmed in my seat and I know he saw me do it. Foley no longer looked bewildered. He glared contentedly from behind his giant stacks of magazines.

"I think, uh—yeah. He's a pitcher, right?"

"Yeah, pretty good one too. Has a fastball in the low nineties, good control as well."

I just nodded, but inside I was panicking. My whole web of deceit was being torn apart. But how did Henrick know?

"Did you know McGann played for me about three years ago?"

"Um, no, I didn't." I hated Henrick's smile. Foley's too. I focused on his little plastic cube of family photos, which featured two goofy-looking kids aged maybe ten or twelve. What did Henrick's wife look like anyway? I wondered.

"Did you know that I keep in touch with my former players?"

"Uh, no, but I think that's good you do." He saw right through my weak attempt at kissing ass. He was going to drop the bomb. And when the smoke cleared I was through.

"Thank you, Scooter, I'm glad you think so. Well, anyway, I spoke to Joe last night and he tells me this story about a kid he met."

I put my head down toward my Timberlands. The prick had already cut me from his team. Did he have to do this too?

"See, this kid comes up to him at Marist as he's walking home from class. You with me, Scooter?"

I wanted to take that boot and see how far I could stick it up his ass.

"And this kid propositions him right there on the sidewalk. What do you think he wants?"

I had another Timberland for Foley. Him and his stupid Irish smirk.

"I'll tell you what he wants, Scooter. He wants to pay Joe twenty dollars to throw him twenty fastballs. A dollar a pitch, as hard as he can."

Oh, shit, Pandora's box was open. How would I explain this mess?

Henrick started yelling. "Do you know who this kid was with the giant McCovey bat and the scar on his left cheek and the long hair and the quilted flannel shirt and the limp?"

Damn! Why not just hook my balls up to electrodes and start cranking up the juice? It couldn't hurt me any more than this form of mental torture. I gave them my best yell.

"What do you want from me? I'm not on your team. I'm not hurting anyone."

"I want the truth!" he screamed.

I got up to leave, but my legs were weak with worry. My whole life had been upended. My greatest secret out. My addiction in the open.

Foley stood up now. He seemed calmer, almost kind as he placed his hand upon my arm.

"We just want to hear your story."

"Why?"

"Because I've been involved in athletics for over twenty years and I've never heard a story quite like this. And McGann told Coach Henrick that you've got the best swing he's ever seen."

Was Foley sucking up to me or had he really heard this? After all, I had hit the pitcher pretty hard. What the hell, I thought. I was tired of living out this lie.

"How much truth can you handle?" I said.

"Give me all you've got."

"That's all I do," I said.

"What is?" Henrick asked.

"That. Travel around. Paying guys to throw to me."

Foley said, "Which guys?"

"Guys who throw ninety or above. That's the cutoff point."

Both of them just stared, waiting. Waiting, I guess, for me to fill in a few more blanks.

"I read the papers, *Sporting News,* talk to scouts at college games, find out who throws hard. Then I go and find them . . . and pay them."

"How long have you been doing this?" Henrick asked.

I thought back to that last day of September in 1973. So many things had happened in the span of that one day. Too much for one teenage boy to handle. How I'd needed that release out behind the Highbridge Community Center. How I'd paid Manny to throw me fastballs. How they'd seemed impossible to hit. Until I finally got wood on one and knew I was hooked. Fastballs, always fastballs. No curves or other useless junk.

"I've been doing this since I was thirteen," I said. "Every chance I get. Whenever I have money."

Foley seemed perplexed. "How come you didn't try out last year if you love the game so much?"

"I never said I loved the game."

"You don't?" Henrick asked.

"No. I think it's boring."

They looked at me like scientists trying to identify some hybrid form of life. Just what were they dealing with? What the hell, I thought. I spilled my guts in Foley's office.

"I don't like the game. I don't like fielding, I don't like running, I don't like bunting, I don't like fungoes, I don't like pepper, I don't like pitchers fooling batters, I don't like batters who don't swing, I don't like curves. I don't like sliders. I don't like stretching, running or doing calisthenics. The only thing I like is swinging as hard as I can at a pitcher throwing as hard as he can. That's it. The rest of it is boring."

Foley's mouth was open. Henrick looked genuinely hurt. But man, it felt good to get that off my chest. I wish I'd had the guts to tell my father back in '65. It would have spared me an awful lot of boring games.

Henrick shook his head in disbelief.

"Scooter, if you don't like the game—why did you try out?"

I gave this one some thought. "Two reasons," I said.

"Okay, let's hear them," Foley said.

"I've worked two jobs since I was fourteen and spent every single cent I made and some of it I've stolen. I'll be seventeen in June. I can't shoplift anymore. I can't afford my habit."

School's final bell went off. Through the glass in Foley's door, I saw kids out in the hallway. Tryouts resumed in twenty minutes. I knew the coach would need to go, but he stayed standing right before me. No longer an interrogator, just a teacher doing his best to understand.

He said, "Did you know that there's a batting cage in Selden that goes up to almost ninety? I believe it's just a dollar."

"It's not the same," I said. "I need a real live pitcher. Man versus man. I need to hear the grunt. I need to feel intensity. I need to see his face when that ball goes flying off my bat."

Henrick scratched his head and then sensed my words were incomplete. "You said you had a second reason—besides running out of money?"

"Yeah, I do," I said.

I looked at both their faces. Hanging on my words. What the hell—I'd gone this far, why turn back now?

"I heard that Lake Grove's got a pitcher who throws ninety-eight—and I'd like to try to hit him."

Henrick made a deal with me. A plea bargain more or less, with Foley as the judge, though I doubted he could find room on that desk to strike a gavel. Unless he struck it on his photo cube and spared me another look at his kids.

He would put me on the team—kind of. I would be kind of like a manager, at least until my hand healed with the help of a new cast. I would observe all the practices and do whatever exercise I could. I would be the team's official scorekeeper, at least until my hand healed. After that I might play, providing I turned over a new leaf at North Milton.

No more fighting, no more absences, no more smoking cigarettes. And if I wouldn't cut my hair, would I at least give some thought to washing it?

I shook hands (with my left) with both my new coach and Dr. Foley. Then I started out the door en route to being the best score-keeper I could be.

[4]

Life had changed tremendously since moving from the Bronx. But of all the things that changed, perhaps none was as dramatic as the change inside my father.

He had not forgotten about the Yankees, but he no longer lived or died by box scores. He'd made good on his promise not to go to any games while they rented space at Shea, but the country's bicentennial had brought the Yankees home and in recent months he'd taken to considering a trip to the newly renovated stadium.

Not without some apprehension, though, as the new stadium had cost New York a bundle, at least a hundred million, while the Bronx was dying all around it. The city told storekeepers to try to spruce up their own places, maybe slap on a coat of paint. As if covering up the problem could erase the underlying cause.

Still, the Bombers had responded well, christening their new home with a pennant for the first time since '64. And while my father's whole demeanor wasn't tied directly to the outcomes as it had been when I was young, he did scream just like a child when Chris Chambliss hit the homer to bring the pennant home.

When fans poured onto the field, he got suddenly nostalgic, saying, "I haven't seen a scene like that since that game in '73." Forgetting for a moment, I thought, that the game he spoke of fondly was a part of what must have been the worst day of his life.

He even bought a car, a green 1970 Dodge Dart Swinger, and though he tried hard not to travel over Robert Moses roads, he didn't seem upset when he had to. But only when he had to. Like on weekly trips to New York City, where he spent entire days without explaining why. Sometimes when snow or rainfall was too heavy, he'd drive me and Patty to the high school, even though the school was just a short walk through the woods.

He'd fought back from his injuries without the aid of pills, and though he limped tremendously—even worse than me—I never heard him complain about it or attempt to place the blame on me.

Several times a week he'd drive himself to rehab and try to get that leg to work. Doctors had been baffled by the symptoms that they'd found. Scans came up with nothing except the old fracture that had somewhat healed. But that leg turned several colors and got so cold that we could feel it—it was not just in his mind. RSD, the doctors called it. Reflex sympathetic dystrophy. Which seemed a fancy way of saying, "We don't have a clue."

God, that leg resulted in so much pain for him, all because of me. Sure, the guy had shot me, but that was accidental. My actions had been deliberate and my intentions had been cruel. And for what? For using the N word and for being mean to paper animals.

I used to hate his weakness—his refusal to stand up to my mother. But by hating him I was hating myself as well, for I'd never really stood up to her either. I think that was my mother's gift—she forced men to overlook her faults in favor of that little bit of decency that lingered in her soul.

Her name came up occasionally, usually from my sister. One night she heard President Carter urging spouses who had left their families to hurry up and go back home.

"Does that mean Mommy's coming home?" Patty asked.

My dad said, "I don't think so."

That night I held her in my arms as she cried herself to sleep.

On this night, however, Patty was just fine. Her eyes were fixed on Anson Williams, who played Potsie on TV. *Happy Days* was all the rage in school and Fonzie was the man. But my sister had eyes only for Potsie, and when someone hit him with a dreaded "nerd" reference, she took it personally. Her face was only inches from the screen and it seemed as good a time as any to bring a subject up that had been haunting me. The subject of my father's leg and why he never spoke of it.

"Dad?"

My father looked up from his paper. "Yes, son?" He actually read the whole paper now, instead of just the sports.

"I stayed after school again."

"You weren't fighting, were you?"

"No—but I did get in an argument."

"An argument?" He put the paper down completely. "Nothing serious I hope."

"No, just about baseball."

On-screen the Fonz had just fixed an ailing jukebox with a quick slap of his hand. Patty may have loved her Potsie, but there was no denying Fonzie's skills.

"Heyyy," my sister said, her thumb up just like Fonzie's.

"Heyyy," we both said back.

Our thoughts turned back to baseball. My father looked at me. "Why were you arguing about baseball?"

"Oh, just a difference of opinion that I had with my coach."

"Your coach?"

"Yeah—I—uh—am going to help out the baseball team. Keeping score, picking up the bases, little things like that."

"That's great, Scooter. Getting involved. I'm proud of you."

"The coach says he might be able to let me play in a game one day."

I got a big pat on my shoulder. "Scooter, that is great. But are you sure that you know how to play?"

I thought of how to handle this. I thought a half truce would suffice. "Well, I've been practicing my swing."

My father slapped me on the knee, the good one, and laughed. "Well, I remember the last time that you swung. Boy, you did some damage."

Damn, was he talking about my would-be homer, back in '69, or the number I had done on him in our living room? I couldn't really tell. Neither one seemed like a laughing matter.

"Yeah," I said. "I'm even exercising with the team."

"That's good," my father said. "Now if you'd just lay off the ice cream."

It was true, I loved my ice cream, and my friend Diane worked at Carvel. Possibly my only friend. Sometimes I'd walk up the street and visit her and she'd give me leftover stuff for free.

I thought to make a joke about my diet but stuck to the plan that I had made. I felt I had to know his secret, why he didn't hold a grudge. It was like he was a cult member or something—like those guys who would drink the Jonestown Kool-Aid in 1978.

Grandpa had gone to his grave without ever revealing the origin of his estrangement from my father. I hoped to someday find the courage to ask my father for his take on their fight, but for now it was all I could do to ask about his leg.

I pondered how best to bring the subject up, trying, I think, to tap into the Fonz's vast reservoir of fortitude. Finally, I spoke.

"I ran a mile today."

"You ran?" my father asked, almost loud enough to jar Patty from her closing credits.

"Yeah, but not too fast."

"Did it hurt?" he asked.

"Just a little, not too bad—how 'bout yours?"

"How 'bout—my leg, you mean?"

"Well, yeah."

"Oh, it's okay, Scooter, you know me. I'm getting by with it."

"I don't think so, Dad," I said. "I see it changing colors. I hear you moan sometimes. I don't think it's okay at all."

My father bit his lip in thought. A habit he had all but lost. It was clear my comment got to him.

"Listen, that's my problem, Scooter. No need for you to get upset."

"It isn't just your problem, Dad," I said, trying not to yell but causing Patty's head to turn.

"It's okay, honey," said my father. "It's just Dad and Scooter talking." My sister turned around, watching a huge Kool-Aid jug with legs crashing through a wall. Kool-Aid seemed so innocent before Jonestown.

I did my best to whisper. "It just seems kind of weird, the way you never mention it. The way you don't ever seem mad at me. The way—"

My father cut me off with a gentle hand placed on my shoulder. "Let your sister watch this next show. Then after she gets ready for bed, read her a little story. When she's gone to sleep—you and I will talk."

I did as I was told. Though I stumbled several times as I read *The Lorax* to my sister. Preoccupied with thoughts of the coming conversation. I'd done a little research on that thing my father had. RSD. I knew sometimes sufferers were treated with medicine for psychos. Was that my father's secret? Had he simply ditched narcotics for psychotics and been too zoned out to care? I hoped our talk would tell.

[5]

"You're probably too young to remember what happened to your grandfather, aren't you?"

"I'm not sure, Dad. A lot of things happened to him."

"Well, this would be in 19—64."

"You mean when you took me to Freedomland and we got the ball signed by Joe D.?"

My father smiled and looked at me intently from across our table. The homes on Flintlock Lane weren't large enough to include both a dining room and a kitchen, so this table served dual purposes. Not counting homework, which was always done on it as well.

He said, "That's quite a memory you've got there, son. Do you . . . remember . . . Grandpa's accident?"

"How could I forget it?"

"Do you know how it happened?" he asked, gently pushing open a door that had remained shut throughout my life.

"I don't know. Maybe faulty wiring. Cigarette in bed. Arson. I never really heard."

"But you're pretty sure he got it on the job?" he asked.

"Yeah, what else could it be?" The statement seemed so obvious.

"Scooter, your grandfather was seventy-eight when he died."

"Yeah?"

"He was seventy years old at the time of the accident."

"I guess."

"Pretty old for a fireman, wouldn't you say?"

Damn, that was pretty old to be lugging heavy gear up walk-ups in the Bronx. "Yeah, I guess so, Dad—but I don't understand the point."

"The point is, Scooter—" He paused and bit down on that lip, obviously wondering how best he should proceed. His eyes were clear, not the look of a guy dependent on psychotics.

"The point is," he repeated, "my father wasn't burned while battling a fire."

"He wasn't?" I was shocked.

"No," my father said.

"Then how?"

"He was battling his demons—" I waited in confused silence for my father to continue.

"Your mother wasn't much on cooking, but she occasionally deep-fried stuff. She had a pot of oil on boil.

"I was in the bathroom toweling off when I smelled something awful burning."

I felt my stomach tie itself quickly in a knot.

"I came out to check it out, towel wrapped around my waist, and there he was, just—melting—with this smile stuck on his face.

"I just assumed it was an accident, that the old fool had just messed up. But in the ambulance, just as we pull into Morrisania, I hear the faintest sound—like Pop, you know, selling peanuts."

"Was he trying to talk?" I asked.

"He was making a confession."

I thought, I thought, I thought I knew, but I had promised not to speak.

"He said he had it coming. Which sounded kind of crazy, like he was in shock, you know?"

"Uh-huh."

"The way he took my hand and patted it. Even in his pain, giving me the consolation. And he said—"

I watched as he dabbed his eye.

"He said it was a price he had to pay."

I wished I could have added words, told of secrets that he'd shared. Of little girls in fiery tombs, locked there by my grandfather. A special child. One special kiss. A true love he held on to. He was battling his demons, and on that one day in '64, the demons had won out.

I sat in a state of stunned silence as my father carried on, finishing his father's story.

"I thought my father had gone crazy, which is why I had him sent to Bronx Psychiatric after he was out of danger."

"The one by Freedomland?"

"Yeah, the one by Freedomland. You have quite a memory." My father smiled. The smile seemed out of place, like a pointed paper party hat at a funeral. But the smile wouldn't leave my father's face.

"What's wrong?" I asked.

"I just wished I'd never shared that thought with your mother, about the old man being crazy."

"Why not?"

"Because I think she let it get to her. She visited him just one time in the hospital—about a week after we met Joe D.—and she swore that he was crazy."

"How come? In what way?"

"She said the entire time she was there, he was staring at her with that one eye. Peering through the gauze as if he was trying to stare right through her."

A chill went down my spine. Something told me I had my answer here. The reason for the fight. The bitter separation of father and son. I tried to speak, wondering how best to frame such a delicate question. The sound of my own name startled me.

"Scooter?"

"Huh?"

"Do you remember my father screaming?"

"Um—yeah, kind of," I said. Although I knew it well.

"Well, I think he took a drastic step to get the screams to stop. He said that only through his suffering could he really be forgiven—but for what, he didn't say."

I struggled with my conscience. Should I let him know the truth? Or honor Grandpa's wishes? I decided not to speak of it.

"Dad? What's that have to do with me and you—that night after the game?"

"Everything, Scooter."

He leaned forward in his seat, resting his elbows on the table, close to me.

"Everyone pays for their sins, son, the only question's when. Your grandfather felt he was paying for some terrible sin the only way that he knew how. Even as that bat was shattering my leg, I felt like I was paying for what I'd done to you. An eye for an eye."

I nodded my head, as if I understood, but in truth I found it a bit confusing. That "eye for eye" stuff always seemed at odds with the "turn the other cheek" stuff later in the same book. But at least it wasn't scary. Which is exactly what I found the idea of my grandfather intentionally melting himself, or my father welcoming a crippling injury, to be. And my father wasn't finished.

"I made some mistakes when I was on the job, son. Some very bad mistakes."

I thought back to his hospital confession.

He said, "Mistakes I'm trying to make up for. Which is where I go sometimes—to work with kids who've got drug problems. Trying to pay up for my sins. But—your sister, Scooter—"

"Dad, I don't need to know," I said firmly. "I was only wondering about your leg. I probably shouldn't have said anything."

He didn't even hear my last remark. He was too focused on this multiple confession. He was like a train rolling down a hill without its brakes, hurtling forward without pause, roaring toward its destination, slowing down for no one.

"I thought that it was just a little bump. I saw worse head wounds every day. There wasn't even any blood. I thought that she'd be fine. But—she wasn't, Scooter. They shone that flashlight in her eye—and I saw the way the doctor looked before they rushed her off. I could have sworn that she was—"

"Dead?" I guessed.

"I'd had so much to drink after Vinnie died. I wasn't thinking straight. But I made it to the car. How, I couldn't tell you. I was hurting pretty bad, you know. My leg, I mean."

I nodded, then glanced down at the leg.

"My head was hurting even worse, though. How could I pay for what I'd done? There was only one way. An eye for an eye, Scooter."

"So there wasn't any robbery?"

He sadly shook his head and confirmed my grave suspicion.

"I wanted for my wife and son to receive my full pension. Death in the line of duty."

He smiled. "So imagine my surprise when I woke up at Morrisania to find out Patty and I were both alive. Neither of us quite the same, but at least we're both still here."

I hopped on that last brief moment of optimism. "So everything's forgiven, right, Dad? No more Bible sayings? No more eyes for eyes?"

"Well, Scooter, I've got a certain sense of peace from knowing that your sister needs me here. And I won't do her any good by pulling my hair out or torturing myself."

"You're right, Dad."

"And I don't think I have to worry about Patty swinging that big bat, looking for revenge."

"No, I don't think you will."

"So I've come to the conclusion that whatever price I pay for what I did to her—won't be paid in this life. It will be paid when I am gone."

Oh, no! Eternal damnation. This was even worse than all that eye-for-eye stuff. I used to like the Bible stuff at Sacred Heart, when Jesus talked in parables and spoke of love and peace and redemption for the sinners. But once they started hammering me about the furnaces of hell, I kind of tuned it out. This talk had gotten heavy. It needed to be lightened.

"Dad?"

"Yes, son?"

"I understand why you're concerned, but I think you kind of overlooked an issue here."

"Oh?"

"Yeah, I think when your time comes you're gonna go up to the gates and I think Peter will have two questions for you."

He smiled. Thank goodness. I didn't want another father-son talk for a very, very long time. "Go ahead, son, tell me."

"First, he's gonna ask, 'Why'd you name the poor kid Scooter?' "

A laugh, oh thank God, a laugh. I thought he'd never laugh again. And then I'd be the one atoning for dragging this stuff out of him.

"And what's the second question?"

"Oh, then Peter's gonna throw his hands up in the air and ask, 'Why'd you tag Scooter out at home?' "

[6]

We played our home games at an elementary school. That's still hard for me to figure out. How a high school like North Milton, with money in its town, could have such a rocky, crappy field. The lacrosse team's sod was perfect. Our practice field at Milton looked like a reject from the Bronx.

So we took the bus to Settlecott School and I shut my mouth and listened while my teammates went to any length to avoid talking of this game.

Farrah was the subject of the day, or more precisely, her left nipple. Apparently the blouse she'd worn on *Charlie's Angels* the night before had left little to the imagination. Blaustein swore he saw a "brown eye" through the shirt and McCarthy said her headlights had been on high beams.

Her poster was the rage back then; it seemed that every kid past fourteen had it. It was almost mandatory, like a teenage rite of passage. That adulthood was not possible unless you'd sacrificed your seed at Farrah's paper altar.

As for me, I was monogamous, a loyal Janet Lupo man, Miss November '75. Let the millions ogle Farrah's hair and her nipples that cut glass—I'd take Lupo's auburn hair, smoldering eyes and cleavage I could get lost in. She looked nothing like Nina had; I think that was the point. To pick a total opposite so her memory wouldn't haunt me.

"You check out the Angels last night, Scooter?" Blaustein asked. "Farrah sure was looking good. Man, I'd like to fix her Fawcetts."

"No," I said, "not me. I forgot that they were on."

"Your loss, Scooter, your loss," he said, and with that our talk was over.

I had been watching television, but it wasn't *Charlie's Angels.* Instead, I'd watched in horror as I saw a former neighbor being robbed on a documentary called "The Fire Next Door." Mrs. Sullivan on Davidson Street, who'd been an old friend of my grandfather's, was talking to the cameras while, unbeknownst to her, vandals stole her things. I'd been so caught up in keeping score of baseball games and helping out with Patty that I'd forgotten that the world still turned and that much of it was bad.

I didn't dare share thoughts like these with my new teammates, though. It was tough enough to be the dirtbag with the weight problem, let alone be known as sensitive.

Henrick's voice prevented me from getting deeper into thought.

And prevented lots of others from explaining in great detail what they'd like to do to Farrah.

"We're almost there!" he shouted in Knute Rockne mode. "Let's start thinking about the game. Just think about the fundamentals and don't get intimidated."

Easy to say, impossible to do. For intimidation hung around that bus like a big White Castle fart. I think that's why the team had been so concerned about their manly plans for Farrah. Trying to convince themselves that they were men before going down like children.

Half the team ate eggs like Rocky—raw and in a glass. That was big back then. And like that movie hero, they weren't hoping for a victory when they took the long walk to the field. Such a thought was sheer insanity with Dan Ferraggo on the mound.

Rocky hoped to find the strength to let him go the distance. Our guys hoped to have some luck so that the ball might find their bats.

It didn't happen very often. Ferraggo had been all but untouchable in his junior year. An ERA of under one, six no-hitters in twelve tries and a staggering strikeout ratio of damn near three per inning.

He also hit a lot of batters. A couple every game. That seemed to be the only knock on him, that he could be a little wild. Some claimed his control was perfect, though, and that he hit batters just for fun.

Bayshore had made headlines opening week when they scored a single run off him. A walk, two steals and one passed ball was the only offense they produced. But they celebrated that one run like it was Bobby Thompson's "shot heard 'round the world" in 1951.

When that player came to bat again, he got a fastball to the ribs that sent him to the hospital. When the game was over, Ferraggo caught his catcher with a sucker punch that knocked the kid's front teeth out.

Coach Henrick kind of liked me, even if I hadn't swung the bat since that opening day of tryouts. My cast had just come off and I told him I was ready. He'd given me the uniform of a former player named Silipo, who was now a lineman at Tulane and weighed in around 290. Which meant the thing was like a tent on me, but it was the only one they had that wouldn't show off my love handles or keep my gut from peering out. So I put it on underneath my new team jacket, which was satin and bright green.

It was "colder than a witch's tit" out there, as Salinger might have said. But despite a temperature reading of just forty, I wore nothing underneath my jersey. Just because you never knew. Perhaps Holden Caulfield was a catcher in the rye while I was a mere scorekeeper on the bench, but if opportunity did come knocking, I planned on basking in its heat.

The taunting of my sister, once a maddening rush, had slowed to a mere crawl. Maybe human decency had finally reared its head. Or maybe my knockout of McCarthy, who had been a tough kid of some distinction, had finally served some notice. My sister enjoyed the new-found calm and liked hanging out with me as I did my best at practice. Collecting balls, limping laps, picking up the bases and keeping score at our first two games—which we'd lost, but not by much.

Henrick had explained to me that Patty couldn't travel on our bus. But he said his wife could take her if it was alright with my father. I was finally going to see her! The coach's wife in all her glory. Would she live up to her billing or would she be a disappointment, like Great White Hope Duane Bobick when he got dropped in just one round by Norton?

An army of pro scouts had descended on Settlecott, like a team of Special Forces invading a political hot zone. But instead of green berets, these scouts wore time-honored fishing hats, and instead of M16's, they carried radar guns. A few veteran scouts sat by themselves, not needing technology or social intercourse to help them in their quest. These guys had seen so many pitches, they didn't even bother with the radar—they could guess the speed of fastballs within a mile or two.

It was generally assumed that Ferraggo would skip college. Players on the borderline often opted for college ball, but guys with arms like his went straight to rookie ball. Besides, as time had shown, an arm could be short-lived. Why waste it in a college town when there were dollars waiting elsewhere?

Some Milton guys were claiming that this was their big chance.

McCarthy claimed he'd get to second at the game and then get to third that night. Blaustein, our pitcher for the game, claimed he'd match Ferraggo's every strikeout and walk back to the bus with a trail of scouts clinging to his ass.

No one was talking about the scorekeeper, and what kind of chance he stood.

Keeping score was relatively easy when our team was up at bat. I might as well have marked a "K" down while each guy walked to the plate. A few guys didn't even swing—hoping just to get to first via a free pass. Alas, no free passes were forthcoming, as Ferraggo's heat was not only awesome, it was accurate as well.

I knew I was a Milton guy, but sitting on the bench I found it hard to root for us. The guy was just amazing. Tall and lanky with room to grow, his left arm like a whip. Firing bullets from a sidearm gun, each one in the upper nineties. Our batters were defenseless as those heaters headed toward them. Fearing for their lives and in-school reputations and hoping through some act of God they'd make the slightest contact.

An average high school pitcher threw high seventies, a good one, eighty-five. Our team did well with them. But to guys accustomed to that weak stuff, Ferraggo's ninety-eight was like my father throwing seventy to kids who'd grown accustomed to Big Will.

McCarthy, to his credit, did single off Ferraggo. To his detriment, however, he got to first only by selling out his soul. The same power-hitting righty who'd taken Smithtown's pitcher semi-deep four days before became Buddy Harrelson right before my eyes. Opting for the smallest metal bat we had, then choking up four inches, McCarthy lost the battle before he ever even swung. Sure, he chopped one off the plate and beat it out at first, then jumped into the air like he'd just won Olympic gold. But to me he was a coward.

Besides McCarthy's wimpy single, our team hadn't done a thing. Except throw their helmets and kick the ground, blaming all their woes on just flat-out rotten luck. Blaustein's predictions seemed a bit ambitious. With Lake Grove touching home four times, the scouts weren't exactly lining up to plant smackers on his butt. The mood on Milton's bench, as we sat down to face Ferraggo in the fourth, was mighty glum indeed.

Betcher went down on three straight swings, on one of which I swore his eyes were closed. Ferraggo's thirteenth of the day. He was on course to break his own state record of eighteen, unless God did see fit to intervene. Dewey came up to bat, his hands halfway up a yellow Murcer bat meant for Little League. I'd seen field mice with more guts. Suitor was our next sacrifice and started warming up, swinging four bats at once as if he might convince himself of something. His face told a different story. An expression of sheer terror, as if he was Patty watching Linda Blair's head spin around.

I turned my head back to the game and saw an expression on Coach Henrick's face that would prove to change my life. It wasn't much at all, just one eyebrow raised slightly. But that arched brow was pointed right at me and I heard it loud and clear and I gave a little smile that he correctly read as "Yeah!"

The Lake Grove scorekeeper thought I was joking when I said our replacement guy was me. News that traveled down their bench and produced a round of belly laughs, as Suitor went down on just four pitches and threw his little metal bat into the dirt.

I had declined Henrick's suggestion to take my warm-up swings. Instead, I had studied the delivery a few last times, while Suitor's bat made its feeble stabs. Then I put my head down and closed my eyes. I didn't leave my thinking pose until the umpire yelled, "Who's next?"

When I stood up I heard the laughs, but also one small cheer. My sister, bless her heart. Either too simple in her mind or too pure in her heart to see it was a joke.

The pants sure didn't help. Hanging like a tent from my ass and legs, they made my 210 pounds look like nothing. The sneakers didn't help me out either. I'd purely been a work boot guy, but had bought a new pair of black canvas Chuck Taylors when I'd been allowed back on the team.

If the idea of the fat kid dressed in rags was a funny one, then the scratchy noise on the cheap PA system was the coup de grâce.

I was walking to the plate with my satin jacket on and canvas bag clutched in my hand when I heard the big announcement.

"Now pinch-hitting for North Milton, the scorekeeper, Scooter Reilly." Even the hometown fans found it humorous, laughing their wealthy-doctor laughs and slapping their overpaid-attorney knees.

"Let's go, Scooter!" I heard one say sarcastically. "Go, scorekeeper!" went another. "Hit it with your hair!" a well-kept mother yelled. My sister's voice was loud and clear and filled with pride. "That's my brother, Scooter." I think those laughs that followed hurt worst of all, and as I stood outside the batter's box, I tried to channel every stuck-up face and every derisive little sound into the shape of just one baseball.

The umpire shook me from my trance, saying, "Son, I can't let you bat with that jacket on." Then, "Or hit without a bat."

The jacket was the first to go. I slowly took it off and heard an escalation of reaction, a growing wave of recognition.

"Oh my God," I heard a mother gasp. The same one who'd made the helpful hair suggestion. "Holy shit!" another said, though I didn't catch its origin. The rest were only muttered murmurs.

I had worn only long sleeves since I'd moved out to Long Island. Right about the time I learned I was grotesque. Not due to long hair or scars or labored limps, however, but because of how they'd grown.

I used to try to leave the world behind while I sat inside my room. Tried to exit with my mind as I held the broomstick in my hand. The strand of twine that once held five pounds had become a thick length of rope. And the weight that dangled from it was damn near sixty pounds. Fifty-seven and a half, to be exact, and the tears would start to fall somewhere around the fifth repetition.

I only did Greenberg's exercise when I was sure I was alone. When no one was around to hear my anguished screams. I wasn't satisfied unless I'd wet my pants. For if I still controlled my body's functions, I was not committed to sheer growth. Pain, suffering, torture, growth. There was no other way.

For somewhere in my mind I wanted more than just fastballs cloaked in secrecy. College guys who threw some heat and collected twenty bucks. I had hoped to find a phenom just like this, a guy almost too good to be real. And I planned on hitting him. And I wanted to be ready.

My forearms were bigger than my biceps easily, almost bigger than my head. Knotted corded bands of muscle, rippling through the skin with every slight move from my hand.

Now it was McCovey's turn, and it didn't disappoint. Drawing oohs and aahs from moms and dads who only moments earlier had mocked my name.

I took my place on the left side of the plate, kicking dust with a black Chuck Taylor. Looking out sixty and a half feet at the intense glare of Ferraggo. I knew no curves were coming. No cheating going on. Just power versus power, the way it ought to be. I smirked at him—he smirked back. I got shivers up my spine. This was all the Rocky training scenes I'd seen a dozen times rolled up into one.

"Go, Scooter!" This time it wasn't funny. Coming from behind my back, from right behind home plate. Mrs. Henrick's voice. Mrs. Henrick knew my name! "Come on, Scooter!" My little sister, Patty—as proud as she was beautiful. I swear that I felt warmth right then, even on that dreary afternoon. I felt warmth from right beside them.

I didn't take my eyes off Ferraggo, who was in the middle of his windup. The left arm whipped across that rangy body, the hand just a fuzzy flash of lightning as it released the ball toward home.

I couldn't swing. I had to see it. Looking down as that white flash whizzed by, I felt for just a moment like some tourist looking up at the Sistine Chapel's ceiling wondering, "How the hell'd he do that?" and knowing true artists didn't know. They just did, that's all—and left others to admire them and ask questions in their wake.

I swear that ball was at a hundred when it popped the catcher's mitt. I felt the scouts raise their mental contract offers and could hear a deep sigh of relief from the Lake Grove bench, just to my right. What had they been thinking? That the scorekeeper had a chance? Against Ferraggo? Come on. Reality had disappeared for just a moment and let fantasy move in. But reality was back and it seemed to state quite clearly that no long-haired, limping, fat scorekeeper was going to get a piece of wood on Dan Ferraggo. No matter what his bat or forearms said.

I stepped out of the box for a few seconds. I took a look up at the scouts, who were looking at their radar guns in awe and shaking their heads in disbelief. I looked at my sister and the coach's wife, caught up in the moment. Both thinking I could do it. Rooting hard and quite believingly. Thinking what—that a guy who hadn't played the game since he was nine stood a chance against 100 mph?

I looked just to their left. Where I thought I felt the warmth. A camera, large and boxy, took up most of her face. A movie camera of some kind, but I could see little things behind it. Long dark hair, golden skin, dark eyes that seemed to peek into my soul. Could it, could it, could it be? The umpire said, "Get back in there, son."

I held my bat up higher than I think I ever had. I'd let one pitch go by just for admiration's sake and to see exactly what real heat felt like. Now it was time to do some damage, and every goose bump on my body told me that I could.

If he'd changed speeds just a little, I might still be corkscrewed in the dirt by home plate at Settlecott School. Or if he'd dropped a curve-ball on me, I would have maybe pooped my droopy pants trying to check my swing. But I knew somehow he wouldn't. I knew his pride just wouldn't let him. He saw that big bat as a challenge and I knew he'd answer it with heat.

He didn't disappoint. If anything, this one was even faster. It may have come in at a hundred, but it left McCovey even faster, traveling off that mighty bat like it had a rocket strapped to it.

If somewhere in the game's long history, a baseball's been hit harder, I've yet to hear its tale. Not Mantle at Forbes Field or Reggie Jackson in Detroit. Not those or any mythical story of kids retrieving home-run balls six blocks from the park. I don't buy it for a second. Maybe McCovey's blast at Shea. Maybe, but I doubt it.

For this one was unreal. I stood there and just watched it, savoring the high inside my forearms that made every tear I'd shed and every set of shorts I'd soaked seem like a tiny price to pay.

It was Grandpa's memory that made me run. He said players who admired their blasts were an insult to the game. That to do so was disrespectful not only to the opposing pitcher but to the entire opposing team, every Hall of Famer and to the very game itself.

So I forced myself to run, thinking that my grandfather might be using that one eye's eerie power to look down on me from heaven. I didn't want to disappoint him. So I limped around those bases as the Milton fans went crazy. I was already rounding first when I heard the baseball land, clanging into a metal playground slide, another world away.

No one was going to catch me here; there was no drunk cop to steal my glory. Only a few kids off in the distance, and unless one had a cannon for an arm and could fire it in a hurry, I'd hit home plate standing up, safe by several hundred feet.

A cannon wasn't hanging out on that playground far away. I think the ball was still rolling out there on that playground when I saw third base approaching. Behind it was pure mayhem. My team was lost in hugs, getting farther with their teammates than they had on several dates with girls. I saw a jumping Dr. Foley pumping a hairy arm up toward the sky. Beside him, his younger son, a chubby kid who had found a new role model. Parents who had showered me with ridicule now serving up their cheers.

I would savor that last ninety feet, anticipating heaven when Chuck Taylor stepped on home. A moment eight years in the making. Too bad my father wasn't here. He'd missed out on his son's finest moment because I'd told him not to come. Assured him that I was just the scorekeeper—that I didn't have a chance to play.

I saw Ferraggo backing up the catcher, waiting for a throw that was two football fields away. I couldn't read his face completely, but as I got closer to home plate I think I saw—denial.

The other faces weren't so hard to guess. Patty's was a giveaway. Sheer and total joy. I don't think I'd ever seen her quite so happy—or anyone else for that matter. Her joy was just so beautiful. Mrs. Henrick seemed quite pleased as well. I'd heard Blaustein tell the team the week before that he liked to close his eyes and think of Betty Henrick when he got to second with his girl. Can't say I blame the guy, having seen both the coach's wife up close—and Blaustein's girlfriend. There it was! Home plate! The next stop on the train. I jumped up in the air intent on feeling both sneakers hit that bad boy at exactly the same time. Now I knew what Dorothy meant. There's no place like home, there's no place like home, there's no place like home!

The team came out to hug me. Hell, a hug just wasn't going to do. They put me on their shoulders. Carried me around. I was hailed as a hero by the doctors. Called a champion by the lawyers. Accepted as a slugger by the team mothers. "How about that?" said the PA, very nearly ruining my moment by both jumping on my bandwagon and ripping off Mel Allen's classic line.

Then I saw her face. First it was her camera pointing straight at me until I saw her and just froze. Her smile was warm and gorgeous. I felt it burning down my neck. The camera lowered just a little and where a camera lens had been I saw brown Latino eyes looking at my soul. How had she found me here? Nina, in Long Island. Except—it wasn't her. At least I didn't think so. But I was so caught up by my teammates and emotion that I couldn't know for sure.

Whoever it was, she had been beautiful and she had big-time eyes for me. I hoped to get to say hello, maybe when the game was over. I sat down on the bench. The wood felt like it was buzzing. A few raindrops touched my face. They wouldn't dampen this historical moment. A small kid on a bicycle brought the ball to me. It cost me my first autograph. I heard Ferraggo's fastball pop the glove.

Dr. Foley slapped my back and said in twenty years spent in athletics he had never seen a thing quite like this. His son stood next to him, his mouth agape. Speechless in the face of such a star. His hero was the scorekeeper. Another fastball found its mark.

Coach Henrick gave a tousle to my long, unruly head of hair. "I've got good news and I've got bad news, Scooter," he said.

I said, "Okay, what's the good news?"

Henrick smiled, savoring this special moment. His team was losing 4–1 and didn't have a prayer of winning but he was ecstatic anyway. Ecstatic just for me—and that his intuition had been right. I had deserved a second chance—and that chance was paying off.

"The good news is, twenty baseball scouts are all writing down your name."

I smiled even wider than I had been, which had been pretty wide already. "And the bad news?"

The catcher's glove popped once again. "Strike three!" yelled the umpire.

"The bad news is—"

"What?" I asked, still smiling wide.

"There's no DH in high school ball. Grab a glove, you're in right field."

[7]

No balls were hit my way in a three up, three down inning that saw Blaustein show some stuff. A decent curve, good control and a tiny bit of movement on his fastball. The hard rain held off as well, giving rise to the unlikely hope that I might hit again. The fans were certainly for it, bringing up loud chants of "Scoo-ter! Scoo-ter!"—which I acknowledged with an uneasy smile.

The hope of a Ferraggo-Scooter sequel seemed a little bleaker when Melville went down in the sixth on two strikeouts and a pop-up to the catcher. Ferraggo urged the guy to let it drop foul, but the catcher didn't hear him. I wondered if the poor kid could expect another sucker punch when they got back to Lake Grove.

He had struck out seventeen with one inning left to play. He was a shoo-in for the record, unless two guys in one inning got aluminum on the ball, which seemed a hopeless prospect. My home run had served to fire Ferraggo up, as if to prove it had been lucky and the Milton nine were going down in ever faster fashion.

Lake Grove led off the seventh with a single. The next batter caught a fast ball solid for a line drive to right field. Hey, that's where I was playing! Oh, man, what should I do? It took one hop and came right to me. I didn't even have to move. I prepared to lob it to the infield when I heard someone holler, "Third!"

I took a step and threw it and followed the arc of my own throw. It bounced one time and went right into McCarthy's glove at third, beating the runner by a step.

I hid my limp as best I could as I trotted in from right to sit down on the bench. McCarthy slapped me five, proving forgiveness need not be a trying proposition. The crowd was chanting "Scoo-ter" even though the rain was heavy now and was changing into snow. Henrick slapped my back and beckoned me to turn around.

"See that?" he asked, gesturing to the scouts who were making notes on pads of paper. "Right now everyone is writing how the kid with all that lefty power has a rocket for an arm."

Dewey looked at three straight strikes, each one harder than the last, and Ferraggo tied his record. Suitor headed to the plate, ready to make history with his little metal bat. He'd be Ferraggo's nineteenth victim unless there was a miracle. Or if the umpire called the game. The flakes were fat and heavy and accumulated on our caps as we waited for the moment to unfold.

Ferraggo had other plans, however, and called his catcher to the mound. An argument ensued, bringing out the Lake Grove coach, who quickly joined the verbal fray. The coach and catcher shook their heads—Ferraggo nodded his. At first it seemed quite comical, like Daffy Duck and Bugs arguing over seasons while Elmer stood close by, rifle poised for game. Rabbit season! Duck season! Rabbit season! Duck season!

Their voices started rising and fingers jabbed the air until Ferraggo threw the ball deep into the woods behind first base and went sulking toward his bench. The coach threw up his hands and asked Ferraggo to come back. Betcher practiced bunting in the on-deck circle, which had to be some kind of first in baseball and would have been cause for ridicule if not for the drama unfolding right before us.

Ferraggo stalked back to the mound, the little tantrum-throwing kid who'd been allowed to have his way. The team was called in to huddle out at the mound and, after conferring for a minute, walked back to their places, their expressions a study in bemusement.

The catcher stood up from his spot behind the plate and gestured with his hand. Ferraggo tossed the ball, slow and three feet wide of Betcher's tiny bat. He was going to put him on base. Which he did on three more pitches. An intentional walk.

He did the same to Dewey, calling for the walk and sending one more man to first. Betcher jogged to second, a smile etched on his face.

The plan Ferraggo hatched made no sense to me until Suitor stepped up to the plate with his little metal bat. Henrick spelled it out. "He's loading up the bases so he can set the record with you batting."

"But why, Coach?" I asked, thinking that such a proposition seemed risky, if not genuinely dumb.

"It's his way to get revenge for you making him look bad."

Suitor had two balls on him and the third was on its way. I was putting on my helmet and picking up my bat when the situation truly hit me. He thought I had been lucky! He aimed to show the world that the home run at Settlecott was nothing short of pure freak luck. And the long-haired boy who'd hit it would be exposed as a mere fraud.

Suitor took his base. The pond was full of ducks, as my grandpa used to say. I was taking off my jacket, giving fans a second peek at the freak show that was me, when Henrick yelled to me, "Home run wins the game!" Indeed, a long ball would, and though I'd never given thought of scouts as incentive for my future, the idea did not escape me that another blast might make me rich. Unless Ferraggo threw me curves, in which case they could bolt their checkbooks closed.

The coach's wife had Patty covered with a blanket she had brought. I've heard that athletes tune out fans to focus on the task at hand. I waved to her and smiled, not an athlete after all, I guess. Just a kid who swung a bat. Man versus man, mano a mano, not counting the young lady with the camera who made heat flash down my neck in spite of falling flakes.

That lens was pointed right at me, and though her face was still obscured, I saw her luscious lips clear as day as they mouthed the words "good luck."

I turned to face Ferraggo, McCovey in my hands, forearms poised to strike.

I had paid so much attention to their faces that I hadn't seen the shift. The reason for the huddle—to inflict some shame on me. I'd heard about the Boudreaux shift, meant to stop pull-hitters like Ted Williams. I'd seen the Mets use it at Shea when McCovey was at bat. Loading up the field to pull, daring guys like Ted and Willie to slap one the other way.

Those shifts were strategic plans but also tributes to the hitters' strengths. Admitting to their power and bestowing honor on their bats. This shift was slightly different in that there was no outfielder in right. All three were playing in shallow left field, as if I had two-sewer power. The first baseman stood on first, but his fellow infielders stood on the left-side grass, as if taking grounders from a toddler.

Henrick was beside himself with anger. Foley had to be restrained. This was a knee to the nuts of sportsmanship, a mockery of decency. Lake Grove's coach threw up his hands. He'd tried to stick up for his principles and had been gunned down by Ferraggo. The kid clearly ran their team and this idea had been his own.

I heard Henrick's voice. "Take this asshole deep." I got goose bumps once again. "Come on, Scooter!" A female voice from back behind her camera.

I wish now that I could take it back, the decision I made. I wish I had just swung the bat the way I knew I could. But that damn shift got the best of me the way it ridiculed my pride. Taunting me, begging me to prove that bastard wrong.

Thick snowflakes and the looming of darkness should have made his fastball just a blur. Whipping from the side, like David and his sling. Trying to slay the giant at the plate who cranked McCovey's bat with horror-movie forearms. I swung the mighty bat and felt the glorious glow of impact.

If that ball could have talked, it would have said "screw you" to Ferraggo and his henchmen, who had heeded his wishes. For it flew at rapid pace, cutting through the snow on its way to outer space. Maybe it wasn't quite as far as the one that hit the slide, but I'd still compare it evenly with Mantle's Forbes Field shot. God, if it would just stay fair, the game was history. Two teammates had already scored and

Suitor rounded third. I stood at home like Carlton Fisk in '75's sixth game, urging that ball fair with all my body language, forgetting all about my grandfather's "run it out" philosophy. I never saw it land, no one did, but the umpire yelled, "Foul ball!"

Did this umpire have some special power? Was he a weatherman by trade? If an umpire could check for shoe polish back in game five of '69, then surely this guy could walk two hundred yards to see where it had landed. But it was not to be. So our runners all got back on base and I got back in the box. Glancing at the scouts who were scribbling on their notepads and knowing right away what was on each mind—the first one was no fluke.

The fielders tried to venture back to normal spots, maybe even play me deep to pull. But Ferraggo threw a fit out on the mound, letting loose with middle fingers and a stream of epithets that left no doubt about his feelings for his comrades—or where they ought to play me.

I thought he'd challenge me again, and I wouldn't screw up twice. I didn't need to pull it down the line to prove that he was mine. I merely had to swing that bat and let mathematics do the rest. Force = mass × speed. I could swing a big bat fast. It doesn't get a whole lot simpler.

It never occurred to me that the guy had other plans. For as I felt his eyes bear down on me, my thoughts were purely on the game. Driving home four runs with one giant swing. Feeling the warmth of all my teammates after stepping once again on home. Looking forward to the camera girl's dark mane of hair and the fullness of her lips.

His release was slightly different. He let it go a little earlier. It might have been a curve for all I knew; after all, I'd never seen one from this vantage point. Heat was all I paid for, so heat was all I'd ever seen. If I'd been a better player, instead of just a swinger, I might have checked the ball for spin. If I'd ever studied Bob Gibson or Don Drysdale I might have guessed what was on tap. But I never saw it coming. Not until it hit me.

I raised my shoulder just slightly. I think the movement saved me. The baseball glanced off it before it made impact with my mouth.

My grandpa had been tuned in to his Philco the night Sugar Ray destroyed La Motta. The St. Valentine's Day massacre. He said no matter what Ray did to him he couldn't put "The Bronx Bull" down. I think that story kept me up that day, although tape would later show that my knee briefly touched the ground. I leaned on Willie's bat and all the balls I had to keep from going down.

"Give him air," Henrick said to the teammates who surrounded me. Why weren't they out there kicking ass, sticking up for me?

I couldn't let them take me out, not while I still had swings to give. A little time and I'd be fine. I just had to clear my head. Life, I knew from living it, was based mainly on perception. I knew that I was screwed up bad, but if I could just put on an air of physical stability, the coach might leave me in. And the next pitch would be mine.

I tried to probe my gums with just my tongue to take stock of dental damage, but the damn tongue let me down. It wouldn't move that way. So I probed with just a finger. Two front teeth gone. There, on the ground, one front tooth sitting in a silver-dollar pool of bright red blood atop the dusting of new snow. I stuck it in my sneaker in case it could be saved. I searched in vain for the other front tooth. Perhaps I swallowed it.

Foley was upon me now, checking on my status, asking me what day it was, where we were and who he was. I tried to speak but couldn't—my mouth had filled with blood. Streaming, flowing rapidly, filling my cheeks up to near Gillespie-esque proportions. Damn, if I didn't answer Foley I'd never finish this at bat. I sucked the red stuff down, chugging my own lifeblood like the Duke in *Rio Bravo* tossing back a brew.

"Tuesday . . . Settlecott School . . . Dr. Foley." My teammates cheered my coherency and Foley asked me further questions, each one prompting a preemptive swig of blood before I mumbled my answer.

I told Foley that I felt fine and that the ball had hit my shoulder. While in truth fine was a long, long way from where I was and my mouth was in some trouble. "Damn," my own blood made me sick, like licking iron skillets. Where was all the blood coming from and would it ever stop?

"Play ball!" the umpire finally yelled, with darkness fast descending. Ferraggo had a record still to chase, and I had bases up in front of me that badly needed clearing. One of us would dine on victory, the other taste defeat.

The umpire tried to grab my bat, but I beat him to it. I felt the thick wood in my hands and dug a canvas sneaker into the frosted batter's box. I raised that barrel tall and proud and looked out at—mass confusion.

Ferraggo screamed more epithets and Lake Grove's coach stormed the plate, meeting Henrick there. An argument ensued; the key point seemed to be that my turn at bat was done. Henrick broke the news. "Scooter, go to first," he said.

"I don't want to go to first," I said. "I want my turn at bat."

"You can't bat anymore, Scooter."

I let another mouthful of blood go sliding down my throat. "Why not?"

"Because those are the rules."

"The rules are wrong," I said, then gulped more blood down. I was feeling queasy now, having drunk a lot of it.

Now the umpire stepped up to me and said, "Take your base now, son."

"But I want my turn at bat," I said, no longer bothering to swallow. This time I let it all ooze out, spraying red with every word. "He threw at me. Don't reward the guy. I should get my choice, and I choose to take my cuts."

My argument was logical but defied the rules of baseball. By now the blood was coming freely down my chin, dripping on my gray North Milton jersey. My head was finally clearing and I read the situation for exactly what it was. I had been hit on purpose in the face with a deadly high-speed weapon. My tongue was cut in half, split straight down the middle and was squirting blood into my mouth at a rate too fast to swallow. And for this—I got to go to first. Whoopee! I took my goddamn base, squirting blood between my missing teeth like the big leaguers do tobacco juice.

Blaustein took strike one. I let blood spill on first base. A second strike popped the catcher's glove. One pitch from the record. Blaustein stepped out of the box to adjust his batting glove. As if it made a difference.

I thought about an argument my father used to have with Grandpa. Back when I was young. Beanballs were the topic. Chin music. High heat. My father found them brutal; my grandfather, a big proponent of the Negro Leagues, which used them frequently, thought them unfortunate but necessary. "A guy's gotta take a ball on the chin once in a while," Grandpa said. "Gotta take it for the team."

It made no sense when I was four; it made less sense at seventeen. Neither did years of batters' manic charges to avenge pitchers' dirty deeds. In all the years I'd seen the game I'd seen the charge yield very poor results. He'd either get out there and miss with his punch, get caught from behind by the catcher, or get the worst of it from a pitcher who had sixty feet six inches to prepare a battle plan. At least Marichal had shown the sense to use a bat. So if indeed he never made the Hall of Fame, he'd be paying quite a price for using common sense.

I used to analyze those situations and thought if a player wanted vengeance, he merely had to wait . . . Blaustein was back in now, Ferraggo kicked his leg—and I took off for the mound. Blaustein took a feeble swipe, the record was Ferraggo's—and Ferraggo's ass was mine.

I had my arms hooked around his waist before he had a clue. The third baseman saw my takeoff and was closing in on me. I had to make my move. I don't know why I wrapped him up when throwing punches was my style. I didn't dare wait longer or the team would grab me and this chance would go to waste.

I acted on pure instinct, squatting low and arching high and letting go of him when he was on a fast trip backward, high above my head. I never saw him land, but I heard the scream on impact. Injury seemed likely, but I couldn't dwell on it. I had one punch I had to land, and I dropped that damn third baseman who had played me on the grass.

It was my last act of the season, but at least I'd made it count.

[8]

It had never crossed my mind as I made my mad dash for the mound that there would be hell to pay. My physical status at the time would surely be a cause for leniency. My tongue took almost forty stitches, and despite the fact that a top surgeon did the work, the tongue was numb and doughy and made my words sound awful dumb. Patty tried to comfort me by saying I sounded just like Rocky.

I thought I'd be alright. Detention for a couple days, maybe miss a game or two. Nothing more than that. I'd only served up just deserts, and besides, I was a star.

Instead, I got a full dose of reality, which tasted every bit as vile and left me feeling just as queasy as the blood that I'd sucked down.

I was finished for the season. Kicked off the team for just one lousy fight. One I hadn't even started. It was blatantly unfair. I'd seen lots of baseball fights and never saw a single player kicked off the team. Hell, Marichal had used a bat and only missed eight games.

Foley said the price was fair considering what I'd done. Ferraggo's collarbone was broken—a brilliant season finished and a career in jeopardy.

I think Henrick took it harder than I did. I swear there were tears in his eyes when he told me, "We'll get 'em next year."

Except there wouldn't be a next year. Not as far as baseball was concerned. I'd had my moment of true greatness and it left me feeling flat. Years of screaming in my room, fighting through the pain, pissing on myself. Traveling, lying, stealing. For what? For a home run and a foul ball and a tongue that didn't work? For a few brief chants from some local businessmen who might talk about the ball I'd hit but not care about my life?

Screw them. Screw baseball. Screw the scouts that wrote their little letters to the school and placed phone calls to my house. I wouldn't allow them to find out that I couldn't touch a curve or field a ball or run the bases. I was giving up their stupid game—and I was going to kick my habit.

It was all McCovey's fault, both the man and his damn bat. I wondered where I'd be if not for that one lousy night at Shea. If my dad had only known that Robert Moses built the place. If I hadn't seen that ball McCovey hit, sailing off into my future.

There would have been no Little League fiasco. Sure, my father had been drunk and thrown a knuckleball to Schwartz, but there would have been no lucky hit of mine and no mad race for home plate. No home run to steal from me, no dream to go unfulfilled.

Maybe I'd have Nina, too, and our one kiss would have grown. I threw away the words that Grandpa gave me when I threw away my chance at love. Instead, I chose her brother and overlooked his ruining of lives for the mere fact that he threw ninety.

That bat had destroyed both my sister's brain and my father's leg. It took me so long just to come to terms with all the damage it had done.

I put the bat up in the attic along with Janet Lupo's *Playboy* and made a solemn vow not to use either one again. And I broke Hank Greenberg's broomstick and tried not to think about my forearms. Like a junkie with his track marks, my arms' grotesque proportions were a sobering reminder of a past that I needed to let die.

As spring gave way to summer, I felt my life was in a vacuum. Nothing seemed to matter. I was dying on the vine. No one dared pick on my sister and no one made fun of my tongue. I didn't give them chances, though, for I rarely spoke a word. Only to my sister. After all, what could she say? She sounded stupid too. I grew my hair out even longer. I wore my front tooth as an earring. I was a scary-looking bastard with a mighty reputation with a bat and with my hands. Kids moved out of my way when I came limping down the hall. They didn't need to, though. I wasn't interested in fighting. I wasn't interested in anything. I was safe in paradise and I didn't give a crap.

[9]

Son of Sam was everywhere. At least that's what Patty thought. She was terrified of him but obsessed at the same time. She loved the TV news and flicked through every channel to see who had new scoops on this guy who stalked New York.

I told her not to worry, that this weirdo only cared about young lovers parked in cars. He didn't hunt down good girls in Long Island—only bad girls in the city. It all seemed so ridiculous, assuaging teenage fears. But God, she took it seriously, and during that long summer Tom Brokaw and Dan Rather replaced Potsie in her heart.

The Bronx was in the news, and not just because of Reggie Jackson. The newest Yankee had raised the ire of all his teammates when he insulted Thurman Munson and raised the fists of Billy Martin when he didn't hustle for a ball. Only my dad's friend Elston Howard and the legendary Yogi, who had become a Yankee coach, prevented further damage.

After seven years of burning, a new Bronx arson squad was formed. After seven years of burning, the president stopped by for a visit, and in the wake of that historic trip the media came calling.

A few weeks later, with the Yankees in the Series, television cameras showed the world exactly how bad the situation was. Just blocks from the refurbished park, an elementary school spewed fire and smoke throughout the broadcast, prompting announcer Howard Cosell to let the world in on a secret: "The Bronx is burning."

The Yankees won that Series, their first since '62, courtesy of Reggie, whose three titanic homers in game six made him a legend for the ages. I saw it on the news. I couldn't bear to watch the games for fear that I might cry. Jackson's every blast would be like a laugh right in my face. A taunting reminder of what once was mine. Like a sick letter from a former friend. "I'm screwing your wife and it feels great." Yeah, I know it does. I was there once too. Remember?

. . .

I rarely saw my father that last half of '77. He might show up to eat dinner, something I had made. Grilled cheese or TV dinners or I'd order up a pizza. Once I made peanut butter and banana and my dad said it tasted awful. He didn't mean it to be hurtful, but it hurt me just the same. I didn't blame my dad, though. How could he have known about his son's emotional attachment to a sandwich he had eaten during game three of the World Series back in '69?

My father spent increasingly more time in the city working with the addicts, atoning for his sins. It became my summer job watching after Patty, and I think I would have been okay if not for that movie and that song.

The movie? It was *Star Wars*—my sister absolutely loved it. I thought it was okay the first time I saw it, even if I had to stand for hours on a line that wrapped around the theater. It wasn't Rocky versus Creed, but I thought it wasn't bad—that first time I saw it.

After that, the whole scenario got old to me real quick. But Patty's love continued. When it came to Luke and Obi-Wan and those little android guys, my sister was insatiable. Every weekend was the same. My dad would drop us off at seven, like we were on a date, and pick us up at nine.

I began dreading Friday nights. While my dirtbag friends were out at Hammerhead's drinking beer with fake ID's and watching Twisted Sister, I was stuck in cinematic purgatory.

One rainy day in late October, the exterminator came. Seems there'd been some roaches found in paradise and the Orkin guy came running to the rescue. My father had his city trip to make and the bug guy needed space, so my father dropped us off at the new multiplex in Commack and said he'd see us in eight hours.

The first six were the longest hours in history. Three straight showings of *Star Wars*—enough to make me wish I'd gotten McCovey from the attic so I could beat the crap out of the screen.

I begged for sympathy. With a tongue that was finally showing life, so it didn't sound so bad. "Anything but this," I said to Patty. "I'll do anything you want, just don't make me watch this movie."

So Patty got my front-tooth earring and we snuck into a different show. We saw the last hour and a half of *Looking for Mr. Goodbar* and, boy, was that an error. I liked it, sure, don't get me wrong, but still it haunted me. Her Son of Sam obsession had been bad enough. But after she saw *Goodbar* I had to hold her hand at night for weeks and assure her that neither Richard Gere nor Tom Berenger was coming after her. Even worse, my sister, innocent and pure, started asking about sex.

The song was even worse. If I'd had the strength to turn back time I would have walked out of that record store without purchasing the song. It seemed so harmless, though. How could I have known that it would try my patience, pound my ears and test my sanity?

I'd heard Patty sing it once or twice, off key but really cute. So I bought the single for her and, man, it made her day. My father wasn't there, as usual, but had he been I'd have made him proud. Patty hugged me hard; she wasn't used to getting gifts. We may have had only twelve hundred square feet, but Long Island wasn't cheap. My father had his pension, but all the work he did with addicts was for free and we just barely made ends meet.

I almost let a tear drop when I heard her sing those first few words. "So many nights I sit by my window."

She sang it with her eyes closed, really belting out the words, believing every lyric until I believed as well. After all I'd done for her, I almost felt as if she was singing "You Light Up My Life" just for me. It was really beautiful. Off key but beautiful.

I walked into my room, truly touched, ready to take on U.S. history. I opened up my book, took a couple notes. I heard the needle of her record player drop. "So many nights I sit by my window." Wow, she was really singing her heart out. "You give me hope to carry ooooonnnn."

I didn't own a record player. Or a record for that matter. I only had my grandfather's ancient Philco, which I'd been given when he died, along with all his Joe D. memorabilia. I kept the radio and sold the rest, procuring myself a grand total of twenty-four Manny Vasquez fastballs back in early '74. I'd give anything to have all that stuff back now. The Philco only got a couple stations. Despite my long hair and dirtbag image, I didn't really like too much hard rock. Led Zeppelin was like cigarettes to me. People just assumed I liked them because all the dirtbags did.

What I really liked was country. WHN on AM. It was kind of hit or miss. I'd turn off "Rhinestone Cowboy" in a second, but I loved to hear the good stuff. I hoped for good stuff now—no offense to Glen Campbell—and I hit the jackpot with ol' Waylon. I turned ol' Waylon up until that Philco was on ten.

Damn, I could still hear my sister! Waylon was like Pop the peanut guy, barely audible. My sister was like a barker with a megaphone—get your peanuts here! I tried to drown her out by singing with ol' Waylon. His song ended moments later. I heard the proud voice of Campbell. "I've been walking these streets so long—singing the same old song." It was time to rake the leaves.

Even with the rustle of the colored leaves and a brisk November wind, I could still hear Patty's voice, never letting up. Giving each new playing of the song her best rendition with a voice that never seemed to tire. I think if I'd had the strength to turn back time, I'd have taken a bat to Pat Boone's 'nads around 1955.

By mid-December I was at a breaking point. I'd seen *Star Wars* twenty-seven times and listened to young, attractive, wholesome Debbie Boone far, far more than that. I thought I might snap. I even yelled once at my sister and could barely live with the ensuing guilt.

That song was like Poe's "Tell-Tale Heart" in that it almost drove me mad. Unlike that fine story, though, the sounds I heard were not my conscience but a real-life symphony of saccharine, complete with sickening strings.

I had to wrest myself free from its vinyl grip. But how? I thought of simply stealing it and letting it fly into the sump by Milton. Or breaking it in pieces and setting up the scene to make it look like robbery. No, my dad would figure that one out. After all, he was a cop and I was sure he'd done more in his career than shoot his son and turn his back on drug deals.

Finally I used the skills I'd learned in electronics shop. I pulled a couple wires and bingo—no more Debbie Boone. Instead, I heard my sister's sobs. Soft at first, then louder, like the singing down in Who-ville on that famous Christmas Day. It drew the attention of my father, who'd been doing paperwork downstairs. He wasn't electroni-cally inclined, though, and after a few more minutes of Patty's sob-bing, I came to save the day. And got punished for it.

"How could you play such a mean trick on your sister?" my father asked.

"I don't know," I said, feeling really bad, looking at her shake, my tooth earring out of place on her pretty, pudgy face.

My father shook his head, contemplating action.

"Patty, do you think Scooter should be punished?"

"No," she said, smiling at me now, unable to sustain the slightest bit of anger.

"Well, that's too bad," my father said, "because I disagree. Scooter is going to take you wherever you want to go tomorrow night."

"Yeah!" my sister said.

Oh, no, her brother thought.

"Where would you like to go with Scooter?"

"*Star Wars!*"

Damn! Of all the rotten luck. Of all the rotten timing. *Saturday Night Fever* had just come out a week before and it had become an immediate sensation. A hit so big it changed the world—or at least my part of Long Island. I'm not sure Highbridge felt the impact, but North Milton did. My fellow smoke shed guys, the dirtbags, who'd pledged allegiance to hard rock, were now jumping ship to disco.

John Travolta single-handedly had made guido-ism cool. Some guys turned hard-core guido right away. Hippie hair gave way to blow-dried bouffants or feathered layers. Zeppelin T-shirts were replaced by silk button-downs meant to show off newly purchased gold medallions. Some guys I knew were bi-musical. Twisted Sister on a Friday night, a mirrored hanging ball and lit-up dance floor on a Saturday.

If North Milton had a slight case of Travolta fever, Lake Grove's was epidemic. It was like a disco bomb had just been dropped and their school was the epicenter. Everyone was hit. My town got the fallout. We were worse off than we'd been, and some of the clothing trends and hairstyles that *Fever* left behind would prove embarrassing in family albums, but nothing terminal.

Lake Grove had it bad, though. I was there to see it at the Smith Haven Mall, which showed two movies every night. That night in mid-December, those two movies were *Fever* with its line snaked out the door . . . and *Star Wars,* now in its seventh month on the big screen, whose audience had dwindled to me, my sister, and a random assortment of big-time science nerds.

Several hundred guidos sat next door getting pumped up by Travolta as he carried paint through Brooklyn's streets, strutting to the Bee Gees. As if it was Stallone doing one-armed push-ups, for crying out loud.

"Scooter, turn around." The voice was right behind me. Wait, I knew that voice. I'd heard it cheer for me. I felt a hot flash shoot down my neck. I quickly turned around to see a face I'd only seen in partial glimpses. The face behind the camera. Her eyes, dark and sensual. Her hair, a long dark mane that spilled over her left shoulder. Her full and luscious lips were whispering my name.

"Scooter, Scooter."

I was like a deer caught in the glare of Obi-Wan's light saber. I tried to talk but couldn't. She looked so much like Nina. Enough to pass for sisters.

"Remember me?" she asked.

I nodded but was speechless. Patty broke the silence.

"Nina, Nina, how are you?"

"I'm fine, honey, but I'm not Nina," the girl gently said. "How have you been, Patty?"

My sister turned back to the screen and in an instant was swept away by the cinematic flair of Mark Hamill. How did Patty know this person? Of course—the game. They'd been sitting next to each other.

"You drive here?" the girl asked, her voice an urgent plea.

"No, my dad drove me." There, my first words to this mystery girl and they were absolutely rotten.

"You got five dollars?" I began to fumble with my wallet. "Not for me," she said. "For you."

"I don't understand."

"Leave now and get a cab." She was almost pleading with me.

"Why?"

"The movie next door lets out in ten minutes. At least a dozen guys want to mess you up. Leave before they get you."

I didn't want to leave. I didn't care if I got beat up. I wanted to stay inside that theater looking at this beauty's face as *Star Wars* shone upon it. The movie wasn't so bad after all, as long as I had my back turned to it.

"Please, Scooter, go. I don't want to see you hurt."

"You don't?" I asked, impressed as hell.

"No. Just do me one small favor first," she said, handing me a pen and her ticket stub for *Fever.*

"Okay."

"Please write down your number. I wanna call you sometime."

I wrote it down with shaking hands. I had a gang of angry guidos out to get me and I was nervous about a girl. I handed her that stub and urged my sister out of her seat. She was slightly less than happy, until I told her if we didn't leave we might be Son of Sam's next victims.

It wasn't until that cab had us out on Jericho that I thought about that stub. How I felt when I had touched it. How I felt when I returned it, following my hurried scribble. How I felt when she had touched me. Had she? Had she? Yes—I thought she had. And I thought it was intentional. Intentional and wonderful.

I fell asleep that night to the sounds of Debbie Boone. I could have tried to drown her out with the Philco to my ear, but in truth, on this night I found Debbie kind of comforting. The words now had new meaning and my life had found new light.

I thought about that number and how I hoped it would be used. I had let my love for Nina Vasquez go up in flames in favor of a fastball, but now my head was clear and my heart was open to the idea of second chances.

"I've been thinking about your touch," she said. Her very first line. Even before "Hello." I was captured right away.

I said, "You mean—"

"At the movies, when you touched me."

"Oh, man," I said. "I've been thinking about it too. But—didn't you touch me?"

"I think we touched each other. Maybe I touched your hand, but I think you touched my heart."

"I did?"

"Yes, you did—can I ask you a question? I know it might sound silly."

"Sure, go ahead."

"Do you believe in destiny?" Her voice was but a whisper, but I heard it loud and clear.

"I'm not sure," I said. "Do you?"

"How about love at first sight?"

"Um—"

"How about grabbing hold of little things and making them get bigger, growing in your grasp until they're so big that they might burst?"

"Uhh—"

She laughed. "Oh, my God, you must think I'm talking about your dick!"

I was so stunned I couldn't answer.

"No, no, no," she said. "I'm talking about the little things—a touch, a glance or just a . . . feeling—that tell you something special's there."

"Yeah, yeah, I do," I said. "I do believe in that. How little things mean a lot."

"Oh, good, otherwise we might as well hang up. I mean, you probably think I'm crazy giving you a warning in the theater and then calling you up to talk about our fingers touching."

"No, I don't think you're crazy. I think that's really nice."

"Listen, Scooter, I don't want to get all weird on you, but I've been trying to call you up."

"You have?" I said.

"Yeah, a couple, three times, but your number isn't listed. And no one seems to know you. You don't think I'm weird yet, do you?"

"No."

"What if I told you that I used to watch you every day? Would you think that's weird?"

I had to think about that one for a second. I did think it was weird but in a good way.

"A little weird, I guess," I finally said, "but also kind of impossible. I would have seen you. Believe me, I could never miss you." Yes! There it was, the boldest line I'd ever used.

"Scooter . . ." A really sexy whisper. A little on the weird side too, but a weird that I could live with.

"Yeah?"

"I used to see you on the video. Remember me with the camera at your game?"

"Uh-huh."

"I used to watch it every day. Not looking for your home run, even though it was awesome. Maybe you could watch it here someday. Would you like to?"

"Um, uh . . . yeah," I said.

"Do you know what I was looking at?"

"No."

"I was looking at you look at me. Just for that brief moment. I used to look at that tape every day just to see that moment. Rewind it, play it, rewind it. Just to see you look at me. And only after several weeks did I admit it to myself, that there was something special there. It may not have been love at first sight, but I knew it was something."

That was when I promised Grandpa's ghost that I would hold on tight this time.

I barely knew this girl. I hadn't even learned her name. I'd only seen her twice, but I was in deep like, bordering on love, right away. I closed my eyes to picture her, and Nina came to mind. But this new girl was different and it wasn't just the accent, pure Long Island. She seemed more confident, more sure of what she wanted. Had this been my stoop in '69, when I was convalescing in my house, she would have pushed my mom right off it and demanded to be seen.

I was so taken with her words that I forgot about my tongue. Granted, I'd only said "uh-huh" and other phrases of equal distinction, but I hadn't been self-conscious.

The talk lasted fifteen minutes. I thought of each and every one, turning it over in my mind like a rotisserie of affection. Letting my feelings touch each word, making sure every one was good and warm before I nodded off.

She said she'd call again. When? She didn't say. I couldn't miss that call. Not now that I knew little things meant so much. I practiced what I'd say, rehearsing like an actor. Running through my lines until I knew all of them by heart. I got my big chance the next day. I grabbed the phone on the fourth ring.

"Hello, Scooter?"

It was her. The mystery girl.

"What's your name?" I asked.

"Angela," she said.

"Are you from Puerto Rico, you know, your family?"

"Puerto Rican?" she laughed. "With a name like Antonelli?"

"My mother used to get them confused."

"Does your mother know you've got a girlfriend?"

"I don't think so."

"Oh." I sensed her disappointment. "I thought you mighta told her about me."

"I think it might be tough to tell her."

"Why? Too scared?"

"No, because she walked out on the family four years ago."

"Oh, I'm sorry," she said. "Wanna tell me why?"

"It's a long story."

"I've got all the time you need, Scooter."

So I let her have it. All of it. It felt damn good to do. I'd held so much in for so long. My thoughts were like one of those wire snakes trapped in a salted-peanuts can, the cap slowly coming unscrewed. Slow, slow, then boing! This is my life.

It was like going to a therapist, but one who really cared. One who didn't charge a dime and didn't stop a session in mid-revelation due to a clock's one extra tick.

I think I heard her cringe when I told her of my leg, and she seemed at a loss for words when she learned of Patty's fate.

So I did. Because she'd asked me to. Because no one ever had before. I told her of Patty's sweetness, of her innocence and faith. How she sometimes seemed too pure for this cruel world with its hurtful words and hate. How she thrived on the slightest display of affection and wanted so badly just to please. How beautiful I thought she was but how remarks about her weight were enough to make her cry. How words of heartless pricks could cut her to the bone as sure as any switchblade used in Highbridge.

I confessed to my guilt. How I was torn between emotions. Between taking care of Patty and having some life of my own. Was that too much to ask? Her condition was partially my fault, but I longed for independence.

"Scooter, I think I've got a plan," she said.

"What is it?"

"I want to see you. I'm not going to lie to you. I told my mother all about you and at first she was kind of shocked, but I told her all good things. She wants to have you over and she wants to cook for you. But your father isn't home much and you can't go out without your sister. Is that right?"

"Pretty much."

"So bring your sister with you."

My face lit up, then dimmed down quite quick. "I don't have a ride."

"I'll pick you up," Angela said. "Six o'clock tomorrow. That sound good?"

"Yeah—great."

"So, I'll see you tomorrow?"

"Yeah."

"Okay, I'd better go."

"Wait, wait," I said, then paused for an awkward moment while I thought about what she'd said. "Angela?"

"Yeah, Scooter?"

"Remember what you asked about, if my mother knew I had a girl-friend?"

"Yeah?"

"Is that—what you are?"

"Only if you want, Scooter. We can just be friends if you're more comfortable—but you'll be missing out."

"No, that's okay. I'm comfortable, I think, being . . . more than friends."

"Good. Because you have no idea what I have in store for you."

"Really?" This was quite possibly the greatest news I'd ever heard.

"Really. No idea at all." Sounded like I might be sliding into second soon. Pulling the strings of Angela Antonelli's sweater puppets. I could almost feel them in my hand.

Her voice jarred me from my imaginary feel-copping process. She said, "It's kind of like *West Side Story*, isn't it?"

"You mean a North Milton boy and the hottest girl in Lake Grove?"

"Exactly." Then she sang a few bars from a song that must have been from the movie, but I'm not really sure, as I'd never actually seen it.

"Angela?"

"Yes, my Jet?" Yeah, the song said something about being a Jet.

"Why was your mother so shocked—you know, to hear about me?"

She laughed as if the very thought of me not knowing was prepos-terous. "Come on, don't kid like that."

"I'm not."

"You really don't know?"

"No."

"Come on, don't kid me."

"I swear, I'm not kidding."

"Scooter—my brother is Dan Ferraggo."

[11]

She drove a candy-apple-red '68 Plymouth Barracuda, almost the spitting image of the car my mother had. The one my dad drove into the pole in his attempt to pay his tab for Patty. An eye for an eye.

She looked good behind the wheel—pretty, sexy, confident, wearing a body-hugging red sweater that showcased her impressive physical assets. A jolly Santa on each breast. Damn! How could I even hope to get to second with my sister Patty hanging around?

"You like Skynyrd?" Angela asked.

The real answer was kinda, but that's not the one I gave, seeing as they were on the eight-track at the moment. "Definitely," I said and tossed my hair to the "Simple Man" guitar solo just to show her I meant business.

"I love your hair," she said.

"I love yours too."

Angela checked her rearview. "I love your hair too, Patty."

"Thank you," Patty said. "I made something for you."

The something she spoke of was a papier-mâché angel that she'd made in art class. The type of simple project that any child could do, but infused with the type of love that no professional artisan could duplicate.

"Well, I'll look forward to opening it when we get to my house."

"I wrapped it myself."

"Patty, what's that hanging from your ear?"

"Scooter's tooth," my sister said, lifting her hair to show it off as if she had the Hope diamond hanging from her lobe.

"My most prized possession," I said, shaking my head. "And I gave it up for a Diane Keaton movie."

"Scooter, let me see you smile," Angela said.

I flashed a gap-toothed grin.

"Sexxxy," she said.

"Really?" I asked.

"Yeah, really," then, "I'm a little tired of these guys. See what other tapes are in the glove box."

I opened up the box and reached into a treasure trove of country outlaws. Waylon. Willie. Johnny Cash. David Allan Coe.

"Are these all yours?" I asked in disbelief.

"You bet they are. You're looking at the only country fan at Lake Grove."

I laughed. "You're looking at the only country fan at Milton."

Out went Skynyrd. In went Willie. We sang poorly but in unison. "If you had not have fallen, then I would not have found you. Angel flying too close to the ground."

I had been teetering already. Willie sealed the deal. I was hopelessly in love and I didn't plan on letting go.

She lived in a house a little smaller than my own. A thousand square feet max. The living room was cluttered with trophies and awards—an altar to her brother. Amid framed articles and photos of Dan the Man, arranged in no particular order on a background of warped brown paneling, I saw a little shot of Angela in a white communion outfit. She looked nothing like her brother and they didn't share a name. Angela was dark of skin; Dan could pass for Irish.

I saw a folded flag in a frame and a photo of a soldier and was trying to match up features when Angela's mother greeted me.

"So, this is your new boyfriend?" she asked. "Five thousand guineas at your school and you hafta pick this guy." Then she laughed, shook my hand and said, "Welcome to our home."

Angie's mother was something of a study in contrasts on that night of our first meeting. Her hair and makeup were perfect, if a bit overdone, but she was dressed in a plain gray sweatsuit, remarkable only for the daringly low hand-ripped neckline that drew instant attention to a gold St. Christopher medallion that seemed in danger of being smothered by a slightly more mature version of her daughter's breasts.

She was young, too young, it seemed, maybe thirty-five. Skin darker than her son's but a few shades paler than her daughter's. Angie looked ready for Old Fezziwig's Christmas blast—her mom looked like she was ready to pump a little iron.

Angie put her arm around me. "Mom, this is my new boyfriend, Scooter."

Angie placed her other arm around Patty, who thrived on the attention. "And this pretty girl is Scooter's sister, Patty."

"Well, hello there, Patty. Isn't that a pretty earring?"

"Thank you. I have a present for you."

Angie's mother unwrapped the gift and marveled at the angel as if it was the Mona Lisa.

"Well, isn't that beautiful," she said. "It will look just perfect on top of our tree."

Patty smiled serenely, floating on a calming pool of compliments. A place she didn't get to hang out very often. "It's Scooter's tooth," she said.

"Well, I'll be," the mother said. "Isn't that a coincidence?" She waited a beat. "My Danny's got a bracelet made out of his own collarbone."

She waited for a second, long enough to make me squirm, and then let go a raucous laugh.

She put an arm around me. "Angie says you'd like to see the hit you got off Danny."

"Yeah, if it isn't any trouble, Mrs.—"

"Oh, just call me Tina. Everybody does."

"Okay."

"Now we just got this extension on our house," she said as she led me down the hall.

"Mom, I'm gonna take Patty to my room so I can do her nails."

"Okay, and I'll put on Scooter's tape. Come on, Scooter."

So I let Tina escort me down the hall, painfully aware of the bobbing braless breast by my side making random contact with my elbow.

"Danny bought this room with his signing bonus. I'm so sorry he's not here. He would have loved to see you."

"Me? Are you sure?"

"Oh, yes. He has nothing but respect for you and I know he feels just terrible that he let that one pitch get away."

I smiled a tight-lipped smile.

She continued, saying, "As I'm sure you must feel for letting your temper get away from you. Okay, let me see."

She began looking through a stack of tapes.

"William Floyd, Smithtown West. Here it is—North Milton."

"Is that a Sony Betamax?" I asked.

"Yes, indeed it is, Scooter. The one Reggie Jackson does commercials for." She put in the tape.

"I hear they're really great." I was trying to sound nonchalant but found it hard to do. When she bent to put the tape in, her left breast became partially exposed. Exposed enough to offer up a nipple that I could probably hit a golf ball off of.

"Oh, they are great," she said, and for just a horny second, I thought she meant her boobs.

"Only problem is we record so many things that I sometimes ruin Danny's games—let's see—"

A blazing fastball popped the catcher's glove. I'd forgotten just how fast he was. And I suddenly wished that I still played the game, that none of this had happened.

"If you want it to go faster, you just jump up and press this button, okay?"

"Okay, thanks."

"Have fun. I'll be out here cooking. I'm preparing a couple dishes for you."

Then I was alone in a room Dan Ferraggo's bonus money paid for, where I'd just seen my first live breast. Watching a videotape of the only game of my high school career.

I got off the couch to press fast-forward, as it seemed early in the game, and with all respect to Dan, the only fastball of his I wished to see was the one that had traveled six hundred feet in the opposite direction.

There! There! There I was. Approaching the plate with McCovey in a bag and my green satin warm-up jacket on. It all came racing back. The forearms. The gasps. The first hundred-mile-an-hour heater.

My heart pounded in my chest. Shivers up my spine. Dryness in my throat. God, it all looked so damn good, like an ice-cold beer at the old stadium on a brutal summer day. I remembered why I loved it so. Why I'd put myself through all the pain.

The camera zoomed in on my face. I saw the look I gave her. When I thought I'd seen the ghost of Nina. No wonder she had read so much into the expression on my face. I looked like a man in love.

Here comes the pitch, and *crack,* there goes that damn ball. I got every bit of that one. The camera shakes and loses sight of that damn ball, but I can hear gasps rising from the crowd and I hear my sister scream and I hear the coach's wife say, "Holy shit!" And then the screen goes fuzzy and hey, there is Tina on TV, her head bobbing up and down, her tongue and lips doing things to some guy that I didn't think were possible.

Whoa, apparently she *had* taped over Danny's game. I wanted to fast-forward—I swear I did—and I know it would have been the proper thing to do. But I didn't move an inch. Well, part of me did. Moved a couple inches. But the rest of me was stationary, looking at my girlfriend's mother do things I'd only seen pencil sketches of in my mother's *Joy of Sex.*

Things had progressed so much in such a short time. A few short minutes earlier, I'd had my first visual encounter with a breast. Just a brief encounter. Now I had the time to study both breasts in striking detail. It was like she'd been given Janet Lupo's breasts and then glued on Farrah's nipples.

Tina called my name from down the hall.

"Scooter?"

"Uh, yeah?" I called.

"How's everything in there?"

"Um, it looks—really good."

"Just call me if you want me."

"Okay."

I watched another minute, enough to know that she had her tech-

nique down pat. This woman had experience. I heard her walking
down the hall.

"Scooter, dinner's ready."

Tina had gone to great lengths to make our dinner a diverse cultural
affair. She'd made corned beef and cabbage, as well as Irish soda bread,
to commemorate my Irish heritage and spaghetti with Italian sausage
to pay tribute to her own family's homeland.

I smiled at Patty, who was eating her spaghetti like she always
did—like Tramp from the Walt Disney film.

"How is it?" Angela asked her.

"Mmm," Patty said. I liked her nails a lot. Little rainbows on
each one.

I tried to look at Tina, but every time she put a sausage in her
mouth I had to turn my head.

[12]

Flintlock Lane was not prone to huge displays of holiday regalia.
Every other house or so had a string of multicolored lights over the
garage or zigzagged in no particular arrangement around the hedges.

It had snowed a week before, but rain and sun and dirt and garbage
had turned the white stuff into a winter not-so-wonderland. Still, I
felt a little of the season's magic work its way into my bones as I listened to Cash sing "Little Drummer Boy" and watched my girlfriend
take the corners like a pro. When she pulled into my drive I couldn't
help but think that the love I felt was real and that the future would
embrace us.

Not a single Christmas light was up, just the dull glow of the streetlight to act as a beacon for us.

Angie smiled at Patty and said, "Did you have fun tonight?"

"Yeah, lots of fun," Patty said, admiring her painted nails as she
had done throughout the drive.

"Would you do me a favor, then?"

"Okay."

"How about going inside and listening to Debbie Boone so I can talk to Scooter outside, okay?"

Patty looked a little apprehensive.

I told her, "It's okay, honey, I'll be right out here. Go ahead, I'll be inside in just a sec."

"You sure?" my sister asked.

"I promise."

Angela said, "I promise too. Cross my heart."

"Hope to die?"

"Hope to die," said Angela.

"Okay," said Patty. "Only because you crossed your heart."

We watched her slowly climb the stairs to my house, both of us smiling at her gentle ways as she turned and waved to us, pointing to her nails as she did it.

"She's really sweet," Angie said.

"Yeah, she's a pain, but she's my sister."

"What's she so afraid of?"

"You're going to laugh," I said.

"Promise."

"She's afraid of Son of Sam."

Angie laughed. "Son of Sam? But he was caught in August. That little pudgy guy."

"Hey, I know it's weird," I said, "but she thinks he's still out there, that they caught the wrong guy somehow."

"Poor kid."

"Yeah, I know. I have to hold her hand at night sometimes."

Angie's eyes were different now. Illuminated by the streetlight, they seemed to be seductive. "So, Scooter, will you hold my hand when I'm scared?"

I knew there was a line in there someplace, but I simply couldn't find it. So I opted for my faithful standby. "Uh-huh."

"You sure you've never had a girlfriend?"

"No, I mean yeah, I'm sure, kinda."

"Did you ever kiss this kinda girl?"

"Only once," I said.

"Did you—you know—get to second with her—or third?"

"No, no, no," I said. "Not even close to them."

"So you got picked off at first, huh?"

She licked her full, soft lips, the lips that looked like Nina's. I thought my chances for a good-night kiss were looking pretty decent, and I wondered if I closed my eyes if her lips would taste like Nina's.

But damn, back then at Yankee Stadium I had full use of my tongue. I'd been able to respond. What if I tried to kiss and couldn't physically pull it off?

"So, Scooter?"

"Yeah?"

"Patty said your mother used to have a car like this."

"Uh-huh." Thank goodness we were off that whole "bases" subject so I could relax again and let my "uh-huhs" flow out naturally.

"Do you think she still drives it somewhere?"

"I doubt it."

"Oh, why's that?"

"That's the one my father drove into the pole."

Angie nodded. "After he brought your sister to the hospital?"

"Right. After I smashed his leg with the baseball bat."

"Which—you did because—you didn't tell me this."

"Because he broke my sister's skull."

"Scooter?"

"Yeah?"

"Your family's a little fucking weird."

I laughed. She did too. She had a way of breaking straight through tension, of putting me at ease.

Angie touched my hand, bringing me straight back to the Smith Haven Mall Theater, where a little thing had happened that meant an awful lot. Like Nina's leg touching mine in '69, a gesture that went unnoticed in that room, let alone this world, but one that meant so much to me.

"Scooter?"

"Yeah?"

"Did you like your mother's car?"

"I don't really know. She only let me ride in it twice."

"You ever check out her backseat?"

I'd heard about those lines. Double contenders, I think. Or double cassandras, or—double—entendres, that's it.

"Scooter?"

"Uh-huh?"

"I'm giving you a hint."

"You are?" She started climbing over the front seat with grace and speed and I tried to follow suit. Damn, my foot was stuck and my foot was numb, so I didn't know it until I'd fought for several seconds.

"Scooter, use the door."

Which I did, but as I closed it I became suddenly aware of a second toe that I could feel. My right pinky toe. It had some feeling.

"Are you sure you've never had a real girlfriend, one that you could—do things with?"

"Uh-huh."

"Is that how your forearms got so big—some special exercise you have?"

"I do have a special exercise," I said excitedly. "When I was just a little—" I had no idea it was a joke until Angie started laughing.

"Relax, Scooter, I'm not going to hurt you. Not unless you ask me to."

"Okay."

"God, you're awful fidgety. Don't you like sitting here with me?"

I saw a couple fellow dirtbags walking down the street. Or maybe *former* dirtbags would be more accurate, as they had blow-dried bouffants now and were walking like they had the Bee Gees' sound track implanted in their brains.

I guess I had to tell her. She would find out anyway eventually.

"I do like being here with you," I said. "It's just that, I, uh—"

"Go on, Scooter, you can tell me anything."

"I know. It's just that, well, ever since that ball hit me, I can't really—use my tongue too well."

"Can I see it?"

"Now?"

"Sure, whip it out."

I stuck it out and saw her squint to see the scars that crisscrossed it. Like a child's picture torn up in a tantrum and pieced together with Scotch tape.

"That's okay," Angie said.

"It is?"

"Sure, because I've got a tongue that works just fine and I'll do all the work."

"Really?"

"Trust me."

I think there are two disparate origins when it comes to big first kisses. Some first kisses are well thought out, aggressively pursued and executed like a redneck bagging bucks. Others are innocent victims of affection. Spontaneous eruptions of desire that arrive without warning. Like my kiss at Yankee Stadium. Mythical. Magical.

That's how this was going to be. Sure, we were in the backseat, and sure, she'd made suggestive comments like that one about my mother's ass, but nonetheless this was spontaneous. The way I closed my eyes actually out of instinct. The way I leaned in oh so slightly, waiting for the soft scent of her Spearmint breath to trigger further motion. I parted my lips just slightly, knowing she would do the work.

A pounding on the window startled me from my state of near bliss, interrupting my life's second kiss just before it got started. At first I thought it was the former dirtbags, trying to get me to see the light, to change my ways, to embrace the guido way of life.

Instead, I saw Patty. She wasn't pounding either, as I had initially thought. Tapping meekly would be more accurate. She had this look of immense concern etched into her features. Angie opened her door.

Patty fumbled for words. "Um, um, you shouldn't be out here, Scooter."

"I'll be right in, hon," I said, trying to be patient but really resenting her presence at that moment.

"But he's going to get you."

"Who?" said Angie. I envied Santa, with his face on Angie's breast. Why couldn't I be Santa?

"Son of Sam," my sister solemnly replied. Angie tried to repress a laugh, but failed.

My sister failed to see the humor. "Scooter says he attacks lovers parked in cars. You two are parked in a car and—and—you're in love." A tear fell from her gentle eye and streaked her innocent face. My romantic night was at an end.

[13]

The ringing awoke me somewhere around nine, interrupting a dream I was having about either Angie or her mother.

"Hello, is Scooter there?" A voice I didn't know, the accent was New England.

"This is Scooter."

"Scooter, this is Jim McGonigle, North Milton's wrestling coach."

"Oh, hello—what can I do for you?"

"Well, we just lost a starter to an injury and we're looking for a new guy."

I thought it was a joke. "Coach, that's nice of you to think of me, but I'm not into wrestling." Actually, I caught the pro stuff every now and then at midnight on Channel 9 and kind of liked it, but I had a feeling that delivering flying elbows and hitting guys with chairs wasn't what this guy meant.

"Scooter, I happened to be at your game last spring and couldn't help but notice how good your technique was on your takedown of that pitcher. I think you'd be an asset to the team. Besides, it would get you in great shape for the baseball season."

"Um, uh, let me think . . ." I said.

"How about watching a practice to see if you like it?"

"Um, okay," I said.

"Practice starts right around twelve."

I figured, what the hell? Why not? So somewhere after eleven, I laced up my Timberlands and limped on over to the school. It was the darnedest thing. Three toes had some feeling. I wasn't really sure because I'd been too wrapped up in love to truly document my finding, but I thought when I'd been mere inches from those luscious lips that I had, just for a moment, felt sensation in my heel.

I'd been limping as a way of life since I was nine years old, but apparently my leg felt better when I was either really mad at pitchers or really horny in a car. Could those two factors be worked into some new form of therapy?

The basketball team had practice in the main gym and was working on a few new twists for their big showdown with Lake Grove. In an average year, the Milton team fulfilled the Dago's theory about white boys, orange balls and decent schools, but this year's team was different. They were legitimate contenders for the Suffolk County crown and had built a rivalry with Lake Grove that threatened to get ugly. The big game was set for Friday night, December 23rd, and anyone who was anyone was expected to show up there. Angie begged me not to go, thinking that an angry crew of guidos might be in Milton's gym to welcome me. Besides, we had tentatively set that date for a romantic pre–Christmas Eve dinner.

I watched a little roundball, staying there just long enough to attract glances from the team. Henrick coached the junior varsity. He gave a little wave and asked, "Scooter, what brings you here?"

"I'm thinking about wrestling."

His face expressed surprise. "Good way to get in shape for baseball."

"I guess—see you later."

I had never been downstairs where Milton's wrestlers toiled. Their room was called "the Dungeon," which I'd assumed was just for fun, until I got down there. Damn, the place was hot and the B.O. was repulsive. That critique coming from a guy who'd been known to skip a shower from time to time.

I'd seen these wrestlers around school, and they seemed kind of like a cult. Like a cult that could use a decent meal. Guys were known to starve themselves to make some kind of weight limit. They sucked on lemons, spit in cups, and wore silver rubber suits, all so they could earn the privilege of rolling around a mat with other guys, ending up in positions that didn't seem all that different from my mother's sex manual.

A voice called out my name. "Scooter!" New England accent— New Hampshire maybe—somewhere way up north. Coach McGonigle. "Glad you could make it."

"This doesn't seem like too much fun."

"How much you weigh there, Scooter?"

"I don't know. Two ten, two fifteen. Maybe a little more with all the Christmas junk I've eaten."

"I figure we'll get you down to one seventy-seven within a month."

"That's over thirty pounds."

"I know. Some exercise, a couple sweatshirts. We'll melt the fat right off. All you'll need is headgear, some wrestling shoes and a haircut."

I saw Coach Henrick as I left.

"So, you think you're going to wrestle?"

"Sure."

"When do you start?"

"As soon as monkeys fly out of my butt. See you, Coach."

[14]

My father left at five—for where he didn't say. The phone rang an hour later, tearing me away from a new book called *The Shining* that Angie said I had to read.

"Hello?"

"Scooter, this is Angie. I think we need to talk." Her voice seemed cold and distant, not at all the one that I'd fallen for so quickly.

"O—K," I said. "What do you want to talk about?"

"Not on the phone. I need to say something to your face. How soon can you be here?"

"I don't know. It all depends on how quickly I get a ride. It could take fifteen minutes; it could take hours. Could you—maybe pick me up?"

"Yes I *could*, but I *won't*. Not after what you did."

What did I do? What did I do? I really didn't know. Damn. Patty was in her room; she'd been in there for hours. She'd go crazy if I left her. Darkness was upon us and Son of Sam was still out there—at least in Patty's mind. I gently tapped her door.

"Patty?" Nothing. Just KC and the Sunshine Band wafting through the door.

"Patty?" I knocked a little harder. I'd be damned if I was going to let KC drown me out. "Patty, open up. Open up!"

KC went way down. "What?" my sister yelled, her voice not all that audible between the music and the door.

"Could you open the door?"

"Scooter, I'm busy," she said. She usually soaked up any drop of affection, but now my attempt just slid right off her, like an indictment on Dick Nixon.

"Listen, Patty, I've got to go somewhere really important, and I'm not going to be able to bring you with me, okay?"

"Okay."

Wait a second, maybe she hadn't heard me right.

"Patty, I'm going to leave for a few hours by myself. Are you okay with that?"

"Uh-huh."

"Patty, I know you get scared, but—"

"Go ahead," cutting off my sentence in mid-concern. "Have fun. I'll be okay here."

"You sure?" I yelled.

" 'Bye."

I lucked out, catching a ride right away from Mrs. Thompson, a lunch lady at the high school, who dropped me off a mere half mile from Angie's.

What exactly had I done? The question pounded at my brain as I walked the last few blocks, feeling something in the sole of my right foot for the first time since I'd been shot.

What the hell was wrong? I thought as I rang her doorbell twice. I saw a Christmas tree through a window, its lights a flashing blue that seemed more big-city Las Vegas than little town of Bethlehem.

I saw Angie emerging from the darkened hall, a can of some kind in one hand, an unknown object in the other. She didn't seem too happy. The flashing blue shed some light on what was in her hands. A Billy Beer in one and, oh shit, she had a beta tape held in the other.

"Hi, Angie, how are you?" I asked when she pushed the front door open.

"I know," was all she said.

"Um, uh—" Not the best defense, but all I could muster.

"I know about the tape," she said, waving it around like a hotshot trial attorney showing off Exhibit A.

"The one where I hit the home run?" I asked, my attempt at nonchalance being spoiled by my quavering voice.

"The one with my mother!"

"I'm not sure I under—"

"Don't bullshit me, Scooter!" she screamed. "I saw the tape this morning. Trying to look at you when you looked at me, so I rewound the tape. And what did I see? Go ahead, Scooter, tell me. What did I see?"

"Um, your mom." I stepped into the house, not wanting her whole neighborhood to be aware of her mother's oral talents.

"Exactly. My mom. And what was Mommy doing?"

"Angie, come on," I said, pleading for some sanity.

"Go ahead now, Scooter, tell me what you saw Mommy do?"

I didn't tell her anything.

"Tell me what you saw!"

I looked straight down at my shoes.

I just saw a flash of her arm in motion and instinctively brought my arm up, concerned that she would hit me. Instead, I saw a full can of Billy Beer sail through the air, pirouetting clumsily in flight, until it crashed into the wall, sending the contents of what was arguably the world's worst-tasting brew splattering in all directions.

"Angie, that's enough!" I yelled, taking the offensive. "It was *your* house. *Your* tape. *Your* tape player. *Your* mother who escorted me in there. *Your* mother who taped over my home run. *Your* mother with the guy."

"Yeah, maybe that was my mother. Maybe it was my mother who worked her ass off her whole life to put a roof over my head. Maybe I prefer a mom like mine to a mom who leaves her family. With her daughter in intensive care. With a husband who can't walk."

Damn, I made her cry. "Come here, come here," I said. She took a step away and then let laughter soothe her pain.

"Look, our first fight. I bet you won't forget it."

"Probably not," I said.

"Can I have a hug?" I opened up for her and held her close to me.

She stepped back and looked at me, a smile lighting up her face. "Ya wanna watch it?"

"Watch what?" I asked. "The tape?"

"Ya wanna?"

"No," I laughed. "That's crazy."

"Come on, I know you want to."

"Angie." An official whine. "How many of those Billy Beers you drink?"

"More than just a couple." She grabbed me by the arm. "Come on, maybe I can pick up a couple pointers."

"Do you think my mother's pretty?" Angie whispered, her mouth dangerously close to mine, the cheap taste of Billy Beer seeming like a vintage French Bordeaux to my uneducated nose. Billy Beer was damn sexy as far as I was concerned.

"What?" I'd completely forgotten what she'd asked me.

"Do you think my mother's pretty?"

It was hard for me to really tell, based on her small-screen likeness. Her head was moving far too rapidly for me to really get a good take on her. I tried to remember what she looked like, but my memories of her had been dominated by the exposed breasts and her on-screen talents. I certainly didn't want to offend Angie, though. I was already in some hot water for the voyeuristic video viewing. So I opted for a safe answer.

"Yes, she is pretty."

"Prettier than me?" Angie asked, inching her body ever closer, so that, oh, God, our legs were touching. My body felt electric once again, like it had during game three in '69. I felt instantly transported to Nina's tattered love seat. It was classic déjà vu, except I didn't have a peanut-butter-and-banana sandwich or a paper plate with which to hide my erection.

Still, that seemed such a minor detail. Her mouth was so near. Her leg was touching mine. The scene was so romantic. My grandfather, bless his heart, had been wrong. There were second chances at first love.

And second chances at lost kisses. No little sister to ruin the big moment. She was safe up in her room, listening to the tender stylings of KC and the Sunshine Band—while I was on the couch with Angie, leaning in, mouth open, eyes closed, in mid-big-kiss delivery. I may have had a tongue that didn't work, but I drew comfort from the assurance that Angie's tongue worked just fine and that she'd do all the work.

I felt the top button of my Levi's give way and a zipper going down.

"Huh."

"Shh," Angie whispered. "Just lean back and enjoy it. I told you I'd do all the work."

My first gut reaction upon this unexpected invitation into the world of oral sex was that I may have overestimated the importance of Nina's sandwich.

My goodness, it felt good. Wait a second, too good. Way, way too good. Things were happening way too fast. I had to push back nature's flow. But how?

I opened my eyes and, leaning forward, took in the visual. Nature's flow was calling and seeing only made things worse. Was this a talent passed down through the genes? Their techniques were very similar.

I looked quickly at the screen to verify my findings. Yes, similar indeed.

I closed my eyes and tried to think of something, anything, to make the moment last.

While in the throes of passion, my answer came to me. Yogi! Yeah! Yogi! With his hand around a Yoo-hoo. Sudsing up his underarm, singing in the shower. Walking out to get the paper clad only in house slippers.

Damn! It was no use. Even Yogi Berra couldn't fight off Mother Nature. Not while Angie's tongue was working on me like she was Rocky on the speedbag. Forget spitting thunder and crapping lightning—this was real talent.

Wait! I had the answer. I'd had it all along. Just like Dorothy and her ruby slippers. She had Good Witch Glinda; I had Dago Vinnie. Who had given me Joe Torre's card, which I carried every day. I didn't have to reach for it; it was with me in my head. So while Angie carried off her big first kiss of sorts, I called on Torre's powers.

Torre, with his Flintstone beard, the kind that grew out every inning. Torre squatting low behind the plate—wearing only Yogi's slippers. Yes, that one was a keeper. Could it be, yes, it was, nature's flow receding, or at the very worst, holding steady. Torre was doing the trick! Joe Torre, the National League MVP back in '71, had never been more valuable than he was on Angela Antonelli's couch in her tiny run-down house on the poor side of Lake Grove. He was kicking Mother Nature's ass. Reminding me of a classic war film I had seen in the last days of the Crest. I shut my eyes even tighter and thought of its battle cry, which I changed to meet my needs. "Torre. Torre. Torre."

On it went for the better part of a minute, maybe more. No, probably not—a minute might be stretching it. But that minute was all I needed. I opened my eyes and realized I was going to participate in that rarest of sexual victories—the mutual orgasm. Me and . . . the guy on television.

"Scooter?"

"Huh?"

"You alright? You looked like you were in a trance."

"Uh, yeah, I'm good, I'm really good."

"How about me?" Angie asked. "Was I good too? Really good?"

"Oh, yeah."

"Better than my mom?"

"Definitely!" I realized that if I wanted her to eventually finish what she'd started, I would be well served to tell a little lie there.

"Did you want me to stop?"

"No, never."

She laughed. "I didn't want to, but as I was doing that to you, I realized I never even apologized for everything."

"Everything?"

"Yeah, you know, everything my brother did to you."

"Oh, that's okay," I said. I couldn't help but think that this conversation could have waited. That damn Torre messed it up for me. Taking my mind off business when the deal was so close to being closed. I looked down at my most private part. Shrinking rapidly. Melting like the Wicked Witch. The on-screen sex, having reached its conclusion, had stopped as well. The Lake Grove–North Milton game was on. Top of the seventh.

"No, it's not okay, Scooter." Her eyes looked damp and sad.

"Angie, I don't understand."

"Look at what he did to you. Because of him, you lost your teeth, even though I kind of like it. Because of him, you talk a little different, even though I think your voice is sexy. Because of him, you can't even kiss your girlfriend, even though I can do all of the work. Right?"

"Almost all of the work," I said, laughing at my own joke.

"This isn't funny, Scooter. For all these years I had to listen to him brag that no one could touch his fastball. Then you reach out and touch it, all the way to the children's playground. So, what's he do? He tries to embarrass you. Make it look like you were lucky. Then you embarrass him, hit the next one even farther. Then he tries to kill you. It's no wonder you hate him."

"I wouldn't say I hate him."

A Lake Grove player lined one into right field. I caught it on one hop and threw a bullet to McCarthy, who applied the tag at third.

"Where's my brother now?" Angie asked.

"I don't know."

"He's getting ready to play rookie ball. He's gonna be a star. He's gonna make big money. How about you, Scooter? Thrown off the team. You don't even talk about next season. Are you even gonna play?"

"I don't think so," I said, feeling bad about that decision for the first time. I looked at the screen to see Francis walking to the bench dejectedly, having just gone down on three straight strikes.

"You shoulda been the star, Scooter. You should be having scouts at every game, throwing offers in your face, just like my brother did."

"Uh-huh."

"And you're trying to say that you don't hate him? I think you're full of it."

I *hadn't* really hated him. In fact, I almost held him blameless. I'd blamed Coach Henrick, Foley, the rules of the game, the doctors and lawyers, and even the bat of McCovey, but I'd held Ferraggo almost blameless. Angela was right. I *should* have been a star. I *should* have had offers at my door. It *was* her brother's fault. Her brother had just walked Betcher intentionally, and was in the process of doing Dewey likewise.

Angie looked at me, eyes narrowed like Eastwood's Dirty Harry. "Do you hate him, Scooter?"

"Kind of, I guess."

" 'Kind of' isn't good enough. Either you hate him or you don't. Either I'm your girlfriend or I'm not. There is no 'kind of,' Scooter."

"Don't you want me anymore?" I said. I watched Suitor head to first on another free pass.

"What I don't want is a liar," Angie said. "If this thing is going to work, we need total honesty, okay?"

I didn't even answer. Instead, we both watched my second massive blast sail through the flakes of snow. Just foul. My last swing of the season. Probably my career.

"Scooter, look at me," she said in a near whisper, lifting my chin up with her thumb until I met her eyes. "Tell me what you feel when you watch that tape."

It was my sister's screams that did it. It was those screams that made me hate him.

As I watched the fateful pitch crash into my face, I had no doubt it was on purpose. No doubt at all. He didn't even pretend to be upset. Didn't even bother to act concerned. He just calmly picked up the weapon he had hurled at me—which had rolled halfway back to the pitcher's mound—and put it in his goddamn pocket.

But he never put me down. One knee touched. That was it. I never went down. I rummaged through the snow-dusted grass, searching for that second tooth I'd lost, but he never put me down.

All the while, I heard Patty scream. High-pitched. Hysterical. I heard Henrick's wife attempt to comfort her. An attempt that didn't work.

"You hate him, don't you?" Angie said, her sexy tone a sharp contrast to the events I had just seen unfold.

"Yes, I do."

"Say it," Angie urged me.

"I hate him."

"Louder, Scooter, so I know you mean it."

"I hate him!" I yelled it. "I hate him!" Even louder.

"Tell me who you hate!"

"Your goddamn brother, Angie. I hate your goddamn brother!"

"Shh, shh, shh, that's enough now, Scooter," Angie said softly, comforting me. I had Dan Ferraggo in my arms on television and was hoisting him high overhead. Damn, it felt good to see him land. Still, my sister's screams, though they had subsided, continued to tear at me.

"Shh, shh, shh," Angie repeated. "Doesn't that feel better? Doesn't it feel good to let it out?"

"Yeah, I guess," I said, though what would make me feel truly better was hatred of a physical sort.

"Good, that's good," Angie said. "Because I know how you can get him back."

"Really? How?"

Angie pushed my hair away and leaned in ever closer, until I felt her hot breath in my ear. Beer. "You really want to know?"

"Yeah."

"Screw his little sister," she whispered.

It was like watching *The Wizard of Oz* in reverse, seeing the Wicked Witch spring back to life. She wasn't melting anymore.

"You like that, Scooter?"

"Uh-huh."

"We'll do it next time."

I walked into the house expecting hell and getting worse.

My father glared at me, a sheet of paper in his hand. "Your sister isn't home."

[15]

"Not home?" I said, hoping that by luck or miracle I hadn't heard him correctly.

My father waved the paper through the air. "It says here that she went out."

"And—?" I asked anxiously.

"And—that's it. I was hoping she'd gone out with you, but I see that's not the case."

"Dad, I'm sure she's fine," I said, my words more wishful thoughts than statements.

My father smiled. "I hope so, son. For your sake, I hope so. But if she's not home in twenty minutes, I'm calling the police."

"You're acting like it's *my* fault."

"Well, you weren't looking out for her."

"Me?" I said indignantly. "I'm not her father, *you* are. Besides, kids at school like Patty fine. Why shouldn't she go out with friends like a normal teenager, Dad?"

"Why?" he asked, his eyebrows arched, his voice's volume slightly higher. "Because she's *not* a normal teenager, Scooter. She's got special needs. She's naive, she trusts too much, she doesn't understand the world. She needs you to take care of her."

"Come on, Dad, that's not fair!" I yelled. "Other kids go out at night. Where do I go? Nowhere. Other kids go out to clubs, get drunk. Me? I stay at home, drink store-brand soda, watch *Happy Days* and tuck my little sister in."

"Do you feel better now?" my father asked.

"No, I don't feel better. I'm drying up. I'm seventeen and I've got no freedom. I didn't ask for this. I deserve a normal life—at least as normal as it gets for a kid whose father shot him."

He didn't take the bait. He wouldn't fire back. I was like an Alabama sheriff taunting Dr. King—and getting no results.

Instead, he sipped his tea. "You went out tonight, didn't you?"

"Well—yeah."

"Was it worth it?"

"Was *what* worth *what*?" I asked.

"Was whatever you did, with whoever you did it, worth what you're feeling now?"

"And what do you think I'm feeling, Dad? Because if you think it's guilt, you're wrong. Because you're the one who should feel guilty, not me."

"I do, son, don't worry," he said without emotion.

"Then do something about it," I said.

"What would you like me to do?"

"Well, how about being a real father for a change? How about being home to cook for us? To take us places—and I'm not talking about *Star Wars* either. How about giving a little less attention to the junkies and a little more to your children?"

Red flashing lights broke up our talk, prompting a clumsy race for the front door. An officer approached us, his arm around my sister, who, cloaked in heavy blankets, was screaming for her mother.

She'd been found running down the street screaming in sheer terror, clad only in her underwear on a cold December night.

Her words had been largely incoherent, but between sobs and primal screams the officers thought they'd pieced together the crime they were pretty sure existed only in her mind.

"Son of Sam, Son of Sam!" she'd screamed, to the confusion of the officers, who, like the rest of America, knew the murderer was locked safely behind bars doing the third month of a prison sentence that had four thousand months left to go.

She'd talked about guns that didn't make a sound, some kind of muted, muzzled flash. Perhaps her ears had failed her—she clearly was in shock and needed medical attention. An officer had found our address in her purse, which, like her clothes, had been discarded behind the old North Country school.

No one needed to mention what the parking lot was for. From the time the school shut down it had served the local populace as a lovers' lane of sorts. It was the sight of frequent raids where teens obeying hormones had Suffolk P.D. flashlights shone on clumsy groping sessions.

Glass was strewn about the lot, an ode to liquid courage that lowered inhibitions and allowed the birds to meet the bees.

So what was Patty doing there, a babe lost in the woods? A child of innocence in a place where such traits came to die? I looked closer at the teardrops that stained a painted face and the night made better sense.

She'd seemed so quick to let me go. Too consumed with something to open her door. I'd thought my leaving her would cause instant panic, but instead she'd seemed relieved. Like she couldn't wait for me to leave.

The police found nothing at the scene. No cars, no blood, no bodies, no bullets fired from silent guns. Just a simple eight-track tape that looked to be brand new. Just a scrape along its side as if it had been flung out of the window by a car moving at slow speed. The eight-track? Debbie Boone.

My sister, beautiful but fragile—a young lady with a small girl's mind, had been starving for affection. Striving for acceptance. Searching for the kind of love that an atonement-seeking father and a freedom-seeking brother were unable to provide.

She thought she'd find it in a parking lot, but found shattered dreams instead. She'd found a carcass-cleaning jackal there, an emotion-sucking vulture. Who fed upon her naiveté and left the bones to run away.

There'd been no murder there—Son of Sam was in her head. No stalker, no abduction, no chalk outline or yellow tape.

My sister would rest peacefully for days with the help of pharmaceuticals. There was no rest for me, however. Not with my conscience as a partner. Keeping me awake. Keeping me from eating. Keeping me alive so I could suffer through the full consequences of my actions.

I longed to feel real pain. Physical in nature. Anything would do as long as it hurt bad. A pistol whipping from a drug dealer. Yeah, that's just what I needed. I touched the scar on my cheek, still there as a reminder. Or a fastball to the mouth. One that would screw up my means of speaking and cost me my front teeth. Where was Don Ferraggo when I needed him to put me in my place? And where was that tooth I'd given Patty? I hadn't seen it dangling in her ear when she'd come home and I didn't dare search through her things. She'd already had her privacy invaded. She didn't need her brother making matters worse.

My heart cried out for Angie. My body did as well. I didn't understand the paradox of wanting a shoulder I could cry on and a body I could love. I guess I wanted both. Both at once. I hated that I felt that way, but I couldn't help myself.

I called Angie's number off and on for a whole day. True love often fell victim to dead silence before the days of answering machines.

I reached her mother on the second day and left a detailed message. Complete with tears and pleas. Her voice was just like Angie's and when I closed my eyes I could almost see her there. The two were somehow linked inside my mind that way.

Tina called me back that night and said her daughter was too distraught to speak. I heard her crying in the background. Angie finally called on Thursday saying she needed me tomorrow—could I meet her over there. She said I'd have to get there on my own as she was too shaken up to risk our lives behind the wheel.

I needed just to bring myself, she said. She'd have everything I needed. A willing ear to listen to my problems and a shoulder I could cry on. And something special she had planned for me, too big a secret to divulge.

[17]

The driving rain that turned the last remnants of snow to slush had tapered off somewhere in the afternoon. When the sun went down the temperature followed suit, dropping into the teens. I could feel the icy results with each measured step I took.

I'd had the foresight to tuck my hair up underneath a Mr. Goodwrench hat, knowing my odds for successful hitchhiking increased if I could avoid looking like a dirtbag.

The wind stung my hand as I assumed the hiking pose, watching as a trail of cars snaked down Old Town Road opposite my destination en route to the big game. I didn't really understand basketball's appeal. At least baseball had the pitcher-hitter confrontation. But it seemed I was alone in that conclusion, as the game was the big news on that last day of school before vacation and anyone who was anyone was making plans to go.

Except for me and Angie, the Romeo and Juliet of Suffolk County. Star-crossed lovers battling the odds, wanting only to explore each other's hearts, souls and bodies. Just thinking of this night was enough to keep me sane. To keep from feeling all alone in this time that tried my soul. Knowing someone understood helped cushion the blows my conscience rained on me. I had a longing just to hold her, to spill my guts like I had in those first few life-affirming phone talks. Perhaps we'd even kiss—I had the feeling it was time.

A pickup truck was merciful; it stopped and I hopped in. I heard Nat King Cole playing low, singing about "The Boy That Santa Claus Forgot." Not a real joyous celebration of the season, but one that got me thinking of my surprise. The one Angie said she had for me.

The pickup guy was talking, saying something about seeing Bruno in the Garden, but my mind was not on Bruno. So I nodded and "uh-huh"ed the guy while I kept thinking about the surprise she had waiting. It was enough to make me smile for the first time since Patty's ordeal had begun.

My dad refused to leave his daughter's side. He was like Kemosabe to her Tonto. Even sleeping in the crummy chairs they had for visitors at St. Charles. I'd been there pretty steady too, but there was only so much depression I could handle. I thought I had a suitcase full of guilt, but my dad was even worse. He'd wait until my sister slept and then get all biblical on me.

The Bible's full of nice quotations, but these escaped my dad. No green pastures or still waters for my father—only fire and brimstone. All directed at himself. I finally couldn't take it anymore and had to tune him out. I'd see his mouth move and watch tears gather in his eyes, but I traveled elsewhere. Kind of like I had with Greenberg's exercise. I just willed myself to leave the room and flew straight to Angie's arms.

There was a note on Angie's door. "Come on in," it read. The house was dark and quiet; the Christmas tree's pale blue twinkling lights guided my careful steps.

"Angie?" I asked with caution, hoping her condition was not so delicate that she'd be unable to see visitors. "Angie?"

"Back here, Scooter." Angie's voice. The thick Long Island accent was music to my ears. Far more soothing than old Nat King Cole and his depressing song about the kid that Santa Claus forgot.

I walked the narrow hallway to the bedrooms with great care, feeling tingling in my toes and sole with every step I took.

"Angie?"

"Right here, Scooter."

I saw a sign, ANGIE'S ROOM, and slowly pushed the door. An unmade bed, black satin sheets, a "Who's Next" poster on the wall. "Angie?"

"Next door," she said. "Come on in, you'll be surprised."

I did as I was told, opening the door to behold in the dim light a cavalcade of trophies, plaques, certificates and balls. Far too many to take in so quick, especially with the shadows and a thick cloud of confusion forming all around me.

"Scooter?"

Her voice gave me a brief scare. I'd been unsure what to think. I thought for just a moment her brother had caught on to us and a showdown might ensue. I accepted it as inevitable at some point down the line. Not tonight, I hoped, for I needed Angie bad.

I could see her on the bed, underneath the sheets, sitting up or kneeling. It was tough to tell there in the shadows. The baseballs loomed like hunter's trophies, row upon row of them, each one representing a treasured moment in Dan Ferraggo's life. Man, I hated him. I couldn't look at his damn things without hearing Patty's screams.

"Scooter?"

Her voice startled me. "Oh, hi," was all I managed to squeak out.

Angie laughed. "Are you gonna come see me, or stare at my brother's balls all night?"

Those damn double entendres always left me speechless. They begged for witty comebacks, but that begging went unheeded. They were like big, fat, hanging curveballs pleading to be taken deep. But the bat stayed on my stupid shoulder. I never did like curveballs.

I flicked on the lightswitch and walked slowly toward my girl. She seemed to be doing a decent job of sheltering her sadness, smiling mischeviously beneath those covers, her long dark hair pulled up beneath a black Lake Grove cap.

"Scooter, turn the light back off," she said.

I did as I was told. I had heard Grandpa tell a story about Cool

Papa Bell, a Negro League ballplayer so fast that he was rumored to be able to flick the light switch in his room and be in bed by the time the lights went out. I had dismissed the story with a laugh back then—after all, the increment of time could be no more than the blink of an eye. On that night in Dan Ferraggo's room, however, that tiny slice of time, that blink of an eye, was all it took to change my world. For as the light went down, I saw, on the dresser next to me, a Polaroid photograph.

"Angie?" I said.

"Yes, my lover?" She practically purred the words, and had I not been in the infant stage of great confusion, I might have melted at the implication of those words—"my lover."

"Angie, I just saw a picture of you and your brother in front of the Christmas tree."

She hesitated for just a moment. "So?"

"So, you said he wasn't home. You said he was playing winter ball somewhere."

"He is, honey, he is. Don't let some old picture keep you from your Christmas present."

"But the lights are the same—those blue lights."

"Scooter, come here."

I sat down at the foot of the bed, my head down like a scolded dog, trying to figure out why I'd been lied to.

"Scooter?"

"Yeah?"

"This house is old."

"So?"

"My mother works sixty-hour weeks just to keep us fed."

"So?"

"There's not much left over for new things. The furniture's old, the paneling's old, the rugs are old, understand?"

"Not really." My head was still drooped, but the warmth of her tone offered encouragement.

"Those lights, Scooter, those ugly blue lights are old. They are in the background of every Christmas picture ever taken in this house. Okay?"

"Okay."

"I know you hate my brother, so why don't you . . ." Her voice trailed off in a mischevious, sexy dead end.

"Why don't I what?"

"Why don't you climb into his bed and have your way with his sister?"

Holy crap! Talk about changing the tempo! Talk about turning the tide! Teenage sex, from what I'd heard, was like an awkward dance. A tango of teasing and testing limits, a waltz of worried backseat warriors that, in a best-case scenario, might lead to a hurried horizontal bop. Angie's somewhat direct approach cut straight through all the experimentation and guesswork.

I flicked my Mr. Goodwrench hat into the darkness and climbed clumsily on top of her.

"No, not yet," she said. "Just keep unwrapping me real slow."

"Is this the surprise?"

"You can think of it that way. Now keep going with that sheet. Nice and slow."

I have a vivid memory, one that captures tiny details, like a camera in my mind. I am also a lover of female breasts, as evidenced by my ability to recall every precious particular of Janet Lupo's perfect pair. Nor will I forget the brief glimpse I caught of Angie's mother's mammary, as she bent over her new Betamax.

But for the life of me, I can't remember Angie's. I imagine they were beautiful, but then again, I think they all are in their own way. Sure, it was dark in her brother's room, on her brother's bed, but not so dark that I couldn't have adjusted my bearings and snapped a mental photograph that I could have treasured for a lifetime. Instead, I just blanked out, so distracted was I by another photograph. The one of Angie and her brother, posed by the Christmas tree. Something about it, about her story, more precisely, didn't quite add up.

"Scooter, where are you going?" Shock, confusion, and annoyance all mingling together.

I turned the light on, causing Angie to retreat beneath her covers, her enigmatic breasts now hidden from my view.

"I just want to look at something."

"Get back here, Scooter!" she yelled. But she was too late. The photograph was now in my hand, and it confirmed my suspicion. At the very moment that Dan Ferraggo's sheet went down, exposing Angela's breasts, I heard the angel call to me. The angel made by Patty. The one she'd been so proud of. The one that sat atop the Christmas tree that my girlfriend and her brother stood happily in front of.

I suppose I should have been mad. After all, I'd been lied to. Been lied to in convincing fashion. Instead, I felt my heart slowly sink into the knot of my queasy gut and I squeezed out the only sound that came to me.

"Why?"

"What do you mean?" Angie replied, feigning ignorance.

"Why did you lie?"

"I didn't."

I felt the queasiness subside, replaced by controlled anger. "The picture's new, Angie."

"I don't know what you—"

"The picture of you and Dan in front of the tree you claimed was old has Patty's angel on top of it. It was taken in the last few days!"

"I can explain," she said.

"Do it."

"I didn't want to upset you, honey," she said. "I mean, you were upset already, with what happened to Patty."

"You lied to me, though."

"But only to protect you."

I tried to study her face. I wished I had Grandpa's ability to read faces. I thought I saw true remorse, but couldn't be sure.

"Look, he stopped by for a few days. It was a surprise, but it *is* his house, right? And he *is* my brother, right? I know you hate him, so I decided not to tell you. Okay? It's no big deal. I'm sorry I lied, but I did it for you. Okay?"

I looked at the picture once again. It bothered me to see Ferraggo's smile, the way it seemed to mock the very innocence and beauty of Patty's angel. There was something else that bothered me about the photo, but I couldn't quite put my finger on it.

"Scooter . . . I'm sorry."

My stomach wasn't quite as knotted. My heart ascended slowly. I may not have had the eyesight necessary to read faces, but I thought I knew true penance when I heard it. And Angie's voice was full of it.

"And Scooter?"

"Yeah?"

"Put that stupid picture down."

"Okay."

"Turn the light off."

"Okay."

"And come over here."

"Okay."

"I've been bad, so you can spank me."

There, that should have done the trick, but the trick was far from done, for even with the permission to spank fully granted, I just couldn't concentrate on Angie. I was still thinking about that damn picture.

She let the sheets slide down her backside, so that nothing stood between me and every horny teenage fantasy. Her beautiful naked ass seemed to be grinning at me, beckoning me, urging me to come forward. Still, I couldn't get into it. The picture haunted me. If Angie's ass was indeed grinning at me, the photo seemed to scream. Look at me! Look at me.

I turned on the light, despite Angie's firm protests. I don't know if she retreated instantly beneath her sheets or not, for I didn't glance her way. Instead, I focused on the Polaroid, seeing in its image what I'd feared the most. What I'd hoped was just imagination turned very real in that one instant. And everything I thought I knew of love simply disappeared.

Just moments earlier, I had gladly swallowed Angie's lies, looking for the slightest alibi to hang my love and faith on. To her credit, she'd been a creative, resourceful liar.

There was no hope in lying this time. Not with Patty's Christmas angel smiling innocently down from its Christmas tree perch at the guy who wore my front tooth in his ear. *My front tooth earring was dangling from Dan Ferraggo's ear.*

"How did he get my earring, Angie?"

"Scooter, look—"

"How?" Louder this time. Quite a bit louder.

"Scooter, please."

"How?" I yelled it this time.

Angie broke into tears. I wish that I had yanked the sheets off the bed, so she could feel as naked and vulnerable as I did at that moment, searching for sensible answers to this nonsensical quandary. What the hell had gone wrong?

"How did he get it from my sister, Angie? I need to know how he got my earring."

"I'm sorry," she cried.

"Sorry's not good enough. I need to know why. Why you did this. Why you lied. And how he got my earring!"

She reached for the side of her brother's bed, rummaging for clothes to hide her shame and her body.

"I'm sorry, Scooter, but he made me promise that I'd help him."

"Promise him what? Help him with what?"

"That I'd . . . get you out of your house for a couple of nights."

"For what? Why would he want me over here? Watching his tapes? Eating his food? Watching his mother?"

Tears were streaming down her cheeks, forging thick mascara trails with every one that fell.

"Why?" I yelled again.

Angie turned her head away from me, seemingly intent on not answering the question. Thinking perhaps that if she avoided the problem long enough, it would just go away.

"Why?" This time I screamed it.

"Because, he—"

"He—what?"

"He wanted to—"

"Wanted to what? Tell me now, Angie, tell me!"

"He wanted to—meet your sister."

I balled up my fist, then took several deep breaths to try to let my hatred subside, so that I would not act on my instinct, which was to lash out at her. I'd shattered my father's leg when I was much smaller and younger and when I'd wielded far less hatred than I felt at that moment for Angie.

She jumped out of bed, suddenly combative, clad only in an old Lake Grove baseball jersey.

"Go ahead, Scooter, hit me!" she screamed. "Go ahead, I don't care. It will be just like old times, when my father was here—and the guy after him, and the guy after him. So go ahead, I deserve it, just fuckin' hit me."

I released the fist and put the hand by my side, resisting the urge to touch her long hair or to wipe away her dark tears. Instead, I looked into her eyes and softly said, "Just tell me why."

She wiped at her tears, leaving a dark streak, like an artist's brushstroke, across her cheek, down toward her chin.

She smiled sadly, then told me a truth I'd never conceived. "Because you screwed it all up."

"What do you mean?"

"Look at our house."

"What about it?"

"It's a shithole, Scooter."

"It's not so bad," I said.

"Maybe not to you, your father's just a crooked cop. But our family deserves a little better. And I would have had it—if not for you."

"But your brother still got drafted," I said defensively.

"Yeah, he did, Scooter. For all of thirty grand. We were looking at two hundred thousand easy, maybe three. We would have had a big house, a new car, nice stuff; all the things we never had. He came into that game the top prospect in the country. Unhittable. A future all-star for sure. And he left with a broken collarbone and a reputation as a head case who gives up home runs to the fuckin' scorekeeper!"

I would have rather taken a Manny Vasquez kick to the groin than to have been doubled over by Angie's verbal blows. I'd been mad enough to hit her just moments earlier, but now I just felt so . . . lost.

"So none of this was real? It was just a way for your brother to get back at me by trying to go out with my sister?"

She gently touched my cheek. I wish I would have pushed her hand aside, but I let it stay for the duration of her impassioned answer.

"All of it was real, Scooter. All of it. I could have never faked the way I felt. I couldn't pretend to be someone that I wasn't. Do you think I would have brought you to my house? Do you think I would have introduced you to my mother? Do you think I would have done what I did in my TV room?"

"You never even kissed me," I said.

She made a quick face as if she'd tasted sour milk, but had a nice comeback, putting her arms around my neck and whispering, "Let me kiss you now."

I almost let her too. I'd longed to feel the way I'd felt in '73, when Nina's lips met mine, and I had been searching for that magic ever since. My dad had gone back to the stadium in pursuit of his lost yesterdays, and I very nearly let Angela Antonelli weave her magic spell on me. But just before our lips touched, I thought of Patty running scared. Topless. Screaming. A chill went down my spine.

"Angie?"

"Kiss me, Scooter."

"Angie?"

"I'll do all the work."

"Was your brother in the car that night?"

I didn't need Grandpa's special power to see the shock in Angie's eyes. "What night?" she asked, although I knew that she knew.

"The night my sister was attacked."

She hesitated, then breathed out a tiny "yes."

"And he knew my sister was slow, but he still tried to take advantage of her."

"Scooter."

"And you sat back and let it happen!"

"I'm sorry, Scooter." Tears began anew. "I just want you to kiss me, Scooter. I'll try to make it up to you—I'll try to make it up to her, I'll try—"

I cut her off. "You said 'a couple of nights.'"

"What," she said, bewildered.

"You said that your brother wanted you to get me out of my house for a couple of nights, right?"

"Uh-huh."

"Which nights?"

"Scooter, don't."

"Which night is it?" I demanded.

"He told me not to let you—"

"Say it, Angie!"

"Go to the game."

"The basketball game?"

"Uh-huh."

"Why?" My sister was in the hospital. He couldn't do her any harm. Yet there had to be a reason he didn't want me at that big game.

"I don't know," Angie said.

"Tell me!" I yelled.

"I swear I don't know."

"You've got to get me there."

"Scooter, let's lay down."

"Take me to the game, Angie."

"It's probably over by now."

My heart was pounding rapidly. I had the feeling that the game was to be the site of some major happening. I needed to get there quickly, but the game was at North Milton, six or seven miles away. I needed Angie's help. I forced myself to speak with a calm that belied the panic racing through my veins.

"Angela, listen."

"Kiss me, Scooter."

"You have messed up bad, understand?"

She tried to lean in for the kiss, forcing me to back away.

"What you and your brother tried to do to Patty is almost too much to forgive."

"But I didn't do anything to her, Scooter."

"Yes, you did, Angie. By standing by and doing nothing, you have done something really bad."

"Scooter, I said I was sorry."

"You can't just say it, Angie, you have to mean it."

"I do mean it, honey."

"Then show it to me."

She began to take her jersey off.

"That's not what I mean." I was no longer in control. The panic that ran in my veins had taken fast control of my words, causing them to fly out in rapid bursts. "Show me that you're sorry. Drive me to Milton. I need your help. I'm asking for your help. Will you give it to me?"

She took the jersey off, exposing once again breasts I never saw. By the time the jersey hit the floor, I was already in the hall, sprinting for her purse out in the kitchen, and the Barracuda's keys.

I was almost out the door when I heard her giving chase, her bare feet on cheap linoleum like a racehorse on a muddied track.

"Give them back!" she yelled.

I hit the sidewalk at a trot, right leg moving better with every passing step. Angie dove for me, naked in the frigid night. She grabbed two handfuls of my hair and tried to pull me back. I kept my hands down at my sides, but dragged her with my hair.

Her bare feet hit slick ice and she fell to the concrete, taking two decent clumps of hair with her as she went.

I climbed into the Barracuda, calling on the skills, or lack thereof, that had resulted in three failed road tests. I turned the key. It fired up and I pulled out of the drive, gunning the car's big engine on an icy winter night. Racing toward an unknown fate.

[18]

It may have been the streakers. The story of three running men wearing only ski masks interrupting graduation ceremonies had become the stuff of legend. They'd done their thing and then took off through the cornfields of Borrella's farm that lay next to the high school. That was '73, when I was still in Highbridge. Streaking never got real big there as far as I could tell, although running from a fire clad only in pajamas was a nightly occurrence.

I floored the pedal on Nesconsett Highway, running the red lights, knowing only fools and sports fans would venture out on such a night.

I made a sharp left at the light on Old Town, the winding narrow road that led down to the high school.

I saw the lot off in the distance, jammed with cars. No trail of exhaust or lights passing by, which meant I had a chance. I pushed the car to eighty, not even shifting gears. That's when I passed the cornfields and looked away just briefly at the ghosts of ski-masked nature boys who'd left behind an angry mob after crashing the biggest party of the year. An off-duty New York City cop had even drawn his gun and fired at the naked fleeing men.

The ice grabbed my attention back when the tires of Angie's car hit a patch of it. I felt the rear end fishtail and was helpless in its wake. A seasoned driver would have turned into the slide, but instead I pulled against it, sending the vehicle into a quick series of 360's. Watching the high school in the distance, the unknown key to Angie's evil mystery, as it passed by me once, twice, almost three times before my progress was abruptly stopped by a decent-sized oak tree.

I saw steam spewing into the cold night air and heard something losing air. A stabbing pain shot through my chest and more air escaped the car. I tried to focus, but saw nothing except my fate sprinting past me, laughing as it went. The school. The school. The school. I had to get there somehow. I willed myself to see it, off somewhere in the distance. Bright white lights were shining now. Shining on the parking lot—its cars lined up in long rows with others on the grass. A huge event, the Lake Grove game. The one I had to get to.

I reached out for the handle, but my left arm no longer moved. I reached over with my right hand and, despite the stabbing pain, felt the handle give and, with all the will and strength I had remaining, rolled out of the car, resting on my knees for just a moment while I tried to gain my bearings and form some kind of plan.

The plan I formed was running. I would cut through Borrella's cornfield, its winter stalks no longer tall or green or suitable for streakers.

Angie's car was in rough shape, but not completely totaled. Steam still burped out of the engine and air still leaked somewhere, sounding very labored, its location unknown. A hose? The tires? I didn't care. All I cared about was leaving it.

The game was running late. Perhaps the start had been delayed to allow for all the cars. I cursed myself for taking time to think when I knew I should be moving. Move first, think later—or let instincts do their job. I limped across the cornfield, the sound of hissing air chasing after me like some psycho movie killer that refuses to stay dead.

It wasn't tires or hoses—it was coming from my lungs. Wheezing, spitting, coughing, sounding like a leaking valve with every step I took. But still I didn't stop.

My left arm dangled uselessly—thank God I didn't need it. I threw punches with the other arm and I paid no heed to defense. I had no idea what to expect but I knew what form the consequences would be delivered in. Big right hands, from way down deep.

I reached up with my right hand, which had been pumping with each stride. I knew it when I felt the bone damn near piercing through the skin. Left collarbone, broken bad—and in that instant I became convinced.

Convinced that I would find him there. That he hadn't just done his thing and left. But what the hell could that thing be and would I be too late to stop it?

With each step more cobwebs seemed to part until my thoughts became quite clear. I heard the air leaking from my lungs, I felt the throbbing of my arm and I felt the brilliant pangs of vengeance. Thinking of Dan Ferraggo, who would not be expecting me. Thinking of his eyes—their fear and panic, when he saw who'd come for him.

Why would God create a man like him? Give him all that talent, that arm that came along just a few times every generation? A Koufax arm, a Ryan arm. Why give him all that talent and leave out the slightest hint of decency? A guy who might throw ninety-eight but didn't have the moral sense to leave an innocent bystander like my sister the hell out of his battles?

The parking lot was closer now and I heard the muffled sounds of thousands cheering as cornstalks passed me by. The left arm no longer hurt. I heard air escape my lungs but no longer felt the knife. Turn the other cheek, the Good Book said. Sorry, God, no deal. I felt adhesions breaking in my leg. Years of inactivity giving way to my sheer will. Toes no longer tingling, simply feeling frozen earth beneath them. An eye for an eye, my father said when he was laid up in his bed. Words that I could finally live by. Words that I could use.

I looked down at my right leg—the one that had been shot. The one that had been sacrificed to my mother's upward social climb. The one that had shaped my life since Cleon Jones caught that last out in '69. That right leg was moving now. Moving up and down. Pumping like a piston. That right leg was . . . running. Racing on toward destiny, whatever it might be.

I heard sounds of pandemonium when I emerged out of the corn-field. I could almost feel the heat.

Cars were everywhere. Every spot was taken. Not a single soul had left. Cars on the playing fields and tennis courts, on the curbs and on the sidewalk. No wonder each was ticketed. Tickets everywhere. But why so many tickets? Surely every car could not face penalties. There were too damn many of them.

No, they must be flyers tucked under every wiper. Hundreds of the things. Someone had spent some time out here making sure their product would receive a whole lot of attention.

I headed for the gym, realizing for the first time that I didn't have a dime and that I'd be at the mercy of security when I showed up without means of gaining entrance.

A flyer floated in the freezing air, pirouetting in the sky as I devised my entry plan. The sky was clear and starry, providing just the right background for the floating flyer. Floating almost at eye level, white paper juxtaposed with pitch-black night, almost like McCovey's mighty blast departing Shea and entering my future. It seemed almost sublime, like an oasis of brief pleasure amid a desert of harsh truths.

Then I saw reality and my oasis disappeared. A brief mirage, an ode to hope replaced by the cruelest truth of all. A photo of my sister. Terrified and naked. Running for her life. Eyes wide in desperation, thinking she was being preyed on by a murderer. Hearing silent gunshots—flashes with no sound. Flashes that took photographs, shot by murderers of innocence. Photographs that had been run off for mass consumption—several hundred times. Waiting to be seen by departing fans who would have a laugh or two, then throw it in the garbage, as good a place as any for my little sister's dignity.

I sometimes wish I'd torn them up. Just grabbed each one I could and destroyed the evidence. Restoring Patty's dignity with each ripping of a page. But I thought there were too many of them and time was running out.

My face began to tremble, my lips to shake in grief. I felt my eyes well up but fought off tears, for I knew I couldn't spare them. Tears, I knew, would fall soon enough. But I could not give in to grief right there, not with its cause in striking distance. I could mourn my sister's innocence when this awful night was over. But as I made a dash across the lobby and forced my way into the gym without permission or a dollar, I knew just what this night was for. It was a night for vengeance, a night to fulfill the words of Exodus. An eye for an eye, a tooth for a tooth.

The gym was hot with passion. Passion for both the game and the towns it represented. I looked up at the clock and then looked to the bleachers. Double overtime, Lake Grove up by one. Eleven seconds left. Milton with the ball. Damn, I wished I knew the layout of the gym—which section was for home team fans, which one for the visitors.

Pompoms shaking, green and gold. Milton colors. Ferraggo must be on the other side. Eight seconds now. There he was. I knew him instantly. Up on the top bleacher now, surrounded by adoring fans like Elvis with his Memphis Mafia.

No one even noticed me, their attention far too focused on the game at hand. I homed in on his pompous face—his eyes, his teeth, his earring. His goddamn earring! There it was. Swinging with his every move, its sole purpose to mock me. A sea of Lake Grove black and yellow ahead, but I was going to swim it. Uphill, upstream, I did not care—I'd move mountains just to hurt him.

I was only on the second step when the jump shot was released with just four ticks left on the clock. I saw nothing except black coats, dark hair and open mouths as I continued on my way.

I heard ball hit rim and cheers and groans and then sensed the bated breath of anticipation. A rebound and then one last shot, its result unseen by me. But then I heard a buzzer and the sea of Lake Grove black became a tidal wave of joy and people all around me were jumping up and down.

I rode the wave unnoticed, moving up the bleachers, getting closer to my target like a shark approaching lunch.

I was three rows from the top when Ferraggo's eyes met mine. Fear and panic swam in those eyes, but my victory was hollow. My element of surprise was gone and I was still a long way from my destination when his cavalry came charging.

I knocked the first one cold with just one punch, his own momentum dooming him by adding to the force. I did not have time to fully pull the next punch from my heels. Instead I caught the guy on the temple with a short straight right that stunned him for a moment. Then I jerked him forward by his collar, pulling off a medallion of some kind and sending him on a crash course down the bleachers, mowing down the Lake Grove student body like a set of dominoes and turning much attention from the celebration on the court to the melee in the stands.

Finally, alone with Dan Ferraggo. Face-to-face with my tormentor, whose plan by now was in effect.

Hundreds must have seen her—seen Patty at her weakest. Would they have a heart and feel for her or would they get off on her pain? Either way her days at North Milton were over. She couldn't face the shame. And I knew I couldn't face myself if I let Ferraggo go.

But go is what Ferraggo did. With terror in his eyes, he made a mad leap from the bleachers. Fifteen feet at least, but the impact was absorbed to some degree by the volume of the crowd. The unsuspecting passersby heading for the exits who'd caught him on their backs.

Bodies raced in all directions, except for those who had been injured in the fall, Ferraggo not among them. He scampered out the door, leaving me without much hope or any option except to follow suit.

There were no backs left on which to jump, so the impact was horrendous. Timberlands slapping wooden floor with over two hundred pounds behind them. Pain shot up both legs like daggers stabbing through the floorboards. My right leg wasn't used to pain—it wasn't used to anything. I didn't like the pain, but I'd gladly choose it over nothingness.

I saw Ferraggo's head above the crowd, bobbing around the people, looking for a hole like a tailback on a sweep. I couldn't take the time to bob around people—I just ran over them instead. I saw that I was gaining ground, but I also saw security trying to close the gap. Suffolk cops, nightsticks drawn, ready to snuff out the altercation before it could get worse.

Leading the charge, however, was Wally Wheet, tearing down the hall like it was a Southeast gridiron, before a surgeon's clumsy hands snatched an NFL contract from his hands and replaced it with a broom.

Ferraggo headed for the rear door. I took a quick right into the cafeteria, knowing that he'd have to run right through the smoke shed to reach the parking lot. I was going to cut him off.

He never even saw me when I emerged from that side door. The door of choice for dirtbags, who longed to have a smoke and empty conversation before going about their business of being ridiculed. If I'd been a second earlier, I could have knocked him out. Could have caught him running with the kind of shot that messed up Rudy T. in the infamous basketbrawl. A Foreman versus Frazier knockout, but unlike Big George's show of force in Kingston, only one punch would be needed.

Instead I tripped him up at the last instant. Shot my arm between his ankles and sent him sprawling into the shed, scattering a litany of pregame party bottles—beer, vodka, J.D.

If I'd known I'd have but one chance to act, I might have used it differently. Thoughts of those wasted potential actions would cause me many sleepless nights. Dan Ferraggo, prone and helpless. What move would I make? I'd been a pretty decent kickball player back in those ancient yesterdays, before my father shot me. Good speed around the bases and a prodigious kicking foot. I think I would have used that prodigious foot to kick Ferraggo's ass. But kicking ass is such a general term. To be a little more specific, I would have kicked his face. A full-force, unobstructed work boot shot to his handsome chiseled features, which would certainly not have remained that way in his post-kick world.

I used that lone chance, instead, to reclaim what had been mine. I strode aside his body, feeling like an old-time gladiator getting ready for the kill. I could hear Ferraggo whimpering, actually goddamn whimpering, when I reached my hand down for it. I suppose I could have slipped it out, but given the hell he'd put me through, I thought it better just to rip it. Tear it out. He screamed loudly when I did it. Blood trickled down his earlobe and I held my tooth aloft.

I should have kept it there—aloft. Had I done so, I'd have been okay. I'd have had a way to block it. Instead, I placed it in my pocket, securing my hard-earned booty. That's how I was posed when Wally Wheet's massive arms wrapped me up—hand stuck in my pocket, right arm trapped within his grasp.

The Suffolk cops arrived just as Ferraggo found his feet, their handcuffs out, nightsticks drawn. Dr. Foley was just a step behind, his crying, chubby kid in tow. The cops could have stopped Ferraggo. But they didn't. For they thought their man was me. I could have bowed or turned my head. But I didn't. For I was momentarily distracted by Foley's little kid. After all, I was his hero.

I never saw the bottle. Which he held in his left hand, which was whipping across his body like a fastball, hard and fast, heading for its target—Scooter Reilly's face. I had only a split second to react, which I used to raise my arms. But neither one went up. My left arm had been rendered useless; my right caught in a trap of bone and muscle.

The two of us, Dan and me, had not, in our history together, exchanged a single word. Our relationship was based solely on physical actions. One physical action cost me two front teeth and the ability to kiss. His current action cost me a bit more—an eye and its ability to see.

1978

[1]

I took off from the suburbs as soon as I got out of the hospital, beating a hasty Long Island Railroad retreat from paradise the night before my official release. After all, I was a wanted man. I knew that Patty would be coming home and that she'd be in need of love, but I thought my need for freedom was the more urgent of the two.

My attempt at gaining vengeance had yielded criminal results. From grand theft auto, to resisting arrest, to three counts of assault, including one on Dan Ferraggo. My father had informed me that things did not look good. In all likelihood, he told me, Ferraggo's bottle assault on me would be seen as self-defense.

As for his humiliation of my sister—no one knew a thing. His entire school shut up, as if they'd taken La Cosa Nostra vows, and as a result, Ferraggo was free and clear. Free to throw his fastball at minor league spring training. And clear of all charges where the case of Patty Reilly was concerned.

But as I caught the number two train from Manhattan to the Bronx on a freezing January night, I made myself a vow—he wasn't free and clear of me.

I got a job at the Bronx Terminal Market, working 4 a.m. till noon, loading produce onto trucks. The market had a long, important history in the Bronx, serving since 1923 as a thoroughfare for produce that arrived from all parts of the world. The market had helped save the produce from going rotten, increasing its availability, making it far more obtainable for the lower working class.

The market also helped give birth to Yankee baseball, as thousands of terminal workers would emerge in early afternoon, direct from working shifts, in the mood for Bombers action.

I didn't feel all that important though, as, with lung and collarbone still on the mend, I lugged case after case of apples, oranges and bananas onto those damn trucks, accompanied only by the endless drone of Latin music and my thoughts of love, lust and revenge.

Angela and Nina were like swordsmen of distinction, their memories dueling for my soul. Nina was a technician, trying hard to win my heart with gentle swipes of true affection. Touching legs, heartfelt words, and one lone kiss were her only weapons in this game. Angela fought her off with the heavy broadsword of hot passion. The tools at her disposal were much more harsh and lethal. How could the simple touching of two lips compete with dirty talk and dueling mother-daughter action. Surprisingly, it did.

I looked for Nina everywhere. With every passing face, I hoped that I would see her, hoped that I would hear her voice, hear it say my name. I didn't like my name at all, except when Nina said it. "Scooter," like a melody.

Perhaps I could return to Nina, though! Perhaps it wouldn't be too late. Her brother, Manny! Why, of course. The Highbridge drug trade was still booming from what I could ascertain. If the zoned-out junkies who lined Jerome were any indication, Manny would be king. Sure, he'd warned me several years ago to leave the girl alone. Sure, he'd pistol-whipped me and caused my balls to swell like grapefruits when I'd disobeyed his words. And sure, he'd taken me on as his ninety-mile-per-hour client only after I'd promised not to see her. But that was years ago. Surely if I saw him after all this time and told him of my undying love for his only sister, he would understand. He would smile that smack-dealing smile, take his fastball-throwing hand and write down those magic numbers. The same numbers I had put to death by fire in my bedroom up on Shakespeare on that night in '73.

I didn't get the number. Manny didn't tell me. He couldn't. He was dead. He'd had his throat slit by a prostitute, who had traded drugs for sex. The Diablos had a new king now—the guy with the big voice, the one who had driven the nail through my foot on my big night to shine. The night when I had passed out on Nelson with a two-by-four nailed to my foot. I doubted that he knew of Nina's whereabouts, and doubted that he'd tell me if he did.

Upon hearing of the fate of Manny Vasquez, I began a slow walk home. I touched the hole where my right eye had been. Stuck the tip of my thumb in and wiggled it about. If I'd stayed in Long Island, I'd have a new one made of glass by now. Instead, I had a hole. I thought of how I lost it, the bottle smashing into my face, jagged glass stuck in my eye. I'd been just one swing away from vengeance, and now I was a world away from hope.

The thought brought about great anger—and the anger made me run. I ran east on 167th, and then I ran up Shakespeare's hill. Maybe my mother had been right; my injury was mental. Maybe I really could run when I was angry. I had charged the mound at Settlecott School without the slightest hesitation, and I had made a dash through Borrella's cornfield without bothering to limp.

If anger was indeed the fuel on which my body ran, I was a lucky man. For I had an unlimited supply. The charge up Shakespeare's hill made my lungs and legs both ache. So I slowly jogged back down, then sprinted up again. Over and over, until my legs simply couldn't move. Drawing from my anger to drive me up the hill.

I began running every day. My days took on new meaning. I worked the eight-hour shift at the market, eating fruit that had been bruised or smashed, then emerged from work in plain gray sweats, flannel shirt and new black Chucks, looking like a one-eyed, long-haired Rocky training on the mean streets of the Bronx for a date with destiny that I hoped would someday come.

In the spring of 1978, those streets were mighty mean indeed. Looking out that taxicab's rear window, four years earlier, on our escape out to the Island, I would not have thought it possible for the Bronx to get much worse. But following the great blackout of July 1977, my thought was proven wrong, and the aftermath was ugly.

My father used to brag about New Yorkers' actions in the wake of a similar blackout in 1965. Crime had actually gone down during the hours that followed, and the helping spirit of the people became a source of immense New Yorker pride. A scant twelve years later, that pride was all but gone, and lawlessness prevailed as the people hit the streets.

The Bronx was hit especially hard, as opportunistic mobs of looters sacked almost five hundred businesses, and dedicated arsonists set three hundred fires. My mother's dear old shopping grounds, the Grand Concourse, did not escape unscathed, as several of its businesses fell victim to the looters' wrath and many store owners opted to just lock up and leave the onetime Park Avenue of the Bronx.

I hit all the sections south of Moses's Cross Bronx masterpiece on my angry runs. Melrose, Motthaven, Highbridge—I didn't give a crap. Even Charlotte Street, where President Carter's autumn visit six months earlier had turned burned-out piles of rubble into a new must-see location. Ted Kennedy would show up there in 1980, in his unsuccessful bid to unseat Carter, as would Ronald Reagan in his more successful one.

Hell, even the pope stopped by Morris Avenue and 151st to give a blessing in Spanish, on his way to saying Mass at the refurbished $150 million stadium, showing that somewhere way up there, God still cared about the Bronx.

Once in a great while, I'd see little signs of hope on my runs—a park where a charred hulk had been demolished, a building lovingly refurbished by local grants and concerned citizens—but these were few and far between.

At first, I took some flak from local riffraff—prostitutes, winos, dealers, junkies—but after I'd charged down their streets every day for weeks, always fueled by anger, they took to cheering me, and no one tried to mess with the white boy with one eye.

[2]

Baseball season rolled around in April, as it always has and always will. Hope may spring eternal for the masses when the nation's pastime awakens from its winter slumber, but for me hope was merely wishful thinking. A wondrous feat of magic that revealed itself as mere illusion the moment I saw Dan Ferraggo with my front tooth hanging from his ear.

I wished I had my magic back. But how, I wondered, how? I thought back to bat day five years earlier, when my father let his secret loose. How he'd been feigning overtime to pursue the magic of his youth. Yankee Stadium. Could it be my answer? The place where I could go to get back what I once had? The place I could feel whole again, just for a couple hours? Maybe by returning to the site of my greatest glory, my life's lone kiss, I could feel whole again.

The Yanks were taking on the White Sox of Chicago in their first home stand of the year. As defending Series champions, the team was a hot ticket and only nosebleed seats remained. But I wasn't settling for the upper deck. I needed seventh row or better, preferably on the first-base side. I made decent money at the market, at least by High-bridge standards, and with the exception of my weekly thirty-dollar rent, I'd saved almost every dime.

It was April 13, 1978, one day after Mayor Koch introduced a $1.5 billion housing plan that, combined with Washington's proposed $55 million economic development plan, was supposed to bail out the South Bronx. What happened to those proposals remains anybody's guess, which seems an awful shame—$1.5 billion could have bought a lot of coats of paint.

I obtained a Yankee Stadium seating chart and, with a fistful of fives meant to satisfy the high-end scalpers, headed for Ruth's new house.

It was a thing of beauty, this refurbished stadium. A truly modern ballpark, but with its heart steeped in Yank tradition, it made my heart jump just to think of recapturing my magic while sitting in its confines. I saw it every day when I loaded crates to earn my living, but it had seemed so cold and distant until the flame of thick nostalgia warmed it up for me.

A fourth-row seat cost thirty bucks—I talked the scalper down ten. I bought a hot dog, peanuts and a program, on which I could keep score. I didn't even pause to think of the last time I'd done that chore, when I'd had my tongue and future ruined by a fastball on that dreary day on that ball field in Settlecott. No, my mind wasn't even thinking '77; it was stuck in '73, when Nina Vasquez kissed me and my dad saved first base for Elston Howard.

Damn, the seats weren't what I'd hoped—they weren't first-base side. No, they were right behind home plate, which I guessed would have to do. What the hell, I thought, I might as well enjoy it. I closed my eye and smiled and inhaled the Yankee air, imagining Nina's perfume's scent, the name of which I never could find out. I hoped that when I opened it, I would see her standing there, beautiful and kind, in her dark blue usher's uniform.

But Nina wasn't there, just a kid who looked quite mortified at the one-eyed freak before him. I couldn't blame the kid, though; I was a little rough on younger eyes. I actually thought that maybe out of respect for those with two eyes, I should wear a patch in public places.

I bit into my "Reggie" bar, a gooey compilation of chocolate, caramel and peanuts, which had been a complimentary token of confectionary affection for all the opening-day fans. All forty-five thousand of them. The bar fulfilled Reggie Jackson's dream of having a candy bar named after him. I put the bar away after a second bite, vowing to return to it if I got really, really hungry.

I was happy for Reggie, really I was. But ballparks just weren't built for candy bars. They were built for dogs. I took a bite and savored it.

A Schickhaus frank with Gulden's mustard—the Yankees' brands of choice. But what difference did it make? Inside the stadium, they were all Yankee dogs to me. I ordered a large beer. A Schaefer beer. A way to honor the memory of my pre–fifth game Series dad. Perhaps through the aid of a beer or two, I could pretend I was in the upper deck, peering out from my pet girder, munching on Pop's peanuts with my dad's arm around my shoulder.

Unfortunately, my order was turned down when I could not produce ID that said I was eighteen. It seems a missing eye and bright red cheek scar, long hair and scraggly beard were not true indicators of my manhood. And when I could not produce the ID, he could not produce the beer. Damn.

So it was with sober eye that I viewed the return of Roger Maris, the man who back in '61 had claimed Babe Ruth's single-season home-run crown. He and Mickey Mantle accepted the Series trophy on behalf of all the Bombers. Grandpa used to tell me that Maris got a lousy deal at the hands of Yankee fans, who never quite forgave him his conquest of Ruth's vaunted crown. He'd left town in '66, vowing never to return, but I guess twelve years can heal a lot of wounds. It was nice to see him receive the type of cheers that, in his old Bronx playing days, had proved to be elusive.

My thoughts turned to the game, which was ready to commence. Did I really care to see the champion Yanks, even from my fourth-row seat? Or would the specter of singles up the middle and perhaps a cheesy home run down the line drive me back to my little hole on Anderson, my lost magic still unfound?

Ed Figueroa readied his first pitch. A nice curveball for a strike. I got my scorer's pencil ready. A second curve missed just outside. Looked like a strike to me though. Wait! Wait a second, I thought. How did I know it was a curve? A fastball found its mark. How could I tell that? I knew when it left his hand. Only three guys in the stadium knew—the catcher, the pitcher and—me. The count was 1 and 2. He'd probably waste a pitch. Try to get the guy to swing at something just outside the zone. Figueroa went into his windup. I saw the baseball leave his hand. Curve! Yes, it was! I could see the damn thing spinning. I could see the red seams rotate, standing out in bold relief like the Rocky Mountains on a U.S. map. Rocky Mountains that were spinning. Low and away, just like I'd thought, but the batter took a swing. Strike three. Forty-five thousand strong voiced their approval, but I sat still and silent. Something was either very wrong, or very right; I couldn't be sure which.

I looked for female ushers—maybe Nina was still here. Third-base side, long hair, dark skin—no, her nose wasn't shaped like Nina's. Upper deck, first-base side. No, skin too light, eyes were green. I took a final look, this time in the bleachers out behind the right field wall four hundred feet away, where Puerto Rican fans had jammed the cheap seats to see Figueroa pitch.

Indeed this Yankee pitching staff was something of a rainbow connection, featuring, among others, a Puerto Rican, a Mexican, a black, and a few decent white guys named Catfish, Gator and Sparky. And while they never did offer to buy the world a Coke, or choose to swap lives with one another, they were effective as a unit.

No, that wasn't Nina. Razor stubble, Adam's apple—not a girl at all.

What the hell was going on? How could I know all this? Was it just a wild hallucination, the effects of a bad hot dog? A rotten peanut, maybe? Had someone accidentally dropped a hit of acid on my still numb and doughy tongue without my knowledge? Was it a bad trip that soon would end?

Figueroa got the sign. Shook it off. Looked again. Nodded. A slider. I knew it right away. The moment it rolled off his fingers, I knew that damn thing was a slider.

I looked up at the owner's box and saw the Yankees' boss, George Steinbrenner. The guy who hadn't quite stuck to building ships, as my father said he would back when he informed me of the Kekich-Peterson transaction. The boss bit into a Schickhaus dog. Gulden's mustard dripped onto his dark blue tie. "Oh, shit," I saw him say. "Oh, shit," I said myself.

Bottom of the first.

Reggie watched two Wilbur Wood knuckleballs dance out of the strike zone before blasting number three over the wall in right center, prompting a celebratory throwing of several thousand candy bars. It was literally raining bars at Yankee Stadium—one of the doggonedest sights I'd ever seen. Even doggoneder (if indeed such a word exists) was the fact that I could see Wood's knuckler so damn clearly. Hovering, floating, darting. No spin at all on those first two. The third just didn't knuckle—it had too much spin on it.

I forgot all about poor Nina. In the midst of heroic cleanup duty, taking place on the ballpark's cool green sod, which was now spotted orange with "Reggie" bars, I left my fourth-row seat. I threw my bar as well—into a blue steel garbage can—as I left the stadium. I left without once looking back, running all the way to my dingy room on Anderson, fueled not by anger but by steadfast resignation. I knew what needed to be done. I grabbed my life savings from beneath my bed and stuffed it in a pillowcase.

I hailed a cab out on Jerome and told him to take the Cross Bronx to Long Island.

I knocked on my old door on Flintlock Lane at 10:50 p.m. My father opened up the door with a shocked but happy face and engulfed me in his arms. "Scooter," he said. "I thought you were gone from me for good."

"Dad," I said clumsily, not quite sure how this next thing would sound, "I want you to teach me to play baseball."

[3]

My father had taken down his FOR SALE sign in mid-February. He, like I, had assumed that Patty's North Milton days were through. That the pain of humiliation would simply be too great for her and that a new start somewhere else would be best for all concerned. It was Patty who had spoken out against the move, saying that Long Island was her home, North Milton was her school and they needed to stay put so that Scooter would be able to find them when he came back home. She apparently had been very sad upon learning of my sudden departure and had taken to looking out the window late at night so she could be the first to see me on my triumphant return to Flintlock Lane.

My sister had asked for me several times a day, my father said, while I'm ashamed to admit that I was so caught up in my thirst for lust and vengeance that I completely disregarded a true love right at home.

I wanted to return to high school, not to study or to socialize, but to act as Patty's enforcer, punching out the sneering mobs who must have undoubtedly showered her with ridicule. I was a good thirty pounds lighter now, thanks to months of anger running, but I was in much better shape and knew I still could punch. I also knew my missing eye and unkempt beard and even longer hair would help keep frightened high school punks at bay.

Except my father swore that things were fine. Patty loved North Milton and North Milton loved her back. Apparently a few kids got cruel early on, but were summoned into Foley's office and had their teenage asses handed to them in a verbal kind of way. A few of my baseball teammates had graduated in '77, but the returning players enveloped my sister in a protective cocoon and a spirit of humanity that quickly became contagious. Patty Reilly, to my surprise, had become a prized pupil at the school.

The legal charges I had feared so much hadn't been pursued. It turned out that two Lake Grove kids with consciences fingered Dan Ferraggo as the perpetrator of the windshield plot, and as a result, his family and his agent thought it might be for the best if the whole night was just forgotten. A sentiment that everybody echoed. Everyone but me, that is, for instead of banishing it from memory, I immersed myself in it, stewed in it, thrived on it, to the point that Dan Ferraggo and the hatred he invoked in me became the focus of my life.

My father said he hadn't seen an eye like mine since the Splendid Splinter, Ted Williams, thirty years before. I didn't try to sell him on my theory of compensation, or alert him to the fact that Grandpa had the same ability. My dad said it was just amazing eyesight, the kind a player seems to grab hold of once a generation.

I asked this man if he would take me on as a student of the game. Now that Patty was doing well, would he consider training me, mentoring me, helping me to learn every aspect of the game? He seemed torn by my request.

I begged him to consider it. "I'm going to use a lighter bat," I said. "And bat righty so I can see." His face took on a Joe D. stoicism. "I won't swing for the fences." Still no sign of giving in. "I'll slap it up the middle." He broke into a wide smile and patted me gently on the chest.

"I'll do it," he informed me, then his smile quickly disappeared. "On one condition."

"Sure, Dad, what is it?"

"You've got to promise that you'll love the game."

"You've got my word on it," I said.

He had the time to offer to me, having cut back his work with Harlem drug addicts to spend time with my sister. Since the incident at North Country, his priorities had changed, and Patty was his focus. But Patty had been faring well, and so he was more than happy to give attention to the son he thought he'd lost, who swore to love the game.

I used a 33-ounce Adirondack bat of white ash, with a Thurman Munson signature burned into the barrel. I'm not ashamed to admit that I choked up on that little bat and gave my dad my undivided attention as he taught me how to rule the strike zone, how to protect the plate with two strikes on the count, and how to use a compact swing to punch it through the holes. We didn't even use a ball for several days, just went through footwork and the basics until I felt like I could make solid contact in my sleep. At night we'd watch the Bombers, and much to my amazement, even the Amazin' Mets when the Yanks weren't on the tube. No, we didn't watch—we studied, with my dad giving postgame quizzes to make sure I'd absorbed the lessons of the night.

Patty even joined us on our quest, on the days she wasn't keeping score on Milton's bench, as Henrick's unofficial assistant coach. She said Henrick often asked for me, wondering if I'd ever catch a home game at the elementary school.

My dad woke me up at five o'clock one morning in late April and said it was time to hit the ball. We drove to the dead end, parked the car and made our way through the woods. My right leg was almost better, the running having helped immeasurably to break free not only of my physical discomfort, but of the mental shackles that had held me captive for so long.

Sadly, my dad was not so lucky. Despite years of rehabilitation, his progress had been minimal, and he moaned aloud with each labored step he took, heavily dependent on his cane. But he made it through and limped out toward the mound, a fielder's glove on one hand, his cane clutched in the other, a bag of balls slung across his shoulder.

The dawn was just beginning to break as he began his first few feeble warm-up tosses. I thought he might fall over or pass out, as each throw elicited a cry of pain that made me wince in empathy.

I said, "Dad, we don't have to do this," and the truth is if he'd called it quits right then, I'd have pulled the plug on my grand plan.

But through clenched teeth he said, "I'm okay. I've just got to get the feel of the mound again."

The last time he'd pitched to me, I'd been a child of nine. A lot had changed since then. Gunshot wounds and broken bones and shattered innocence. A missing eye and a missing son, but still, through it all, we had emerged—incomplete but hanging on, a semblance of a family. A father and his son, playing the timeless game of baseball, handing down a legacy of loving the great game.

"Go ahead, Scooter, get in there," he said. "I'll try to put it right over. See if you can slap it up the middle."

I stepped to the right side of the plate, and choked up on the little bat. I did as I was told, making solid contact with my father's timid pitch, slapping it up the middle. I was so intent on watching the ball roll into center field that I almost didn't see him as he wiped a tear off his cheek.

Every single pitch was a testament to one man's courage, as each one produced an anguished grunt. If I'd been a better son, I'd have admitted to my true intentions and asked for his forgiveness. Instead, I stood tight-lipped, content to watch him put himself through hell because he thought I loved the game.

His leg turned purple that first day after practice and I urged him to take something, anything, to take away his pain. He paid no heed to my advice. Just said he needed rest to get him ready for the next day's practice.

He lay down in his bedroom, and even above the crackling of my Rice Krispies in cold milk, I could hear him as he moaned.

By day three he was a master, left leg kicking high, cutting through the air, right arm snapping off sharp curves that I learned to take to right field or to punch through the holes. Had it not been for the cries of pain, I'd have sworn that he was fine. Every night I'd hear him moan, though, and every morning, right at five, I'd be surprised to feel him wake me, Cap'n Crunch fresh on his breath, a delighted father's smile glued on his face, saying, "Sun's almost out. Time to take your swings."

And every day I'd do just that, driving my father's cavalcade of breaking pitches through the holes and up the box for sure base hits. I learned to know those pitches in an instant, depending on the spin, or other telltale movements of the ball. Curveballs, sliders, sinkers— knucklers too. Every single day for weeks, until he felt that I was ready. All except the fastball, which remained a question mark. He'd never thrown especially hard, the memory of those seventy-mile-an-hour bullets whizzing in from forty-five feet notwithstanding. Out there on North Milton's rocky field, he just couldn't push off hard enough to generate real heat.

My schedule was demanding. Batting practice at dawn, followed by defensive drills back at home, nightly baseball games to study and late-night distance runs, during which I'd cover six miles at a clip all around the town. I did it five days every week, taking weekends off to get some extra work in at the Terminal Market.

The acrid taste of anger still fueled those late-night runs. Had I not been so consumed with angry thoughts, I might have been propelled by love. My house on Flintlock Lane was overflowing with it, but despite my keen Ted Williams eye, I was just too blind to see. A sister who would not stop hugging me and telling me how much she missed me when I left. A dad who sacrificed his sweat and tears just to teach his son the game.

I turned eighteen on June 17th—officially a man. Old enough to buy a drink. Old enough to know the truth. For years I'd thought about that day on Townsend Street—the day my father left in tears. For years I'd tried to guess the big fight's origin, and my mind had produced some mighty far-fetched themes.

Maybe my father liked men and Grandpa had found out. Perhaps the friendship of my dad and the Dago had gone too far one night.

Sure, it was gross, but what's an active mind bound to do but jump to paranoid, baseless conclusions?

Maybe my mother had been involved with a man and my grandfather knew. Why not? She always seemed to have an eye for a sale. Maybe a little sexual respite from her plain old street cop husband seemed like quite a bargain to her.

I even wondered from time to time if I was my father's son. I'd done the math a thousand times and the numbers were suspect. Maybe I was just born prematurely—or maybe I wasn't. Maybe my mother the nurse had been knocked up by a doctor, or some Concourse highbrow, and then got poor Patrick O'Brien to foot the fatherhood bill.

I needed the truth. When my father walked into the kitchen, all smiles at 2 p.m., I decided to get it.

I really hoped he'd take my inquiry well. He'd suffered way too much already—no need to make things worse. His smile was really hurting me, the way it shone with hope. He'd lost his father to a knife, his mother to a needle, his wife to the almighty dollar, his daughter's mind to an errant swing and his son's leg to a virgin gun. But still the guy believed in hope. Despite the steadfast belief that God might not judge him very favorably when his turn came to go, he still saw the future as a friend. And I was going to shatter that friendship.

"Happy Birthday, son," he said. "Patty will be home real soon."

"I know." I was sitting at the table, trying not to look at him.

"Where would you like to go? It's your day, so it's your choice."

"I don't really want to go out, Dad," I said.

"That's okay," he said, optimism still shining through, despite his labored, cane-assisted steps. "We'll just open up your presents here."

"I don't really need presents, Dad."

"No?" he asked, surprised.

"No, all I want's the truth."

His face wrinkled in confusion. "The truth?" he said.

"About that day at Grandpa's house."

My comment caught him unaware and left him speechless. Indeed, had it not been for his cane, he might very well have fallen.

"You know," I said. "The fight. The day you stopped—"

"I know it well, Scooter," he interjected. "Not a day goes by that I don't think of it."

"Well, I want to know," I said.

"Can I sit down?" He did so with great effort.

"Will you tell me?"

He seemed like a mouse caught in a maze. Confused, frightened, panicked. Nowhere to run, nowhere to turn to where he wouldn't run into dead ends.

"Will you?" I repeated.

The mouse started to laugh.

"Dad?"

My father was laughing. A weird laugh. A Scrooge on Christmas Day laugh. Like he'd just lost his mind.

"Dad? Dad? Are you alright?"

The laughter subsided, long enough for my father to spit out a few words.

"It's gonna sound—"

"Sound what, Dad? It's gonna sound what?"

"It's gonna sound—"

"Yeah?"

"Crazy."

"Crazy?" I said, shocked. "What does that mean? Why will it sound crazy?"

"Because my father thought your mother was—"

"Was what?" Having an affair? A lesbian? A communist? Knocked up with some rich guy's child?

"Evil."

"What?" I must admit, I'd never expected that one.

"Evil," my father reconfirmed. "Your grandfather said your mother was evil."

"That's what he said in '68?"

"Well, he said it in '68, but he'd known it for years, he said, since the day your mother visited him at Bronx Psychiatric."

"What do you mean, he knew it?" I asked, although I thought I knew.

My father let out a laugh. Not a Scrooge laugh, just a nervous one.

"He said he could see it in her eyes. He said he held on to that thought as long as he could, until he simply couldn't keep it quiet anymore. It was like he could read minds or something."

Or faces, I thought.

"Scooter?" my father said.

"Yeah, Dad?"

"Does that sound crazy to you?" His tone was sad, but oddly hopeful. Hoping that I'd confirm the insanity of my grandfather's hospital vision.

"No, Dad, not really."

For a moment I thought he might cry. Or laugh. Instead, he looked up at the ceiling, biting his lip and shaking his head. "I loved her, Scooter," he said.

"I know you did, Dad."

"I believed in her."

"I know."

"Any word against her was worth fighting for—even with your grandfather. But now, after all these years, I've come to see that I was blind, and my father, with just one eye, could somehow see it all."

My sister bounded in the door, dressed in long pink shorts and my black canvas Chucks, with Joe Silipo's huge North Milton jersey—the one I'd hit my big home run in. The high school year was winding down and kids were encouraged to dress up according to some goofy themes. Patty's ensemble was part of "Wacky Day," when, for one day only, students could dress "Wacky." Patty proudly showed off a pale blue ribbon she had won, signifying she'd been voted "Wackiest of All."

There was just no way a serious father-son talk could compete with that type of news. So, despite my recent contention that I didn't feel like going out, my dad packed the family in the old Dart Swinger and headed to the Ground Round on Nesconsett Highway, where we ate burgers of outrageous size, opened up my presents and threw peanut shells on the oak plank floor.

· · ·

The next morning, I went down to the courthouse, where I had my name changed legally. I was no longer Scooter Reilly. I looked at choices for a glass eye and was fitted for a partial denture—a flipper, as it's known. A week later, I trimmed my facial hair into a well-groomed beard, had my mop of unruly hair shaved into a crew cut, and took the Long Island Railroad into Queens, where I caught a subway to Shea, for a massive New York–Penn League open tryout.

[4]

I became a real-life, honest-to-goodness Yankee. An Oneonta Yankee, that is. An Oneonta Yankee in the New York–Penn League, a Class A minor league affiliate of the one and only Bombers. There had been other open tryouts, but I didn't bother with them. It *had* to be New York–Penn. Simply *had* to.

The minors held these open tryouts from time to time, usually after the draft, just in case a prospect who may have been overlooked during the arduous scouting process stood out in their minds. On that day at Shea, I was that man. Sure, I'd been the slowest guy in cleats (I couldn't very well wear Chuck Taylors at Shea Stadium), and I'd almost been sent packing when they saw me run the forty. I'd come a long way from being the kid who took the bullet, so my limp was barely noticeable, but I was still far from fast.

Then I took the field and misplayed two routine fly balls and was told my day was through. I pleaded with the scouts, however, to let me take my swings and made their eyes light up when I sprayed that ball around. Several pitchers tried their luck, but none could solve the puzzle of my compact swing, throwing pitches that seemed to float for days, so that I could read the seams every bit as easily as if they'd been the Sunday funnies and I was laughing on the couch.

I was signed up to a deal before I even stepped into the dugout—the same dugout McCovey had descended to after rolling me his bat. A three-thousand-dollar signing bonus and three hundred bucks a week.

I wish Grandpa could have seen me, honoring my roots by taking on his name. Number 15 for the Oneonta Yankees, Hugh O'Brien. He might have shed a tear from that one remaining eye. Had he known my plans, however, he'd have rolled over in his grave.

[5]

I hardly played at all those first few weeks, so I tried to concentrate on the fine points of the game. Hit-and-runs, double steals, how to work the count. But mostly I studied, visualized, hoped and prayed.

I studied pitchers from my dugout perch, looking not just at their release points, grips and spins but at their entire body language. By inning two, I'd have them nailed, catching on to every smirk, blink, frown, facial tick and physical twitch that telegraphed their pitches. Eight times out of ten, I could guess what was coming before it ever left their hands. I may have just turned eighteen, but I felt like Kenny Rogers's wizened "Gambler," a man who'd "made a life out of reading people's faces, knowing what their cards were by the way they held their eyes."

I visualized the fateful pitch, the one I knew was coming soon. Watching it approach, letting fly the wood, feeling the contact, waiting for it to reach its destination. Over and over, I saw it happen in my mind. Could actually feel the heat, smell the ball's impact on my bat, rejoice over the unparalleled high of a white sphere on the sweet spot, and watch the crowd recoil as that white sphere came to rest.

I hoped that Grandpa's story about transcending what was believed to be possible had some truth to it. Could it be? And if so, could one man, through constant visualization, pick the time to make it happen? If that one man applied everything, could he create his own destiny?

I prayed for guidance in my quest. After all, this wasn't prayer for profit or some trivial pursuit. If anything, I had God's blessings on this one. Buried deep in the book of Exodus, its meaning sometimes garbled through the test of time and hands of men. But in my specific

case, the words could not have been much clearer. "An eye for an eye."
End of story.

I batted in the winning run with a pinch-hit single up the middle
against the Newark Orioles. It was the last day of July, with Patty and
my father in the stands. They both were filled with joy, showering me
with affection that I neither deserved nor could enjoy.

I went three for four that next day in my first start of the season.
The curveball seemed to levitate, almost long enough for me to read
SPALDING before punching it through the holes. By the fifth, I knew
exactly what the pitcher would throw by the way he bit his lip. Slider,
low, a bit outside, but I swung the white ash anyway and drilled it
down the line, first-base side, for a stand-up double. I was really on my
way. Two more weeks until we headed to Elmira, for three games with
the Red Sox. My prayers were out there on the wind. I hoped they
would be heard.

[6]

Elmira, New York. Just a few short miles from the charming town of
Horseheads, which always makes me think of the first *Godfather.* Con-
federate soldiers called it "Hellmira" for the inhumane conditions
their prisoners endured there. For me, however, Elmira would be
heaven-sent, or so I hoped. I knew that God was busy, but if he
believed in his own written words, I hoped he could grant a wish at
the ballpark so that justice could be served.

Our team was really rolling. We'd won five straight and were
breathing down the necks of the Red Sox for the New York–Penn
League crown. Kind of echoing the pennant race in the majors, where
the Yanks had overcome a sluggish start and bickering to challenge
Boston down the stretch. A challenge they would ultimately meet
when their light-hitting shortstop blooped a homer just over the
Green Monster to ensure that Boston's "curse of the Bambino" lived to
see another day.

I was something of a phenom in the league. Hugh O'Brien, a man who arrived upon the baseball scene with no known past and no known batting weakness, even if defensively I was slightly less than vacuumlike. A few sure outs found new life when they were hit in my direction. I was lining singles left and right and up the box, punching it up the middle, slapping it through the holes. Then came the game out in Batavia, when I'd gone down three times on strikes. And another one in Jamestown, where I'd struck out twice on feeble swings, like I'd been Suitor in Settlecott.

All it took was those two games for word to spread around the league. O'Brien had a weakness. Superman had kryptonite, Joe D. had Marilyn—and Hugh O'Brien had the fastball. I could read the seams on curves and spot the red dot on sliders, but I couldn't hit the real heat.

Which didn't bode well for me in Elmira, where a lanky lefty brought the heat at ninety-nine. For the first time since I'd lost my eye, I'd get a look at Dan Ferraggo.

We stopped for gas in Binghamton, at a Shell next to the Greyhound stop. I saw a bus bound for Long Island and wondered how my family was. I wondered if my sister liked her job at the dog shelter where she tended to the strays. Or if my dad's leg had recovered from the hell he'd put it through to get me to this point. Or if his poor mind would eventually recover when he learned of my true plan. Surely I could make him understand; after all, he'd put the words in play when lying in his hospital bed in Morrisania. "An eye for an eye."

I heard my teammates hoot and holler. They pointed out the window at the Broome County Arena, which sat off in the distance. Was there a concert there? Perhaps Fleetwood Mac, whose singer, Stevie Nicks, was like a mythic goddess to young men. Or Meat Loaf, whose "Paradise by the Dashboard Light" had turned my former namesake, Phil Rizzuto, into a cult hero for the ages. He might never make the Hall, I thought, but at least he'd done the play-by-play of Meat Loaf getting laid.

There was no concert there. The marquee said MEMORABILIA SHOW, which didn't seem so grand. Underneath those words lay the answer, though. HAPPY DAYS STARS, BASEBALL CARDS, PLAYMATES. And unless the Oneonta Yankee bus was filled with Richie Cunningham fans or collectors looking for a rookie Honus Wagner card, I guessed the boys were cheering for the girls.

The show was going on all weekend. I briefly contemplated running off the bus to procure an Anson Williams keepsake for my sister. Since returning from the hospital, she'd kind of lost her thing for newsmen and was back to her old crush on Richie's dreamy pal.

Our manager, Norm Darrow, put an end to my brief thought, yelling, "All aboard!" before dealing out a muffled fart and spitting brown tobacco juice into his ever-present pin-striped coffee mug. Like roughly two-thirds of his managerial counterparts in every league in existence, Norm was known as "Skip"—short for "Skipper"—which was either a synonym for manager or a testament to the enduring popularity of the Alan Hale Jr. character on *Gilligan's Island.*

I pushed Potsie from my mind. The Skipper's farts as well. I had a date to think about. A date with destiny. A pitch to visualize. Transcending still to do. Hopes that needed nurturing. Prayers that needed to be answered. Too bad I couldn't hit the hard stuff.

He had torn up the instructional league in Florida. He'd overwhelmed the hapless batters he had faced in rookie ball. He was sent to play A ball in Elmira, with his next stop due real soon—Boston's Fenway Park. Dan Ferraggo had battled back from his broken collarbone and was making the thirty grand he'd been signed for seem like the biggest steal since Ryan for Fregosi. He looked right at me when I took my batting practice swings and didn't have a clue. I was a kid who couldn't touch his fastball, no need to study me. But I sure studied him.

Damn, the guy threw hard. Just as hard as I'd remembered, perhaps even slightly harder. He had a nasty curveball too, one that seemed to drop right off the table, as they say. But he released it slightly higher, almost from three-quarters, and I knew that if he served one up, I could slap it through the holes. I knew I wouldn't see one, though. The word on me was out. Nothing but fastballs for O'Brien.

I studied his every move for two and a third innings, resisting the urge to search out his family members, whose talents I was quite familiar with. One I'd seen in action, the other I had felt, and I'd often stopped to wonder if that whole Betamax thing was planned. If doting mommy Tina had set up the whole damn thing to screw up my poor brain. If it was a plan, it worked. In an odd way, I think Grandpa would have admired them—both willing to take balls on the chin for the good of the team.

Mom and Sis were not a factor in my thoughts on this specific night, however, for even when my turn to bat came and I looked at three straight strikes, I was deep into my studies. Getting good looks at all three pitches for plans in my near future.

Skip nearly foiled it all, saying he'd have to take me out. "You just can't hack his heater, Hughie," he said. "I'm gonna sit you down."

I begged him for a second chance. Literally begged. My display must have changed his mind. "Alright, I'll leave you in. But get the bat off your damn shoulder. Take some swings up there." A pause, then, "What's this green duffel bag doing in the dugout? We got enough crap in here already."

It had been a brutal summer. Hot, sticky. A summer meant for Houston or New Orleans, not upstate New York. Still, I dressed for every game the same. Long-sleeved undershirt beneath my Oneonta jersey, the largest size they made. I'd stretched those shirtsleeves out as well, to better hide my arms. I hadn't toiled with Greenberg since I'd been beaned by Dan Ferraggo. But all those years had left their mark, and my forearms, though not quite the size they used to be, still bordered on grotesque.

Our number seven hitter, a little guy named Imbriani, led off our top half with a pop-up foul behind the plate, where the catcher hauled it in. I guessed Ferraggo no longer punched catchers out for unassisted putouts.

"The batter, Number 15, Hugh O'Brien." Ferraggo looked in for the sign, a mere formality. I knew what I was getting. Heat, and plenty of it. I locked in on his eyes. He had no idea. But why would he? How could he know what I had planned? Everything was different. My name, my hair, my beard, my eye, my teeth, my weight, my batting stance, the bat I used. He didn't have a clue. And if the Fates were smiling on me, he didn't have a chance.

I closed my one eye as I dug in from the right side, crouching slightly in the box, choking up on my small bat. I saw the whole thing in my mind, just as I'd done a million times. I tasted Grandpa's words, savoring their possibilities, hoping they could be taken to a higher level so I could transcend on command. Come on, God, be with me now, just like the Good Book says. Exodus. Chapter 21, verse 24. "An eye for an eye."

Fastball, high and tight. Blazing heat. I managed an ultra-weak check swing and watched the ball roll slowly foul. Skip just shook his head and shot a stream of thick brown juice, disgusted, disregarding his faithful mug for the convenience of the dugout floor. This guy just threw too fast—at least to the naked eye he did.

Not to my eye, though. From my vantage point, that heat looked like a beach ball slowly spinning in the air. Floating, floating, waiting to be smacked. Instead, I'd hit a dribbler—just as I had planned.

Another blazing fastball, another check-swing foul. Another shrug from Skip. Another foul brown stream. Beech-Nut, maybe Red Man. There really was no difference. They all made taking postgame showers seem like tiptoeing through a minefield, hoping to avoid a foul brown stain on newly showered toes.

I saw Ferraggo grin. I knew I could expect more of the same. Much more. Besides, I knew what his cards were by the way he held his eyes. I was getting only heat.

Another floating beach ball. Another check-swing foul. To Dan Ferraggo's eyes, it seemed like I was barely hanging on. To my vengeful, hateful mind, I was following a plan. A plan I had hatched the day I saw the Yankee boss say "Oh, shit" when mustard soiled his tie. The day I'd seen the red seams on the baseball look like the Rocky Mountains. The day I'd gone looking for my past, that little kiss, but found destiny instead.

A guy named Wee Willie Keeler once said, "Hit 'em where they ain't." If Ted Williams hadn't been so damn proud, he could have followed that advice and hit .400 every year. Keeler had another claim to fame, however. He had a rule instated just for him. If a player bunts foul with two strikes on him, that player is called out. The "Wee Willie" rule, although it's never called that. For Keeler had such good bat control, he could bunt forty pitches foul, maybe more, destroying pitchers' arms in just one turn at bat.

I was paying homage to Wee Willie. I knew I couldn't bunt Ferraggo's pitches foul, but I could do the next best thing; I could check-swing little dribbles foul. No one would know a thing. At least not until I let them. At which point—vengeance would be mine.

Time and again, Ferraggo fired. Time and again, I checked my swing. I could see him losing patience; just a few more and he'd be mine. As soon as he came in tight, I'd get the handle on the ball, right above the hands. His heat would saw the bat in half, of that much I was sure. Where the ball would go, however, was not for me to know. That was up to luck and fate—and God as well, if he was alive there in Elmira. I trusted that he would be there for me; after all, those words were his. An eye for an eye.

The bat was cut clean in half, a thing of beauty, really. Unlike the sweet-spot long balls I'd launched out at Settlecott School that caused rejoicing in my body, this one hurt like hell. Enough to make me wince.

Our batboy jogged out on the field, collected the splintered Munson bat and offered me a new one. I shook my head. He attempted once again, and again I shook him off. "Time," I said to the umpire. Time was granted.

I walked slowly to the dugout, wincing in pain, favoring my hand, knowing that a feigned injury would buy the time I needed. Time enough to slip into the clubhouse and slip off my sweat-soaked long-sleeved undershirt. Time enough to stare down at the forearms that still dominated the landscape of my body. Time enough to put on my short-sleeved Oneonta jersey, before heading back to work. The transformation was complete—almost.

I grabbed the old green duffel bag and slowly reached inside. Wood. Beautiful. Thick and strong. I withdrew it from the bag, like

Excalibur from its stone, and held it aloft just long enough so my teammates could get a look. The hush was deafening.

I then reached into my pocket, for a body part I'd given up for far too long. I slid that earring in and let my front tooth dangle. Hugh O'Brien had walked off Elmira's diamond. Scooter Reilly walked back out, McCovey in his hands, prepared to swing from way down at the heels.

Even with the mighty bat held aloft, he didn't really know. At least, not until I took my stance—from the left side of the plate. I focused on his eyes so I could take a mental snapshot the moment he caught on. That snapshot is now a prized possession. For in the instant when he realized it, a small piece of Dan Ferraggo died. I saw it slowly pass away. His will, his nerve, his joy for life—something in him left. And now, unless he ran off the mound for safer pastures, I was going to seize the moment and make my hopes and prayers come true.

Ferraggo didn't run. But he did back off the mound to catch his breath. And in those brief few moments, I closed my eye and saw it happen one last time before making it come true.

My lefty stance was now wide open, my right foot pointing toward first base so I could see the mound with my left eye. This stance served another purpose though, and awkward as it seemed, it would prevent the ball from being pulled. No, I didn't want to pull it; I wanted to drive it up the box. Up the box and at eye level.

I remembered '69 at Shea and the "Say Hey Kid," Willie Mays, literally hiding behind the Met first baseman. It seemed silly at first. A game of hide-and-seek in front of forty thousand fans. My father's words made Mays's move make much more sense. "That's because the big bastard hits so hard. He could ruin a face with one swing of the bat."

I was going to ruin Dan Ferraggo's face. Had this not been both our fates, the odds of such a feat would have been astronomical. But I'd seen it in my mind a million times. Seen it, felt it, dreamed it. Visualized, hoped and prayed. Prayed for the power to do damage. The power to just one time propel a ball off McCovey's mighty bat into a human face. Dan Ferraggo's face. A face that might one day learn to chew or speak with a numb and doughy tongue. A face that might one day hear chirping birds or, at the very least, beeps and bells in hospitals, where he'd be given the bad news. "You'll never see again." "An eye for an eye," you piece of shit. Bring the heat. I'm ready.

My father couldn't push off hard enough to help me hit the hard stuff. But my high-heat savior came to me one day while I was hauling crates out at the market. Former major leaguer Mike McHenry, who'd been sweeping up for sixteen years, had asked me for a smoke. I saw an All Hallows ring on a thick, calloused finger and it all made perfect sense. He didn't throw high eighties anymore, but it didn't really matter.

I remembered how damn fast my father's heat had seemed when I was nine years old. Grandpa said he only threw seventy, "but to a nine-year-old boy from forty-five feet, I'm sure it did look like it was shot from a gun."

McHenry threw high seventies to me from Little League distance out on that same Macombs Dam field I'd almost homered on. I didn't even pay him cash. I just gave him butts and beers and did a great deal of his sweeping up.

I gradually moved McHenry in, closer to the plate. From forty-five to forty-two, and then on to thirty-nine. By the time I left for Oneonta, I was swinging from the heels at seventy-eight-mile-per-hour heaters thrown from thirty-seven feet. Making contact, too. From sixty feet, six inches, Ferraggo's ninety-nine seemed to travel in slow motion.

But that next pitch wasn't ninety-eight. Wasn't even close. He may have thrown his arm out when I fouled off all those pitches. Or he may have lost his speed when he lost his will or nerve. But whatever the reason, despite the fact he wound up extra long, kicked his leg up extra high and delivered his pitch with an exultation of great air, that ball had nothing on it.

Grandpa's words flashed through my mind. "We all end up paying for our sins—the only question's when." He'd been talking about the Yankees' woes specifically, but even upon hearing them at the tender age of nine, I'd sensed the words had deeper meaning.

My dad! My dad had said those same words too, in reference to the leg that I had shattered. I'd been doing him a favor. Helping him pay up. The key to life, it seemed, was the payment of one's sins. "The only question's when."

For Dan Ferraggo, doom was fast impending. Forty feet, thirty-five. Thirty feet till payment time. Twenty-five, twenty. Was a fastball ever any fatter? Had there ever been a more perfect way to even up the score? Fifteen, ten. I could almost hear Rizzuto make the call. "Holy cow! Will you look at that! That huckleberry O'Brien just evened up the score with one swing of the bat!"

Except I didn't swing.

For a little while, I couldn't figure out why I couldn't. Belt-high and down the pipe, traveling eighty, maybe eighty-five. For a while I thought I'd chosen the moral high ground, that I'd forgiven him his trespasses. That I'd let little bygones like my right eye and my sister's mental health be forgotten. That I'd figured out that violence, even in extreme situations like my own, was never the right answer. Or even that the Bible passage Exodus 21:24 is perhaps the most misused and misunderstood quote in the history of written language. I loved my father dearly, but he was wrong in quoting Exodus. He didn't deserve to have his leg crippled or his life taken in his car that night as he had wished. And Grandpa should have searched for other ways to make the screaming stop. Somewhere in that book, between the "eye for an eye" of Exodus and the "turn the other cheek" of Matthew, chapter 6, verse 39, I'm sure an answer lies.

Perhaps Dan Ferraggo will one day pay up for his sins. Perhaps he'll spend a lifetime in search of true atonement, or simply wake up screaming, cold and sweating, and put an ice pick in his eye. He might even pay up in another life. I don't know. I do know that I couldn't force-feed that payment to him.

I laid down a bunt instead. A genuine, Phil Rizzuto bunt. Dropped it right in front of the mound, and as Ferraggo headed toward it; I thought for just a moment about running for that mound, meeting him halfway, driving my knee into his face just as he bent down for the ball. Feeling his face shatter from the force.

I ran it out instead. Beat the throw by half a foot. Then went to second on a walk, third on a wild pitch and scored on a double down the line. I saw a Red Sox scout staring at his radar gun, as if the thing was broken. The gun read eighty-one. It had been a fastball, too.

I walked into the clubhouse and took off the uniform. At least I'd been a Yankee, if only in A ball. Clad only in a jockstrap, sitting on a plain wood bench amid tobacco juice, drink cups and a potpourri of sweat and liniment, I hung my head and cried.

I had wasted my one moment. I had worked so hard to create my one defining moment, then threw it all away on a shitty little bunt. All my thoughts of Exodus and Matthew had been but camouflage for cowardice. I'd been Grandpa back in 1912. I'd been Scooter Reilly, circa 1973, standing idly by while my father's life was threatened.

Grandpa told me epitaphs were written based on moments circumstances define. Whatever the hell that means. What circumstance best defined me? That I'd looked destiny square in the eye and blinked? That I'd had my chance and chickened out? That I'd failed to heed my own damn rule—always go down swinging?

I stepped into the shower, coward's tears still clinging to my face. I thought about my epitaph, the one my circumstances would define. "Here lies Scooter Reilly. Lousy son. Lousy brother. Lousy grandson. Liar—Coward—Thief."

Water beat down on me, cleaning off the dirt, if not the guilt that I'd brought in from the game. The game of baseball. Yes, the game. The game itself was my answer—a mythic force preventing me from completing my plan.

It's true, I was a lousy son. A lousy grandson too. I'd destroyed my father's leg. I'd hocked Joe D.'s sacred ball for money, and done likewise with Grandpa's Mr. Coffee. I'd even put my dad through hell for months so he could show me how to play the game. The game.

I could be forgiven for all those selfish crimes, in most cases, gladly so. But if I'd followed through on my well-laid plans, I'd have broken my father's heart. The game he loved reduced to a means of vengeance. No, he would not have forgiven me that. Nor would Grandpa's memory.

It might seem a cheap excuse, a cop-out, an overly sensitive rationalization. But I've come to understand, and have a firm belief, that I didn't swing that bat against Dan Ferraggo in Elmira out of respect for all three—my father, Grandpa's memory and the very game itself.

I was lacing up my new black canvas Chucks when Skip came running in. "O'Brien, dammit, you're up next, what the hell do you think you're doing?"

"Ferraggo still out there?" I asked.

"Jesus, no," Skip lashed out. "He got tagged for five more runs. Now get your gear on and get back out."

"Sorry, Skip, I'm done," I said. "I'm going to leave the game."

"Leave the game?" Skip yelled out. "What the hell does that mean?"

I thought for just a second, then put McCovey back in his duffel bag and smiled broadly at the skipper. "I'm going to leave the game to those who love it."

[7]

I thumbed a ride with a dejected Red Sox scout, who dropped me off in Binghamton on his way to check out a couple outfielders up in Syracuse. The guy had showed up in Elmira to confirm Ferraggo's greatness and had left with shaking head, wondering just how he could explain the tale of the guy who'd lost his heat.

The scout seemed a bit surprised that I'd just packed it in and quit, but then said in all honesty that I'd made a decent choice.

"No use delaying the inevitable, kid," he said, his face a haggard map of every mile he'd logged in pursuit of next big things.

"No, sir, I guess not."

"No use at all," he reiterated.

"Sir?"

"Yeah, kid?"

"What is the inevitable?"

"Hell, you can't hit a fastball."

I fought the urge to laugh, then sat still while he expanded on his view.

"Look, kid, word's out on you already. Ya gotta great eye. Ya can't be fooled by breaking pitches. But ya just can't take the heat."

"No, sir, I guess not."

"But I gotta admit, ya got the doggonedest set of forearms I think I ever seen. Forearms like Hank Greenberg."

I smiled all the way to Binghamton, knowing that the choice I'd made indeed was decent, even if the reasons for it were my own.

I didn't love the game. As time went on, that factor would have spelled the end for me. I could fake my way through a couple months of backyard practices and a few weeks in the minors, but with the ghost of Dan Ferraggo exorcised, I'd have quickly lost my drive. And once that drive was gone, I'd have been a sad sight at the plate and a sad case off the field, and the kid with the eyesight of Ted Williams would have been bypassed by kids with the will of Rose or Munson.

I had made a decent choice when I vowed to leave the game—to the guys who love it.

[8]

There was nothing in that bag for Dorothy. The Wizard kind of sort of followed through on the promises he'd made to the Lion, the Tin Man and the Scarecrow, but he never did send Dorothy home.

That's kind of how I felt on the heels of my great heroic inaction. I may have shown my respect to Grandpa and my father, but not swinging at Ferraggo's pitch had done nothing for my sister. I was still a lousy brother. In fact, I'd never once perceived my New York–Penn League plans as payback for my sister. It had been strictly about me. Just like always.

God knows I'd had my chances. She'd been knocked unconscious by my father's errant swing, and when I'd had my chance to help her, I'd helped myself instead. I'd looked for my own vengeance in her time of need.

I'd seen her naked body on the flyer at the game. There's no way I could have torn up every one, but I didn't even try. I would have failed, but at least I would have done so swinging from the heels, putting every ounce of energy into every precious second. I had let the bat rest on my shoulder, seeking retribution instead of helping out my sister.

I would have my whole life to make it up to her. A lifetime to show my sister how much I cared and how much I regretted the backward order of my past priorities. Family would be number one to me—as soon as I thought it right to return back to the fold.

I needed time to think. Time to sort things out. I hadn't swung the bat. For that much I was proud. I certainly had misled my father into thinking the game was my life's love. If he learned the truth, he would be badly hurt. So I resolved to simply perpetuate the idea that I was still an A league player. How could he possibly find out? I'd just send a postcard now and then from New York–Penn League towns. Just for a couple weeks. Until I sorted things out. Then I'd fake an injury—I'd say it was the leg he'd shot—and he'd welcome me home with open arms and heavy heart.

I would come home with a surprise, I thought. An Anson Williams autograph. A glossy eight-by-ten of Potsie. Maybe the whole damn gang. I took a cab to the arena to check out the memorabilia show. It might not merit full forgiveness, but at least it would be a start.

But Potsie wasn't there. Neither was the Fonz. Nor was Richie C. Not a single cast regular was in attendance. The reason given was a canceled flight, which didn't make much sense. The show ran throughout the weekend. Surely there were other flights to bring the guys to Binghamton.

Which is not to say the show's promoters didn't try to make things right. They'd brought in stars from the show's early days. Chuck was there—the older brother with the crew cut whose character simply stopped appearing, without an explanation or the slightest mention of his name. Sticks was there—the drummer in Richie's band, whose black skin prevented all the kids in racist fifties Wisconsin from coming to the party. Bag was there as well, though I have no idea who he was.

Attendance was slight, save for a big crowd at the far end of the arena. This was 1978—a few years before the memorabilia craze set in.

Before a guy like Mickey Mantle could pull in more cash on a weekend than he had in an entire season in his prime.

There were a couple bona fides from the sitcom world who did draw decent lines. Gilligan. The Professor. I asked the Professor if either of the girls was there, Mary Ann or Ginger. "No," he said, but he was kind enough to engage me in a discussion of the two.

"Mary Ann or Ginger?" the Professor said, sounding just as wise as ever. "Which one does it for you?"

"Oh, I've got to go with Ginger," I told him.

"You like the redheads, do you?"

"Definitely."

The Professor smiled. A smile more conspiratorial than intellectual. He leaned in just a bit. "You know, there's a redhead at the *Playboy* table."

I turned my head quickly and, using my Teddy Ballgame eye, detected a slight movement of auburn hair, even among a throng of admirers who were lined up at the table, snaking backward toward the sitcom guys. Binghamton didn't care about their minor *Happy Days* has-beens, but they sure seemed to like their Playmates. I tried to see things clearer, but there were just too many horny upstate New Yorkers in the way. I may have had the type of sight that comes only once a generation, but I wasn't Superman. I headed for the auburn hair, the quest to gaze at Miss November '75 replacing family in my thoughts.

The Playmates had the back wall to themselves. There must have been a dozen total, but I had eyes (or in my case, eye) for only one. I was pretty traditional that way, kind of like my father with his Yankees. I'd had romantic feelings for only three girls in my life. One had touched my heart and mind and had been dropped in favor of a dealer who threw ninety. One had broken my heart and screwed up my mind. One, until this day, had existed only on paper. That was going to change.

I took my place in line, maybe fifteen deep, then scanned Broome Arena.

There were a few Mets sitting by some baseball memorabilia. Bats and balls and baseball cards—things like that. Ron Swoboda, the guy who'd made the "Lulu" of a catch, had a decent line, although I couldn't for the life of me see how a red-blooded male could choose Swoboda over Janet Lupo.

Ten more guys to go. Then I'd be up at the table full of photographs available for purchase. I'd allocated twenty dollars for Fonz and Potsie stuff, and since those guys hadn't showed (or more likely had never been told about the show) I fully intended to spend it all on Janet.

Was that a Yankee over there? Yes, it was. Horace Clarke. He who bailed out into center field when turning double plays. The guy had caused my father many heartaches during his Yankees heyday, but I thought I'd grab an autograph anyway. Besides, Horace didn't have a line.

I turned my attention back to Miss November and was met with one of the great disappointments of my life. Janet Lupo had the ugliest cleavage I'd ever seen. Simply hideous. Wait, that wasn't Janet, that was the crack of some guy's sizable ass bending over Janet's table for a Polaroid with the busty beauty. Whew, that one was close. I wondered if I'd lost my gift—if my one eye's sight had betrayed me somehow. Mistaking a big fat hairy ass for Janet Lupo's brilliant breasts was no minor league snafu.

Hell, I thought, even Ted Williams must have screwed up every now and then. Thought a slider was a fastball or took a swing at some bad pitch. It was probably just nerves. Just one more guy in front of me. The guy had a hundred-dollar bill clenched in his extended hand, and he planned to do some shopping. This guy was going to take a couple minutes. Janet was now visible, but I turned my head away. I'd waited this long to get a look at her, I might as well bide just a bit more time, so my first look would be a clear one. So I could take in every luscious inch of her before handing over twenty dollars for the honor of her photographs and memories.

I looked back quickly at Horace Clarke. Still no line to see the former Yankee second baseman. The man whose very name had come to symbolize the team's early seventies woes. "The Horace Clarke Years," they were called. My dad had lightened up on him, however, after learning that "ol' Hoss" used to walk to Yankee Stadium from his small South Bronx apartment and even as a semi-star of sports' most storied franchise never pulled in much more than twenty grand.

I stared intently at the guy from a distance of some forty feet, trying to read his face for sadness, for the bruising of an ego that a lack of fans might bring. My intensity wavered. I never really locked in on him too well, as I was distracted by some memorabilia right behind him. Baseballs in a glass case, each in a separate holder. One ball grabbed my attention and refused to let it go.

At first I thought my eye had let me down again—that my gift indeed was gone and my mind was playing cruel tricks on my conscience. Because I could have sworn I saw . . . the ball.

I focused even harder, disregarding Horace Clarke, just like the rest of Binghamton. My eye became blurred for just a moment as a tear had formed inside it. Formed the moment that I saw the smudge. The bloodstain. Joe D.'s bloodstain. The ball he'd signed at Freedomland for Grandpa had somehow found its way to Binghamton after fourteen years in limbo.

I heard a voice in front of me say, "Come on, baby, drop the top for Tietam and I'll give you an extra twenty." That voice might just as well have been a dream and I paid it little mind. Not while Joe D.'s ball was on the market. I saw the distinctive, elegant arcs and knew it was legit. I had to have that ball. I had a twenty in my pocket but more tucked inside my sneaker, underneath the insole. I could have my cake and eat it too. DiMaggio and Janet—I wouldn't have to choose. A man approached the vendor at the glass, no real need to worry.

"Next." The smoky voice shook me from my trancelike state. The voice belonged to Janet Lupo, who was every bit as beautiful in person as she'd been on the pages of a magazine. Her dark brown eyes were nothing less than dazzling. Sparkling. Smoldering. Burning holes into my pounding heart, setting loose a school of butterflies to flutter deep inside me.

It was really her. The object of my affection, or at the very least, my lust. Our clandestine affair had helped soothe the pain of an absent mother and a long-lost chance at love. Now I was next to her, for real, not just in a magazine.

"Excuse me." Janet's voice again.

"Um, yeah?" I said. My first words to Janet Lupo and, man, I'd come up with some good ones.

"Are you okay?" she said.

"Uh-huh." Yes! Another one.

"Most men don't stare at just my eyes."

I instinctively looked down. Oh my goodness. Cleavage I could get lost in, for a whole week, maybe more. I felt terrible for comparing other breasts to hers. There was only one set of true Janet Lupo breasts, and I was staring at them. Blatantly, and unapologetically.

Janet laughed. A very pretty laugh. "Just don't try to touch, like that last guy, okay?"

"Uh-huh."

"Now, what would you like?"

So many photos to choose from. Formal shots. Bikini shots. Topless shots. I couldn't choose just one. I shot a quick look behind me at the baseballs. The vendor had a ball out of the glass case, showing it to that same prospective buyer. I took a better look, summoning my gift of sight like it was the bionic eye of Majors. All I needed was the sound effects. Damn! I'd feared the worst and got it. Grandpa's ball!

"Have you decided?"

"Huh?" I wheeled around to see Janet's face, her expression warm but slightly restless, as if she'd grown weary of my slick one-liners.

"What would you like?"

"Um, um." I looked over the photos then checked on Grandpa's ball. Thankfully, the vendor was putting the ball back in its case as the prospective buyer walked away.

"Honey?"

Had she just called me honey? The coast was clear. Joe D.'s ball would still be waiting for me when I was through at Janet's table. The chances of some guy grabbing it in those next few minutes bordered on the microscopic.

"What can I get you, honey?"

It was a chance I couldn't take.

"Nothing," I said.

"Nothing?"

"Nothing."

She smiled. She wasn't mad, just intrigued at this seemingly normal horny teenager, who wanted "nothing" from her.

"You waited in this line for quite a while, didn't you?"

"Uh-huh."

"And now you're at the front, and you decide that you don't want anything?" she said, leaning in toward me so that her breasts rested on the table, an image I would take with me and keep, kind of like an eight-by-ten, but cheaper.

"Uh-huh."

She leaned back, pretending to be sad. "Oh, you're going to make me cry."

"I'm sorry, I really am, but I really have to go."

"Where are you going?"

"Home," I said, then took one last look at Janet Lupo before sprinting for the ball.

A NOTE ON THE TYPE

This book was set in Adobe Garamond. Designed for the Adobe Corporation by Robert Slimbach, the fonts are based on types first cut by Claude Garamond (c. 1480–1561). Garamond was a pupil of Geoffroy Tory and is believed to have followed the Venetian models, although he introduced a number of important differences, and it is to him that we owe the letter we now know as "old style." He gave to his letters a certain elegance and feeling of movement that won their creator an immediate reputation and the patronage of Francis I of France.

Composed by Creative Graphics
Allentown, Pennsylvania
Printed and bound by Berryville Graphics
Berryville, Virginia
Designed by Virginia Tan